"Like Umberto Eco's classic, *The Name of the Rose*, Rowland's novel is an excellent whodunit. Highly recommended for all mystery fans."
—*Booklist*

BUNDORI

"BUNDORI is one of those mysteries in which the itch to find out whodunit recedes before the pleasures of prowling through a different world."
—*The Washington Post Book World*

"An appealing character in a fascinating setting in a book enhanced by creative plotting and highly professional writing."
—*Washington Times*

SHINJŪ

"This impressive first novel features a plot that's perfectly adapted to its historical background: Sano's growing terror of humiliation and dishonor comes across more keenly than any contemporary setting would allow."
—*Kirkus Reviews* (starred)

"[A] remarkably self-assured debut . . . [Rowland] evokes the claustrophobic atmosphere of Edo and of the rigidly hierarchical society that was 17th-century Japan with aplomb: the sights, the smells, and the layout of the walled city are as palpable as their counterparts in Ed McBain's 82nd precinct of New York."
—*San Jose Mercury News*

"Rowland is a sturdy, persuasive storyteller, and well worth keeping an eye on."
—*The Washington Post Book World*

Also by Laura Joh Rowland

The Samurai's Wife
The Way of the Traitor
Bundori
Shinjū
Black Lotus

The Concubine's Tattoo

LAURA JOH ROWLAND

St. Martin's Paperbacks

THE CONCUBINE'S TATTOO

Library of Congress Catalog Card Number: 98-7910

ISBN: 0-312-96922-8

Printed in the United States of America

t. Martin's Press hardcover edition / December 1998
. Martin's Paperbacks edition / April 2000

9 8 7 6 5 4

To Pamela Gray Ahearn,
With appreciation

Edo

Genroku Period,
Year 3, Month 9
(Tokyo, October 1690)

"It is my privilege to open this ceremony in which *Sōsakan* Sano Ichirō and Lady Ueda Reiko shall be united in marriage before the gods." Pudgy, nearsighted Noguchi Motoori—Sano's former superior and the go-between who had arranged the match—solemnly addressed the assembly gathered in Edo Castle's private reception hall.

On this warm autumn morning, sliding doors stood open to a garden resplendent with scarlet maple leaves and brilliant blue sky. Two priests, clad in white robes and tall black caps, knelt at the front of the hall before the alcove, in which hung a scroll bearing the names of the *kami*—Shinto deities. Below this, a dais held the traditional offerings of round rice cakes and a ceramic jar of consecrated sake. Two maidens, wearing the hooded cloaks of Shinto shrine attendants, stood near the priests. On the tatami to the left of the alcove knelt the bride's father and closest associates: stout, dignified Magistrate Ueda and a few relatives and friends. To the right, the groom's party consisted of Shogun Tokugawa Tsunayoshi, Japan's supreme military dictator, dressed in brocade robes and the cylindrical black cap of his rank, attended by several high officials; Sano's frail, elderly mother; and Hirata, Sano's chief retainer. All eyes turned to the center of the hall, the focus of the ceremony.

Sano and Reiko knelt side by side before two small tables—he in black ceremonial robes stamped with his fam- ily's gold flying-crane crest, his two swords at his wai she in a white silk kimono and a long, white silk drape completely covered her face and hair. They faced porcelain dish containing a miniature pine and plum bamboo grove, the statues of a hare and a crane: s of longevity, pliancy, and fidelity. Behind them, Noguchi and his wife knelt at a table reserved for the go-between. As the priests stood and bowed to the altar, Sano's heart pounded. His stoic dignity hid a turmoil of emotion.

The last two years had brought him continuous upheaval: the death of his beloved father; the move from his modest family home in the Nihonbashi merchant district to Edo Castle, Japan's seat of power; a dizzyingly rapid rise in status and all the associated challenges. At times he feared his mind and body couldn't withstand the relentless onslaught of change. Now he was marrying a twenty-year-old girl he'd met exactly once before, more than a year ago, at the formal meeting between their two families. Her lineage was impeccable, her father one of the wealthiest and most powerful men in Edo. But they'd never spoken; he knew nothing of her character. He barely remembered what she looked like, and wouldn't see her face again until the end of the ceremony. To Sano, the tradition of arranged marriage now seemed like sheer madness—a potentially disastrous pairing of strangers. What perilous turn had his fate taken? Was it too late to escape?

From her tiny bedchamber in the Edo Castle women's quarters, the shogun's newest concubine heard hurrying footsteps, slamming doors, and shrill feminine voices. The dressing rooms would be littered with opulent silk kimonos and spilt face powder, the servants rushing to finish dressing the two hundred concubines and their attendants for the *sōsakan-sama*'s wedding feast. But Harume, weary of the suffocating presence of so many other women after only eight months at the castle, had decided to skip the celebration. Privacy was almost nonexistent in the crowded women's quarters, but now her chambermates were gone, the palace officials busy. The shogun's mother, whom Harume attended, hadn't required her services today. No one ould miss her, she hoped—because Harume meant to take advantage of her rare solitude.

he latched the door, then closed the shutters. On a low she lit oil lamps and incense burners. The flickering cast her shadow against the mullioned paper walls;

the incense smoked, sweetly pungent. A hushed, secretive atmosphere permeated the room. Harume's pulse quickened with a dark excitement. She set a rectangular black lacquer box, its lid inlaid with gold irises, and a porcelain sake decanter and two cups on the table. Her movements were slow and graceful, befitting a sacred ritual. Then she tiptoed to the door and listened.

The noise had diminished; the other women must have finished dressing and started toward the banquet hall. Harume returned to the altar she'd created. With eagerness rising in her breast, she pushed back her glossy, waist-length black hair. She loosened her sash and parted the skirts of her red silk dressing gown. She knelt, naked from the waist down.

She contemplated herself with pride. At age eighteen, she was as ripe of flesh as a mature woman, yet with youth's fresh radiance. Flawless ivory skin covered her firm thighs, her rounded hips and stomach. With her fingertips Harume stroked the silky triangle of pubic hair. She smiled, remembering his hand there, his mouth against her throat, their shared rapture. She reveled in her eternal love for him, which she would now prove beyond any possible doubt.

One of the priests swished a long wand tasseled with white paper strips, crying, "Evil out, fortune in! Whoosh! Whoosh!" to purify the room. Then he chanted an invocation to the Shinto gods Izanagi and Izanami, revered procreators of the universe.

Hearing the familiar words, Sano relaxed. The timeless ceremony lifted him above doubt and fear; anticipation soared in him. No matter the risks, he wanted this marriage. At the advanced age of thirty-one, he was at last ready to make the decisive step into official adulthood, to take his place in society as the head of his own family. And he was ready for a change in his life.

His twenty months as the shogun's *sōsakan-sama*–most honorable investigator of events, situations, and pe ple—had been a nonstop cycle of criminal cases, trea hunts, and spying assignments, culminating in a catastrophic trip to Nagasaki. There he had investigat murder of a Dutch trader—and been shot, almost burned to death, charged with treason, and nearly executed before clearing himself. He'd returned to Edo seven days ago, and while he hadn't lost his desire to pursue truth and deliver criminals to justice, he was tired. Tired of violence, death, and corruption. The aftermath of a tragic love affair the previous year had left him lonely and emotionally drained.

Now, however, Sano looked forward to a respite from the rigors of his work. The shogun had granted him a month's holiday. After a year-long betrothal, Sano welcomed the prospect of a private life with a sweet, compliant wife who would provide a haven from the outside world. He yearned for children, especially a son who would carry on his name and inherit his position. This ceremony was not just a social rite of passage, but a gateway to everything Sano wanted.

The second priest played a series of high-pitched, wailing notes on a flute, while the first beat a sonorous accompaniment on a wooden drum. Now came the most solemn, sacred part of the wedding ritual. The music ceased. One attendant poured the consecrated sake into a long-handled brass ewer and brought it to Sano and Reiko. The other attendant set before them a tray containing three flat wooden cups, graduated in size, nested together. From the ewer, the attendants filled the first, smallest cup, bowed, and handed it to the bride. The assembly waited in hushed expectation.

Harume opened the lacquer box and took out a long, straight razor with a gleaming steel blade, a pearl-handled knife, and a small, square black lacquer jar with her name painted in gold on the stopper. As she arranged these objects before her, a tremor of fear fluttered in Harume's throat. She dreaded pain, hated blood. Would someone interrupt this ceremony—or worse, discover her secret, for-
·idden liaison? Dangerous intrigues shadowed her life, and
·ere were people who might wish to see her disgraced
· banished from the castle. But love demanded sacrifice
·necessitated risk. With unsteady hands she poured sake
·he two cups: one for herself; a ritual one for her absent

lover. She lifted her cup and swallowed the drink. Her eyes watered; her throat burned. But the potent liquor enflamed her courage and determination. She picked up the razor.

With careful strokes Harume shaved bare her pubic area, brushing the cut black strands onto the floor. Then she set aside the razor and lifted the knife.

Reiko, her face still concealed beneath the white headdress, lifted the sake cup to her lips and drank. The process was repeated three times. Then the attendants refilled the cup and passed it to Sano. He drank his three drafts, imagining that he felt the transient warmth of his bride's dainty fingers on the polished wood and tasted the sweetness of her lip rouge on the rim: their first, albeit indirect, touch.

Would their marriage be, as he hoped, a union of kindred souls as well as sensual satisfaction?

A collective sigh passed through the assembly. The *san-san-ku-do*—the "three-times-three-sips" pledge that sealed the marriage bond—never failed to arouse poignant emotion. Sano's own eyes burned with unshed tears; he wondered if Reiko shared his hopes.

The attendant set aside the cup and filled the second one. This time Sano drank first, three times, then Reiko did. After the third, largest cup was passed and the liquor sipped, the flute and drum music resumed. Joy nearly overwhelmed Sano. He and Reiko were now joined in wedlock. Soon he would see her face again . . .

Touching the knife's sharp blade to her tender, shaved skin, Harume flinched at the coldness of the steel. Her heart thudded; her hand trembled. She put the knife down and took another drink. Then, closing her eyes, Harume summoned the image of her lover, the memory of his caresses. The incense smoke steeped her lungs in the scent of jasmine. Ardor flooded her with daring. When she opened her eyes, her body was still, her mind calm. She took up the knife again. On her pubis she slowly cut the first stroke, just above the cleft of her womanhood.

Crimson blood welled. Harume let out a sharp hiss of pain; tears stung her eyes. But she wiped away the blo with the end of her sash, took another drink, and cut the next stroke. More pain; more blood. Eleven more strokes, and Harume sighed in relief. The worst part was done. Now for the step that would bind her irrevocably to her lover.

Harume opened the lacquer jar. The stopper was fitted with a bamboo-handled brush, its soft bristles saturated with gleaming black ink. Carefully she brushed the ink onto the cuts, enjoying its cool wetness, balm to her pain. With her bloody sash she blotted up the excess ink and stoppered the bottle. Then, sipping more sake, she admired her work.

The complete tattoo, the size of her thumbnail, etched in black lines, now adorned her private place: an indelible expression of fidelity and devotion. Until the hair grew back, she hoped she could keep herself covered, hiding her secret from the other concubines, the palace officials, the shogun. But even after the tattoo was safely obscured, she would know it was there. As would he. They would treasure this symbol of the only marriage they would ever celebrate. Harume poured herself another cup of sake, a private toast to eternal love.

But when she drank, she couldn't swallow; the sake leaked from her mouth, running down her chin. A strange tingling began in Harume's lips and tongue; her throat felt strangely thick and numb, as if packed with cotton. An eerie, cold sensation crept across her skin. Dizziness washed over her. The room spun; the lamp flames, unnaturally bright, whirled before her eyes. Frightened, she dropped the cup. What was happening to her?

Sudden nausea gripped Harume. Doubling over, hands pressed against her stomach, she retched. Hot, sour vomit clogged her throat, shot up her nose, and spewed onto the floor. She wheezed and coughed, unable to get enough air. In a panic, Harume rose and started for the door. But the muscles of her legs had gone weak; she stumbled, scattering incense burners, razor, knife, and ink bottle. Lurching and limping, all the while struggling to breathe, Harume managed to reach the door and open it. A hoarse cry burst from her numb lips.

"Help!"

The corridor was empty. Clutching her throat, Harume

staggered in the direction of voices that sounded distorted and far away. Ceiling lanterns burned as bright as suns, blinding her. She grabbed the walls for support. Through a haze of dizzy nausea, Harume saw winged black shapes pursuing her. Claws snatched at her hair. High-pitched shrieks echoed in her ears.

Demons!

Now the attendants served sake to Sano's mother and Magistrate Ueda, honoring the new allegiance between the two families, then passed cups of liquor to the assembly, which proclaimed in unison, "*Omedetō gozaimasu*—congratulations!"

Sano saw happy faces turned toward him and Reiko. His mother's loving gaze warmed him. Hirata passed a self-conscious hand over the black stubble on his head—shaved during their Nagasaki investigation—and beamed. Magistrate Ueda nodded in dignified approval; the shogun grinned.

From the table before him, Sano picked up the ceremonial document and read in an unsteady voice, "We have now become united as husband and wife for all eternity. We vow to execute our marital duties faithfully and spend all the days of our lives together in never-ending trust and affection. Sano Ichirō, the twentieth day of the ninth month, Genroku year three."

Then Reiko read from her identical document. Her voice was high, clear, and melodic. This was the first time Sano had ever heard it. What would they talk about, alone together, tonight?

The attendants handed Sano and Reiko branches of saka tree with white paper strips attached, leading the couple to the alcove to make a traditional wedding offering to the gods. Small and slender, Reiko barely came up to Sano's shoulder. Her long sleeves and hem trailed on the floor. Together they bowed and laid the branches on the altar. The attendants bowed twice to the altar, then clapped their hands twice. The assembly followed suit.

"The ceremony is successfully completed," announce

the priest who had performed the invocation. "Now the bride and groom can begin to build a harmonious home."

Pursued by the demons, Harume somehow found her way through the winding passages of the women's quarters, to the door leading to the main palace. There stood the castle ladies, dressed in bright, colorful kimonos, attended by servants and a few male guards. Harume's strength was fading. Wheezing and choking, she crashed to the floor.

In a loud rustle of silk garments, the crowd turned. A flurry of exclamations arose: "It's Lady Harume!" "What's wrong with her?" "There's blood all over her mouth!"

Now a shifting collage of shocked, frightened faces hovered over Harume. Ugly purple blotches obscured the familiar features of these women she knew. Noses elongated; eyes burned; fanged mouths leered. Black wings sprouted from shoulders, fanning the air. Silk garments became the lurid plumage of monster birds. Claws reached out to grab.

"Demons," Harume gasped. "Don't come any closer. No!"

Strong hands seized her. Authoritative male voices gave orders. "She's ill. Get a doctor." "Don't let her disrupt the *sōsakan-sama*'s wedding." "Take her to her room. . . ."

Panic infused strength into Harume's muscles. As she kicked and thrashed and gasped for breath, her voice burst from her in a scream of terror: "Help! Demons! Don't let them kill me!"

"She's mad. Stay back—out of the way! She's violent."

Down the corridor they carried her, trailed by the screeching, flapping horde. Harume struggled to free herself. Her captors finally set her down, pinning her arms and legs. She was trapped. The demons would rip her to shreds, then devour her.

Yet even as these fearsome thoughts flashed through Harume's mind, a more terrifying power gathered within her body. A gigantic convulsion surged through bone, muscle, and nerve; stretched sinews; drew invisible chains tight around internal organs. Harume screamed in agony as her back arched and her stiff limbs shot out. In a cacophony of shrieks, the demons let go, thrown off by the force of her involuntary movements. A second, stronger convulsion, and darkness seeped across her vision. External sensations receded; she couldn't see the demons or hear their voices. The wild, erratic pounding of her own heart filled her ears. Another convulsion. Mouth open wide, Harume couldn't draw another breath. Her final thought was of her lover: With a grief as agonizing as the pain, she knew she would never see him again in this life. Then one last gasp. One more unspoken plea:

Help . . .

Then nothingness.

Sano barely heard the assembly's murmured blessings, because the attendants were lifting the white drape away from his new wife's head. She was turning toward him . . .

Looking even younger than her twenty years, Reiko had a perfect oval face with a delicate chin and nose. Her eyes, like bright, black flower petals, shone with somber innocence. On her high, shaved brow arched the fine lines of painted eyebrows. White rice powder covered smooth, perfect skin, contrasting with the satiny black hair that fell from a center part all the way to her knees. Her beauty took Sano's breath away. Then Reiko smiled at him—the merest shy curving of dainty red lips before she demurely lowered her gaze. Sano's heart clenched with a fierce, possessive tenderness as he smiled back. She was everything he wanted. Their life together would be sheer conjugal bliss, which would begin as soon as the public formalities ended.

The assembly stood as the attendants escorted Sano and Reiko from the altar to their families. Sano bowed to Magistrate Ueda and thanked him for the honor of joining the clan, while Reiko did the same to Sano's mother. Together they thanked the shogun for his patronage, and the guests for coming. Then, after many more congratulations, thanks, and blessings, the party, led by the shogun, moved through the carved doors and down the wide corridor toward the hall where the wedding banquet would take place and more guests waited.

Suddenly, from deep within the castle's interior, came loud, high-pitched screams, then the sound of running footsteps. The shogun paused, halting the procession.

"What is that noise?" he asked, his aristocratic features darkening in annoyance. To his officials, he said, "Go and, ahh, determine the cause, and put a stop to—"

Down the corridor toward the wedding party stampeded hundreds of shrieking women, some dressed in brilliant silk robes, others wearing the plain cotton kimonos of servants, all holding their sleeves over their noses and mouths, eyes wide with terror. Palace officials stormed after them, shouting commands and trying to restore order, but the women paid no heed.

"Let us out!" they cried, shoving the bridal procession up against the wall as they rushed past.

"How dare these females treat me in this disrespectful manner?" Tokugawa Tsunayoshi wailed. "Has everyone gone mad? Guards—stop them!"

Magistrate Ueda and the attendants shielded Reiko from the mob, which quickly expanded to include panicky guests pouring out of the banquet hall. They crashed into Sano's mother; he caught her before she fell.

"We're all doomed if we don't run!" shrilled the women.

Now an army of guards appeared. They herded the hysterical women back to the castle interior. The wedding party and guests clustered in the banquet hall, where tables and cushions had been arranged on the floor, a troupe of frightened musicians clutched their instruments, and maids waited to serve the feast.

"What is the meaning of this?" The shogun straightened his tall black cap, knocked atilt in the scuffle. "I, ahh, demand an explanation!"

The guard commander bowed to Tokugawa Tsunayoshi. "My apologies, Your Excellency, but there's been a disturbance in the women's quarters. Your concubine Lady Harume just died."

The chief castle physician, dressed in the dark blue coat of his profession, added, "Her death was caused by a sudden violent illness. The other ladies fled in panic, fearing contagion."

Murmurs of dismay rose from the assembly. Tokugawa Tsunayoshi gasped. "Contagion?" His face paled, and he covered his nose and mouth with both hands to keep the spirit of disease from entering. "Do you mean to say there is an, ahh, epidemic in the castle?" A dictator of delicate health and with little talent for leadership, he turned to Sano and Magistrate Ueda, the men present who ranked next below him in status. "What is to be done?"

"The nuptial festivities must be canceled," Magistrate Ueda said with regret, "and the guests sent home. I will see to the arrangements."

Sano, though shocked by this calamitous end to his wedding, hastened to his lord's aid. Contagious disease was a serious concern in Edo Castle, which housed hundreds of Japan's highest-ranking officials and their families. "In case there really is an epidemic, the ladies must be quarantined to prevent its spread." Sano instructed the guard commander to manage this, and told the castle physician to examine the women for symptoms. "And you, Your Excellency, should stay in your chambers to avoid illness."

"Ahh, yes, of course," said Tokugawa Tsunayoshi, obviously relieved to have someone else take charge. Hurrying in the direction of his private suite, the shogun summoned the officials to follow, while shouting orders to Sano: "You must personally investigate Lady Harume's death at once!" In his fear for himself, he seemed indifferent to the loss of his concubine and the fate of his other women. And he'd apparently forgotten all about Sano's promised holiday. "You must prevent the evil spirit of disease from reaching me. Now go!"

"Yes, Your Excellency," Sano called after the retreating despot and his entourage.

Hirata hurried to join him. As they started down the corridor toward the women's quarters, Sano looked over his shoulder and saw Reiko, white bridal gown trailing behind her, being escorted out by her father and attendants. He felt extreme annoyance at the shogun for reneging on his promise, and regret for the delayed wedding celebrations, both public and private. Had he not earned a little peace and happiness? Then Sano suppressed a sigh. Obedience to his lord was a samurai's highest virtue. Duty prevailed; once again, death commanded Sano's attentions. Marital bliss would have to wait.

The women's quarters in Edo Castle occupied a private inner section of the main palace known as the Large Interior. The route to it led Sano and Hirata through the outer, public areas of the palace, past audience halls, government offices and conference rooms, through convoluted passages. An ominous pall had stilled the castle's normal bustle of activity. Officials huddled in clusters from which rose uneasy mutters as news of the concubine's shocking death spread. Armored guards patrolled the corridors in case of further unrest. The great Tokugawa bureaucracy had ground to a halt. Imagining the serious repercussions that an epidemic in Japan's capital might have for the nation, Sano hoped that Lady Harume's sickness would prove to be an isolated incident.

A massive oak door, banded in iron and decorated with carved flowers, sealed the entrance to the women's quarters, home to the shogun's mother, wife, and concubines, their attendants, and the palace's cooks, maids, and other female servants. Two sentries guarded the door.

"We're here on His Excellency's orders to investigate the death of Lady Harume," Sano said, identifying himself and Hirata.

The sentries bowed, opened the door, and admitted Sano and Hirata into a narrow, lantern-lit corridor. The door closed behind them with a soft, reverberant thud.

"I've never been in here before," Hirata said, his voice hushed with awe. "Have you?"

"Never," Sano said. Mingled interest and trepidation stirred inside him.

"Do you know anyone in the Large Interior?"

In his capacity as the shogun's *sōsakan,* Sano had free

access to most of the castle. He was familiar with its walled passages and gardens, keep, ancestral shrine, martial arts training ground, and forest preserve, the Official Quarter where he lived, the outer section of the palace, and even the shogun's private chambers. But the women's quarters were closed to all men except a few carefully chosen guards, doctors, and officials. These did not include Sano.

"I know some of the servants and minor officials by sight," he said, "and I once headed a military escort to convey the shogun's mother and concubines on a pilgrimage to Zōjō Temple. But my duties have never involved direct contact with anyone from the Large Interior."

Now Sano had the disconcerting sense of entering alien territory. "Well, let's get started," he said, driving confidence into his voice as he regretted his postponed nuptial festivities. How much longer before he and Reiko could be together? Sano started down the corridor, resisting the urge to tiptoe.

The polished cypress floor gleamed, dimly reflecting Sano's and Hirata's distorted images. Painted flowers adorned the coffered ceiling. Unoccupied rooms were crammed full of lacquer chests, cabinets, and screens, charcoal braziers, mirrors, scattered clothing, dressing tables littered with combs, hairpins, and vials. Gilt murals covered the inner walls. In abandoned bathchambers, round wooden tubs steamed. The corridor was deserted, but behind the latticed wood and paper walls, countless shadowy figures moved. As Sano and Hirata passed, doors cracked open; frightened eyes peeked out. Somewhere a samisen played a melancholy tune. The high murmur of feminine voices filled the air, which felt warmer and smelled different than in the rest of the palace, sweet with the scent of perfume and aromatic unguents. Sano thought he could also detect the subtler smells of women's bodies: sweat, sexual secretions, blood?

In this crowded hive, the very walls seemed to expand and contract with female breath. Sano had heard rumors of extravagant entertainments held here, of secret intrigues and escapades. But what practical expertise could he bring to a mysterious case of fatal disease in this private sanctum? Sano glanced at Hirata.

The young retainer's wide, boyish face wore a look of nervous determination. He walked self-consciously, shoulders hunched, putting one foot in front of the other with exaggerated care, as if afraid to make noise or occupy space. Despite his own discomfort, Sano smiled in rueful sympathy. Both of them were beyond their depth here.

Sano, the son of a *rōnin*—masterless samurai—had once earned his living as an instructor in his father's martial arts academy and as a tutor to young boys, studying history in his spare time. Family connections had secured him a position as a senior police commander. He'd solved his first murder case and saved the shogun's life, an act that had led to his current post.

Twenty-one-year-old Hirata's father had been a *doshin,* one of Edo's low-ranking police patrol officers. He'd inherited the position at age fifteen, maintaining order in the city streets until becoming Sano's chief retainer a year and a half ago, when they'd investigated the notorious Bundori Murder case. Their humble origins, personal inclinations, and past experience ill suited them for this assignment. Yet, as Sano reminded himself, they'd emerged victorious from other difficult situations.

"What should we do first?" Hirata asked, his cautious tone echoing Sano's misgivings.

"Find someone who can show us the scene of Lady Harume's death."

This, however, proved unnecessary. A great commotion drew Sano and Hirata deeper into the shadowy maze of rooms inhabited by countless unseen women who whispered and sobbed behind closed doors. Blue-robed physicians rushed about, carrying medical chests; servants followed with trays of tea and herbal remedies. Voices chanted and called; bells tinkled; drums throbbed; paper rustled. The sweet, tarry odor of strong incense wafted through the corridors. Sano and Hirata easily located the focus of activity, a small chamber at the end of a hallway. They entered.

Inside, five saffron-robed Buddhist priests rang bells,

chanted prayers, beat drums, and shook paper-tasseled wands to drive away the spirits of disease. Maids sprinkled salt on the windowsill and around the perimeter of the room, laying down a purifying boundary, across which death's contamination could not pass. Two middle-aged female palace officials, dressed in the somber gray robes of their station, waved incense burners. Through the asphyxiating haze Sano could barely see the shrouded body on the floor.

"Please wait outside for a moment," Sano told the priests, maids, and officials. They complied, and Sano said to Hirata, "Get the chief physician."

Then he opened the window to admit sunlight and clear away the smoke. He took a folded cloth from beneath his sash and covered his nose and mouth. After wrapping his hand with the end of his sash to protect himself from physical disease and spiritual pollution, he squatted by the corpse and pulled back the white shroud.

There lay a young woman, full and robust of body, skirts parted to expose naked hips and legs. She had an oval face whose smooth skin and softly curved features must have once been beautiful, but were now smeared with the blood and vomit that also stained her red silk kimono and the tatami around her. Sano swallowed hard. Earlier this morning he'd been too nervous about the wedding to eat; now, the sensation of nausea on an empty stomach was almost overpowering. He shook his head in pity. Lady Harume had died in the bloom of her youth. Then Sano frowned, noticing the corpse's odd condition.

Her whole body looked as rigid as if she'd been dead for many hours, instead of just moments: spine arched, fists tight, arms and legs stiffly straight, jaws clenched. With his covered hand, Sano palpated her arm. It felt hard and unyielding, the muscles frozen in a permanent spasm. And Harume's wide-open eyes seemed too dark. Leaning over for a closer look, Sano saw that the pupils were dilated to maximum size. And her shaved pubis bore what appeared to be a freshly tattooed symbol, still red and puffy around the inked black cuts—the character *ai*:

At the sound of footsteps in the corridor, Sano looked up to see Hirata and the castle physician enter the room. They crouched beside him, cloths held over their noses and mouths, studying Lady Harume's corpse.

"What disease was this, Dr. Kitano?" Sano spoke through his own cloth, which was now wet with saliva.

The doctor shook his head. He had a lined face, and thin gray hair knotted at his nape. "I don't know. I've been a physician for thirty years, but I've never seen or heard of anything like this before. The sudden onset, the violent delirium and convulsions, the dilated pupils, the rapid demise . . . It's a mystery to me; I know of no cure. The gods help us if this disease should spread."

Hirata said, "During my first year in the police service, a fever killed three hundred people in Nihonbashi. Not with those symptoms, or so quickly, but it caused serious trouble. Shops were deserted by owners who had died or run for the hills. Fires started because people burned candles and incense to purify their homes and keep away the fever demon. Bodies lay in the streets because they couldn't be taken away fast enough. The smoke from all the funerals made a big, black cloud over the whole city."

Sano covered Harume's corpse with the shroud, stood, and put away his facecloth, as did his companions. He remembered the epidemic and dreaded an even more disastrous repeat here, in the heart of Japan's government. But because of his observations, another, equally disturbing alternative occurred to him.

"Had Lady Harume displayed any signs of illness before now?" he asked Dr. Kitano.

"Yesterday I personally conducted her monthly examination, as I do for all the concubines. Harume was in perfect health."

Even as Sano's fear of an epidemic waned, he felt a

growing sense of unease. "Are any of the other women sick?"

"I haven't examined them all yet, but the chief lady official tells me that although they're upset, they're physically well."

"I see." Though this was Sano's first visit to the Large Interior, he knew of its crowded conditions. "The women live together, sleep together, bathe together, eat the same food, and drink the same water? And they and the staff are in constant contact with one another?"

"That is correct, *sōsakan-sama,*" the doctor said.

"Yet no one else shares Lady Harume's symptoms." Sano exchanged glances with Hirata, whose face showed dawning—and dismayed—comprehension. "Dr. Kitano, I think we must consider the possibility that Lady Harume was poisoned."

The doctor's worried expression turned to one of horror. "Lower your voice, I beg you!" he said, though Sano had spoken softly. Casting a furtive glance toward the corridor, he whispered, "In this day and age, poison is often a possibility in a case of sudden, unexplained death." Indeed, Sano knew that it was used commonly in peacetime by people who wanted to attack their enemies without open warfare. "But are you aware of the dangers of making such a claim?"

Sano was. News of a poisoning—whether actual or conjectured—would create an atmosphere of suspicion just as destructive as an epidemic. The legendary hostilities in the Large Interior would escalate, and might even turn violent. This had happened in the past. Shortly before Sano came to the castle, two concubines had ended an argument in a brawl, the winner stabbing the loser to death with a hairpin. Eleven years ago, an attendant had strangled a female palace official in the bath. Panic could spread to the rest of the castle, intensifying existing rivalries and provoking fatal duels among samurai officials and troops.

And what if the shogun, ever sensitive to challenges to his authority, should perceive the murder of a concubine as an attack upon himself? Sano envisioned a bloody purge of potential culprits. Seeking a possible conspiracy, the *bakufu*—Japan's military government—would investigate every official, from the Council of Elders down to the most humble clerks; every servant; every daimyo—provincial lord—and all their retainers; even the lowliest *rōnin*. Politically ambitious individuals would try to advance themselves by casting aspersions upon their rivals. Evidence would be manufactured, rumors circulated, characters maligned, until one or many "criminals" were executed. . . .

"We have no proof that Lady Harume was murdered," Dr. Kitano said.

Noting the man's pallor, Sano knew he feared that, as chief physician, with a knowledge of drugs, he would be the prime suspect in a crime involving poison. Sano himself had no desire to face the *bakufu*'s scrutiny, because he had a powerful enemy eager for his ruin. The image of Chamberlain Yanagisawa flashed through Sano's mind. Sano now had a wife and in-laws, also vulnerable to attack. In Nagasaki he'd learned the dire consequences of indulging curiosity by probing sensitive matters. . . .

Yet, as always at the beginning of an investigation, Sano found himself entering a realm where higher concerns outweighed personal, practical ones. Duty, loyalty, and courage were the cardinal virtues of Bushido—the Way of the Warrior—the foundation of a samurai's honor. But Sano's personal concept of honor encompassed a fourth, equally important cornerstone: the pursuit of truth and justice, which gave his life meaning. Despite the risks, he had to know how and why Lady Harume had died.

Also, if she had been murdered, there might be more deaths unless he took action. This time his personal desires coincided with the interests of security and peace in Edo Castle, for good or bad.

"I agree that we can't rule out disease yet," Sano said to Dr. Kitano. "An epidemic is still a possibility. Finish your examination of the women, keep them quarantined, and report any cases of illness or death to me immediately. And please have someone take Lady Harume's body to Edo Morgue."

"Edo Morgue?" The doctor gaped. "But *sōsakan-sama*, high-ranking castle residents don't go there when they die;

we send them to Zōjō Temple for cremation. Surely you know this. And Lady Harume cannot be removed yet. A report documenting the circumstances of her death must be filed. The priests must prepare the body for the funeral, and her comrades keep an overnight vigil. It's standard procedure."

During such rituals the corpse would deteriorate, and evidence possibly get lost. "Arrange Lady Harume's transport to Edo Morgue," Sano said. "That's an order." Unwilling to say why he wanted the concubine taken to a place where dead commoners, outcasts, and victims of mass disasters such as floods or earthquakes went, Sano knew that a show of authority often yielded better results than explanations.

The doctor hurried off. Sano and Hirata surveyed the room. "The source of the poison?" Hirata said, pointing at the floor near Lady Harume's shrouded corpse. Two delicate porcelain cups lay on the tatami; their spilled contents had darkened the woven straw. "Maybe someone was with her, and slipped the poison into her drink."

Sano picked up a matching decanter from the table, looked inside, and saw that a bit of liquor remained. "We'll take this, and the cups, as evidence," he said. "But there's more than one way to administer poison. Perhaps she breathed it." Sano gathered lamps and incense burners. "And what do you make of the tattoo?"

"The character *ai*," Hirata said. " 'Love.' " He grimaced in distaste. "Yoshiwara courtesans mark themselves this way to prove their love for their clients—even though everyone knows they really do it to get more money from the men. But I would have thought that the shogun's concubines were too elegant and refined to stoop to such a low-class custom. Do you think the tattoo has anything to do with Lady Harume's death?"

"Perhaps." Sano contemplated the razor, blood-tipped knife, and shaved pubic hairs on the floor. "It looks as though she'd just finished the tattoo before she died."

He collected the tools, then found the ink bottle lying in the corner and placed it with the other items. Then he and Hirata began searching the room.

Cabinets and chests contained folded quilts and futons; kimonos and sashes; toiletries, hair ornaments, makeup; a samisen; writing brush and inkstone—the miscellany of women's lives—but no food, drink, or anything resembling a poisonous substance. Wrapped inside a white under-kimono Sano found a book the size of his hand, bound in silk printed with a pattern of pale green intertwined clover stems and blossoms on a mauve background, and tied with gold cord. He leafed through sheets of soft rice paper covered with tiny characters written in a feminine hand. The first page read, "The Pillow Book of Lady Harume."

"A diary?" Hirata asked.

"It looks like it." Since the reign of the Heian emperors five hundred years ago, court ladies had often recorded their experiences and thoughts in books like this. Sano tucked the diary under his sash for later perusal, then said quietly to Hirata, "I'm taking the sake, lamp oil, incense, tools, and ink to Dr. Ito at Edo Morgue—perhaps he can identify the poison, if it's there." He carefully bundled the articles in the garment that had contained the diary. "While I'm gone, please supervise the removal and transport of Lady Harume's body; see that no one tampers with it."

From outside the room, Sano heard the priests' muttered conversation, the chatter and weeping of women in nearby chambers. Lowering his voice even more, he continued, "For now, the official cause of death is illness, with an epidemic still a possibility. Have our men distribute the news to everyone who lives in the castle, instructing them to stay in their quarters or at their posts until the danger has passed." Over the past year, Sano's personal staff had grown into a team of one hundred detectives, soldiers, and clerks, enough to handle this large task. He added, "That should help prevent rumors from spreading."

Hirata nodded. "If Lady Harume died of a contagious disease, we need to know what she did, where she went, and whom she saw just before she died, so we can trace the sickness and quarantine her contacts. I'll set up appointments with the chief lady palace official, and His Excellency's Honorable Mother."

The shogun's wife was a reclusive invalid who kept to

her bed, her privacy and health guarded by a few trusted physicians and attendants. Therefore Tokugawa Tsunayoshi's mother, Lady Keisho-in, his constant companion and frequent adviser, ruled the Large Interior.

"But if it was murder," Hirata continued in a lower voice, "we'll need information about Lady Harume's relations with the people around her. I'll make discreet inquiries."

"Good." Sano knew he could trust Hirata, who had demonstrated impressive competence and unswerving loyalty during their association. In Nagasaki, the young retainer had helped solve a difficult case—and saved Sano's life.

"And *sōsakan-sama*? I'm sorry about the wedding banquet." They left the room, and Hirata bowed. "My congratulations on your marriage. It will be a privilege to extend my service to the Honorable Lady Reiko."

"Thank you, Hirata-*san*." Sano also bowed. He appreciated Hirata's friendship, which had supported him through a lonely period of his life. One of the hardest things about his job had been learning to share responsibility and risk, but Hirata had taught him the necessity—and honor—of both. They were united in the ancient samurai tradition of master and servant, absolute and eternal. Glad to leave matters in trustworthy hands, Sano left the palace, bound for Edo Morgue.

The gate to Sano's mansion in the Edo Castle Official Quarter stood open to the bright autumn afternoon. Up the street, past the estates of other high *bakufu* officials, porters carried wedding gifts from prominent citizens hoping to win favor with the shogun's *sōsakan*. Servants transferred the bundles across the paved courtyard, through the wooden inner fence, and into the tile-roofed, half-timbered house. There maids unpacked; cooks labored in the kitchen; the housekeeper supervised last-minute preparations for the newlyweds' residency. Members of the *sōsakan*'s elite detective corps passed among the surrounding barracks, the stables, and the house's front offices, and through the gate, carrying on business in their master's absence.

Isolated from this clamor of purposeful activity, Ueda Reiko, still wearing her white bridal kimono, knelt in her chamber in the mansion's private living quarters, amid chests filled with personal belongings brought from Magistrate Ueda's house. The newly decorated room smelled sweetly of fresh tatami. A colorful mural of birds in a forest adorned the wall. A black lacquer dressing table with matching screen and cabinet, inlaid with gold butterflies, stood ready for Reiko's use. Afternoon sunlight shone through latticed paper windows; outside, birds sang in the garden. Yet the pleasant surroundings, and even the fact that she was now living at Edo Castle—the goal of all ladies of her class—failed to lift the unhappiness that weighed upon Reiko's spirit.

"There you are, young mistress!"

Into the room hurried O-sugi, Reiko's childhood nurse and companion, who had moved to the castle with her.

Plump and smiling, O-sugi regarded Reiko with affectionate exasperation. "Daydreaming, as usual."

"What else is there to do?" Reiko asked sadly. "The banquet was canceled. Everyone is gone. And you said not to unpack, because there are servants to wait on me, and it would make a bad impression if I did anything for myself."

Reiko had counted on the festivities to take her mind off her homesickness and fears. The death of the shogun's concubine and the possibility of an epidemic seemed trivial in comparison with these. How could she, who had never left her father's house for more than a few days, live here, forever, with a man who was a stranger to her? Although Sano's absence delayed the scary plunge into the unknown future, Reiko had nothing to do but worry.

The nurse clucked her tongue. "Well, you could change your clothes. No use hanging about in bridal kimono, now that the wedding is over."

With O-sugi's assistance, off came the white robe and red under-kimono; on went an expensive kimono from Reiko's trousseau, printed with burgundy maple leaves on a background of brown woodgrain, yet dull and somber compared to her customary gay, bright maiden's clothing. Its sleeves reached only to her hips—unlike the floor-length ones she had worn until today—suitable for a married woman. O-sugi pinned Reiko's long hair atop her head in a new, mature style. As Reiko stood before the mirror, watching the trappings of her youth disappear and her reflection age, her unhappiness deepened.

Was she doomed to a secluded existence within this house, a mere vessel for her husband's children, a slave to his authority? Must all her dreams die on the first day of her adult life?

Reiko's unusual girlhood had disinclined her for marriage. She was Magistrate Ueda's only child; her mother had died when she was a baby, and he had never married again. He could have ignored his daughter, consigning her to the complete care of servants, as other men in his situation might have, but Magistrate Ueda had valued Reiko as all that remained of the beloved wife he'd lost. Her intelligence had secured his affection.

At age four, she would toddle into his study and peer at the reports he wrote. "What does this say?" she would ask, pointing to one character after another.

Once the magistrate taught her a word, she never forgot. Soon she could read simple sentences. She still remembered the joy of discovering that each character had its own meaning, and that a column of them expressed an idea. Abandoning her dolls, she spent hours inking her own words on large sheets of paper. Magistrate Ueda had encouraged Reiko's interest. He'd employed tutors to instruct her in reading, calligraphy, history, mathematics, philosophy, and the Chinese classics: subjects that a son would have been taught. When he'd found his six-year-old daughter wielding his sword against an imaginary foe, he'd hired martial arts masters to instruct her in *kenjutsu* and unarmed combat.

"A samurai woman must know how to defend herself in case of war," Magistrate Ueda had told the two *sensei*, who'd been reluctant to teach a girl.

Reiko recalled their disdainful treatment of her, and the lessons intended to dissuade her from this manly pursuit. They'd brought bigger, stronger boys to serve as her opponents in practice matches. But Reiko's proud spirit refused to break. Hair disheveled, white uniform stained with sweat and blood, she'd battered at her opponent with her wooden sword until he went down under a storm of blows. She'd wrestled to the floor a boy twice her size. Her reward was the respect she saw in the teachers' eyes—and the real, steel swords her father had given her, replacing each pair with longer ones every year as she grew. She loved stories of historical battles, envisioning herself as the great warriors Minamoto Yoritomo or Tokugawa Ieyasu. Reiko's playmates were the sons of her father's retainers; she scorned other girls as weak, frivolous creatures. She was sure that, as her father's only child, she would one day inherit his position as magistrate of Edo, and she must be ready.

Reality had soon cured her of this notion. "Girls don't become magistrates when they grow up," scoffed her teachers and friends. "They marry, raise children, and serve their husbands."

And Reiko had overheard her grandmother telling Magistrate Ueda, "It isn't right to treat Reiko like a boy. If you don't stop these ridiculous lessons, she'll never learn her place in the world. She must be taught some feminine accomplishments, or she'll never get a husband."

Magistrate Ueda had compromised, continuing the lessons but also engaging teachers to instruct Reiko in sewing, flower arranging, music, and the tea ceremony. And still she had clung to her dreams. Her life would be different from other women's: She would have adventures; she would achieve glory.

Then, when Reiko was fifteen, her grandmother had persuaded the magistrate that it was time for her to marry. Her first *miai*—the formal meeting between a prospective bride and groom and their families—had taken place at Zōjō Temple. Reiko, who had observed the lives of her aunts and cousins, didn't want to marry at all. She knew that wives must obey every command and cater to every whim of their husbands, passively enduring insults or abuse. Even the most respected man could be a tyrant in his own home, forbidding his wife to speak, forcing physical attentions upon her, begetting one child after another until her health failed, then neglecting her to dally with concubines or prostitutes. While men came and went as they pleased, a wife of Reiko's social class stayed home unless given her husband's permission to attend religious ceremonies or family functions. Servants relieved her of household chores, but kept her idle, useless. To Reiko, marriage seemed like a trap to be avoided at all cost. And her first suitor did nothing to change her mind.

He was a rich, high-ranking Tokugawa bureaucrat. He was also fat, forty, and stupid; during a picnic under the blossoming cherry trees, he got extremely drunk, making lewd remarks about his patronage of the Yoshiwara courtesans. To Reiko's horror, she saw that her grandmother and the go-between didn't share her revulsion; the social and financial advantages of the match blinded them to the man's flaws. Magistrate Ueda would not meet Reiko's gaze, and she sensed that he wanted to break off the negotiations but couldn't find an acceptable reason for doing so. Reiko decided to take matters into her own hands.

"Do you think there was any way Japan could have conquered Korea ninety-eight years ago, instead of having to give up and withdraw the troops?" she asked the bureaucrat.

"Why, I—I'm sure I don't know," he blustered, eyeing her with surprise. "I never thought about it."

But Reiko had. While her grandmother and the go-between stared in dismay and her father tried to hide a smile, she stated her opinion—that Japanese victory over Korea could have been achieved—giving explanations at great length. The next day, the bureaucrat ended the marriage negotiations with a letter that read, "Miss Reiko is too forward, impertinent, and disrespectful to make a good wife. Good luck finding someone else to marry her."

Subsequent *miai* with other unattractive men had ended similarly. Reiko's family protested, scolded, and finally gave up in despair. She rejoiced. Then, on her nineteenth birthday, Magistrate Ueda summoned her to his office and said sadly, "Daughter, I understand your reluctance to marry; it's my own fault for encouraging your interest in unfeminine pursuits. But I won't be able to take care of you forever. You need a husband to protect you when I am dead and gone."

"Father, I'm educated, I can fight, I can take care of myself," Reiko protested, though she knew he spoke the truth. Women did not hold government posts, run businesses, or work as anything other than servants, farm laborers, nuns, or prostitutes. These options repelled Reiko, as did the prospect of living on the charity of relatives. She bowed her head, acknowledging defeat.

"We've received a new marriage proposal," Magistrate Ueda said, "and please don't ruin the negotiations, because we may never get another. It's from Sano Ichirō, the shogun's most honorable investigator."

Reiko's head snapped up. She knew of *Sōsakan* Sano, as did everyone in Edo. She had heard rumors of Sano's courage, and a great but secret service he'd performed for the shogun. Her interest stirred. Wanting to see this famous wonder, she consented to the *miai*.

And Sano didn't disappoint her. As she and Magistrate Ueda strolled the grounds of Kannei Temple with the go-between, Sano, and his mother, Reiko eyed Sano covertly. Tall and strong, with a proud, noble bearing, he was younger than any of her other suitors, and by far the handsomest. As formal custom dictated, they didn't speak directly to each other, but intelligence shone in his eyes, echoed in his voice. Best of all, Reiko knew he was leading the hunt for the Bundori Killer, whose grisly murders had plunged Edo into terror. He wasn't a lazy drunk who neglected duty for the revels of Yoshiwara. He delivered dangerous killers to justice. To Reiko, he seemed the embodiment of the warrior heroes she'd worshipped since childhood. She had a chance to share his exciting life. And when she looked at Sano, an unfamiliar, pleasurable warmth spread through her body. Marriage suddenly didn't look so bad. As soon as they got home, Reiko told Magistrate Ueda to accept the proposal.

When the wedding date was set, however, Reiko's doubts about marriage resurfaced. Her female relatives counseled her to obey and serve her husband; the gifts—kitchen utensils, sewing supplies, home furnishings—symbolized the domestic role she must assume. Her books and swords remained at the Ueda mansion. Hope had flared briefly at the wedding, inspired by the sight of Sano, as handsome as she remembered; but now Reiko feared that her life would be no different from any other married woman's. Her husband was out on an important adventure; she was home. She had no reason to believe that his treatment of her would be different from any other man's. Panic squeezed her lungs.

What had she done? Was it too late to escape?

O-sugi fetched a tray, which she set upon Reiko's dressing table. Reiko saw the short bamboo brush, mirror, and ceramic basin; the two matching bowls, one containing water, the other a dark liquid. Her heart contracted.

"No!"

O-sugi sighed. "Reiko-*chan,* you know you must dye your teeth black. It's the custom for a married woman, proof of her fidelity to her husband. Now come." Gently but firmly she seated Reiko before the table. "The sooner over with, the better."

With leaden reluctance, Reiko dipped the brush in the bowl and opened her mouth in an exaggerated grimace. When she painted the first stroke across her upper teeth, some of the black dye dripped onto her tongue. Her throat spasmed; saliva gushed into her mouth. The dye, composed of ink, iron filings, and plant extracts, was terribly bitter.

"Ugh!" Reiko spat into the basin. "How can anyone stand this?"

"They all do, and so will you. Twice a month, to maintain the color. Now continue, and be careful not to stain your lips or your kimono."

Wincing and gagging, Reiko applied layer after layer of dye to her teeth. Finally she rinsed, spat, then held the mirror before her face. She viewed her reflection with dismay. The dead, black teeth contrasted sharply with the white face powder and red lip rouge, highlighting her skin's every imperfection. With the tip of her tongue, Reiko touched her chipped incisor, a habit in times of strong emotion. At age twenty, she looked ancient—and ugly. Her days of study and martial arts practice were over; hope of romance withered. How could her husband want her for anything besides obedient servitude now?

Reiko choked down a sob, and saw O-sugi regarding her with sympathy. O-sugi had been married at fourteen to a middle-aged Nihonbashi shopkeeper who'd beaten her daily, until the neighbors complained that her cries disturbed them. The case had come before Magistrate Ueda, who sentenced the shopkeeper to a beating, granted O-sugi a divorce, and hired her as nurse to his infant daughter. O-sugi was the only mother Reiko had ever known. Now the bond between them strengthened with the poignant similarity in their situations: one rich, one poor, yet both prisoners of society, their fate dependent upon men.

O-sugi embraced Reiko, saying sadly, "My poor young lady. Life will be easier if you just accept it." Then, in an effort to be cheerful, "After all this wedding excitement, you must be starving. How about some tea and buns—the pink kind, with sweet chestnut paste inside?" This was

Reiko's favorite treat. "I'll bring them right away."

The nurse limped out of the room: Her brutal husband had permanently crippled her left leg. Seeing this ignited angry determination inside Reiko. Then and there she refused to let marriage cripple her own body, or mind. She would not be imprisoned inside this house, talents and ambitions wasted. She would live!

Reiko rose and fetched a cloak from the wardrobe. Then she hurried to the front door, where Sano's staff was unloading the wedding gifts.

"How may I serve you, Honorable Madam?" asked the chief manservant.

"I don't need anything," Reiko said. "I'm going out."

The servant said haughtily, "A lady cannot just walk out of the castle alone. It's against the law."

He arranged an escort of maids and soldiers. He summoned a palanquin and six bearers and installed her inside the ornate, cushioned sedan chair. He gave the escort commander the official document that allowed Reiko passage in and out of the castle, then asked her, "Where shall I tell the *sōsakan-sama* you've gone?"

Reiko was appalled. What could she do while hampered by a sixteen-person entourage that would undoubtedly report her every move to Sano and everyone else at Edo Castle? "To visit my father," she said, accepting defeat.

Trapped in the palanquin, she rode through the castle's winding stone passages, past guard towers and patrolling soldiers. The escort commander presented her pass at the security checkpoints; soldiers opened gates and let the procession continue downhill. Mounted samurai cantered past. Windows in the covered corridors that topped the walls offered brief glimpses of Edo's rooftops, spread out on the plain below, and the fiery red-and-gold autumn foliage along the Sumida River. Against the distant western sky, Mount Fuji's ethereal white peak soared. Reiko saw it all through the small, narrow window of the palanquin. She sighed.

However, once outside the castle's main gate and past the great walled estates of the daimyo, Reiko's spirits rose. Here, in the administrative district, located in Hibiya, south of Edo Castle, the city's high officials lived and worked in office-mansions. Here Reiko had enjoyed the childhood whose end she now regretted so keenly. But perhaps it wasn't entirely lost.

At Magistrate Ueda's estate, she alit from the palanquin. Leaving her entourage outside the wall among the strolling dignitaries and hurrying clerks, she approached the sentries stationed at the gate's roofed portals.

"Good afternoon, Miss Reiko," they greeted her.

"Is my father home?" she asked.

"Yes, but he's hearing a case."

Reiko wasn't surprised that the conscientious magistrate had returned to work when the wedding banquet was canceled. In the courtyard she wove through a crowd of townspeople, police, and prisoners awaiting the magistrate's attention, into the low, half-timbered building. She slipped past the administrative offices and shut herself up inside a chamber adjacent to the Court of Justice.

The room, once a closet, was barely big enough to hold its one tatami mat. With no windows, it was dim and stuffy, yet Reiko had spent some of her happiest hours here. One wall was made of woven lattice. Through the chinks, Reiko had a perfect view of the court. On the other side of the wall her father occupied the dais, wearing black judicial robes, his back to her, flanked by secretaries. Lanterns lit the long hall, where the defendant, his hands tied behind him, knelt on the *shirasu,* an area of floor directly before the dais, covered with white sand, symbol of truth. Police, witnesses, and the defendant's family knelt in rows in the audience section; sentries guarded the doors.

Reiko knelt to watch the proceedings, as she'd done countless times before. Trials fascinated her. They showed a side of life that she could not experience firsthand. Magistrate Ueda had indulged her interest, letting her use this room. Reiko's tongue touched her chipped tooth as she smiled in fond memory.

"What have you to say in your own defense, Moneylender Igarashi?" Magistrate Ueda asked the prisoner.

"Honorable Magistrate, I swear I did not kill my partner," the defendant said with earnest sincerity. "We fought over the favors of the courtesan Hyacinth because we were drunk, but we settled our differences." Tears ran down the defendant's face. "I loved my partner like a brother. I don't know who stabbed him."

During discussions of cases, Reiko had impressed Magistrate Ueda with her insight; he'd come to value her judgment. Now she whispered through the lattice, "The moneylender is lying, Father. He's still jealous of his partner. And now their whole fortune is his. Push him hard—he'll break and confess."

She'd often given her advice during trials this way, and Magistrate Ueda had often followed it, with good results, but now his shoulders stiffened; his head turned slightly. Instead of interrogating the defendant, Magistrate Ueda said, "This session will adjourn for a moment." Rising, he left the courtroom.

Then the door to Reiko's chamber opened. There in the corridor stood her father, regarding her with consternation. "Daughter." Taking Reiko's arm, he led her down the hall, into his private office. "Your first visit home shouldn't take place until tomorrow, and your husband must accompany you. You know the custom. What are you doing here, alone, now? Is something wrong?"

"Father, I—"

Suddenly Reiko's brave defiance crumbled. Sobbing, she poured out her misgivings about marriage; the dreams she could not forsake. Magistrate Ueda listened sympathetically, but when she'd finished and calmed down, he shook his head and said, "I should not have raised you to expect more from life than is possible for a woman. It was an act of foolish love and poor judgment on my part, which I deeply regret. But what's done is done. We cannot go back, but only forward. You must not watch any more trials, or assist with my work as I've mistakenly allowed you to do in the past. Your place is with your husband."

Even as Reiko saw the door to her youth close forever, a gleam of hope brightened the dark horizon of her future. Magistrate Ueda's last sentence recalled her fantasy of sharing *Sōsakan* Sano's adventures. In ancient times, samurai women had ridden into battle beside their men. Reiko remembered the incident that had ended the wedding festivities. Earlier, preoccupied with her own problems, she'd given hardly a thought to Sano's new case; now, her interest stirred.

"Maybe I could help investigate Lady Harume's death," she said thoughtfully.

Concern shadowed Magistrate Ueda's face. "Reiko-*chan*." His voice was kind, but stern. "You're smarter than many men, but you are young, naïve, and far too confident of your own limited abilities. Any affair involving the shogun's court is fraught with danger. *Sōsakan* Sano will not welcome your interference. And what could you, a woman, do anyway?"

Rising, the magistrate led Reiko out of the mansion to the gate, where her entourage waited. "Go home, daughter. Be thankful you needn't work to earn your rice, like other, less fortunate women. Obey your husband; he is a good man." Then, echoing O-sugi's advice, he said, "Accept your fate, or it will only grow harder to bear."

Reluctantly Reiko climbed into the palanquin. Tasting the bitterness of the dye on her teeth, she shook her head in sad acknowledgment of her father's wisdom.

Yet she possessed the same intelligence, drive, and courage that had made him magistrate of Edo—the post she would have inherited if she'd been born male! As the palanquin carried her briskly up the street, Reiko called to the bearers: "Stop! Go back!"

The bearers obeyed. Disembarking, Reiko hurried into her father's house, to her childhood room. From the cabinet she took her two swords, long and short, with matching gold-inlaid hilts and scabbards. Then she returned to the palanquin and settled herself for the trip back to Edo Castle, hugging the precious weapons—symbols of honor and adventure, of everything she was and wanted to be.

Somehow she would make a purposeful, satisfying life for herself. And she would begin by investigating the strange death of the shogun's concubine.

In the slums of Kodemmachō, near the river in the northeast sector of the Nihonbashi merchant district, Edo Jail's complex of high stone walls, watchtowers, and gabled roofs hulked over its surrounding canals like a malignant growth. Sano rode his horse across the bridge toward the iron-banded gate. Sentries manned the guardhouse; *doshin* herded miserable, shackled criminals into the jail to await trial, or out of it toward the execution ground. As always when approaching the prison, Sano imagined that he felt the air grow colder, as if Edo Jail repelled sunlight and exuded a miasma of death and decay. Yet Sano willingly braved the danger of spiritual pollution that other high-ranking samurai avoided. In the city morgue, housed inside the peeling plaster walls, he hoped to learn the truth about the death of Lady Harume.

The sentries opened the gate for Sano. He dismounted and led his horse through the compound of guards' barracks, courtyards, and administrative offices, past the jail proper, where the howls of prisoners drifted from barred windows.

In a courtyard near the rear of the jail, Sano secured his horse outside the morgue, a low building with scabrous plaster walls and a shaggy thatched roof. He took the bundled evidence from Lady Harume's room out of his saddlebag. Crossing the threshold, he braced himself for the sight and smell of Dr. Ito's gruesome work.

The room held stone troughs used to wash the dead; cabinets containing the doctor's tools; a podium in the corner, piled with books and notes. At one of the three waist-high tables, Dr. Ito assembled a collection of human bones in their relative positions. His assistant, Mura, cleaned a pan of vertebrae. Both men looked up from their work and bowed when Sano entered.

"Ah, Sano-*san*. Welcome!" Dr. Ito's narrow, ascetic face brightened with glad surprise. "I did not expect to see you. Is this not the day of your wedding?"

Dr. Ito Genboku, Edo Morgue custodian, whose scientific expertise had aided Sano in many investigations, was also a true friend—rare in the politically treacherous Tokugawa regime.

Shrewd of gaze and keen of mind at age seventy, Dr. Ito had short, abundant white hair that receded at the temples. His long, dark blue coat covered a tall, spare frame. Once esteemed physician to the imperial family, Dr. Ito had been caught practicing forbidden foreign science, which he'd learned through illicit channels from Dutch traders in Nagasaki. Unlike other *rangakusha*—scholars of Dutch learning—he'd been punished not by exile, but by being sentenced to permanent custodianship of Edo Morgue. Here, though the living conditions were squalid, he could experiment in peace, ignored by the authorities.

"I was married this morning, but the wedding banquet and my holiday were canceled," Sano said, laying his bundle on an empty table. "And once again, I need your help." He explained about Lady Harume's mysterious death, the shogun's orders for him to investigate, and his suspicion of murder.

"Most intriguing," Dr. Ito said. "Of course I shall assist in any way I can. But first, my congratulations on your marriage. Allow me to present you with a small gift. Mura, will you please fetch it?"

Mura, a short man with gray hair and a square, intelligent face, set aside his pan of bones. He was an *eta*, one of society's outcast class who staffed the jail, acting as corpse handlers, jailers, torturers, and executioners. *Eta* also performed such dirty work as emptying cesspools, collecting garbage, and clearing away dead bodies after floods, fires, and earthquakes. Their hereditary link with such death-related occupations as butchering and leather tanning rendered them spiritually contaminated, unfit for contact with other citizens. But shared adversity forged strange bonds; Mura was Dr. Ito's servant and companion. Now the *eta* bowed to his master and Sano and left the room. He returned with a small package wrapped in a scrap of blue cotton, which Dr. Ito handed to Sano.

"My gift in honor of your marriage."

"*Arigatō,* Ito-*san.*" Bowing, Sano accepted the package and unfolded the wrapping. Inside the cloth lay a flat, palm-size circle of black wrought iron: a guard meant to fit between the blade and hilt of a samurai's sword. The filigree design was a variation on Sano's family crest, with a crane's elegant, long-beaked head in profile, a slit for the blade cut through its body, and elaborately feathered, upswept wings. Caressing the smooth metal, Sano admired the gift.

"It's just a poor, humble thing," Dr. Ito said. "Mura gathered scrap iron in the city. One of the janitors was a metalsmith before being convicted of thievery and sentenced to work here. He helped me make the sword guard at night. It's not really good enough for—"

"It's beautiful," Sano said, "and I'll treasure it always." Carefully he rewrapped the sword guard and tucked the package in his drawstring pouch, more moved by Ito's thoughtful gesture than by any of the lavish presents he'd received from strangers currying favor. Then, to fill the awkward silence that ensued, he opened his bundle and explained the circumstances of Lady Harume's death. "Her corpse won't arrive for examination until later. But there's a strong possibility that she was poisoned." Sano set out the lamps, incense burners, sake decanter, razor, knife, and ink jar. "I want to know whether one of these things is the source of the poison."

At the doctor's orders, Mura fetched six small, empty wooden cages, and a larger one containing six live mice. Dr. Ito lined the cages up on the table. In the first two small ones, he lit a lamp and incense burner from Lady Harume's room, placed a wriggling gray mouse into each cage, and covered them with cloths.

"This method should expose the mice to any poison in the oil or incense," Dr. Ito said, "while protecting us from dangerous fumes."

In the third cage he set a dish of the sake that Harume had apparently imbibed shortly before her death, and a third mouse. To test the razor, Dr. Ito shaved a patch of hair off a fourth mouse's back; with the pearl-handled knife he made a shallow cut on the fifth mouse's belly, then dropped the animals into separate cages.

"And now the ink." From a cabinet Dr. Ito took one of his own knives. "I'll use a clean blade to avoid introducing extraneous contamination." He made a scratch on the sixth mouse's belly, unstoppered the lacquer jar, and brushed black ink onto the wound. Then he dropped the mouse into its cage and said, "Now we wait."

Sano and Dr. Ito watched the cages. Faint scratchings came from within the two cloth-covered ones. The third mouse sniffed the liquor, then began to drink. The razor-shaved mouse roamed his cage while the others licked their wounds. Suddenly a high shriek rang out.

"Look!" Sano pointed.

The mouse with ink on its cut belly writhed, back arching, tiny claws grasping the air, tail whipping back and forth. Its chest heaved as if trying desperately to suck air into the lungs; its eyes rolled. The little pink mouth opened and closed, emitting cries of agony, then a gush of blood. Sano indicated the symptoms which matched the castle physician's description of those suffered by Lady Harume: "Convulsions. Vomiting. Shortness of breath."

A few more squeals and gasps, a final paroxysm, then the mouse lay dead. Sano and Dr. Ito bowed their heads in respect for the animal that had given its life to the pursuit of scientific knowledge. Then they checked the other cages.

"This mouse is intoxicated," Dr. Ito said, observing the creature that staggered around the now-empty sake dish, "but otherwise healthy." The shaved animal and the knife-cut one scampered about their cages. "No apparent ill effects here, either." Dr. Ito lifted the cloths off the last two cages, releasing clouds of pungent smoke and revealing two groggy but living mice. "Or here. The ink alone contained poison."

"Could this have been suicide?" Sano asked, still hoping for an easy resolution to Lady Harume's death.

"Possibly, but I think not. Even if she had wanted to die, why choose such a painful method, instead of hanging or drowning herself? Those are the more common means of female suicide. And why bother putting the poison in the ink, instead of simply swallowing it?"

"So Lady Harume was murdered." Dismay tempered Sano's gratification at having his suspicions confirmed. He must report the news to the shogun, the chief castle physician, and palace officials; it would then spread throughout Edo. To prevent destructive consequences, Sano must identify the poisoner, fast. "What substance kills so quickly and horribly?"

"When I was physician to the Imperial Court in Kyōto, I made a study of poisons," Dr. Ito said. "The symptoms caused by this one match those of *bish,* an extract of a plant native to the Himalayan region. *Bish* has been used in India and China for almost two thousand years as an arrow toxin, both for hunting and in warfare. As you can see, a small amount introduced into the blood is fatal. People have also died after mistaking the plant's roots for horseradish. But the plant is extremely rare in Japan. I've never heard of any such poisoning cases here."

"Where could the poison that killed Lady Harume have come from?" Sano asked. "Am I looking for a murderer with special knowledge of herbs? Such as a sorcerer, priest, or doctor?"

"Perhaps. But there are druggists who illegally sell poisons to any customer able to pay." Dr. Ito told Mura to remove the mice. Then his expression turned thoughtful. "These merchants usually offer common poisons such as arsenic, which can be mixed with sugar and dusted onto cakes, or antimony, which is administered in tea or wine. Or fugu, the poisonous blowfish.

"But there was one man who became a legend among physicians and scientists: an itinerant peddler who traveled around Japan, collecting remedies from remote areas and in port cities where the locals possess medical knowledge gleaned from foreigners before Japan was closed to free international trade. His name was Choyei, and I used to buy medicine from him when he passed through Kyōto. He knew more about drugs than anyone I've ever met. Mostly he dealt in beneficial substances, though he also sold poisons to scientists who, like myself, desired to study them. And there were rumors that his merchandise had caused the deaths of several high *bakufu* officials."

"Could he be in Edo now?" Sano asked. If the poison dealer named a recent purchaser of *bish,* Lady Harume's murder could be solved.

"I haven't seen Choyei—or heard anything of him—in years. He must be about my age now, if he's still alive. An odd, reclusive individual who wandered wherever fancy took him, according to no particular schedule, disguised as a tramp. I heard he was a fugitive from the law."

Though discouraged by this story, Sano didn't lose hope. "If Choyei is here, I'll find him. And there's another possible route to the killer." Sano held up the ink jar. "I'll try to discover where Lady Harume got this, and who could have put poison into it."

"Perhaps the lover for whom she tattooed herself?" Dr. Ito suggested. "Unfortunately, Lady Harume didn't cut his name on her flesh, as courtesans often do, but she would have wished to obscure his identity, if he was someone other than the shogun."

"Because a concubine could be dismissed, or even executed for infidelity to her lord," Sano agreed. "And the place she chose for the tattoo suggests that she wanted secrecy." He rewrapped the evidence. "I plan to interview the shogun's mother and her chief lady palace official. Maybe they can provide information about people who might have wanted Lady Harume dead."

Dr. Ito accompanied Sano outside to the courtyard, now shaded by the coming twilight. "Thank you for your help, Ito-*san,* and for the gift," Sano said. "When Lady Harume's corpse arrives, I'll return for the examination."

After loading the evidence into his saddlebag, Sano mounted his horse, eager to continue the investigation, yet reluctant to return to Edo Castle. Would he find the killer before fear heightened the dangerous personal and political tensions there? Could he avoid becoming a casualty of the inevitable plots and schemes?

Autumn twilight descended upon Edo. Clouds sketched swirls across a pale gold western sky, like script written in smoke. Lanterns burned above gates and in the windows of peasant houses, merchant dwellings, and great daimyo mansions, the Edo residences of landowning lords. A gibbous moon rose amid early stars, distant beacons heralding night and guiding a hunting party that tramped through the Edo Castle forest preserve. Porters laden with chests of supplies followed servants leading horses and barking dogs. Ahead, the hunters, armed with bows, moved on foot among the trees, above which birds soared in prenocturnal flight.

"Honorable Chamberlain Yanagisawa, is it not getting a bit late for hunting?" Senior Elder Makino Narisada hurried to catch up with his superior. The other four members of Japan's Council of Elders followed, huffing and gasping. "There is a most unpleasant chill in the air. And soon it will be too dark to see anything. Should we not go back to the palace and continue our meeting in comfort?"

"Nonsense," Yanagisawa retorted, drawing his bow and sighting along the arrow. "Night is the best time to hunt. Though I cannot see my prey clearly, neither can he see me. It's much more of a challenge than hunting in the unsubtle light of day."

Tall, slender, strong—and, at age thirty-three, at least fifteen years younger than any of his comrades—Chamberlain Yanagisawa moved swiftly through the woods. Night's mystical energy always stimulated his senses. Vision and hearing gained power and clarity until he could detect the slightest motion. In the forest's pine-scented shadows, he heard wings flap softly as a bird landed on a nearby bough. He froze, then took aim.

Hunting aroused Yanagisawa's killing instinct. What better condition in which to conduct affairs of state? He let fly the arrow. With a thump, it struck a tree. The bird flew off unharmed. Squawks arose as a nearby flock took wing in panic.

"A marvelous shot," Senior Elder Makino said anyway. The other elders echoed his praise.

Chamberlain Yanagisawa smiled, not caring that he'd missed his target. He was after larger, more important prey. "Now, what is the next subject on our agenda?"

"The *sōsakan-sama*'s report on his successful murder investigation and capture of a smuggling ring in Nagasaki."

"Ah. Yes." Fury filled Yanagisawa like a geyser of corrosive fluid, tapping the deeper anger that had burgeoned in him ever since Sano Ichirō had come to Edo Castle. Sano was a rival he'd failed to eliminate, a man who stood between him and his heart's desire.

"His Excellency was very impressed with the *sōsakan-sama*'s victory," Makino said, a hint of sly satisfaction coloring his obsequious manner. "What do you think, Honorable Chamberlain?"

With emphatic, deliberate movements, Yanagisawa took another arrow from his quiver and kept walking. "Something must be done about Sano Ichirō," he said.

Since his youth, Yanagisawa had been the shogun's lover, using his influence over Tokugawa Tsunayoshi to gain the exalted position of second-in-command, actual ruler of Japan. Yanagisawa's administrative skills kept the government functioning while the shogun indulged a passion for the arts, religion, and young boys. Through the years, Yanagisawa had amassed great riches by skimming money from tributes paid to the Tokugawa by daimyo clans and taxes collected from merchants, and by charging fees for access to the shogun. Everyone bowed to Yanagisawa's authority. Yet all this wealth and power wasn't enough. Recently he had formulated a plan for becoming a daimyo, the official governor of an entire province. Four months ago he'd banished *Sōsakan* Sano to Nagasaki, thinking he'd seen the last of his enemy, believing that he'd permanently secured his position as the shogun's favorite.

However, his plan had backfired. Sano had survived exile—as he had Yanagisawa's past attempts to discredit him—and returned a hero. Today he'd married the daughter of Magistrate Ueda, who also had more influence with the shogun than Yanagisawa liked. Tokugawa Tsunayoshi, peeved at him for sending Sano away, had so far refused Yanagisawa's bid to enlarge his domain. Sano's status at court had risen. So had that of another rival, whose influence Chamberlain Yanagisawa had easily counteracted in the past. And now, with the shogun finally aware of the animosity between his advisers, Yanagisawa dared not use against Sano the method he'd employed to dispose of past enemies: assassination. The risk of exposure and subsequent punishment was too great. Still, he must somehow destroy his competition.

"Honorable Chamberlain, if the *sōsakan-sama* protects Japan from corruption and treason, isn't this a good thing?" said Hamada Kazuo, an increasingly enthusiastic partisan of Sano. "Should we not support his efforts?"

Murmurs of timid agreement came from all the elders except Makino, Yanagisawa's chief crony. Panic flared in Chamberlain Yanagisawa. The elders had once accepted his pronouncements without any objection. Now, because of Sano, he was losing control over the men who advised the shogun and set government policy. But he wouldn't let it happen. No one must impede his rise to power.

"How dare you contradict me?" he demanded. Speeding his pace, he forced the elders to walk faster as they offered hasty apologies. "Hurry up!"

Oh, how he savored their obedience, a reminder of his authority—and how he dreaded its slightest weakening, which threatened to plunge him into the nightmare of his past. . . .

His father had been chamberlain to Lord Takei, daimyo of Arima Province, and his mother the daughter of a merchant family that had sought advancement through union with a samurai clan. Both parents had viewed children as tools to improve the family's rank. Money and attention were lavished upon their upbringing, but only as means to an end: a position in the shogun's court.

In Yanagisawa's clearest early memory, he and his brother Yoshihiro knelt in his father's gloomy audience chamber. He was six, Yoshihiro twelve. Rain pattered on the tile roof; it seemed that the sun never shone in those days. Upon the dais sat their father, a grim, towering figure dressed in black.

"Yoshihiro, your tutor reports that you are failing all your academic subjects." Contempt laced their father's voice. To Yanagisawa he said, "And the martial arts master tells me that you lost in a practice sword match yesterday."

He didn't mention the fact that Yanagisawa could read and write as well as boys twice his age, or that Yoshihiro was the best young swordsman in town. "How do you expect to bring honor to the family this way?" His face purpled with anger. "You're both worthless fools, unfit to be my sons!"

Grabbing the wooden pole that always lay upon the dais, he battered the boys' bodies. Yanagisawa and Yoshihiro cringed under the painful beating, fighting tears which would further enrage their father. In an adjacent chamber their mother punished their sister, Kiyoko, for her failure to excel at the accomplishments she must master before they could marry her off to a high-ranking official: "Stupid, disobedient girl!"

The sound of slaps, blows, and Kiyoko's weeping echoed constantly through that house. No matter what the children achieved, it was never enough to please their elders. Still, the punishment might have been bearable if they'd found consolation in the company of people outside the family, or in one another's love. However, their parents had made this impossible.

"Those brats are beneath you," Yanagisawa's mother would say, isolating him and his siblings from the young offspring of Lord Takei's other retainers. "One day you'll be their superiors."

The children learned that they could avoid punishment by passing the blame for misbehavior. Therefore, they hated and distrusted one another.

Through all those terrible years, Yanagisawa remembered crying only once, on the cold, rainy day of his brother Yoshihiro's funeral. At age seventeen, Yoshihiro had committed *seppuku.* While priests chanted, Yanagisawa and Kiyoko wept bitterly, the only people in the crowd of mourners to show emotion.

"Stop that!" whispered their parents, administering slaps. "Such a pathetic display of weakness. What will people think? Why can't you bring honor to the family, like Yoshihiro did?"

But Yanagisawa and Kiyoko knew that their brother's ritual suicide wasn't a gesture of honor. Yoshihiro, the eldest son, had succumbed to the pressure of being the chief repository of the family's ambitions. Always falling short of his parents' expectations, he'd killed himself to avoid further anguish. Yanagisawa and Kiyoko wept not for him but for themselves, because their parents had traded their lives for a higher place in society.

Kiyoko, fifteen and married to a wealthy official, had lost a child during one of her husband's beatings, and was pregnant again. And Yanagisawa, eleven, had served three years as Lord Takei's page and sexual object. His anus bled from the daimyo's assaults; his pride had suffered even worse mortifications.

Then, as the smoke from the funeral pyre drifted over the cremation ground, a change took place inside Yanagisawa. The weeping drained a reservoir of accumulated misery from his heart until there was nothing left except a bitter core of resolve. Yoshihiro had died because he was weak. Kiyoko was a helpless girl. But Yanagisawa vowed that someday he would be the most powerful man in the country. Then no one could ever use, punish, or humiliate him again. He would exact revenge upon everyone who had ever hurt him. Everyone would do his bidding; everyone would fear his anger.

Eleven years later, Tokugawa Tsunayoshi heard reports of a young man whose looks and intelligence had facilitated his rapid advancement through the ranks of Lord Takei's retainers. Tsunayoshi, enamored of beautiful males, summoned Yanagisawa to Edo Castle. Yanagisawa had grown to splendid maturity; he was arrestingly handsome, with intense dark eyes. When the palace guards escorted Yanagisawa into Tsunayoshi's private chamber, the twenty-nine-year-old future shogun dropped the book he was reading and stared.

"Magnificent," he said. Wonder dawned on his soft, effeminate features. To the guards, he said, "Leave us."

By this time, Yanagisawa knew his own limitations and assets. The relatively low status of his clan impeded his entry into the *bakufu*'s upper ranks, as did lack of wealth, but he'd learned how to use the talents given him by the gods of fortune. Now, gazing into Tokugawa Tsunayoshi's eyes, he saw lust, weakness of mind and spirit, and a craving for approval. Inwardly Yanagisawa smiled. He bowed without bothering to kneel first, taking the first of many liberties with the future shogun. Tokugawa Tsunayoshi, humble in his awe, bowed back. Yanagisawa walked to the dais and picked up the older man's book.

"What are you reading, Your Excellency?" he asked.

"The, ahh, ahh—" Stammering with excitement, Tokugawa Tsunayoshi trembled beside Yanagisawa. *"The Dream of the Red Chamber."*

Boldly Yanagisawa sat on the dais and read from the classic, erotic Chinese novel. His reading, perfected by childhood study and punishment, was flawless. He paused between passages, smiling provocatively into Tsunayoshi's eyes. Tsunayoshi blushed. Yanagisawa held out his hand. Eagerly the future shogun grasped it.

There was a knock at the door, and an official entered. "Your Excellency, it's time for your meeting with the Council of Elders. They're to brief you on the state of the nation and solicit your opinion on new government policies."

"I, ahh . . . I'm busy now. Can't it wait? Besides, I don't think I have any opinions on anything." Tsunayoshi looked to Yanagisawa, as if for rescue.

At that moment, Yanagisawa saw his path to the future he'd envisioned. He would be Tsunayoshi's companion, and furnish the views that the foolish dictator lacked. Through Tokugawa Tsunayoshi, Yanagisawa would rule

Japan. He would wield the shogun's power of life and death over its citizens.

"We'll both attend the meeting," he said. The official frowned at his impertinence, but Tsunayoshi nodded meekly. As they left the room together, Yanagisawa whispered to his new lord, "When the meeting is over, we shall have all the time in the world to become acquainted."

When Tokugawa Tsunayoshi assumed the position of shogun, Yanagisawa became chamberlain. Former superiors fell under his control. He seized Lord Takei's lands, turning the daimyo and all his retainers—including Yanagisawa's father—out to fend for themselves. Yanagisawa received urgent letters from his impoverished parents, begging for mercy. With a gleeful sense of vindication, he denied aid to the family that had brought him up to be exactly what he was. Yet Yanagisawa never forgot how precarious a position he held. The shogun doted on him, but new rivals vied constantly for Tsunayoshi's changeable favor. Yanagisawa dominated the *bakufu,* but no regime lasted forever.

Senior Elder Makino's crackly voice drew Chamberlain Yanagisawa out of his ruminations. "We should discuss the possible epidemic and plan how to prevent serious consequences."

"There will be no epidemic," Yanagisawa said. As the sky's brightness diminished, forest trails vanished into the tangle of trees, but Yanagisawa maintained his pace. "Lady Harume was poisoned."

The elders gasped and exclaimed. "Poisoned?" "But we've heard nothing of this." "How do you know?"

"Oh, I have ways of learning things." Chamberlain Yanagisawa had spies in the Large Interior, as well as everywhere else in Edo. These agents maintained surveillance on important people, eavesdropping on their conversations and riffling through their belongings.

"There will be trouble," Makino said. "What shall we do?"

"We needn't do anything," Yanagisawa said. "*Sōsakan* Sano is investigating the murder."

Suddenly a brilliant plan burst into his mind. By using

Lady Harume's murder case, he could destroy Sano—and his other rival. Yanagisawa wanted to rejoice aloud, but the plan required extreme discretion. He needed the sort of accomplice not offered by the present company.

Halting the procession in a clearing, Chamberlain Yanagisawa told his entourage, "You may go home now." The elders departed in relief; only Yanagisawa's personal attendants remained. "I wish rest and refreshment," he said. "Put up my shelter."

The servants unloaded supplies and erected an enclosure like those used by generals as battlefield headquarters: white silk curtains hung from a square frame, open to the sky. Inside they spread futons, lit lanterns and charcoal braziers, and set out sake and food. With bodyguards stationed outside, Yanagisawa smugly reclined on a futon. He had no real need for this makeshift shelter, with the entire castle at his disposal. But he loved the spectacle of other men toiling for his comfort, the clandestine air of a night rendezvous outdoors. And was he not akin to a general, marshaling his troops for an attack?

"Bring Shichisaburō here," Chamberlain Yanagisawa ordered a servant, who ran off to comply.

As Yanagisawa waited, the sensual thrill of lust increased his excitement. Shichisaburō, leading actor of the Tokugawa No theater troupe, was his current paramour. Schooled in the venerable tradition and practice of manly love, he also had other uses. . . .

Soon the silk curtains parted, and Shichisaburō entered. Fourteen years old, small for his age, he wore his hair in the style of a samurai boy: crown shaven, with a long forelock tied back from his brow. His red and gold brocade theatrical robe covered a figure as gracefully slender as a willow sapling. Kneeling, Shichisaburō bowed.

"I await your orders, Honorable Chamberlain," he murmured.

Yanagisawa sat upright as his heartbeat quickened. "Rise," he said, "and approach." He tasted desire, raw and salty as blood. "Sit beside me."

The youth obeyed, and Yanagisawa gazed possessively upon his face, admiring the exquisite nose, tapered chin, and high cheekbones; smooth, childish skin; rosy lips like a delicious fruit. Shichisaburō's wide, expressive eyes, aglow in the lantern light, reflected a gratifying eagerness to please. Yanagisawa smiled. Shichisaburō came from a distinguished theatrical family that had entertained emperors for centuries. Now the family's great talent, concentrated in this youth, was Yanagisawa's to command.

"Pour me a drink," Chamberlain Yanagisawa ordered, adding magnanimously, "and one for yourself."

"Yes, master. Thank you, master!" Shichisaburō lifted the sake decanter. "Oh, but the liquor is cold. Please allow me to warm it for you. And may I serve other refreshments for your delectation?"

Yanagisawa looked on with delight as the young actor set the decanter on the charcoal brazier and laid rice cakes on a plate. At the beginning of their affair, Shichisaburō had spoken and behaved with adolescent gaucheness, but he was intelligent, and had quickly adopted Yanagisawa's speech patterns; now, the big words and long, complicated sentences issued from him with mature fluency. When not abasing himself as custom dictated, he also assumed the chamberlain's bearing: head high, shoulders back, movements swift, impatient, but smoothed by natural grace. This flattering mimicry pleased Yanagisawa greatly.

They drank the warm sake. His face rosy from the liquor, Shichisaburō said, "Have you had a difficult day ruling the nation, master? Shall I soothe you?"

Chamberlain Yanagisawa lay down on the futon. Shichisaburō's hands moved over his neck and back, easing the stiff muscles, arousing desire. Though tempted to roll over and pull the boy against him, Yanagisawa resisted the urge. They had business to discuss first.

"It's an honor to touch you." Fingers rubbing, stroking, teasing, Shichisaburō whispered close to Yanagisawa's ear: "When we're apart, I yearn for the time when we can be together again."

Yanagisawa knew he was only acting and didn't mean a word of what he said, but this didn't bother Yanagisawa at all. How wonderful that someone respected him enough to exert all this effort to please!

"At night I dream of you, and—and I must confess an embarrassing secret." Shichisaburō's voice trembled convincingly. "Sometimes my desire for you is so great that I caress myself and pretend you are touching me. I hope that this does not offend you?"

"Far from it." Yanagisawa chuckled. The actor, despite his talent and heritage, was a commoner, a nobody. He was weak, naïve, pathetic, and another man might consider his words an insult. Yet Chamberlain Yanagisawa relished the charade as proof that he was no longer the helpless victim, but the omnipotent user of other men. He had flunkies instead of friends. He'd married a wealthy woman related to the Tokugawa clan, but kept a distance from her and their five-year-old daughter, for whom he'd already begun seeking a politically advantageous match. He didn't care if everyone despised him, as long as they obeyed his orders. Shichisaburō's pretense aroused Yanagisawa; power was the ultimate aphrodisiac.

Now Chamberlain Yanagisawa reluctantly deferred his pleasure. "I need your help with a very important matter, Shichisaburō," he said, sitting upright.

The young actor's eyes brimmed with happiness, and Yanagisawa could almost believe he truly felt flattered by the request, which was actually an order. "I'll do anything for you, master."

"This is a matter of utmost secrecy, and you must promise to tell no one about it," Yanagisawa warned.

"Oh, I promise, I promise!" Sincerity radiated from the boy. "You can trust me. Just wait and see. Pleasing you means more to me than anything else in the world."

Yet Yanagisawa knew that it was not devotion but the threat of punishment that held Shichisaburō in thrall to him. Should the actor disobey, he would be stripped of his status as star of the Tokugawa theater troupe, banished from the castle, and put to work in some squalid highway brothel. The chamberlain smiled. *Everyone will do* my *bidding and fear* my *anger . . .*

Bending close, Chamberlain Yanagisawa whispered to Shichisaburō. Inhaling the boy's fresh, youthful scent, Yanagisawa felt his manhood lift within his loincloth. He finished conveying his orders, then let his tongue trace the delicate whorl of Shichisaburō's ear. The actor giggled and turned to Yanagisawa in delighted admiration.

"How clever you are to think of such a wonderful plan! I'll do exactly as you say. And when we're done, *Sōsakan* Sano will never trouble you again."

From above the enclosure came a flutter of wings. On impulse, Chamberlain Yanagisawa fitted an arrow to his bow and aimed upward, scanning the cobalt sky, the black filigree border of trees. Against the moon's luminescent silver disc hovered a dark shape. Yanagisawa released the arrow to invisible flight. A screech pierced the evening calm. Into the enclosure plummeted an owl, the arrow stuck in its breast. Its own prey—a tiny blind mole—was still gripped in the sharp talons.

Shichisaburō clapped his hands gleefully. "A perfect shot, master!"

Chamberlain Yanagisawa laughed. "By attacking one, I also claim the other." The symbolism was as perfect as his aim, the shot an auspicious omen for his scheme. Triumph fed Yanagisawa's desire. Dropping the bow, he extended his hand to Shichisaburō. "But enough of business. Come here."

The young actor's eyes faithfully mirrored Yanagisawa's need. "Yes, master."

The wind's hushed breath stirred the forest; the rising moon swelled. On the silk walls of the enclosure, two shadows fused into one.

When Sano arrived at his residence after the long, tiring ride from Edo Jail, Hirata came out through the gate to meet him. "The shogun's mother has agreed to speak with us before her evening prayers. The *otoshiyori*—chief lady palace official—will answer questions, but she has to make her night tour of inspection around the Large Interior soon."

Sano cast a longing look at his mansion, which held the promise of food, a hot bath, and the company of his new bride. With what peaceful, feminine pursuits had she occupied the time since their wedding? Sano pictured her sewing, writing poetry, or perhaps playing the samisen—an oasis of calm amid violent death and palace intrigue. He yearned to enter that oasis, to become acquainted with Reiko at last. But night was rapidly descending upon the castle and Sano couldn't keep Lady Keisho-in and her *otoshiyori* waiting, or delay informing the shogun that there would be no epidemic because Lady Harume had been murdered.

Leaving his horse with the guards, Sano said to Hirata, "We'd better hurry."

Through stone-walled passages they ascended the hill, past patrol guards carrying flaming torches. Out of cautious habit they didn't speak until they'd cleared the last security checkpoint and were approaching the palace, whose many-gabled tile roof gleamed in the moonlight. Torches flared against its half-timbered walls and sentries guarded the doors. The garden lay deserted under the moonlight. Here, among the gravel paths and shadowy trees, Sano told Hirata the results of Dr. Ito's test.

"The residents and staff of the Large Interior are potential murder suspects," Sano said. "Did your inquiries turn up anything?"

"I spoke to the guards and their commander," Hirata said, "as well as the chief administrator of the Large Interior. The official story is that Harume's death is a tragedy, which they all mourn. No one would say otherwise."

"Because it's the truth, or to protect themselves?" Sano mused. With the fact of murder established, he and Hirata could probe beyond official stories later. The women were the people closest to Harume, with the easiest access to her room and the ink jar. Sano and Hirata needed the cooperation of Lady Keisho-in and the *otoshiyori* before they could interview the concubines and attendants.

Gaining admission to the palace, they walked past silent, dark offices to the shogun's private chambers. The guards stationed there told Sano, "His Excellency is not available. He left word that you should report to him first thing tomorrow."

"Please tell him there's no epidemic," Sano said, so that Tokugawa Tsunayoshi need worry about illness no longer.

Then he and Hirata continued deeper into the palace's labyrinth. As they approached the Large Interior, a high-pitched hum pervaded the quiet. When the guards opened the door to the women's quarters, the hum exploded into a din of shrill female voices, chattering to the accompaniment of slamming doors, running footsteps, splashing water, and the rattle of crockery.

"Merciful gods," Hirata said, covering his ears. Sano winced at the noise.

In the hours since their first visit, the Large Interior had assumed what must be its normal condition. Walking toward Lady Keisho-in's private suite at the center, Sano and Hirata passed chambers jammed with pretty, gaudily dressed concubines eating meals off trays, preening before mirrors, or playing cards while arguing with one another and calling orders to their servants. Sano saw nude women scrubbing themselves or soaking in high wooden tubs, and blind masseurs massaging naked backs. All the women met his gaze with a curious passivity that reflected a stoic acceptance of their lot. Sano was reminded of Yoshiwara's courtesans: the only difference seemed to be that those women existed for public pleasure, and these for only the shogun's. When he and Hirata passed a chamber, conversation and activity ceased momentarily before resuming with undiminished noise. A gray-robed female official patrolled the corridors beside a male guard. In this feminine prison, life went on, even after the violent demise of an inmate.

Yet Sano wondered if one or more of the women knew the truth about Lady Harume's death, and the identity of the killer. Perhaps they all did, including their mistress.

The door to Lady Keisho-in's private chambers, located at the end of a long corridor, was like the main portal of a temple: solid cypress, rich with carved dragons. A lantern burned above; two sentries stood like guardian deities a discreet twenty paces away. As Sano and Hirata approached, the door slid open. A tall woman stepped out and bowed.

"Madam Chizuru, chief lady official of the Large Interior," Hirata said.

He introduced Sano, who studied the *otoshiyori* with interest. She was in her late forties; white strands threaded the hair piled neatly atop her head. Her drab gray kimono draped a body as strong and muscular as a man's. Madam Chizuru's square face also had a masculine cast, emphasized by a cleft chin, thick, unshaven brows, and a shadowing of dark hairs on her upper lip. Sano knew that the *otoshiyori*'s most important duty was to keep a vigil outside Tokugawa Tsunayoshi's bedchamber whenever he slept with a concubine, to ensure that no woman extorted favors during his vulnerable moments. Like the other female palace officials, she would have once been a concubine herself—probably to the previous shogun—but the only visible feminine charm was her mouth, as dainty as that of a courtesan in a woodblock print. Arms folded, she regarded Sano with a bold, level gaze that brooked no misbehavior.

"You cannot see Lady Keisho-in yet," Madam Chizuru said. Her voice was deep, but not unpleasant. "His Excellency is with her now."

So that was where the shogun had gone. "We'll wait," Sano said. "And we need to speak with you, too."

As Madam Chizuru nodded, a pair of younger female officials arrived. An unspoken form of communication—oblique glances, nods, a twitch of lips—passed between them and their superior. In this alien territory, even the language was different. Then Madam Chizuru said to Sano and Hirata, "Urgent business demands my attention. But I shall return shortly. Wait here."

"Yes, master," Hirata said under his breath as the *otoshiyori,* flanked by her lieutenants, strode away. To Sano he said, "These women will be running the country someday if we men don't watch out."

The *otoshiyori* had left Lady Keisho-in's door open a crack. Murmurs came from within. Curiosity overcame Sano. He stole a look. In the shadowy chamber, a ceiling lantern formed a nimbus of light around a woman seated upon silk cushions. Small and dumpy, she wore a loose, shimmering gold satin dressing gown printed with blue waves. Long black hair, untouched by gray, spilled around her shoulders, giving the sixty-four-year-old Keisho-in a strikingly youthful appearance. Sano couldn't see her face, which was bent over the man cradled in her plump arms.

Tokugawa Tsunayoshi, Japan's supreme military dictator, pressed his face against his mother's ample breasts. His black court robes swaddled his bent knees; his shaved crown, minus the customary black cap, looked as vulnerable as an infant's. Mumbles and whimpers issued from him: ". . . so afraid, so unhappy. . . . People always wanting things from me . . . expecting me to be strong and wise, like my ancestor, Tokugawa Ieyasu . . . never know what to do or say . . . stupid, weak, unworthy of my position . . ."

Lady Keisho-in petted her son's head, emitting soothing sounds. "There, there, my dear little boy." Her crusty voice betrayed the age that her appearance belied. "Mother is here. She'll make everything all right."

Tokugawa Tsunayoshi relaxed; his whimpers turned to a purr of contentment. Lady Keisho-in took up the long, silver pipe that lay on the smoking tray beside her, puffed, coughed, and addressed her son gently. "To earn happiness, you must build more temples, support the clergy, and hold more sacred festivals."

"But Mother, that sounds so difficult," the shogun whined. "How shall I ever manage it?"

"Give money to Priest Ryuko, and he'll take care of everything."

"What if Chamberlain Yanagisawa or the Council of Elders object?" Tokugawa Tsunayoshi's voice quavered with fear of his subordinates' disapproval.

"Just tell them that your decision is the law," said Lady Keisho-in.

"Yes, Mother," sighed the shogun.

At the sound of footsteps in the corridor, Sano quickly moved away from the door, embarrassed and appalled by what he'd observed. The rumors about Keisho-in's influence over Tokugawa Tsunayoshi were true. She was a fervent Buddhist, dominated by the ambitious, self-aggrandizing Ryuko, her favorite priest—and, Sano had heard, her lover. No doubt Ryuko had convinced her to ask the shogun for money. That such power lay in their hands posed a serious threat to national stability. Throughout history, the Buddhist clergy had raised armies and challenged samurai rule. And how ironic that Tsunayoshi had officials to protect him from unscrupulous concubines, but not from the most dangerous woman of all!

Madam Chizuru rounded the corner and approached her mistress's suite. She put her head inside the door. At some signal from within the chamber, she turned and said, "Lady Keisho-in will see you now."

They entered the room. There Lady Keisho-in sat alone, puffing on her pipe. There was no sign of the shogun, but the brocade curtains at Keisho-in's back moved, as if someone had slipped through them. Sano and Hirata knelt and bowed.

"*Sōsakan* Sano and his chief retainer, Hirata," Madam Chizuru announced, kneeling near Lady Keisho-in.

The shogun's mother studied her visitors with frank interest. "So you are the men who have solved so many baffling mysteries? How exciting!"

Viewed up close, she didn't look as young as she had

at first. Her round face, with its small, even features, might have once been attractive, but the white powder didn't completely mask deep creases in her skin. Bright cheek and lip rouge lent a semblance of vitality that the veined, yellowish whites of her eyes belied. A double chin bulged above a full bosom that had sagged with age. Her black hair had the uniform, unnatural darkness of dye. Her smile revealed cosmetically blackened teeth with two gaps in the top row, which gave her a rakish, common appearance. And commoner she was, Sano thought, recalling her history.

Keisho-in was the daughter of a Kyōto greengrocer. When her father had died, her mother became servant and mistress to a cook in the household of the imperial regent prince. There Keisho-in formed a friendship with the daughter of a prominent Kyōto family. When the friend became concubine to Shogun Tokugawa Iemitsu, she took Keisho-in to Edo Castle with her, and Keisho-in also became Iemitsu's concubine. At age twenty, she had borne his son Tsunayoshi and secured herself the highest position a woman could attain: official consort to one shogun, mother of the next. Ever since then, Keisho-in had lived in luxury, ruling the women's quarters.

"My honorable son has told me so much about your adventures," Lady Keisho-in said, "and I'm delighted to make your acquaintance." Batting her eyes at Sano and Hirata, she displayed the coy charm that must have enticed Tokugawa Tsunayoshi's father. Then a sigh rattled in her throat. "But what a sad occasion that brings you here: Lady Harume's death. A tragedy! We women are all afraid for our own lives."

However, it was apparently not Keisho-in's nature to remain sad for long. Smiling flirtatiously at Sano, she said, "But with you here to save us, I feel better. Your assistant told Madam Chizuru that you desire our help in preventing an epidemic. Just tell us what we can do. We're eager to be of use."

"Lady Harume didn't die of a disease, so there won't be an epidemic," Sano said, relieved to find the shogun's mother so complaint. With her rank and influence, she could oppose his investigation if she chose; all inhabitants of the Large Interior were suspects in this politically sensitive crime, including herself. About Madam Chizuru's feelings, Sano wasn't sure. The *otoshiyori*'s expression remained neutral, but her rigid posture indicated resistance. "Lady Harume was murdered, with poison."

For a moment, both women stared; neither spoke. Sano detected a flicker of unreadable emotion in Madam Chizuru's eyes before she averted them. Then Lady Keisho-in gasped. "Poison? I'm shocked!" Eyes and mouth wide, she fell back against the cushions, panting. "I can't breathe. I need air!" Madam Chizuru hurried to her mistress, but Lady Keisho-in waved her away and beckoned to Hirata. "Young man. Help me!"

Casting an uneasy glance at Sano, the young retainer went over to Lady Keisho-in. He picked up her fan and began fanning her vigorously. Soon her breaths evened; her body relaxed. When Hirata helped her sit up, she leaned against him for a moment, smiling into his face. "So strong and handsome and kind. *Arigatō.*"

"Dō itashimashite," Hirata mumbled. He hastily returned to his place next to Sano with a sigh of relief.

Sano eyed him with concern. Usually Hirata could face with aplomb witnesses of either sex or any class; now, he knelt with his head down, shoulders hunched. What was the problem? For now, Sano considered the women's reactions. Was the poisoning really news to them? Keisho-in's swoon had seemed genuine, but Sano wondered if the *otoshiyori* had known or guessed about the murder.

"Who would want to kill poor Harume?" Keisho-in said in a plaintive voice. She puffed on her pipe, and a tear rolled down her cheek, leaving a track in the thick white makeup. "Such a sweet child; so charming and vivacious." Then Keisho-in's flirtatious manner returned. With a dimply smile at Hirata, she said, "Harume reminded me of myself when I was young. I was once a great beauty, and a favorite with everyone."

She sighed. "And Harume was the same. Very popular. She sang and played the samisen wonderfully. Her jokes made us all laugh. That's why I chose her to be one of my attendants. She knew how to make people happy. I simply adored her, like a daughter."

Sano looked at Madam Chizuru. The *otoshiyori* pressed her lips together; a single breath eased from her: it was obvious that she didn't share Keisho-in's view of the dead girl. "What did you think of Lady Harume?" Sano asked Chizuru. "What kind of person did she seem to you?"

"It's not my place to have opinions about His Excellency's concubines," Madam Chizuru said primly.

Sano sensed that Chizuru could tell him plenty about Lady Harume, but didn't want to contradict her mistress. "Did Lady Harume have any enemies in the palace who might have wanted her dead?" he asked both women.

"Certainly not." Keisho-in blew out an emphatic puff of smoke. "Everyone loved her. And we're all very close here in the Large Interior. Like sisters."

But even sisters had disagreements, Sano knew. Past quarrels in the Large Interior had resulted in murder. For Keisho-in to claim that five hundred women, crowded into such a tight space, lived together in complete harmony, she must either be quite stupid—or lying.

Madam Chizuru cleared her throat and said hesitantly, "There was a feud between Harume and one of the other concubines. Lady Ichiteru. They . . . didn't get along."

Keisho-in gaped, showing her missing teeth to unfortunate advantage. "No! This is the first I've heard of it."

"Why didn't Lady Ichiteru and Lady Harume get along?" Sano asked.

"Ichiteru is a lady of fine lineage," Chizuru said. "She's a cousin of the emperor, from Kyōto." This was where the imperial family lived in genteel poverty, though stripped of political power and under the complete domination of the Tokugawa regime. "Before Harume came to Edo Castle eight months ago, Lady Ichiteru was the honorable shogun's favorite companion . . . at least, among the women."

Stealing a nervous glance at her mistress, Chizuru put a hand to her mouth. Tokugawa Tsunayoshi's preference for men was common knowledge, but not, apparently, discussed in his mother's presence.

"But when Harume came, she replaced Lady Ichiteru in the shogun's affections?" Sano guessed.

Madam Chizuru nodded. "His Excellency stopped requesting Ichiteru's company at night and started inviting Harume to his chamber."

"Ichiteru should not have minded," Lady Keisho-in announced. "My darling son has the right to enjoy any woman he chooses. And it's his duty to beget an heir. When Ichiteru failed to produce a child, he was correct to try another concubine." Keisho-in giggled. Winking at Hirata, she said, "One who is young and saucy and fertile—like I was when I met my dear, deceased Iemitsu. You know the kind of girl, don't you, young man?"

A bright red spot of embarrassment burned on each of Hirata's cheeks as he blurted, "*Sumimasen*—excuse me, but was there anyone among the servants, guards, or attendants who didn't get along with Lady Harume?"

Shaking her head, Keisho-in waved away the question with her pipe, scattering ash onto the cushions. "The staff are people of excellent character and disposition. I personally interviewed them all before they were permitted to work in the Large Interior. None would have attacked a favored concubine."

Madam Chizuru set her jaw and looked at the floor. Sano saw a disturbing fact emerging: Lady Keisho-in was oblivious to what happened around her. The *otoshiyori* handled the administration of the Large Interior, just as Chamberlain Yanagisawa managed the government for Tokugawa Tsunayoshi. That both leaders of Japan's ruling clan were so weak and dull-witted—there seemed no better term for it—boded ill for the nation.

"Sometimes people are not what they seem," Sano hinted. "Someone may hide his true nature, until something happens. . . ."

Chizuru seized on this opening: she was obviously torn between fears of contradicting Lady Keisho-in and of lying to the shogun's *sōsakan-sama*. "The palace guards are all men who come from good families and have good service records. Usually they're of good character, too. But one of them, Lieutenant Kushida . . . Four days ago, Lady Harume registered a complaint. She said he was behaving in an improper fashion toward her. When the palace officials weren't watching, he would loiter around her, trying to start conversations about . . . inappropriate things."

Meaning sex, Sano interpreted.

"Lieutenant Kushida sent offensive letters to Lady Harume, or so she said," continued Madam Chizuru. "She even claimed that he spied on her while she bathed. She said she told him again and again to leave her alone, but he persisted, then finally got mad and threatened to kill her."

"Disgusting!" Lady Keisho-in made a face, then said indignantly, "Why does no one tell me anything?"

Chizuru's pained glance at Sano told him that she had informed the shogun's mother, who had forgotten.

"What happened then?" Sano asked.

"I was reluctant to believe the accusations," Chizuru said. "Lieutenant Kushida has worked here for ten years without causing any trouble. He is a fine, upstanding man. Lady Harume had been here only a short time." The *otoshiyori*'s tone indicated that she had thought Harume less fine and upstanding, and the likely source of the problem. "However, this kind of accusation is always treated seriously. The law forbids male staff to bother the women, or engage in any improper relations with them. The penalty is dismissal. I reported the matter to the chief administrator. Lieutenant Kushida was temporarily relieved of his duties, pending an investigation of the charges."

"And was this investigation performed?" Sano asked.

"No. And now that Lady Harume is dead . . ."

The charges, without her to substantiate them, must have been dropped, which explained why the chief administrator had neglected to tell Hirata about them. How fortunate for Lieutenant Kushida that his accuser's death had averted the disgrace of losing his post. He, as well as the envious Lady Ichiteru, definitely merited an interview.

"Jealous concubines, rude guards," lamented Keisho-in. "Dreadful! *Sōsakan-sama,* you must find and punish whoever killed my sweet little Harume and save us all from this evil, dangerous person."

"I'll need to have my detectives search the Large Interior

and speak with the residents," Sano said. "May I have your permission?"

"Of course, of course." Lady Keisho-in nodded vigorously. Then, with a grunt, she pushed herself upright and beckoned Madam Chizuru to help her stand. "It's time for my prayers. But please come and see me again." She dimpled at Hirata. "You, too, young man."

They made their farewells. Hirata almost ran from the room. Sano followed, wondering about his retainer's uncharacteristic bashfulness and looking ahead to all the work they must do. Yet as they left the palace, he was glad that the hour was too late to begin calling on suspects or witnesses, and that they needn't meet with the shogun until tomorrow. At home, Reiko waited. This was their wedding night.

Servants greeted Sano in the entryway of his mansion when he arrived home. They relieved him of his cloak and swords and ushered him into the parlor, where charcoal braziers and lanterns burned, and wall murals depicted a serene mountain landscape. Resting upon silk floor cushions, Sano felt the tensions of the day dissolve and happy anticipation swell within him. Hirata had gone to give orders to the detective corps and secure the estate for the night. Sano's time was his own, until tomorrow. His marriage could begin.

"Would you like a meal?" the chief manservant asked.

Sano nodded, then said, "Where is . . . my wife?" The phrase felt strange on his lips, but as satisfying as a drink of water after a long, dry journey.

"She has been told that you're home, and she's coming right away." The servant bowed and left the room.

As Sano waited, his heart beat faster; his stomach tightened. Then the door slid open. Sano sat up straight. Into the room walked Reiko. Dressed in a dull orange silk kimono printed with golden asters, her long hair pinned up, his bride carried a porcelain sake decanter and two cups on a tray. Eyes demurely lowered, she glided over to Sano, knelt before him, set down the tray, and bowed.

"Honorable Husband," she murmured. "May I serve you?"

"Yes. Please," Sano said, admiring her youthful beauty.

The pouring of liquor smoothed the awkward moment—someone must have instructed Reiko on what to do when alone with her husband for the first time—but her hands trembled when she passed the cup to Sano. Sympathy eased his own nervousness. This was his domain. It was up to him to make Reiko feel comfortable here.

"I hope you're feeling well?" he said, filling the other cup with sake and offering it to her.

Cautiously, as if afraid to touch his hand, Reiko took the cup. "Yes, Honorable Husband."

They drank, and Sano saw that her teeth had been dyed black. An unexpected surge of warmth flooded his groin. He'd never given much thought to this familiar custom of married women; now, seeing Reiko thus transformed awakened his desire. It reminded him that she was his in body as well as spirit.

"Are your rooms satisfactory?" Sano tasted liquor and arousal. Reiko's upswept hair accentuated her graceful neck and sloping shoulders. More than a year had passed since he'd been with a woman . . . "Have you gotten settled?"

"Yes, thank you."

A tentative smile encouraged Sano: beneath the placid demeanor of a well-bred lady, she was not without feeling for him. Just then, a servant entered, gave Sano a hot, damp cloth for wiping his hands, and set before him a lacquer meal tray. When he and Reiko were alone again, she quickly removed the lids from his dishes of sashimi, steamed trout, and vegetables, then poured his tea. She would have eaten earlier, the better to serve him. Her wifely subservience delighted Sano.

"I hope you'll be happy here," he said. "If there's anything you want, just ask."

Reiko lifted an eager, shining face to him. "Perhaps—perhaps I could help you investigate the death of the shogun's concubine," she blurted.

"What?" The morsel of fish Sano had lifted to his mouth fell from his chopsticks as he stared in surprise.

Gone were his bride's self-effacing pose and appealing shyness. Head high, back straight, she looked Sano directly in the face. Her eyes flashed with nervous daring. "Your work interests me very much. I've heard rumors that Lady Harume was murdered. If it's true, I want to help catch the killer." She gulped, then continued in a rush: "You said that if there was anything I wanted, I should ask."

"That's not what I meant!" Dismay jolted Sano. From deep within his memory rose scenes from his childhood: his mother cooking, cleaning, and sewing at home while his father ventured out into the world to earn their living. Experience had formed Sano's notion of a proper marriage. A host of additional reasons forbade him to grant Reiko's request. "I'm sorry," he said gently. "I appreciate your offer, but a murder investigation is no place for a wife."

He expected her to accept his decision, as his mother had all of his father's. But Reiko said, "My father told me you'd think that, and he agrees. But I want to work, to be useful. And I can help you."

"But how?" Sano asked, increasingly bewildered as his dream of conjugal felicity evaporated around him. Who was this strange, obstinate girl he'd married? "What could you possibly do?"

"I'm educated; I can read and write as well as any man. For ten years I've watched my father's trials in the Court of Justice." Reiko's dainty chin trembled, but she didn't yield before Sano's disapproval. "I understand the law, and criminals. I can help figure out who killed Lady Harume."

Growing up in Magistrate Ueda's mansion, Reiko must have seen more criminals than Sano himself! Ashamed to be outdone by his young bride, Sano also hated to imagine what spectacles of violence and human depravity she'd witnessed. Worse, he hated the thought of allowing these elements of his work to intrude on his private life. How could home be a haven if Reiko shared his knowledge of the world's evils?

"Please . . . calm down and let me explain," Sano said, raising his hands in a placating gesture. "Detective work is dangerous. You could get hurt—or even killed." This had happened to many other people during his past cases. His protective instincts rallied in protest against letting his own wife fall victim to his search for justice. "It would be wrong for me to let you have anything to do with the murder investigation." With an air of finality, Sano resumed eating.

"You think I'm weak and stupid because I'm a woman," Reiko persisted, "but I know how to fight. I can defend myself." Ardor lit her lovely, petal-shaped eyes. "And since

I am a woman, I can go places where you can't. I can learn things from people who would never talk to you. Just give me a chance, and you'll see!"

Now Sano grew angry. He recalled his docile mother cooking the foods her husband preferred, managing the household to accommodate his needs without ever asking anything for herself. In a samurai's world of unstinting duty to the Tokugawa regime, his own home was the only domain under his absolute control. Now Sano felt this precious control slipping, his manly authority weakening in the face of Reiko's challenge. Fatigue strained his patience. Although the last thing he wanted was a quarrel on his wedding night, his temper snapped.

"How dare you contradict your husband?" Sano demanded, throwing down his chopsticks. "How dare you even suggest that you, a silly, headstrong girl, can do anything better than I can?"

"Because I'm right!"

Reiko leapt to her feet, eyes sparking with a fury that matched Sano's. Her tongue touched her chipped incisor; her hand went to her waist as if reaching for a sword. This unfeminine, aggressive response incensed Sano—and aroused him deeply. Anger turned Reiko's delicate beauty into the raw, female power of a goddess. Her rapid breathing and flushed cheeks suggested sexual excitement. Despite Sano's dislike of her impertinence, he admired her courageous spirit, yet he couldn't believe her capable of investigating a murder—or let her undermine his masculinity by talking back to him. He shoved aside his tray and stood, glaring at his young wife.

"I order you to stay home where you belong, and not to interfere with my work," he said, though aghast at the hostile turn their relationship had taken. He wanted them to be happy together, and hurting Reiko's feelings wouldn't achieve that. But what else could he do? "I'm your husband. You will obey me. And that's final!"

Scorn narrowed Reiko's eyes. "And what will you do if I disobey?" she demanded. "Beat me? Send me back to my father? Or kill me?" A bitter laugh burst from her throat. "I wish you would, because I'm sorry I married you. I'd rather die than submit to you or any other man!"

Her repudiation stabbed Sano like a knife to the heart. Wounded and furious, he experienced an overwhelming urge to assert his power by taking physical possession of her. His manhood sprang erect. He stepped forward and seized her shoulders.

At once, Reiko's brave defiance dissolved. She shrank within Sano's grasp. Towering over her, he felt the fragility of her bones. Terror filled her eyes, and he knew it wasn't blows or death she feared. It was the crueler injury a man could inflict upon a woman—the personal assault on the most sensitive parts of her body. Yet as their gazes locked, Sano sensed in her an unfathomed appetite for that intimate, brutal engagement. Reiko's lips were wet; her breaths came hard and fast. Before Sano shimmered a vision of the two of them naked and entwined, resolving all argument in the primitive mating rite. And he could tell from the shocked expression on Reiko's face that she shared it—and wanted it—too.

Slowly Sano lifted his hand and touched her soft cheek. Their breath mingled for a long, tense moment. Then suddenly she twisted out of his grasp and ran from the room.

"Reiko. Wait!" Sano called.

Her rapid footsteps receded down the passage. A door slammed. His emotions in chaos, his body still engorged with desire, Sano stood frozen, hands holding the emptiness she'd left behind.

In the sanctuary of her private chamber, Reiko latched the door and breathed a tremulous sigh. Her heart still beat wildly in her breast; her muscles quaked. Feverish in her agitation, she hurried through the outer door and stepped onto the veranda.

A lopsided ivory moon poured soft illumination over the garden's trees, boulders, and pavilion. Crickets chirped; dogs barked. Somewhere in the night, guards patrolled the estate and castle; footsteps, hoofbeats, and low voices carried through clear, cold air that smelled of frost and charcoal smoke. In chilly solitude Reiko paced, trying to sort out her tumultuous feelings.

How she hated Sano for disregarding her wishes, for mocking her intelligence and abilities! And how angry she was at herself for badly handling the situation. She should have taken things more slowly, playing the submissive wife and winning his affection before pleading her cause. But she sensed that it wouldn't have made any difference. Sano was like all other men, and she'd been mad to think otherwise.

"Pompous, ignorant samurai!" she muttered, seething with anger. "Ordering me around as if I were a servant, or a child." Beneath her anger was the leaden misery of disappointment. How naïve and foolish seemed her dream of solving crimes and achieving glory. "Better that I should have committed *seppuku* than ever marry!"

As Reiko paced, a warm trickle of moisture slid down her inner thigh. Thinking she'd begun her monthly bleeding, she felt under her skirts. Her hand came up smeared with a clear, musk-scented secretion: the fluid of arousal, her body's involuntary response to the confrontation with Sano. Horror gripped Reiko as she became aware of a heaviness in her lower abdomen, the dull, hot pulse between her legs. Crouching on the veranda, she faced the sum of her fears.

She didn't fear beating, the common punishment for unruly wives—martial arts training had given her a high tolerance for pain—and she knew instinctively that Sano wasn't the kind of man who would hurt a woman in anger. Yet she dreaded the sexual act, a battleground where nature had made her vulnerable to a man's violation. And desire could make her the thrall of the husband who already owned her, destroying her precious independence.

Even so, she was terrified that Sano would divorce her. If he did, everyone would blame her for the marriage's failure; no other man would have her. She and her family would suffer public humiliation. The specter of a bleak future as a disgraced spinster living on the charity of relatives loomed before Reiko. And despite her anger at Sano's tyranny, she didn't want to leave him. She wanted to experience love's dangerous pleasures. Body and spirit yearned for it, even as her mind recoiled at the prospect of a life of domestic seclusion and boredom.

Reiko watched the branches of a tall pine capture the rising moon. Through the tangle of conflicting emotions she identified one certainty: She must make the marriage work—but on her own terms.

She went inside her chamber and knelt before her writing desk. On a shelf above it lay the swords she'd retrieved that afternoon. Reiko ground ink, readied paper, and took up her brush. Desperation strengthened her resolve. She would prove to Sano that a wife could be a detective. She would show him that it was in his best interest to make her a partner in his work instead of a glorified house slave. She would make him love her for herself, not for his idea of what she should be.

With her tongue touching her chipped tooth, Reiko began listing plans for her secret inquiry into the murder of Lady Harume.

Alone, Sano reluctantly decided against going after Reiko: In his current state of anger, confusion, and unsatisfied desire, he would only make things worse between them. He finished eating, though the food had grown cold and he'd lost his appetite. Wearily he rose, went to his room, and shed his clothes. In the bathchamber he scrubbed, rinsed, soaked in the tub, then wrapped himself in a cotton robe. He walked down the corridor, past the empty suite where he'd planned to spend his first night with his bride. Next door, the paper wall of her private chamber glowed with lamplight. Sano paused outside.

Reiko's hazy shadow moved, shrugging off garments, combing her hair. She evidently intended to sleep there. Desire welled in Sano's loins. Fierce possessiveness enflamed his anger. Despite their quarrel, she was his wife. He had the right to command her presence in the marriage bed. Sano grasped the door handle . . .

. . . then let his hand fall away, shaking his head as reason tempered angry lust. He could not subdue Reiko through physical strength, because he didn't want a resentful mate who obeyed him only because society decreed that woman must submit to man. He still yearned for a union of mutual love. It had been a long, difficult day, probably no less for Reiko than him. They'd gotten off to a bad start, but tomorrow they would begin again, after a good night's sleep. He would show her every kindness. She would realize that her place was in their home, not in a murder investigation. And she would learn to love him as her husband and superior.

Reluctantly Sano went to his bedchamber, but with his mind replaying his argument with Reiko and thinking of what he should have said, he felt too tense to sleep. Amid the folds of discarded clothing on the floor lay the diary he'd taken from Lady Harume's room. Sano picked it up with a sigh. There was nothing like work to take his mind off domestic troubles, and he might actually learn something useful from the murdered concubine's record of her life and private thoughts. He lay down on the futon and pulled the lamp near. Propping himself on his elbow, he opened the diary's mauve-and-green, clover-printed cloth cover and turned to the first page.

The text was written in an awkward hand, with lots of crossed-out mistakes. Like many women, Lady Harume had been barely literate. Maybe this was for the best, Sano thought, considering how Reiko's superior education had fostered her contrary nature. However, as Sano scanned the diary, Harume's natural flair for descriptive prose emerged:

> I enter the Large Interior. The guards lead me through the corridors like a prisoner to her cell. Hundreds of women stand and watch. They stop chattering as I pass, and they're staring at me: such disdain! Staring, staring—greedy, caged animals wondering if the newcomer's arrival means less food for them. But I hold my head up. I may be poor, but I'm prettier than anyone I see. Someday soon I will be the shogun's favorite concubine. And no one will dare disdain me again.

None of the entries was dated, but this first one must have been written just after the New Year, eight months ago, when Harume came to Edo Castle. Sano skimmed passages describing the routines and irritations of the Large Interior, Harume's various amusements, and her increasingly frequent visits to the shogun's bedchamber.

> This place is so crowded that we must eat and bathe in shifts. There is always someone bumping into me whenever I move, always someone in the privy when I have to go, someone's finger in my business, someone's stink in my nose. The bathwater is always scummy by the time it's my turn, and the noise never stops, even at night, because someone is always talking, snoring, coughing, or weeping. But although I long for solitude, I am dying of loneliness. The others treat me as an outsider, and I don't like them either. And there's nothing to do except the same things. Every day is like the last, and we don't get to go out often enough.
>
> Yesterday was very hot, with thunder grumbling like angry dragons. We went for a picnic in the hills. I wore my green kimono with the willow leaf pattern. We drank sake and were very merry until all of a sudden, pouring rain! We shrieked and hurried into the palanquins while servants ran around packing up the food. What great fun to see those haughty senior concubines drenched and squawking like wet hens!—particularly after they had mocked my rustic manners.
>
> Last night I entertained His Excellency again. I wore my red satin kimono printed with lucky characters so that I might bear him a son and be rich and happy for the rest of my life, like Lady Keisho-in.

As Sano had expected, Harume's pillow book resembled those written by imperial court ladies of centuries past, who had documented the trivia of life rather than important historic events. About such great occasions as the last, Harume gave no details: Even naïve young girls knew that any careless remark about the shogun could bring harsh censure, including dismissal or even death. Harume must also have feared that nosy comrades would read her pillow book and take revenge for unfavorable portrayals. Lady Ichiteru and Lieutenant Kushida appeared only in the middle of a long list entitled "Things I Dislike About Living in Edo Castle":

39. Being served the tough, crusty rice from the bottom of the pot because the senior concubines get the best food.
40. Ichiteru, who thinks she's better than everyone else just because she's the emperor's cousin.
41. The monthly health examinations, and Dr. Kitano's cold hands on my private parts.
42. Lieutenant Kushida—a terrible pest.

In subsequent passages there was no indication of any particular animosity or quarrel that could have led to her murder. Sano was growing drowsy. He turned to the last page.

Yesterday we went on a pilgrimage to Kannon Temple. I love the Asakusa district because the streets are so busy that the guards and palace officials can't keep a close watch over us. We can escape them and wander through the marketplace, buying food and souvenirs at the stalls, having our fortunes told, watching the pilgrims, priests, children, and sacred doves: Freedom!

I hurry along the narrow lanes to the inn. As usual, there's a room already reserved for me, so I slip through the pine groves and bamboo thickets that surround the inn like a small forest. My room is in the rear building—very private. I go inside, close the door, and wait. Soon I hear footsteps crunching on the gravel path. They stop outside my room—

Sano was now wide awake and fully alert. So Lady Harume had used her freedom for secret assignations.

—and I see his tall, thin shadow on the paper window. There's a hole in the pane, and his eye appears.

But he doesn't speak, and neither do I. Pretending I'm alone, I slowly take off my cloak. I untie my sash and let my outer- and under-kimonos drop to the floor, facing the window so he can see me, but never meeting his eye.

His shadow stirs. Naked, I run my hands over my breasts, sighing and licking my lips. His garments rustle as he parts them and loosens his loincloth. I lie on the floor cushions. I spread my legs wide, my womanhood open to him. I caress myself with my fingers. Faster and faster, moaning, arching my back, tossing my head with a pleasure I don't really feel. He gasps and grunts. When I cry out, he does, too—an ugly sound, like a dying animal.

Then I lie still, my eyes half closed. I watch his shadow move past the window and out of sight. When I'm sure he's gone, I dress quickly and hurry back to the market before the palace officials discover I'm not with the other girls. I could be beaten, dismissed, or even killed for what I've done. But he's very rich and powerful. Soon he travels to Shikoku, and we won't meet again for at least eight months. I must get what I can now, from him, no matter the risk.

Aroused by this erotic scenario, Sano felt like a voyeur himself, spying on a dead woman's intimate life. He closed the book and pondered the meaning of what he'd just read. Harume had probably thought that anyone who happened to read the story would deem it a fantasy, but it had the quality of truth. Who was her partner in the bizarre game, and why had she played when she got no pleasure from it? What else might have happened between them? Sano considered the clues: a tall, thin man who was rich, powerful, and bound for an eight-month stay on that southern island . . .

Then he smiled. He knew of someone who fit the hints Harume had dropped about her paramour. Sano blew out the lamp, lay down with his head on the wooden neck rest, and pulled the quilt over him. Tomorrow he and Reiko would reconcile their differences and begin their happy marriage. And tomorrow, sometime between reporting to the shogun, attending the examination of Harume's corpse at Edo Morgue, and interviewing Lady Ichiteru and Lieutenant Kushida, Sano would visit the latest suspect in Lady Harume's murder: Lord Miyagi Shigeru, daimyo of Tosa Province.

Their breath frosting the morning air, Sano and Hirata strode through Edo Castle's winding passages and security checkpoints on their way to report to the shogun. It was another crisp, clear day, though colder than the previous one. Sunlight glittered on the tile roofs of the walled passages, flashed through wind-tossed pine boughs above, and reflected off the armor of patrolling guards. Shadows were as precise as paper cutouts, and every sound rang clear: horses' hooves on stone paths; marching footsteps; voices calling. Geese winged across the vast, cloudless blue sky, trailing a streamer of honks over the castle. An invigorating tang of fallen leaves and charcoal smoke spiced the air.

"Did you sleep well?" Hirata asked, alluding to Sano's wedding night with a meaningful look.

"Fine, thank you," Sano said tersely, hoping Hirata wouldn't pursue the subject. He hadn't seen Reiko today. Unwilling to risk another disastrous scene before work, he'd decided to postpone their next meeting until tonight.

Hirata, ever sensitive to Sano's moods, said, "The men and I had a little celebration planned for you last night. I guess it's just as well that we decided to put it off and let you rest."

Knowing what wedding night festivities were like, Sano fervently agreed. He hoped the meeting with the shogun would progress more smoothly than his marriage. But although he'd assumed the news that there was no epidemic would have allayed the shogun's concerns, he soon discovered otherwise. Tokugawa Tsunayoshi, ensconced in his private sitting room amid guards and attendants, greeted Sano and Hirata's arrival with an anguished cry.

"Ahh, *sōsakan-sama,*" he wailed. "The murder of my

concubine has distressed me so much that I could not sleep last night. Now I have the most terrible headache. I feel sick at my stomach, and my, ahh, entire body pains me."

Tokugawa Tsunayoshi lay on the dais, supported by cushions, wearing a bronze silk dressing gown. The fact of Harume's death having belatedly sunk into his mind, he looked shriveled, pale, and much older than his forty-four years. An attendant placed a screen by the window, shielding him from the sunlit paper panes. Others stoked charcoal braziers, heating the room to an ovenlike warmth. A priest chanted prayers. Dr. Kitano hovered beside the shogun with a cup of steaming liquid.

Sano and Hirata knelt and bowed. "I apologize for intruding upon you in your illness, Your Excellency," Sano said. "If you'd like to wait until later for me to report the status of the murder investigation—"

The shogun waved away this suggestion with a feeble hand. "Stay, stay." He raised himself to drink from Dr. Kitano's cup, then eyed it suspiciously. "What is this?"

"Bamboo-ash tea, to soothe your stomach."

"You. Come here!" Beckoning a servant, Tokugawa Tsunayoshi commanded, "Taste this, and, ahh, make sure there's no poison."

"But I prepared it with my own hands," Dr. Kitano said. "It's perfectly safe."

"With a poisoner loose in Edo Castle, one cannot be too careful," the shogun said darkly.

The servant drank. When he remained alive and well after several moments, the shogun finished the tea. Attendants ushered in the masseur, a bald, blind man. Tokugawa Tsunayoshi pointed at the jar of oil the masseur carried. "Try that out on, ahh, someone else first."

A guard smeared the oil on his arm. More guards brought caged birds to detect noxious fumes; servants tasted cakes for the shogun. He obviously didn't care about Lady Harume. It was his own vulnerability that worried him, with good reason: Assassination was a time-honored method by which ambitious warriors overturned regimes and seized power.

"The poison that killed Lady Harume was in a bottle of

ink marked with her name," Sano said. "She was clearly the murderer's target—not you, Your Excellency."

"That makes no, ahh, difference." The shogun grunted as his attendants stripped off his robe, exposing sagging white flesh. A loincloth covered his sex and cleaved the withered buttocks. Lying facedown, he said, "The poisoning was an indirect attack on me. The murderer will not stop at killing a worthless concubine. I am in, ahh, grave danger."

The masseur's hands kneaded his back. Servants fed him cakes and tea, while guards placed the birdcages around the room. Sano didn't agree with Tokugawa Tsunayoshi's self-centered view of the murder, but at this stage could not completely dismiss the shogun's fears. Political intrigue was a possible motive behind the crime. Sano gave the results of his interview with Lady Keisho-in and Madam Chizuru and outlined his plans to question Lady Ichiteru and Lieutenant Kushida. He mentioned that Lady Harume's pillow book indicated an additional suspect, whose identity he would determine.

An abrupt stillness fell over the room. Servants and guards ceased their activities; the masseur's hands froze on Tokugawa Tsunayoshi's body. Hirata inhaled sharply. Sano's nape prickled in response to the same inaudible signal that had alerted the others. He turned toward the door.

There stood Chamberlain Yanagisawa, regal in brilliant robes, an enigmatic smile on his handsome face. Servants, guards, attendants, and masseur prostrated themselves in obeisance. Behind Sano's calm façade, his heart seized. Yanagisawa must have been listening next door, and come to obstruct this investigation as he had others.

"Ahh, Yanagisawa-*san*. Welcome." Tokugawa Tsunayoshi smiled affectionately at his former protégé and longtime lover. "*Sōsakan* Sano has just reported on his inquiry into Lady Harume's murder. We would appreciate your advice."

Viewing Sano as a rival for Tokugawa Tsunayoshi's favor, for power over the weak lord and thus the entire nation, Chamberlain Yanagisawa had in the recent past deployed assassins to kill Sano and spies to unearth information to use against him. Yanagisawa had spread vicious rumors about Sano and ordered officials not to cooperate with his inquiries. He'd sent Sano to Nagasaki, hoping he would get in enough trouble there to destroy him forever. And Sano knew that Chamberlain Yanagisawa was furious because the ploy hadn't worked.

Upon Sano's return, the shogun and many high officials had gathered at the palace to welcome him. As he passed down the receiving line, Chamberlain Yanagisawa had flashed him a look that evoked images of spears, guns, and swords, all aimed straight at him.

Now Sano braced himself for a new attack while Yanagisawa crossed the room and knelt beside him. He felt Hirata stiffen, alert to the threat. His trained senses absorbed the chamberlain's scent of wintergreen hair oil, tobacco smoke, and the distinctive, bitter undertone of corruption.

"It seems as though *Sōsakan* Sano has matters admirably under control," Chamberlain Yanagisawa said.

Sano waited for the jabs at his character, thinly disguised as praise; ridicule masquerading as solicitude; hints at his negligence or disloyalty—all designed to manipulate the shogun into doubting Sano, while saying nothing he could openly refute. Neither by word nor gesture had Sano ever indicated a desire to steal Yanagisawa's power. Why couldn't they coexist peacefully? Anger shot fire through Sano's blood, preparing him for a battle he always lost.

However, Yanagisawa smiled at Sano, enhancing his masculine beauty. "If there's any way in which I can be of assistance, please let me know. We must cooperate to eliminate the potential threat to His Excellency."

Sano regarded the chamberlain with suspicion. Yet he saw no malice in Yanagisawa's dark, liquid gaze, only an apparently genuine friendliness.

"Ahh, that is what I like to see—my best men working together for my benefit," the shogun declared, flopping over so the masseur could work on his chest. "Especially since I was beginning to get the idea that you two did not, ahh, get along. How silly of me." Tokugawa Tsunayoshi chuckled.

Throughout Yanagisawa's war on Sano, their lord had remained blithely oblivious. Yanagisawa didn't want his quest for power exposed. For Sano to speak against the shogun's chief representative was tantamount to speaking against the shogun himself: treason, the ultimate disgrace, punishable by death. Now Sano wondered what new strategy Yanagisawa had devised for his ruin.

"I am glad for your protection," the shogun continued, "because the murder of Lady Harume signals a dire threat to my whole, ahh, regime. By killing one of my favorite concubines, someone wants to ensure that I never beget an heir, thereby leaving the succession uncertain and allowing the opportunity for a rebellion."

Chamberlain Yanagisawa said, "That's a very insightful interpretation of the crime."

The shogun beamed, flattered by the praise. When Yanagisawa exchanged with Sano a veiled glance of mutual surprise at their lord's unexpected perspicacity, Sano's suspicion grew. This was the first time any hint of comradeship had arisen between them. Hope rose in Sano despite their troubled history. Could the chamberlain have changed?

"I have been continually thwarted in my, ahh, quest for a son," Tokugawa Tsunayoshi lamented. "My wife is a barren invalid. Two hundred concubines have failed to produce any children either. Priests chant prayers night and day; I've given a fortune in offerings to the gods. On my honorable mother's advice, I issued the Dog Protection Edicts."

Priest Ryuko had convinced Lady Keisho-in that in order for the shogun to father a son, he must atone for the sins of his ancestors. Since he'd been born in the year of the dog, he must do this by protecting dogs. Now any person who injured one was imprisoned; anyone who killed a dog was executed. The situation illustrated Ryuko's influence over Keisho-in, and hers over the shogun, both of which had strengthened despite his continued failure to beget an heir.

"But all my efforts have been fruitless." Tokugawa Tsunayoshi's head lolled as the masseur kneaded his shoulders. "Perhaps the concubines are all as inadequate as my wife, or my ancestors' sins were too great for me to, ahh, overcome."

Sano privately thought that the trouble was neither the women nor ancestral misdeeds, but Tsunayoshi's preference for manly love. He kept a harem of young peasant boys, samurai, priests, and actors with whom he spent much of his leisure time. Was he even capable of impregnating the concubines? However, since it wasn't Sano's place to contradict his lord, he remained silent, as did Yanagisawa.

A cold touch of foreboding disturbed Sano as he saw how Yanagisawa stood to gain by the shogun's lack of a successor. Without one, Tokugawa Tsunayoshi couldn't retire; control of the *bakufu* couldn't pass from the chamberlain to a new regime. Had Yanagisawa ordered Lady Harume's murder to extend the duration of his supremacy? Was this the reason for whatever scheme he was now deploying? Remembering the Bundori Murder case, in which Yanagisawa had been a suspect, Sano dreaded a repeat of the scenario that had almost cost him his life and honor. How he longed to believe Yanagisawa had reformed!

"My past troubles with begetting an heir can be attributed to fate," Tokugawa Tsunayoshi whined. "But the poisoning of Lady Harume was an act of human evil—an intolerable outrage! She was young, strong, and healthy; I had great hopes that she would succeed where my other women had, ahh, let me down. *Sōsakan* Sano, you must catch her murderer quickly and deliver him to justice."

"Yes, you must," Chamberlain Yanagisawa said. "Rumors of conspiracies are circulating around the castle. There will be serious trouble if the murder case isn't resolved soon."

Here it comes, thought Sano, wincing inwardly as he prepared to combat another of Yanagisawa's attempts to make him look incompetent. Then the chamberlain turned to him and said, "My suggestion is to trace the route of the ink jar from its origin to Lady Harume, and determine when and where the poison was introduced."

This logical strategy had already occurred to Sano, who watched his enemy in growing amazement as Yanagisawa continued, "If you need help, I shall be glad to make my staff available to you."

Even more suspicious, Sano replied, "Thank you, Honorable Chamberlain. I'll keep your offer in mind."

Yanagisawa rose and bowed his farewells to the shogun, then to Sano and Hirata, who also took their leave. "Spare no effort or expense in catching Lady Harume's murderer," Tokugawa Tsunayoshi commanded between grunts and gasps as the masseur pummeled his chest. "I am counting on you to save me and my regime from destruction!"

Outside the palace, Hirata said, "Why is Chamberlain Yanagisawa acting so nice? He must be up to something. You're not going to accept his help, are you?"

Sano winced at his blunt-spoken retainer's mention of a sensitive issue. Caution and wishful thinking pulled him in opposite directions. He knew Yanagisawa, and didn't trust him. Yet how much easier his work would be with the chamberlain's cooperation!

"Maybe he's decided to call a truce," Sano said as they walked through the garden.

"*Sumimasen*—excuse me, but I can't believe that!"

Caution won out. Sano said, "Nor can I. I'll send out spies to check up on him. Now, in the interest of saving time, we'd better split up to interview Lieutenant Kushida and Lady Ichiteru. Which one do you want?"

Hirata's expression turned pensive. "My great-grandfather and Kushida's fought in the Battle of Sekigahara together. Our families still visit on New Year's Day. I'm not close to Kushida—he's fourteen years older than I am—but I've known him as long as I can remember."

"Then you'd better take Lady Ichiteru," Sano said, "so your lack of objectivity won't affect the investigation."

After a moment's hesitation, Hirata nodded.

"Is everything all right?" Sano asked.

"Yes, of course," Hirata said quickly. "I'll speak to Lady Ichiteru right away."

Sano dismissed his misgivings. Hirata had never let him down before. "One of Ichiteru's attendants is a girl named

Midori," Sano said. "I know her from my first murder case."

Midori, a daughter of Lord Niu of Satsuma Province, had helped Sano identify her sister's killer, an act that had resulted in her banishment to a distant nunnery. Sano had used his influence to bring her back to Edo and secured her a post as an Edo Castle lady-in-waiting, a desirable situation for girls from prominent families. He hadn't seen Midori again, but she'd sent a letter expressing the desire to repay his kindness.

After explaining this to Hirata, Sano said, "Be sure to talk to Midori, and tell her you're working for me. Perhaps she can provide some useful information about affairs in the Large Interior."

They separated, Hirata bound for the women's quarters to see Lady Ichiteru and Midori, and Sano to locate Lieutenant Kushida, the palace guard who had threatened to kill Lady Harume.

Sano rode his horse through the narrow streets of the Nihonbashi merchant district, past commoners' houses and open storefronts that sold sake, oil, pottery, soy sauce, and other products. Merchants haggled with customers. Laborers, craftsmen, and housewives thronged lanes patrolled by troops. Sano crossed a bridge that led over a willow-edged canal to a greengrocer's shop, a stationer's store, and several food stalls. Pedestrians called friendly greetings to him: by a not entirely surprising happenstance, his quest for Lieutenant Kushida had led him to his own home territory.

When he'd questioned the palace guard commander regarding Kushida's whereabouts, the man had said, "Lieutenant Kushida has been reinstated to his post, but he doesn't go back on duty until tomorrow. However, I've heard that since he was suspended, he's been hanging around the Sano Martial Arts Academy."

This was the school founded by Sano's deceased father. Sano had once taught there and had planned to run it after his father's retirement, but when he'd joined the police force, his father had turned the academy over to an apprentice. Yet Sano had never lost his love for the place where he'd learned the art of swordsmanship. His mother, who didn't want to move to Edo Castle, still lived in quarters behind the school. Upon Sano's promotion to the post of *sōsakan-sama,* he'd spent some of his large stipend on improving the academy. Now, as he dismounted outside the long, low building, he proudly surveyed the results.

The leaky, sagging tile roof had been replaced, and the façade given a coat of fresh white plaster. A new, larger sign announced the academy's name. The space had also expanded to fill two adjacent houses. Sano entered. Inside, rows of samurai dressed in white cotton uniforms wielded wooden practice swords, staffs, and spears in simulated combat. Shouts and stamps echoed in a thunderous cacophony, the background noise of Sano's childhood. The familiar reek of sweat and hair oil permeated the air. However, the enrollment had increased from a handful of students to over three hundred, and the teaching staff from one to twenty.

"Sano-*san*! Welcome!" Toward Sano walked Aoki Koemon, once his childhood playmate and his father's apprentice, now proprietor and chief *sensei*. He bowed, then shouted to the class: "Attention! Our patron is here!"

Combat ceased. In perfect silence, everyone bowed to Sano, who was embarrassed yet gratified. His own reputation had enhanced the academy's status. Once only *rōnin* and low-class retainers of minor clans had studied here. Now Tokugawa vassals and samurai from the great daimyo families came, hoping to curry favor with Sano and acquire his famous fighting skills in the classes he sometimes taught.

"Continue as you were," Sano ordered, sad that his rank set him above the place of his childhood, yet pleased to honor his father's spirit by sharing his success with the academy.

Activity and noise resumed. "What brings you here today?" said Koemon, a stocky, pleasant-faced man.

"I'm looking for Kushida Matsutatsu."

Koemon pointed toward the back of the room, where a group of students was taking a lesson in *naginatajutsu*—the art of the spear—from a short, thin samurai. His bamboo practice weapon had a narrow, curved wooden blade padded with cotton. "That's Kushida," Koemon said. "He's one of our best students, and often acts as instructor."

As Sano moved closer to watch, Lieutenant Kushida demonstrated strokes to the class. He appeared about thirty-five years of age, and wore ordinary white practice clothes. His face was creased like a monkey's, with glowering eyes beneath a low forehead. A jutting jaw, long arms and torso, and short legs increased his simian appearance. He seemed an incongruous suitor for a beautiful young woman like Lady Harume.

Kushida arranged his twelve students in two parallel lines. Then he crouched, spear held in both hands. "Attack!" he shouted.

With blood-curdling yells, the students rushed him, spears outthrust. Originally used by warrior monks, the *naginata* had been adopted some five hundred years ago by military clans such as the Minamoto. Spearmen had scattered armies during Japan's civil wars; until Tokugawa law restricted dueling, bands of enthusiasts had roamed the land, training with different masters and challenging rivals. Now, as Lieutenant Kushida sprang into action, Sano gained a new appreciation for the power of the *naginata* and a respect for this man who wielded it.

In a dizzyingly fast circular dance, Kushida whirled amid his attackers, his spear carving the air. He used every part of his weapon, parrying blows with the haft, slicing opponents with the padded blade, jabbing the blunt end into chests and stomachs. As bodies thudded to the floor around him, Kushida seemed to gain stature; his monkey face acquired a blazing ferocity. The students cried out in pain. But Kushida continued fighting, as if for his life. Sano glimpsed in Kushida the type of samurai who kept his emotions under tight control and found release at times like this. By now he must know about Lady Harume's death. Was this brutality his way of showing grief? Or the expression of murderous tendencies that had led him to kill her?

Within moments, every student lay defeated, groaning and rubbing their bruises. "Weaklings! Lazy oafs!" Kushida berated them. He was breathing hard; sweat dripped off his shaved crown. "If this had been a real battle, you would all be dead now. You must practice harder."

Then he caught sight of Sano. His body tensed and he raised his spear, as though preparing for another battle. Glowering, he said, "*Sōsakan-sama*. It didn't take you long to find me, did it?" His normal speaking voice was quiet and tight. "Who told you about me? That cow, Madam Chizuru?"

"If you know why I'm here, then wouldn't you rather

go outside where we can talk in privacy?" Sano said with a pointed glance at the curious students.

Shrugging, Kushida stalked to the door. He moved with a taut, wiry grace; the muscles in his thin arms and legs were like steel cords. From a wooden bucket he dipped a cup of water. Sano followed him onto the veranda, where they sat. A continuous parade of peasants and mounted samurai filled the street.

"Tell me what happened between you and Lady Harume," Sano said.

"Why do we have to talk about it, when you must already know?" Kushida threw down his spear, drank deeply from his cup, then glared at Sano. "Why don't you just arrest me? I've been suspended from duty; I've disgraced myself and my family name. How could things possibly get worse?"

"The penalty for murder is execution," Sano reminded him. "I'm giving you a chance to tell your side of the story—and perhaps escape further disgrace."

Sighing in resignation, Kushida put down his cup and leaned back on his elbows. "Oh, well," he said. "When Lady Harume came to the castle, I was . . . attracted to her. Yes, I know the rules against improper behavior with the shogun's concubines, and I've always obeyed them before."

Sano recalled what Kushida's commander had told him when asked about the lieutenant's character: "He's a quiet, serious one—he doesn't seem to have any friends or much of a life beyond work and martial arts. The other guards don't like his air of superiority. Until now, Kushida has controlled himself around the concubines so well that everyone thought that he didn't care for women. He assumed his post at age twenty-five, when his father retired from it. We were a little uneasy about letting such a young fellow loose in the Large Interior; usually we choose men who are past their prime. But Kushida has lasted ten years—longer than many other men, who've been transferred because they got too friendly with some lady."

"Never before had I ever allowed myself to be tempted by any of the women. But Harume was so beautiful, with such a lively, charming manner." Kushida's gaze softened in reminiscence. More to himself than to Sano, he said, "At first, I was content just to look at her. I listened to her talk to the other women and take her music lessons. Whenever she left the castle, I volunteered to be part of the military escort. Anything just to be near her.

"But soon I wanted more." His voice gained intensity; he seemed eager for confession. "I found excuses to start conversations with Harume. She was pleasant to me. Yet I still wasn't satisfied. I wanted to see her naked body." Lust burned behind the gaze Kushida turned on Sano. "So I started spying on her. I'd stand outside her room while she undressed, and watch her shadow move against the paper walls. Then one day she accidentally left the bathchamber door open a crack. And I saw her shoulders and legs and breasts." Lieutenant Kushida's voice grew hushed with awe, his expression bemused. "The sight drove all caution from me."

Had Harume really left the door open by mistake, or had she been playing the same game with Kushida as described in her diary? As yet, Sano had an incomplete sense of her character; he must learn more about her. But now, seeing on Kushida's ugly face the haunted look of obsessive love, Sano felt his heartbeat quicken in excitement. Such obsession could lead to murder. "So you made advances toward Lady Harume?" he prompted.

The lieutenant frowned, as though angry at himself for speaking too freely. Hunching over, arms folded upon his knees, he stared at the ground and said, "I sent Harume a letter, saying how much I admired her. But she never answered, and she began avoiding me. I was afraid I'd made her angry, so I wrote another letter, apologizing for the first one and begging to be her friend." Kushida's voice tightened; his fingers dug into his arms. "Well, she didn't answer that one, either. I hardly ever saw her anymore; she stopped speaking to me.

"I was so desperate, I cast aside discipline and wisdom. I wrote her another letter, saying I loved her. I begged her to run away with me so we could be with each other as man and wife for a night, then die together and spend eternity in paradise. Then I waited for her reply—for five whole, miserable days! I thought I would go mad." A high, shaky laugh burst from Kushida. "Then, while I was patrolling the corridor, I happened to run into Harume. I grabbed her shoulders and demanded to know why she hadn't answered my letters. She yelled at me to let go. I was past caring who saw or heard. I said I loved her and wanted her and couldn't live without her. Then—"

Kushida rested his forehead upon his arms. Palpable waves of unhappiness emanated from him. "She said I should have guessed from her behavior that she didn't share my feelings. She ordered me to leave her alone." The lieutenant raised his face, a mask of bleak misery. "After all my dreams, she rejected me! I became so angry my vision turned black. For that ungrateful whore I'd sacrificed discipline, risked my position and my honor!

"I started shaking her. I heard my own voice saying, 'I'll kill you, I'll kill you.' Then she broke free and ran away. Somehow I managed to pull myself together and resume my duties. Eventually my commander told me Harume had reported everything that had happened. The guards threw me out. I never saw Lady Harume again." Kushida exhaled forcefully and looked out on the busy street. "End of story."

But was it? Sano wondered. A forbidden love, nurtured over a period of eight months, didn't just suddenly die, even after official censure. Deprived of all hope, it could fester into an equally obsessive hatred.

"How much time passed between that encounter with Lady Harume and your expulsion from Edo Castle?" Sano asked.

"Two days. Long enough for Madam Chizuru to hear Lady Harume's complaint and notify my superiors so they could punish me."

And long enough for Lieutenant Kushida to exact revenge on the woman who had rejected him. "Have you ever seen this before?" From his pouch Sano removed the ink jar—now empty and rinsed—and gave it to Kushida.

"I heard that it was a poisoned bottle of ink that killed her. So this is it?" Lieutenant Kushida cradled the jar in his palm, bending his head so that Sano couldn't see his expression. His fingertip traced the gilt characters of Harume's name. Then he handed the jar back to Sano, grimacing with impatience. "I know what you're thinking: that I killed Harume. Weren't you paying attention when I told you what happened between us? She despised me. She would never have tattooed herself for me. And no, I've never seen that jar before." He added bitterly, "Harume didn't make a habit of showing me gifts from lovers."

Sano wondered if Kushida had lied about his relations with Harume. What if she had really welcomed his advances, and they'd become lovers? In spite of the disparaging reference to him in her diary, it wasn't impossible that the lonely, bored concubine would have accepted an unattractive suitor if he was the only diversion available. Maybe she'd agreed to tattoo herself as proof of her love for Kushida, and he'd brought the ink. Then, afraid they would be discovered and punished, had she tried to break with him? When Lieutenant Kushida objected, Harume might have reported him in hopes of saving herself. But Sano still planned to question the lord of Tosa Province, of whom he believed Harume had written in her diary. And the lieutenant's last remark offered another possible motive.

"You knew Harume had a lover, then?" Sano said.

"I'm only assuming now that she must have, because of the way she died." Rising, Kushida leaned on the veranda railing, his face averted from Sano. "How could I have known before? She didn't confide in me."

"But you watched her, followed her, eavesdropped on her conversations," Sano said, standing beside Kushida. "You might have guessed what was going on. Were you jealous because she not only rejected you, but had another man? Did you see them together when you escorted her away from the castle? Did you poison the ink he gave her?"

"I didn't kill her!" Kushida snatched up his spear and brandished it menacingly. "I didn't know about the ink. The rules forbid palace guards to go into the concubines' rooms except during emergencies, and never alone." Emphasizing his words by jabbing his spear in the direction of Sano's face, Kushida said, "I did not kill Harume. I loved her. I would never have really hurt her. And I still love her now.

If she had lived, she might have come to love me. I had no reason to wish her dead."

"Except that her death resulted in the charges against you being dropped, and your reinstatement to your post," Sano reminded him.

"Do you think I care about that?" Kushida shouted, his face livid with rage. Curious pedestrians stared. "What do position, money, or even honor mean to me now that Harume is gone?"

Sano backed away, hands raised palms outward. "Calm down," he said, realizing how dangerously love, grief, and anger had unbalanced the lieutenant's mind.

"Without her, my life is over!" Kushida yelled. "Arrest me, convict me, execute me if you will—it doesn't matter to me. But for the last time: *I did not kill Harume!*"

Kushida forced the last words through bared teeth, spacing them with hissing breaths as if pumping himself up with ire. His face took on the ferocious expression he'd worn during the practice match. He lunged at Sano, spear thrusting. Sano grabbed the spear's haft. As they grappled for control of the weapon, Kushida spat curses.

"No, Kushida-*san*. Stop!" Koemon and the other teachers rushed out the door. They grabbed the lieutenant, pulled him away from Sano, and seized his weapon. As Kushida howled and thrashed, they wrestled him to the veranda floor. It took five men to pin him down. Students watched in dismay. Bystanders hooted and cheered. Kushida burst into loud, hysterical laughter.

"Harume, Harume," he wailed. Sobs wracked his body.

A castle messenger hurried up to the academy. A flag bearing the Tokugawa crest waved from a pole attached to his back. Bowing to Sano, he said, "A message for you, *sōsakan-sama,*" and proffered a lacquer scroll case.

Sano opened the case and read the enclosed letter, which had been sent to his house earlier that morning and forwarded to him. It was from Dr. Ito. Lady Harume's corpse had arrived at Edo Morgue. Ito would perform the examination at Sano's convenience.

"See that Kushida gets home safely," Sano told Koemon. Later he would order the Edo Castle guard commander to delay Kushida's reinstatement: Innocent or guilty, the lieutenant was in no shape for active duty.

After stopping to see his mother, Sano rode toward Edo Morgue while mulling over his interview with Kushida. How easily hurt and jealousy could have turned the disturbed lieutenant's love for Harume to hatred. Yet there was one critical factor that argued against Kushida's guilt. From what Sano had observed, his temper manifested itself in sudden, violent outbursts. The spear was Kushida's favored weapon—if he wanted to kill, wouldn't he use it? Lady Harume's murder had required cold, devious forethought. To Sano, poisoning seemed more like a woman's crime. He wondered how Hirata was doing on his interview with Harume's rival concubine, Lady Ichiteru.

The Saru-waka-chō theater quarter was located near Edo's Ginza district, named for the Tokugawa silver mint. Bright signs advertised performances; music and cheers rang out from the open upper-story windows of the theaters. In framework towers atop the roofs, men beat drums to attract audiences. People of all ages and classes lined up at ticket booths; teahouses and restaurants were filled with customers. Hirata left his horse at a public stable and continued on foot through the noisy crowd. On Sano's orders, he'd already dispatched one team of detectives to search for the itinerant drug peddler Choyei, and another to search the Large Interior for poison and other evidence. Upon going to the women's quarters to question Lady Ichiteru, he'd been informed that she was spending the day at the Satsuma-za puppet theater. Now, as he neared the theater, a growing apprehension sped his heartbeat.

He'd lied when he had told Sano everything was all right, trying to reassure himself that he was capable of handling the interview with Lady Ichiteru. Women didn't always intimidate him the way Lady Keisho-in and Madam Chizuru had last night; he liked them, and had enjoyed many romances with maids and shopkeepers' daughters. However, the ladies of powerful men tapped a deep sense of inadequacy within him. Usually Hirata took pride in his humble origin and what he'd achieved in spite of it. In courage, intelligence, and martial arts skill, he knew he equalled many a high-ranking samurai; thus, he could face his male superiors with aplomb. But the women . . .

Their elegant beauty inspired in him a hopeless longing. A bachelor at the late age of twenty-one, Hirata had deferred marriage in the hope of one day advancing high enough to wed a fine lady who would never have to slave like his mother had, keeping house and caring for a family without benefit of servants. As Sano's chief retainer, he'd achieved that goal; his family had received proposals from prominent clans seeking a closer association with the shogun's court, offering their daughters as Hirata's prospective brides. Sano would act as go-between and arrange a match. Yet still Hirata delayed his wedding. Ladies of high class made him feel coarse, dirty, and inferior, as if none of his accomplishments mattered—he would never be good enough to associate with them, let alone deserve one as a wife.

Now Hirata stopped outside the Satsuma-za, a large, open-air arena comprised of wooden walls built around a courtyard. Above the entrance, five plumed arrows—symbol of the puppet theater—pierced a railing hung with indigo curtains bearing the establishment's crest. Vertical banners announced the names of current plays. An attendant seated on a platform collected admission fees, while another guarded the doorway, a narrow horizontal slot in the wall that prevented theatergoers from entering without paying. Hirata made up his mind that he would not let Lady Ichiteru upset him as the shogun's mother had. Poisoning—a devious, indirect crime—was the classic method of female killers, and Ichiteru was therefore the prime murder suspect.

"One, please," Hirata told the attendant, offering the requisite coins.

Ducking through the door, he found himself in the theater's entryway. He'd come in at an intermission during the daylong series of plays, and the space was jammed with patrons buying tea, sake, rice cakes, fruit, and roasted melon seeds from food stalls. Hirata left his shoes beside a row of others and eased his way through the crowd, wondering how to find Lady Ichiteru, whom he'd never met.

"Hirata-*san*?"

He turned at the sound of a female voice calling his name. Before him stood a young lady several years his junior. Clad in a bright red silk kimono printed with blue and gold parasols, she had glossy shoulder-length black hair, round cheeks, and bright, merry eyes. She bowed, then said, "I'm Niu Midori." Her voice was high, lilting, girlish. "I just wanted to convey my respects to your master." A smile curved her full, rosy lips and dimpled her cheeks. "He once did me a big favor, and I'm truly grateful to him."

"Yes, I know—he told me." Hirata smiled back, charmed by her unaffected manner, which he hadn't expected from a woman of Midori's social status. Her father was an "outside lord"—a daimyo whose clan had suffered defeat at the Battle of Sekigahara and later sworn allegiance to the victorious Tokugawa faction. The Niu, though stripped of their ancestral fief and relocated to distant Kyūshū, remained one of the wealthiest, most powerful families in Japan. But Midori seemed as natural as the girls Hirata had romanced. Feeling suddenly lighthearted and cocky, he bowed and said, "I'm delighted to meet you."

"The pleasure is all mine." Now Midori's expression grew wistful. "Is the *sōsakan-sama* well?" When assured that Sano was in perfect health, she said, "So he's married now." Her sigh told Hirata that she liked Sano and had once cherished hopes of a match with him. Then she regarded Hirata with lively interest. "I've heard lots about you. You were a policeman, weren't you? How exciting!"

At a food stall, Midori bought a tray of tea and cakes. "Here, let me help you," Hirata said.

She dimpled. "Thank you. You must be very brave to be a detective."

"Not really," Hirata said modestly. They moved to a vacant spot, and he related some heroic tales of his police career.

"How wonderful!" Midori clapped her hands. "And I've heard how you helped capture a band of smugglers in Nagasaki. Oh, I do wish I could have seen that."

"It was nothing," Hirata said, preening under her frank admiration. She was really very pretty and sweet. "Now I'm investigating the murder of Lady Harume, and I need to speak with Lady Ichiteru. I have some questions for you, too," he added, recalling Sano's instructions.

"Oh, good! I'll tell you whatever I can." Midori smiled. "Come and sit with us. We can talk until the play starts."

As Hirata followed her into the theater, his confidence soared. He'd found it so easy conversing with Midori; he should do just fine with Lady Ichiteru.

In the sunny theater courtyard, tatami mats covered the ground. Charcoal braziers warmed the air. The audience knelt in chattering groups. At the front, the stage consisted of a long wooden railing, from which hung a black curtain to conceal from view puppeteers, chanter, and musicians. Midori led Hirata toward the choice seating area directly in front of the stage, which was occupied by a row of richly dressed ladies with their maids and guards.

"That's Lady Ichiteru at the end." Suddenly Midori seemed shy, uncertain. "Hirata-*san*. Please forgive me if I'm interfering, but—I must warn you to be careful. I don't know anything for sure, but I—" She continued stammering, but just then, Lady Ichiteru turned and caught Hirata's eye.

With a long, tapering face, high-bridged nose, and narrow, tilted eyes, she was a classic beauty from ancient court paintings—or from the cheap booklets advertising the courtesans of the Yoshiwara pleasure quarter. Everything about her reflected this startling combination of high-class refinement and common sensuality. Dainty red lips had been painted over a mouth that was full, lush, and not quite hidden beneath the white makeup that covered her face. Her hairstyle, looped up at the sides and long in the back, was simple and severe, but anchored with an elaborate ornament of silk flowers and lacquer combs in the style of a high-ranking prostitute. Her burgundy brocade kimono slid off her shoulders in the latest, provocative fashion, yet the skin of her long neck and rounded shoulders looked pure, white, and untouched by any man. Ichiteru's gaze was at once veiled and remote, sly and knowing.

Hirata felt his knees tremble, and an embarrassing flush spread heat over his body. Like a dream walker he moved toward Lady Ichiteru. He was barely conscious of Midori performing introductions and explaining his presence. His surroundings receded into blurry shadow, while Ichiteru alone remained vivid and distinct. A profound arousal stirred in his loins. Never before had he been so immediately attracted to a woman.

Lady Ichiteru spoke in the trailing, mannered speech of a highborn woman: ". . . pleased to make your acquaintance. . . . Of course I shall help with your inquiry in any way I can . . ."

Her voice was a husky murmur that insinuated its way into Hirata's mind like dark, intoxicating smoke. She raised a silk fan, covering the lower half of her face. By lowering her eyelids and inclining her head, she invited Hirata to sit beside her. He did so, with an absentminded glance at Midori when she took the tea tray from him and began passing out refreshments to the party, her face unhappy. Then Hirata forgot Midori completely.

"I—I want to know—" he floundered, trying to collect his wits. Lady Ichiteru's perfume cloaked him in the potent, bittersweet scent of exotic flowers. Hirata felt horribly conscious of his cropped hair; the disguise that had saved his life in Nagasaki made him look more peasant than samurai. "What was your relationship with Lady Harume?"

"Harume was a pert little thing . . ." Ichiteru shrugged delicately, and her kimono slid further off her shoulders, exposing the tops of her full breasts. Hirata, wrenching his gaze back to her face, felt himself grow erect. ". . . but she was a common peasant. Hardly a person with whom a member of the imperial family . . . such as I . . . should have cared to associate." Ichiteru's nostrils flared in haughty disdain.

Through a haze of desire, Hirata recalled Madam Chizuru's statement. "But weren't you jealous when Harume came to the castle and—and—took your place in His Excellency's, uh, bedchamber?"

The last word was no sooner spoken than he longed to snatch it back. Why couldn't he have said "affections," or some other polite euphemism for Lady Ichiteru's relations with the shogun? Mortified by his own crassness, Hirata regretted that nothing in his police experience had prepared him for discussing intimate matters with women of high class. He should have let Sano question Lady Ichiteru! Now, against his will, Hirata imagined a scene in Tokugawa Tsunayoshi's private suite: Lady Ichiteru on the futon, disrobing; and in place of the shogun, Hirata himself. Excitement heated his blood.

A hint of a smile played upon Lady Ichiteru's lips—did she know what he was thinking? Eyes lowered meekly, she said, "What right have I . . . a mere woman . . . to mind my lord's choice of companion? And if Harume had not succeeded me, someone else would have." A shadow of emotion crossed her serene features. "I am in my twenty-ninth year."

"I see." Hirata recalled that concubines retired after that age, to marry, become palace officials, or return to their families. So Ichiteru was eight years older than he. Suddenly the chaste young girls he'd considered as prospective brides seemed dull, unattractive. "Well, ah," he said, groping for the line of inquiry he'd begun.

A maid passed Lady Ichiteru a plate of dried cherries. She took one, then said to Hirata, "Will you partake of refreshment?"

"Yes, thank you." Grateful for the distraction, he popped a cherry in his mouth.

Ichiteru pursed her lips and opened them. Slowly she inserted the fruit, pushing it in with her fingertip. Hirata gulped, swallowing his cherry whole. He'd often seen women eat this way, careful not to touch food to their lips and smear the rouge. But on Lady Ichiteru, it looked so erotic. Her long, smooth fingers seemed made for holding, stroking, and inserting into bodily orifices . . .

Shamed by his thoughts, Hirata said, "There were reports that you and Lady Harume didn't get along."

"Edo Castle is full of gossips who have nothing better to do than malign other people," she murmured. Face averted, she daintily extracted the cherry pit from her mouth.

On its own volition, Hirata's hand reached out. Ichiteru dropped the seed into his palm. It was warm and moist with her saliva. He gazed at her in helpless lust until the loud, insistent clacking of wooden clappers sounded. He looked up to see that the audience now filled the theater; the play was about to start. A man dressed in black walked in front of the stage and announced, "The Satsuma-za welcomes you to the premier performance of *Tragedy at Shimonoseki,* which is based upon a true story of recent events." He recited the names of the chanter, puppeteers, and musicians, then shouted, "*Tōzai*—hear ye!"

From behind the curtain came melancholy samisen music. A painted backdrop showing a garden appeared above the curtain. The chanter's disembodied voice uttered a series of wails, then intoned, "In the fifth month of Genroku year two, in the provincial city of Shimonoseki, the beautiful, blind Okiku awaits the return of her husband, a samurai who is in Edo attending his lord. Her sister Ofuji comforts her."

The audience cheered as two female puppets with painted wooden heads, long black hair, and bright silk kimonos made their entrance. One had a sad, pretty face; her eyes were closed to indicate Okiku's blindness. While she simulated weeping, the chanter's voice altered to a high, feminine pitch: "Oh, how I miss my dear Jimbei. He's been gone so long; I shall perish of loneliness."

Her sister Ofuji was plain, with a frown slanting her brows. "You're lucky to have such a fine man," the chanter said in a lower tone. "Pity me, with no husband at all." Then he informed the audience, "In her blindness, Okiku does not see that Ofuji is in love with Jimbei, or that her sister envies her good fortune and wishes her ill."

Okiku sang a sad love song, accompanied by samisen, flute, and drum. The audience stirred in expectancy; a loud buzz of conversation arose: silence during performances was not a habit of Edo theatergoers. Hirata, still clutching Lady Ichiteru's cherry pit, forced his thoughts back to the investigation.

"Did you know that Lady Harume was going to tattoo herself?" he asked.

". . . I was not on such intimate terms with Harume that she would confide in me." From behind her fan, Ichiteru favored Hirata with a glance that slid over him like a warm breath. "I have heard shocking rumors. . . . Tell me, if I may be so bold to ask. . . . Where on Harume's person was the tattoo?"

Hirata gulped. "It was on her, uh," he faltered. Did she really not know the location of the tattoo? Was she innocent? "It was, uh—"

The faintest amusement curved Lady Ichiteru's lips.

"Above her crotch," Hirata blurted. Shame washed over him like a tide of boiling water. Had Ichiteru deliberately manipulated him into using the crude term? She was so provocative, yet so elegant. How would he ever finish this interview? Wretchedly, Hirata stared at the stage.

Okiku's song had ended. Now a sly, handsome samurai puppet sidled onto the stage. "Jimbei's younger brother Bannojo is secretly in love with Okiku and wants her for himself," the chanter narrated. Bannojo beckoned to Ofuji. Unobserved by the blind Okiku, the pair conspired. Jealous Ofuji agreed to let the covetous Bannojo into the house that night. The music turned discordant. Murmurs of anticipation swept the audience. Hirata grasped at the shreds of his professional demeanor. "Had you been in Lady Harume's room prior to her death?" he asked.

"It would degrade one to enter the chamber of a vulgar peasant. One just . . ." insinuation filmed Ichiteru's covert glance ". . . doesn't."

If she hadn't gone into Harume's room, did that mean she couldn't have poisoned the ink? Despite his police training, Hirata was unable to think clearly or follow the logic of the interrogation, because Lady Ichiteru's remark had pierced the heart of his insecurity. He felt vulgar in her presence; it seemed she was rejecting him, as she had Harume, as unworthy of her regard. Humiliation edged his desire.

Onstage, a new backdrop appeared: a bedchamber, with a crescent moon in the window to indicate night. Beautiful Okiku lay asleep while Ofuji let Bannojo into the room. Warning cries came from the audience.

Okiku stirred and sat up. "Who's there?" The chanter made her voice high, frightened.

"It is I, Jimbei, home from Edo," the chanter answered for Bannojo. Then he explained, "His voice is so like his brother's, and her longing for her husband so great, that she believes his lie."

The couple sang a joyous duet. Then they tugged each other's sashes loose. Garments fell away, revealing her large breasts, his upright organ. This was the advantage of puppet theater: scenes too explicit for live actors could be shown. Bawdy cheers filled the courtyard as Okiku and Bannojo embraced. Hirata, already too aroused, could hardly bear it. His manhood fully erect now, he feared that Lady Ichiteru and everyone else would notice his condition. Trying to sound businesslike, he said, "Have you ever seen a square, black lacquer bottle of ink with Lady Harume's name written in gold on the stopper?"

An involuntary gulp caught in his throat. While Ofuji watched from outside the door, Bannojo mounted Okiku. Amid sinuous music, the chanter's moans, and the audience's raucous exclamations, the puppets simulated the sexual act. Hirata squirmed, but Ichiteru viewed the drama with tranquil detachment.

"When one sees a fancy container of ink . . . one naturally assumes that it is for writing letters . . ." Another veiled glance. "Perhaps letters of . . . love."

The last word, spoken on a whisper, sent a shiver through Hirata. Lady Ichiteru raised her hand to her temple, as if to brush away a stray hair. Without looking at him, she lowered her hand, letting the wide sleeve of her kimono fall across Hirata's lap. His loins throbbed at the sudden pressure of its heavy fabric; he gasped. Had she done it by accident, or deliberately? How should he respond?

He tried to concentrate on the continuing drama onstage, where morning had come, bringing the unexpected arrival of Okiku's husband, Jimbei. Ofuji triumphantly informed him that his wife and brother had betrayed him. Jimbei, the stern, noble samurai, confronted his wife. Okiku tried to explain the cruel trick played upon her, but honor demanded revenge. Jimbei stabbed his wife through the chest. Ofuji begged him to marry her, swearing eternal love for him, but Jimbei stormed off in search of his duplicitous brother.

Under cover of her sleeve, Lady Ichiteru's hand moved onto Hirata's thigh. She began to massage it. Hirata felt her touch as if against his naked flesh, warm and smooth.

Breathing hard, he hoped the audience was too engrossed in the play to see. Lady Ichiteru's impassive expression didn't change. But now he knew that her provocation was intentional. She had maneuvered their whole encounter to this point.

In the city marketplace, Bannojo learned of Okiku's death. He rushed to the house and slew the treacherous Ofuji. Just then Jimbei arrived. Accompanied by wild music, the chanter's cries, and shouted encouragement from the audience, the brothers drew their swords and fought. Hirata, almost oblivious to the drama, felt his own excitement rise as Lady Ichiteru's hand crept stealthily to his groin. This shouldn't be happening. It was wrong. She belonged to the shogun, who would have them both killed if this dalliance became known. Hirata knew he should stop her, but the thrill of forbidden contact held him immobile.

Ichiteru's finger circled the tip of his manhood. Hirata swallowed a moan. Around and around. Then she grasped the rigid shaft and began to stroke. Up and down. Hirata's heart thudded; his pleasure mounted. Onstage, the wronged husband, Jimbei, delivered the fatal slash to his brother. Bannojo's wooden head flew off. Up and down moved Ichiteru's hand, her movements expert. Tense and breathless, Hirata approached the brink of climax. He forgot the murder investigation. He no longer cared if anyone saw.

Then Jimbei, overcome with grief, committed *seppuku* beside the corpses of his wife, brother, and sister-in-law. Suddenly the play was over, the audience applauding. Ichiteru withdrew her hand.

"Farewell, Honorable Detective . . . this has been a most interesting meeting." Eyes modestly downcast, fan shielding her face, she bowed. "If you need my further assistance . . . please let me know."

Hirata, denied the release he craved, gaped in helpless frustration. From Ichiteru's demeanor, the incident might never have taken place. Too confused to speak, Hirata rose to leave, struggling to recall what he'd learned from the interview. How could a woman he wanted so much be a cold-blooded killer? For the first time in his career, Hirata felt his professional objectivity slipping.

From behind the stage curtain, the chanter's solemn voice intoned, "You have just seen a true story of how treachery, forbidden love, and blindness caused a terrible tragedy. We thank you for attending."

Eta corpse handlers placed the shrouded body on the table in Dr. Ito's workroom at Edo Morgue. Sano and Dr. Ito watched as Mura unwrapped the white folds of cloth from Lady Harume. Her eyes had dulled, and encroaching decay had blanched her skin. The foul, sweet odor of rot tainted the air. She still wore the soiled red silk dressing gown; blood and vomit still smeared her face and tangled hair. Hirata had indeed made sure that no one tampered with the evidence. Having known what to expect, Sano experienced only a momentary pang of revulsion, but Dr. Ito seemed shaken.

"So young," he murmured. As morgue custodian, he had examined countless bodies in worse condition; yet lines of pain deepened in his face, aging him. He said in a bleak voice, "I had a daughter. Once."

Sano recalled that Ito's youngest child had died of a fever at about the same age as Harume. He'd also lost contact with his other children upon his arrest. Sano and Mura stood silent, heads bowed in respect for their friend's grief, so seldom expressed. Then Dr. Ito cleared his throat and spoke in his normal brisk, professional manner. "Well. Let us see what the victim can tell us about her murder."

He walked around the table, studying Harume's corpse. "Dilated pupils; muscular spasm; vomiting of blood—symptoms that confirm my original diagnosis of poison by Indian arrow toxin. But perhaps there is more to learn. Mura, would you please remove her garment?"

Despite his unconventional nature, Dr. Ito followed the custom of letting the *eta* handle the dead. Hence, Mura performed most of the physical work of examinations, under his master's supervision. Now he took a knife and cut the robe away from Harume's rigid form. The dark nipples and tattoo contrasted harshly with her waxen pallor. Her limbs were smooth and shaved hairless, her skin without blemish. Sano felt rude to violate the privacy of this woman who had obviously taken care over her personal grooming.

Dr. Ito bent over the corpse's midsection, frowning. "There's something here." He spread a white cotton cloth over Lady Harume's abdomen, then pressed his hands against her, the cloth shielding him from the polluting contact with death. His fingers palpated and squeezed.

"What is it?" Sano asked.

"A swelling. It may be an artifact of the poison, or some other unrelated abnormality." Dr. Ito straightened, his expression grave as he met Sano's eyes. "But I've treated many female patients in my medical career. Unless I'm mistaken, Lady Harume was in the early stages of pregnancy."

A heavy weight of dismay thudded inside Sano's chest like an iron clapper in a temple bell. Pregnancy would have serious ramifications for the murder case, and for Sano as well.

Dr. Ito's gaze conveyed unspoken concern and understanding, but he was not a man to shy away from the truth. "A dissection is the only way to tell for sure."

Sano drew a deep breath and held it, containing the fear that burgeoned within him. Dissection, a procedure associated with foreign science, was just as illegal as when Dr. Ito had been arrested. During other investigations, Sano had risked banishment and disgrace for the sake of knowledge. So far the *bakufu* hadn't discovered his involvement in taboo practices—even the most avid spies avoided Edo Morgue—but Sano feared that his luck would run out. He dreaded verification of Harume's condition, and the consequential danger. However, a pregnancy offered myriad possible motives for Harume's murder. Without exploring these, Sano might never identify her killer. And he never evaded the truth, either. Now he exhaled in resignation.

"All right," he said to Dr. Ito. "Go ahead."

At a nod from his master, Mura fetched a long, thin knife from a cabinet. Dr. Ito removed the cloth from Lady

Harume's abdomen. In the air over it, he sketched lines with his forefinger: "Cut here, and here, like so." Carefully, Mura inserted the sharp blade into the dead flesh, making a long horizontal slash below the navel, then two shorter, perpendicular cuts at each end of the first. He drew back the flaps of skin and tissue, exposing coiled pink bowels.

"Remove those," Dr. Ito instructed.

A strong fecal odor arose as Mura cut away the bowels and placed them in a tray. Nausea clutched Sano's stomach; the unclean aura of ritual contamination enveloped him. No matter how many times he observed dissections, they still sickened his body and spirit. He saw, within the cavity of Lady Harume's corpse, a fleshy, pear-shaped structure about the size of a man's fist. From this extended two thin, curved tubes, the ends fanning out in fibrous growths resembling sea anemones, meeting two grapelike sacs.

"The organs of life," Dr. Ito explained.

Shame exacerbated Sano's discomfort. What right had he, a man and stranger, to look upon the most private parts of a dead woman's body? Yet growing curiosity compelled his attention while Mura sliced into the womb, then laid it open. Inside nestled a frothy inner capsule of tissue. And curled within this, a tiny unborn child, like a naked pink salamander, no longer than Sano's finger.

"So you were right," Sano said. "She was pregnant."

The child's bulbous head dwarfed its body. The eyes were black spots in a barely formed face; the hands and feet mere paws attached to frail limbs. Threadlike red veins chased the skin, which stretched across ridges of delicate bone. A twisted cord connected the navel to the womb's lining. The vestige of a tail elongated the diminutive rump. As Sano stared at this new wonder, awe overcame him. How miraculous was the creation of life! He thought of Reiko. Would their troubled marriage succeed and produce children who would survive, as this one had not? His hopes seemed as fragile as the dead infant. Then professional and political concerns eclipsed Sano's domestic problems.

Had Lady Harume died because the killer had wanted to destroy the child? Jealousy might have compelled Lady Ichiteru or Lieutenant Kushida, rival and rejected suitor.

However, a more ominous motive came to Sano's mind.

"Can you determine the sex of the child?" he asked.

With the tip of a metal probe, Dr. Ito uncurled the infant and surveyed the genitals, a tiny bud between the legs. "It is only about three months old. Too early to tell whether it would have become a boy or a girl."

The uncertainty didn't alleviate Sano's worries. The dead child could have been the shogun's long-desired male heir. Someone might have murdered Lady Harume to weaken the chances of continued Tokugawa reign. This scenario posed a serious threat to Sano. Unless . . .

"Could the shogun have sired a child?" Dr. Ito voiced Sano's unspoken thought. "After all, His Excellency's sexual preference is well known."

"Lady Harume's pillow book mentioned a secret affair," Sano said, then described the passage. "Her lover could be the father of the child—if they didn't limit their activities to the kind Harume wrote about. Maybe I can prove it when I visit Lord Miyagi Shigeru today."

"I wish you good luck, Sano-*san*." Dr. Ito's face reflected Sano's hope. The stakes had risen; mortal danger now overshadowed the investigation. If the child belonged to another man, then Sano was safe. But if it was the shogun's, then Lady Harume's murder was treason: not just the killing of a concubine, but of Tokugawa Tsunayoshi's flesh and blood, a crime that merited execution. And if Sano failed to deliver the traitor to justice, he himself could be punished by death.

Through the streets of Nihonbashi moved a procession of soldiers and attendants, all wearing the gold flying-crane crest of the Sano family, escorting a black palanquin with the same symbol emblazoned on its doors. Inside the cushioned sedan chair sat Reiko, tense and anxious, oblivious to the colorful sights of mercantile Edo. To disobey her husband's orders would surely bring divorce, and shame to the whole Ueda clan. But she was still determined to pursue her illicit inquiry. She must prove her competence to herself as well as Sano. And to gain the necessary information, she must use every resource she possessed.

Under the surface of Edo society ran an invisible network composed of wives, daughters, relatives, female servants, courtesans, and other women associated with powerful samurai clans. They collected facts as efficiently as the *metsuke*—the Tokugawa spy agency—and spread them by word of mouth. Reiko was herself a link in the loose but effective network. As a magistrate's daughter, she'd often exchanged news from the Court of Justice for outside information. This morning she'd learned that Sano had identified two murder suspects, Lieutenant Kushida and Lady Ichiteru. Social custom prevented Reiko from meeting two strangers without introduction by mutual acquaintances, and she dared not risk Sano's anger by approaching them directly. However, the strength of the female information network lay in its ability to bypass such obstacles.

The procession skirted the central produce market, where vendors manned stalls heaped with white radish, onions, garlic bulbs, ginger-roots, and greens. Memory brought a smile to Reiko's lips. At age twelve, she'd begun sneaking out of her father's house in search of adventure.

Dressed in boys' clothes, a hat covering her hair, swords at her waist, she'd blended with the crowds of samurai who roamed Edo's streets. One day, here in this very market, she'd come upon two *rōnin* who were robbing a fruit stall and beating the helpless merchant.

"Stop!" cried Reiko, drawing her sword.

The thieves laughed. "Come and get us, boy," they goaded her, weapons unsheathed.

As Reiko lunged and slashed, their amusement turned to surprise, then fury. Their blades clashed with hers in earnest. Shoppers fled; passing samurai entered the melee. Horror filled Reiko. Unwittingly she'd started a full-scale brawl. But she loved the thrill of her first real battle. As she fought, someone's elbow slammed her face; she spat out a piece of broken tooth. Then the police arrived, disarmed the swordsmen, subdued them with clubs, bound their hands, and marched them off to jail. A *doshin* grabbed Reiko. While she struggled, her hat fell off. Her long hair spilled down.

"Miss Reiko!" the *doshin* exclaimed.

He was a friendly man who often stopped to talk to her when he visited the magistrate's house on business. Thus Reiko soon found herself not in jail with the other troublemakers, but kneeling in her father's courtroom.

Magistrate Ueda glared down at her from the dais. "What is the meaning of this, daughter?"

Quaking with fear, Reiko explained.

Her father's face remained stern, but a proud smile tugged his mouth. "I sentence you to one month of house arrest." This was the usual punishment for brawling samurai when no fatalities were involved. "Then I shall provide a more suitable outlet for your energy."

Hence the magistrate had begun letting her observe trials, on the condition that she stayed off the streets. The broken tooth, though an embarrassment, was also Reiko's battle trophy, the symbol of her courage, independence, and rebellion against injustice. Now, as the palanquin carried her into a lane of shops with colorful signs above curtained doorways, she felt the same thrill that she'd known during that long-ago battle and the trials she'd watched. She might lack detective experience, but she knew instinctively that she'd at last found the right use for her talents.

"Stop!" she commanded her escorts.

The procession halted, and Reiko alit from the palanquin. As she hurried down the street, her escorts tried to follow. But Reiko soon lost them in the crowd, which was composed mainly of women, like flocks of chattering birds in their gay kimonos. These shops sold beauty potions and hair ornaments, makeup and perfume, wigs and fans. The few men present were shopkeepers, clerks, or ladies' escorts. Reiko ducked under the indigo doorway curtain of Soseki, a popular dealer of unguents, and stepped inside.

The showroom, lit by barred windows and open skylights, contained shelves, cabinets, and bins of every imaginable beautifying substance: medicinal balms, hair oils and dyes, soap, and blemish removers, as well as brushes and sponges for applying them. Clerks waited on their female customers. Reiko left her shoes in the entryway, then moved through the crowded aisles. She halted at the bath-oil display.

There stood a woman in her late thirties, wearing the blue kimono of a *joro*—second-rank palace official. Thin to the point of emaciation, hair piled atop her head, she addressed the clerk in an authoritative manner. "I'll take ten bottles each of the pine, jasmine, gardenia, almond, and orange-scented oils."

The clerk wrote up the order. Gathering her attendants, the *joro* prepared to leave. Reiko approached.

"Good morning, Cousin Eri-*san*," she said, bowing.

This was a distant relative from her mother's side of the family, once concubine to the last shogun, Iemitsu. Now Eri was in charge of supplying the personal needs of the women's quarters, and thus a minor functionary whom Sano would no doubt relegate to the bottom of his list of witnesses. But Reiko knew that Eri was also the center of the Edo Castle branch of the female gossip network. Through the servants, Reiko had traced Eri to Soseki, and she meant to benefit from her cousin's knowledge. Still, Reiko addressed Eri with cautious diffidence.

"Might I please have a word with you?" Since her

mother's death, the Ueda clan had maintained infrequent contact with Eri's family. Eri's position had further isolated her, and Reiko guessed that she might resent a younger, prettier, and well-married relative.

But Eri greeted Reiko with a gasp of delight. "Reiko-*chan*! It's been such a long time. You were just a little girl the last time I saw you; now you're all grown up. And married, too!" A former beauty, Eri had lost her youthful good looks. Middle age showed in the gray roots of her dyed hair and the gaunt planes of her face. Yet the warmth of her eyes and smile was undiminished. When Eri looked at you, Reiko remembered, you felt special, as though you had her complete interest. No doubt this was how she'd charmed her lord—and how she got people to tell her secrets. Now Eri said, "Come along, where we can talk in private."

Soon they were settled comfortably in a back room of the shop, with sake, dried fruit, and cakes supplied by the proprietor. Since high-ranking ladies couldn't drink in public teahouses or eat at food stalls, many establishments in this district provided areas in which customers could refresh themselves. These rooms, where men were not allowed, often served as stations for the exchange of gossip. Through the paper walls, Reiko could see other women's shadows, hear their chatter and giggles.

"Now tell me everything that's new with you," Eri said, pouring them each a cup of heated liquor.

Soon Reiko had told her cousin all about the wedding, what gifts she'd received, and how her new home was furnished. She only just managed to stop herself before revealing her troubles with Sano, marveling at Eri's talent for extracting personal information. What a fine detective she would make! But Reiko couldn't afford to go away having told more than she'd learned.

"I'm very interested in the murder of Lady Harume," she said, nibbling a dried apricot. "What do you know about it?"

Sipping from her cup, Eri hesitated. "Your husband is investigating the murder, isn't he?" A sudden wariness cooled her manner, and Reiko sensed Eri's distrust of men in general, and the *bakufu* in particular. "Did he send you to question me?"

"No," Reiko confessed. "He ordered me to stay out of the investigation. He doesn't know I'm here, and he would be furious if he did. But I want to solve the mystery. I want to prove that a woman can be as good a detective as a man. Will you help me?"

A mischievous sparkle lit Eri's eyes. She nodded, then held up a hand. "First you must promise to tell me everything you can learn about your husband's progress on the case."

"Done." Reiko suppressed a twinge of guilt over her disloyalty toward Sano. Fair was fair; she must pay the price of the information she needed—and by refusing her assistance, hadn't Sano earned the punishment of having his activities known to every woman in Edo? Even as the memory of her desire for him fluttered Reiko's heart, determination steeled her resolve. She reported the news gleaned from the maids who eavesdropped on Sano's detectives while cleaning the barracks: "Today my husband interviews Lieutenant Kushida and Lady Ichiteru. Could they have poisoned Harume?"

"The women in the Large Interior are laying bets that one or the other did," Eri said, "with most of them favoring Lady Ichiteru."

"Why is that?"

Eri smiled sadly. "Concubines and ladies-in-waiting are young. Romantic. Naïve. The plight of a rejected suitor touches their soft little hearts. They don't understand how a man can love a woman as much as Kushida did Lady Harume, and at the same time hate her enough to kill her."

"But there must be evidence that has persuaded other women to believe Kushida is guilty?"

"My, you sound just like a police officer, Reiko-*chan*. Your husband is a fool not to accept your help." Eri laughed. "Well, I'll tell you something he probably doesn't know and won't find out. The day before Lieutenant Kushida was suspended, a guard caught him in Lady Harume's room. He had his hands in the cabinet where she kept her undergarments. Apparently Kushida was stealing them."

Or planting the poison? Reiko wondered.

"The incident was never reported," Eri continued. "Kushida is the guard's commanding officer, and he forced the man to keep quiet. No one would have known about it, except that a maid overheard them arguing and told me. The guard will never talk, because he could lose his post if the palace administration found out he protected someone who broke the rules." Eri paused. "And I never spread the story because Kushida had never made trouble before, and it seemed like a minor, harmless thing. Now I wish I'd gone to Madam Chizuru. If I had, Harume might not have died."

Through Eri's excuses, Reiko saw her real reason for keeping silent: Despite her worldly experience, her heart was as soft as those of the young concubines; she also sympathized with Lieutenant Kushida. But she'd established his opportunity for murder.

"Why is Lady Ichiteru considered the better suspect?" Reiko asked.

Eri's mouth tightened; she evidently disliked the concubine as much as she pitied Kushida. "Ichiteru hides her emotions well—from her manner, you'd never guess that she felt anything toward Harume besides disgust for a lowly peasant. She'll never admit how furious she was when the shogun stopped sleeping with her because he preferred Harume.

"But one day last summer, the ladies went on an outing to Kannei Temple. I was rounding them up for the trip home, when I heard screams in the woods. I hurried over and found Ichiteru and Harume on the ground, fighting. Ichiteru was on top of Harume, hitting her, shouting that she would kill Harume before she took Ichiteru's place as the shogun's favorite. I pulled them apart. Their clothes were dirty, their faces scratched and bloody. Harume was crying, and Ichiteru mad with rage. I separated them, then told everyone they'd hurt themselves by falling down in the woods."

"And this incident wasn't reported, either?"

Eri shook her head. "I might have lost my post for failing to keep order among my charges. Ichiteru didn't want anyone to know she'd behaved in such an undignified manner. And Harume was afraid of getting into trouble."

In Reiko's opinion, Lady Ichiteru had a much clearer motive for murder than Lieutenant Kushida. The concubine had also threatened Harume, and might have followed up the attack by poisoning her. "Did anyone see Lady Ichiteru in or near Harume's room shortly before she died?"

"When I asked the women, they all said no. But that doesn't mean Ichiteru wasn't there. She could have sneaked in when no one was looking. And she has friends who would lie for her."

Motive, and possible opportunity, Reiko decided. Lady Ichiteru was looking better and better as a suspect, but to prove her guilt, Reiko needed a witness, or evidence. "Can you let me talk to the other women and help me search Ichiteru's room?" she asked.

"Hmmm." Eri looked tempted, then frowned and shook her head. "Better not take the chance. It's against the rules to bring an outsider into the Large Interior. Even your husband will need special permission—though I doubt that he'll find anything. Ichiteru is smart. If she's the murderer, she would have gotten rid of any leftover poison."

Reiko was disappointed, but not unduly. She would just have to find a way around the rules, lies, and subterfuge that protected the Large Interior.

Eri was watching her with concern. "Cousin, I hope you won't go too far with playing detective. There are other men in the *bakufu* besides your husband who don't like women interfering in matters that are none of their business. Promise me you'll be sensible."

"I will," Reiko promised, though Eri's slighting reference to her pursuit bothered her. When a man investigated murder, it was considered work, for which he earned money. But a woman could only "play" at the same job. Impulsively, Reiko said, "Eri, I think it would be wonderful to have a real job in the castle, the way you do. Are you glad you became a palace official instead of marrying?"

Her cousin's mouth twisted in a smile of affectionate pity for her naïveté. "Yes, I'm glad. I've seen too many bad marriages. I enjoy my authority. But don't idealize my position, Reiko-*chan*. I got it by pleasing a man, and I serve under the rule of other men. Really, I'm no more free than you, who serve only your husband."

This depressing truth further convinced Reiko that she must find her own path through life. Then, seeing a sudden distracted expression on Eri's face, she said, "What is it?"

"I just remembered something," Eri said. "About three months ago, in the middle of the night, Lady Harume became violently ill with stomach pains. I gave her an emetic to make her vomit, then a sedative to put her to sleep. I thought that her food must have disagreed with her, and didn't bother reporting the illness to Dr. Kitano because she was better by morning. And Harume was almost struck by a flying dagger in a crowded street in the Asakusa district, on Forty-six Thousand Day." This was a popular temple festival. "No one knows who threw it. I never thought the two events were related, but now . . ."

Reiko saw Eri's point. In hot summer weather, spoiled food often caused sickness. Weapons let loose during battles between gangsters or dueling samurai endangered innocent bystanders. However, in view of Harume's murder, another possible explanation connected her two earlier misfortunes.

"It looks as though someone had been trying to kill Harume even before yesterday," Reiko said.

But was it Lady Ichiteru, Lieutenant Kushida, or some other, unknown person?

After leaving the Satsuma-za puppet theater, Hirata rode aimlessly around town. Hours slipped by while he relived every moment spent with the woman he desired but could never have. He couldn't think of anything except Lady Ichiteru.

Eventually, however, his physical excitement subsided enough for him to grow aware of his actions. Instead of working on the murder investigation, he'd wasted a whole morning on hopeless daydreams! And he'd automatically traveled to his old territory: police headquarters, located in the southernmost corner of Edo's administrative district. Seeing the familiar high stone walls and the stream of *doshin,* prisoners, and officials passing through the guarded gates restored Hirata's wits. He realized what had happened, and cursed himself for a fool.

Lady Ichiteru had avoided answering every single one of his questions. How would he explain to Sano why he'd failed to establish whether Ichiteru had motive or opportunity for Lady Harume's murder? He'd made a complete mess of the crucial interrogation of a prime suspect. Now he could admit that Ichiteru's evasion indicated her guilt. And, Hirata thought miserably, a woman of Lady Ichiteru's class wouldn't dally with a man of his, unless for unscrupulous purposes.

Still, the knowledge didn't stop Hirata from wanting her, or from hoping she was innocent—and that she wanted him, too. Though he feared another episode of failure and humiliation, he longed to see her again. Should he go back to the theater and demand straight answers? Hot blood filled his loins at the thought of being with Ichiteru, of finishing what they'd started. Reluctantly he decided he was in no shape to conduct an objective interrogation; he must first regain control over his feelings. And Hirata had other leads to investigate besides Lady Ichiteru. Fortunately his detective instincts had brought him to a good starting place.

Hirata entered the police compound. After giving his horse to a stableboy, he crossed the yard lined with the barracks where he'd once lived as a *doshin,* then went inside the main building, a rambling wooden structure. Officers signed on or off duty and delivered criminals in the reception room. From a raised platform, four clerks dispatched messages and dealt with visitors.

"Good day, Uchida-*san,*" Hirata greeted the chief clerk.

Uchida, an older man with a humorous face, gave Hirata a welcoming smile. "Well, look who's here again." The police station was always a font of information, and Uchida, across whose desk all this information passed, had proved a valuable source many times. "How's life at Edo Castle?"

After exchanging pleasantries, Hirata explained why he'd come. "Any reports of an old peddler selling rare drugs?"

"Nothing official, but I heard a rumor you might be interested in. Some youths from wealthy merchant families in the Suruga, Ginza, and Asakusa districts have supposedly gotten hold of a substance that induces trances and makes sex more fun. Since there's no law against it, and the users aren't suffering or causing any harm, the police haven't arrested anyone. The dealer is reportedly a man with long white hair and no name." Uchida chuckled. "The *doshin* are looking for him, mainly, I think, so they can try the drug themselves."

"A man with pleasure potions might also have poisons," Hirata said. "It sounds like he could be the one I'm looking for. Let me know if there's any word on his whereabouts."

"Be glad to—if you'll recommend me to your important friends when they hand out promotions." Uchida winked.

Hirata left police headquarters, mounted his horse outside the gate—and immediately thought of Lady Ichiteru. He forced himself to concentrate on the work at hand. Suruga, Ginza, and Asakusa were separated by considerable distance; apparently the nameless drug dealer ranged all over Edo, and might have moved on by now. Instead of questioning the *doshin* who had reported on him, Hirata would exploit a better, albeit unofficial, source of information.

Perhaps the activity would keep his mind off Lady Ichiteru.

The great wooden arch of the Ryōgoku Bridge spanned the Sumida River, linking Edo proper with the rural districts of Honjo and Fukagawa on the eastern banks. Below, fishing boats and ferries glided along the water, a shimmering mirror that reflected the vivid autumn foliage along its banks and the blue sky above. Temple bells tolled, their peals sharply vibrant in the clear air.

The hooves of Hirata's mount clattered on the bridge's wooden planks as he joined the stream of traffic bound for the far end of the bridge, an area known as Honjo Mukō—"Other Side"—Ryōgoku. This had developed in recent years as Edo's population had overflowed the crowded city center. Marshes had been drained; warehouses and docks now lined the shore. In the shadow of the Temple of Helplessness—built upon the burial site of the victims of the Great Fire thirty-three years ago—a flourishing merchant quarter had sprung up. Honjo Mukō Ryōgoku had also become a popular entertainment center. Peasants and *rōnin* thronged the wide firebreak, patronizing teahouses, restaurants, storytellers' halls, and gambling dens where men played cards, wagered on turtle races, or hurled arrows at targets to win prizes. Lurid signs above a menagerie depicted wild animals. Barkers shouted come-ons; peddlers sold candy, toys, and fireworks. Hirata headed for a popular attraction, where a large crowd had gathered before a raised platform. There stood a man of remarkable appearance.

He wore a blue kimono, cotton leggings, straw sandals, and red headband. Coarse black hair covered not only his scalp, but also the other exposed parts of his body: cheeks, chin, neck, ankles, the backs of his hands and tops of his feet, and the wedge of chest at the neckline of his garment.

Shaggy brows nearly obscured his beady eyes; a sharp-toothed mouth grinned within his whiskers.

"Come to the Rat's Freak Show!" he called, waving toward the curtained doorway behind him. "See the Kantō Dwarf and the Living Bodhisattva! Witness other shocking curiosities of nature!"

The Rat was no less an oddity than his freaks. He came from the far northern island of Hokkaidō, where cold winters caused men to sprout copious body hair. The Ainu, as they were called, reminiscent of apes, very primitive, and usually much taller than other Japanese. Short and wiry, the Rat must have been a runt of his tribe—and an ambitious one. He'd come to Edo as a young man to seek his fortune. A tobacco merchant had let him live in the back of his small shop, charging customers money to see him. The Rat's rodentlike visage had earned him his nickname; his business acumen had turned the merchant's sideline into this lucrative, notorious freak show. Some twenty years later, the Rat now owned the establishment, which he'd inherited upon his master's death.

"Step inside!" he invited. "Admission is only ten *zeni*!"

Coins in hand, the audience lined up outside the curtain. The Rat leapt off the platform to usher them inside; his assistant, a hugely muscled giant, collected admission fees. Hirata joined the queue. Seeing his empty hands, the giant growled, frowning.

"It's you I've come to see," Hirata told the Rat.

"Ah, Hirata-*san*." The Rat's beady eyes took on a gleam of avaricious cunning; he rubbed his hairy paws together. "What can I do for you today?"

"I need some information."

The Rat, who roamed Edo and the provinces in an ongoing hunt for new freaks, also collected news. He supplemented his income by selling choice information. While a police officer, Hirata had caught the Rat during a raid on an illegal brothel, and the Rat had bartered his way out of an arrest by telling Hirata the whereabouts of an outlaw who had eluded Edo police for years. Since then, Hirata had often used the Rat as an informant. His prices were high, but his service reliable.

"Better come inside," the Rat said now. "Show's about to start, and I have to announce the acts." He spoke with an odd, rustic accent. "We can talk during them."

Hirata followed him into the building, where the audience had gathered in a narrow room with a curtained stage. The Rat jumped onto this. Extolling the wonders of what was to come, he whipped the crowd into a noisy, eager frenzy, then announced, "And now I present the Kantō Dwarf!"

The curtain opened and out walked a grotesque figure, half the height of a normal man, with a large head, stunted body, and short limbs. Dressed in bright theatrical robes, he sang a song from a popular Kabuki drama. The audience cheered. The Rat joined Hirata at the side of the stage.

"I'm looking for an itinerant drug peddler named Choyei," Hirata said, relating the meager background material that existed on the man.

The Rat's feral grin flashed. "So you want to know who sold and who bought the poison that killed the shogun's concubine. Not easy, finding someone who doesn't want to be found. Plenty of hiding places in Edo."

Hirata wasn't fooled. The Rat always began negotiations by stressing the difficulty of obtaining a particular piece of information. "Thirty coppers if you find him by tomorrow," Hirata said. "After that, twenty."

On stage, the dwarf's song ended. "Excuse me," said the Rat. He bounded onto the stage and announced, "The Living Bodhisattva!" Amid more cheers, a woman appeared. She wore a sleeveless garment to show off her three arms. She struck poses reminiscent of statues of the many-armed Buddhist deity of mercy, then invited audience members to bet on which of three overturned cups hid a peanut. The Rat rejoined Hirata. "A hundred coppers, no matter when I find your man."

Other acts followed: a dancing fat man; a hermaphrodite singing the male and female parts of a duet. The negotiations continued. At last Hirata said, "Seventy coppers if you find him within two days, fifty thereafter, and nothing if I find Choyei first. That's my final offer."

"All right, but I want an advance of twenty coppers to cover my expenses," the Rat said.

Hirata nodded, handing over the coins. The Rat stuffed them into the pouch at his waist, then went to announce the final act. "And now, the event you've all been waiting for: Fukurokujo, god of wisdom!"

Out walked a boy about ten years old. His features were as tiny as a baby's, his eyes closed, his head elongated into a high dome that resembled that of the legendary god. Gasps of surprise came from the audience.

"For an added charge of five *zeni,* Fukurokujo will tell your fortune!" cried the Rat. Eagerly the audience pressed forward. The Rat said to Hirata, "To seal our bargain, I'll give you a free fortune." He led Hirata onto the stage and placed Hirata's hand on the boy's forehead. "Oh, great Fukurokujo, what do you see in this man's future?"

Eyes still closed, the "god" said in a high, childish voice, "I see a beautiful woman. I see danger and death." As the audience emitted oohs and ahs, he keened, "Beware, beware!"

The memory of Lady Ichiteru came rushing back to Hirata. He saw her lovely, impassive face; felt her hand upon him; heard again the wild music of the puppet theater underscoring his desire. He experienced anew the stirring mixture of lust and humiliation. Even as he recalled her trickery and the penalty for consorting with the shogun's concubine, he yearned for Ichiteru with a frightening passion. He knew he must see her again—if not to repeat the interview and salvage his professional reputation, then to see where their erotic encounter would lead.

The gilt crest above the gate of Lord Miyagi Shigeru of Tosa Province represented a pair of swans facing each other, their wings spread around them in a feathered circle, touching at the tips. Sano arrived at dusk, when homebound samurai trooped through the darkening streets. An elderly manservant led Sano into the mansion, where he left his shoes and swords in the entryway. Edo's daimyo district had been rebuilt since the Great Fire; hence, the Miyagi estate dated from a recent period. Yet the interior of the house seemed ancient, the woodwork of the corridor dark with age and probably salvaged from an older structure. A faint smell of decay hung in the air, as if from centuries of moisture, smoke, and human breath. In the reception room, an eerie melody ended as the servant ushered Sano inside and announced, "Honorable Lord and Lady Miyagi, I present Sano Ichirō, the shogun's *sōsakan-sama.*"

Four people occupied the room: a gray-haired samurai, reclining on silk cushions; a middle-aged woman who knelt beside him; and two pretty young maidens seated together, one holding a samisen, the other a wooden flute. Sano knelt, bowed, and addressed the man.

"Lord Miyagi, I'm investigating the murder of the shogun's concubine, and I must ask you some questions."

For a moment, everyone regarded Sano with silent wariness. Cylindrical white lanterns burned, giving the room an intimate, late-night ambience. Charcoal braziers warmed away the autumn chill. The Miyagi swan insignia was repeated in carved roundels on the ceiling beams and pillars, in the gold crests on the lacquer tables and cabinets and the man's brown silk dressing gown. Sano had the distinct sense of a self-contained world, whose inhabitants perceived other people as outsiders. An aura of perfume, wintergreen hair oil, and a barely perceptible musky odor formed a cocoon around them, as if they exuded their own atmosphere. Then Lord Miyagi spoke.

"May we offer you some refreshment?" He gestured toward a low table, which held teapot, cups, smoking tray, and sake decanter, plus a lavish spread of fruit, cakes, and sushi.

Observing social convention, Sano politely refused, was persuaded, then graciously accepted.

"I wondered whether you would find out about me." Lord Miyagi had a thin, lanky body and long face. His downward-tilted eyes were moist and luminous, his full mouth softly wet. Loose skin wattled his neck and cheeks. His drawling voice reflected his languid posture. "Well, I suppose I might have expected that my connection with Harume would become known eventually; the *metsuke* is most efficient. I am just glad that it happened after her death, when it can hardly matter anymore. Ask me whatever you please."

Preserving the possible advantage of keeping Lady Harume's diary a secret, Sano did not correct the daimyo's impression that Tokugawa spies had uncovered the relationship. "Perhaps we should talk alone," Sano said, eyeing Lady Miyagi. He needed the intimate details of the affair, which Lord Miyagi might want to hide from his wife.

However, Lord Miyagi said, "My wife will stay. She already knows all about Lady Harume and myself."

"We are cousins, joined in a marriage of convenience," Lady Miyagi explained. Indeed she did bear a striking family resemblance to her husband, with the same skin, facial features, and thin figure. Yet her posture was rigid, her eyes a flat, lusterless brown, her unpainted mouth firmly set. She had a deep, mannish voice. While everything about Lord Miyagi bespoke weakness and sensuality, she seemed a stern, dry husk within her brocade kimono. "There is no need for us to keep secrets from each other."

Then she added, "But perhaps we do require a bit more privacy. Snowflake? Wren?" She beckoned to the maidens, who rose and knelt before her. "These are my husband's concubines," Lady Miyagi said, surprising Sano, who had assumed they were the couple's daughters. With a motherly pat to the cheek of each girl, she said, "You may go now. Continue practicing your music."

"Yes, Honorable Mistress," the girls chorused. They bowed and left the room.

"So you knew that your husband was secretly meeting Harume in Asakusa?" Sano asked Lady Miyagi.

"Of course." The woman's mouth curved in a smile, baring her cosmetically blackened teeth. "I am in charge of all my lord's amusements." Beside her, Lord Miyagi nodded complacently. "I select his concubines and courtesans. Last summer I made an acquaintance with Lady Harume and introduced her to my husband. I organized their every rendezvous, sending Harume letters telling her when to be at the inn."

Some wives went to extraordinary lengths to serve their men, Sano thought. While this arrangement caused him a prickle of distaste, he wished Reiko possessed some of Lady Miyagi's willingness to please. "You took a big risk by sporting with the shogun's concubine," he told Lord Miyagi.

"I find much enjoyment in danger." The daimyo stretched luxuriously. His tongue came out, moistening his lips with saliva.

A true devotee of fleshly delights, he seemed acutely conscious of every physical sensation. He wore his robe as though he felt the soft caress of silk against his skin. Picking up a tobacco pipe from the metal tray, he drew on it with slow deliberation, sighing while he expelled the smoke. In his frank pleasure, he appeared almost childlike. Yet Sano saw a sinister shadow behind the veiled eyes. He recalled what he knew of the Miyagi.

They were a minor clan, more renowned for sexual debauchery than political leadership. Rumors of adultery, incest, and perversion haunted both male and female members, though their wealth purchased freedom from legal consequences. Apparently the present daimyo followed the family tradition—which had sometimes included violence.

Addressing both husband and wife, Sano said, "Did you know that Lady Harume planned to tattoo herself?"

Lord Miyagi nodded and smoked. His wife answered, "Yes, we did. It was my husband's wish that Harume prove her devotion by cutting a symbol of love for him upon her body. I wrote the letter asking her to do so."

Sano wondered whether Lady Miyagi's stiff bearing reflected a sexual coldness that precluded normal marital relations between her and her husband. Certainly she possessed none of the physical attractions valued by a man such as him. But perhaps she pursued her own carnal thrills by procuring her husband's; she, too, was a member of the infamous clan. From the cloth pouch at his waist, Sano removed the black lacquer bottle whose ink had poisoned Harume. "Did she get this from you, then?"

"Yes, that is the bottle we sent with the letter," Lady Miyagi said calmly. "I bought it. My husband wrote Harume's name on top."

So they both had handled the bottle. "And when was this?" Sano asked.

Lady Miyagi considered. "Four days ago, I believe."

That would have been before Lieutenant Kushida's suspension from duty in the Large Interior, but after Lady Harume's complaint. But Kushida claimed to have had no prior knowledge of the tattoo, and Sano didn't yet know about Lady Ichiteru. Presumably Hirata would obtain the information. For now, the Miyagi seemed the ones with the best opportunity to poison the ink.

"Were you on good terms with Lady Harume?" Sano asked Lord Miyagi.

The daimyo shrugged languorously. "We had no quarrels, if that's what you mean. I loved her as much as I'm capable of loving anyone. I was getting what I wanted from the affair, and I presumed she was, too."

"What was it that she wanted?" The diary explained how Lord Miyagi achieved gratification, but Sano was curious to know why the beautiful concubine had risked her life for sordid, joyless encounters with an unattractive man.

For the first time, Lord Miyagi looked uncomfortable; his Adam's apple bobbed in the loose flesh of his throat, and he looked to his wife. Lady Miyagi said, "Harume had a craving for adventure, *sōsakan-sama*. The forbidden liaison with my husband satisfied it."

"And you?" Sano asked. "How did you feel about Lady Harume and the affair?"

The woman smiled again—a curiously unpleasant expression that emphasized her homeliness. "I was grateful to Harume, as I am to all my husband's women. I consider them my partners in serving his pleasure."

Sano suppressed a shudder of revulsion. Lady Miyagi reminded him of a Yoshiwara brothel owner, catering to clients' sexual whims with professional skill. She didn't even seem to care how vulgar or perverted she might appear. From down the corridor drifted faint strains of music, and the concubines' voices, singing. Sano suddenly became aware of how quiet the house was. He heard none of the sounds usually associated with a provincial lord's estate—no troops patrolling; no officials conducting business; no servants at work. The solidly built mansion shut out street noises, reinforcing Sano's impression of a closed world. What an odd household this was!

"So you see," the daimyo said with a tired sigh, "neither my wife nor I had reason to kill Lady Harume, and we didn't. I shall sadly miss the pleasure she provided me. And my dear wife has never been jealous about my liaisons with Harume or anyone else." Raising himself from his cushions, he made a weak gesture toward the refreshment tray.

Quickly Lady Miyagi said, "Let me help you, Cousin," and poured tea for him. She put the cup in his left hand, a persimmon in his right. For a moment, their arms joined in a circle, and Sano was struck by their resemblance to the Miyagi double-swan crest. A mated pair, mirror images of each other, wings touching, locked in a strange but mutually agreeable union . . .

The musky odor grew stronger, as though produced by the couple's contact. Sano perceived between them a deep, emotional connection that did not exclude passion. Weighing the statements they'd given, he found that he believed Lady Miyagi's story of accepting and even abetting her husband's infidelity, but Lord Miyagi's claim of love for

Harume rang less true. Had she somehow threatened the marriage? Had one or both spouses wished her dead?

"Who else had access to the ink bottle before it reached Lady Harume?" Sano said.

"The messenger who carried it to Edo Castle," said Lady Miyagi, "as well as everyone in the house. The retainers; the servants; Snowflake and Wren. When I brought the bottle home, my husband wasn't here, so I left it on his desk while I attended to other business. Some hours passed before we sent it off. Anyone could have tampered with the ink without our knowledge."

Was she simply relating facts, or shielding herself and Lord Miyagi by directing suspicion toward other residents of the estate? Perhaps one of them had borne a grudge against Harume. "My detectives shall come and question everyone in your household," Sano said.

Nodding indifferently, Lord Miyagi ate his fruit. The juice ran down his chin; he licked his fingers. "As you wish," Lady Miyagi said.

And now for the delicate, critical part of the interrogation, Sano thought. "Have you any children?" he asked the couple.

Neither husband nor wife altered expression, yet Sano's trained senses detected a sudden pressure in the air, as though it had expanded to push against the walls. Lady Miyagi sat motionless, her gaze fixed straight ahead, a tightness about her jaw muscles. Lord Miyagi said, "No. We do not." Regret permeated his words. "Our lack of sons has forced me to name a nephew as my heir."

From the strained atmosphere between the Miyagi couple, Sano guessed that he'd touched a vulnerable spot in their marriage. He suspected that each harbored different feelings about their childlessness. And the answer to his question disappointed Sano. Harume's pillow book portrayed Lord Miyagi as a voyeur who preferred self-stimulation to bedding a woman. Did this tendency, combined with his lack of offspring, mean that he was impotent? Was the shogun—weak, sickly, and inclined toward manly love—the father of Harume's child after all?

Sano dreaded both telling Tokugawa Tsunayoshi that his

unborn heir had died with the concubine, and the added pressure to solve the murder case. If he failed, the shogun's unreliable affection wouldn't save him from disgraceful death. And so far, this interview had not incriminated Lord or Lady Miyagi. Yet Sano would not give up hope.

"Lord Miyagi, I understand that Harume would undress and touch herself, while you watched through the window," Sano said bluntly. He couldn't spare the daimyo's feelings at the expense of his own salvation.

"My, but the *metsuke* are efficient," Lord Miyagi drawled. "Yes, that is correct. But I fail to see how my private habits are any of your business." Lady Miyagi neither moved nor spoke, and the couple didn't look at each other, but hostility radiated from them both: Though open about the daimyo's affairs, they resented Sano's quest for details.

"Did you ever penetrate Lady Harume?" Sano asked.

The daimyo gave a nervous chuckle, looking at his wife. When she offered no help, he said feebly, "Really, *sōsakan-sama,* this intrusion verges on disrespect toward me, and Lady Harume as well. What bearing can our relations have upon her death?"

"In a murder investigation, anything about the victim's life can prove significant," Sano said. He couldn't mention Harume's pregnancy before first informing the shogun, who would be angry to hear such important news via gossip instead of directly from Sano. "Answer the question, please."

Lord Miyagi sighed, then shook his head, eyes downcast. "All right. No—I did not penetrate Harume."

"Of course he didn't!" Lady Miyagi's outburst startled Sano, as well as Lord Miyagi, who jerked upright. Glaring at Sano, she demanded, "Do you think my husband would be so foolish as to violate the shogun's concubine? And risk death? He never touched her; not even once. He wouldn't!"

Wouldn't—or couldn't? Here was the passion Sano had sensed in Lady Miyagi, though he didn't understand her vehemence. "You say that you organized your husband's affair with Harume. Aside from the danger, why does the thought of his touching her bother you?"

"It doesn't." With an obvious effort, Lady Miyagi regained her composure, though an unattractive flush stained her cheeks. "I believe I've already explained my attitude toward my lord's women," she said coldly.

In the ensuing silence, the daimyo shrank into his cushions as if he wished to disappear behind them. His fingers played with a fold of his robe, savoring the feel of silk. Lady Miyagi sat rigidly still, biting her lips. From down the corridor came the concubines' tinkly laughter. Sano could tell that husband and wife were lying about something: their relationship with Harume, or their feelings toward her? Did they already know about the pregnancy because the daimyo was responsible for it? And why hide the truth? To avoid scandal and punishment for the forbidden liaison—or murder charges?

"It's getting late, *sōsakan-sama*," Lady Miyagi said at last. Her husband nodded, relieved that she'd taken charge of the situation. "If you have any further questions, perhaps you would be so good as to return some other time."

Sano bowed. "I may do that," he said, rising. On impulse, he said to Lord Miyagi, "What inn did you and Lady Harume use for your meetings?"

Lord Miyagi hesitated, then answered, "The Tsubame, in Asakusa."

As the manservant escorted Sano from the room, he looked back to see the Miyagi watching him with grave inscrutability. Once outside the gate, he could almost feel their strange, private world close against him, like a membrane sealing shut. A creeping, unclean sensation lingered, as though contact with that world had polluted his spirit. Yet Sano must probe its secrets, by indirect means if necessary. Perhaps when Hirata traced the poison dealer, the search would lead back to the Miyagi. And there was another side to the story of Lord Miyagi and Lady Harume's affair: hers. An investigation into her life might provide answers that would avert the threat of failure and death that shadowed Sano. But now his thoughts turned homeward.

Mounting his horse, Sano headed up the boulevard. Lanterns burned at the guarded portals of daimyo estates. The moon rose in the evening sky over Edo Castle, perched on its hill, where Reiko waited. The thought of her beauty and youthful innocence came to Sano like a purifying force that washed away the contamination of his encounter with the Miyagi. Perhaps tonight he and Reiko could settle yesterday's quarrel and begin their marriage anew.

The baying of dogs echoed across Edo, as if a thousand beasts heralded the hour that bore their name. Night submerged the city in wintry darkness, extinguishing lights, vacating streets. Moonlight turned the Sumida River into a ribbon of liquid silver. At the end of a pier far upstream from the city rose a pavilion. Lanterns suspended from the upturned eaves of its tile roof illuminated banners bearing the Tokugawa crest and walls decorated with carved gilt-and-lacquer dragons. The water reflected its glittering, inverted image. Soldiers stood watch on the pier and in small craft anchored off the forested shoreline, guarding the safety and privacy of the pavilion's lone occupant.

Inside, Chamberlain Yanagisawa sat on the tatami-covered floor, studying official documents in the flickering light of oil lamps. The remains of his evening meal littered a tray by his side; from a charcoal brazier, smoke drifted out the slatted windows. This was Yanagisawa's favorite site for secret meetings, away from Edo Castle and any eavesdroppers. Tonight he'd heard reports from *metsuke* spies who'd just returned from assignments in the provinces. Now he awaited his final rendezvous, which concerned the most important matter of all: the status of his plot against *Sōsakan* Sano.

Voices and footsteps sounded on the pier. Yanagisawa tossed his papers on a cushioned bench and stood. Peering out the window, he saw a guard escorting a small figure along the pier toward the pavilion. Yanagisawa smiled when he recognized Shichisaburō, dressed in multicolored brocade theatrical robes. Anticipation quickened his heartbeat. He threw open the door, admitting a rush of cold air.

Up the pier came Shichisaburō, moving with ritual grace

as if entering a No stage. Seeing his master, his eyes lit in convincing delight. He bowed, chanting:

"Now I will dance the moon's dance,
My sleeves are trailing clouds,
Dancing, I will sing my joy,
Again and again while the night endures."

This was a quote from the play *Kantan,* written by the great Zeami Motokiyo, about a Chinese peasant who has a vivid dream of ascending the throne of the emperor. Yanagisawa and Shichisaburō often enjoyed performing scenes from a favorite drama, and Yanagisawa responded with the next lines:

"And yet while the night endures,
The sun rises bright,
While we think it is still night,
Day has already come."

Desire spread warmth through Yanagisawa. The boy was a masterful actor—and so arrestingly beautiful. But for now, business took precedence over pleasure. Drawing Shichisaburō into the pavilion and closing the door, Yanagisawa asked, "Have you carried out the orders I gave you last night?"

"Oh, yes, my lord."

In the lamplight, the young actor's face radiated happiness. His presence infused the room with the fresh, sweet fragrance of youth. Intoxicated, Chamberlain Yanagisawa inhaled hungrily. "Did you have any trouble getting inside?"

"None at all, my lord," Shichisaburō said. "I followed your instructions. No one stopped me. It was perfect."

"Were you able to find what we needed?" Despite the fact that they were alone, Yanagisawa followed his usual practice of speaking in a circumspect manner.

"Oh, yes. It was right where you said it would be."

"Did anyone see you?"

The young actor shook his head. "No, my lord, I was

careful." His mouth quirked in a mischievous smile. "And even if someone had seen me, they wouldn't have guessed who I was, or what I was doing."

"No. They wouldn't." Remembering their ploy, Yanagisawa smiled, too. "Where did you put it?" The actor stood on tiptoe to whisper in his ear, and he chuckled. "Superb. You've done very well."

Shichisaburō clapped his hands with glee. "Honorable Chamberlain, you're so brilliant! The *sōsakan-sama* is sure to fall into the trap." Then doubt furrowed his childish brow. "But what if he happens to miss it somehow?"

"He won't," Yanagisawa said confidently. "I know how Sano thinks and acts. He'll do just as I've predicted. But if for some reason he doesn't, I'll help him." Yanagisawa chuckled. "How appropriate that my other rival should provide the tool for the destruction of them both. All we have to do is wait and be patient. Right now, I can think of a pleasant way to pass the time. Come here."

Yanagisawa grasped Shichisaburō's hand, pulling him close. But the boy playfully resisted. "Wait, my lord. I have a surprise for you. If you will please permit me?"

With a tantalizing smile, he unknotted his sash and let it drop to the floor. Ceremoniously he shrugged off his outer kimono, one sleeve at a time. He stepped out of his flowing trousers. Desire welled in Chamberlain Yanagisawa's throat and groin. No one else undressed with such graceful flair. He couldn't wait to see what new erotic delight the actor had in store for him.

Shichisaburō's eyes glowed, reflecting his master's excitement. Prolonging their pleasure, he paused for a dramatic moment in his white under-robe. Then he peeled the robe away from his shoulders and let it fall. Triumphantly he flung out his arms, displaying himself for Yanagisawa's inspection. Yanagisawa gasped; his heart lurched.

Raw gashes marked Shichisaburō's chest. Recent and unhealed, the cuts were red, caked with darkening blood, lurid against the fair, smooth skin. The cruelest one bisected his left nipple. Another ran down through his navel, into his loincloth. He looked like the victim of a savage attack.

"I did it for you, my lord!" Shichisaburō exclaimed. "To

show that I'm willing to endure pain and suffering for your sake."

Ritual self-mutilation, performed with swords or daggers, was an age-old practice by which samurai lovers demonstrated their loyalty and devotion to each other. Therefore, Shichisaburō's action didn't really surprise Yanagisawa, now that the initial shock had passed. Amused by the boy's eagerness to please, he laughed.

"You've done well," he said.

Shichisaburō knelt. Taking Chamberlain Yanagisawa's hand, he pressed it against the wound on his breast. His skin felt feverish. "With my blood, I pledge my eternal love for you, my lord," he whispered.

His eyes blazed with passion—genuine, unfeigned passion. The laughter died in Yanagisawa's throat. Stunned, he said, "You really mean it, don't you?" Deep within him, something trembled, like the ground during an earthquake. "Everything you say about your feelings for me, it's all true. You're not just acting. You mean every word!"

The boy nodded. "At first I was acting," he admitted. "Then I grew to love you." His smile was full of yearning affection. "You're so beautiful and strong, so intelligent and powerful. You're everything I want, everything I could wish to be. I would do anything for you!" He raised Yanagisawa's hand to his face, pressing his mouth to its palm.

A torrent of emotion flooded Yanagisawa. First came disbelief that anyone would make such a gesture of self-sacrifice for him. Into his mind flashed a vivid memory. On the day he'd achieved the post of chamberlain, he had hosted a lavish gala at Edo Castle, with music, dancers, Kabuki skits, the best food and sake. All the male guests were subordinates who wanted favors from him. All the women were courtesans bought with his new wealth. No family—he remained estranged from them; no friends—he had none. The guests with whom he'd celebrated cared nothing about him, except for the power he wielded. In the midst of insincere smiles and congratulations, Yanagisawa had experienced a feeling of complete emptiness.

Now that same emptiness opened into a vast, yawning cavern inside him. From it howled the voice of his soul, demanding the love he craved but had never known. Tears rushed to Yanagisawa's eyes—tears he thought had been spent at his brother's funeral, but had instead accumulated into a huge reservoir of loneliness. Shichisaburō's tribute moved him to the core. He wanted to embrace the boy and sob out his gratitude, to feel tender arms around him while the armor shielding his heart crumbled.

Then, across the distance of time, he heard his father's voice: ". . . lazy, unfit to be my son . . . pathetic, dishonorable . . ." Yanagisawa recalled the blows with the wooden pole. Again he experienced the feeling of sheer worthlessness, the feeling that he didn't deserve love. Hating the awful sensation, wanting to make it go away, he forced himself to remember who he was: the shogun's second-in-command. And who Shichisaburō was: just a little peasant, foolish enough to injure his own body for another person. How could he have the temerity to love the ruler of Japan?

Yanagisawa's yearning and gratitude turned to rage. Jerking his hand away from Shichisaburō, he demanded, "How dare you treat me in this impertinent manner?" He slapped Shichisaburō's face. The young actor gasped; hurt filled his eyes. "I never ordered you to love me." Anyone capable of loving him was beneath contempt. "How dare you?"

The lessons of a lifetime filled him with a fear that increased his anger. Love made a person vulnerable, dependent; love could only lead to misery. Hadn't his parents spurned his childhood efforts to please them and win affection? The rejection had hurt even worse than the blows. In Shichisaburō's love, Yanagisawa glimpsed the terrible promise of future rejection, more pain—unless he did something to avert the threat.

"I'm your lord, not your paramour," Yanagisawa shouted, his voice ragged as he fought to control his warring emotions. "Show some respect! Bow down!"

With a swipe of his arm, he knocked the actor off his knees. Shichisaburō sprawled on the floor. Horrified by his own cruelty, Chamberlain Yanagisawa stifled the urge to apologize, to give in to his craving for love. But the need for self-preservation outweighed all other needs.

"I'm sorry, my lord." Shichisaburō was sobbing. "I didn't mean to offend you. I thought you'd be pleased by what I did. A thousand apologies!"

He raised himself on his elbows. Chamberlain Yanagisawa struck his jaw, and he fell again. By bringing Yanagisawa's loneliness to the surface, by making him vulnerable, the actor had demeaned him, reversed their positions. Yanagisawa couldn't tolerate the shift in the balance of power. It presaged suffering and ruin that he didn't want to imagine.

Roughly he tore away the white cotton band that bound Shichisaburō's loins and cleaved his buttocks. Then he stripped off his own robes. Shoving the young actor face-down on the tatami, he straddled Shichisaburō.

"I'll show you who is master and who is the slave!" Yanagisawa shouted.

Trembling with fear, Shichisaburō wept. They'd often indulged in rough sexual play—but this was not play, and he knew it. "If it please my lord, I'll never speak of my love again," he cried. "Let's forget what happened and go back to the way we were before!"

They could never go back; everything had changed between them. Chamberlain Yanagisawa pummeled Shichisaburō's back with his fists. Shichisaburō moaned, but didn't struggle. The lack of resistance further incensed Yanagisawa. He grabbed the boy's hair and slammed his face repeatedly against the floor, while fumbling to liberate his erection from his loincloth.

"You can do—whatever you wish—to me," Shichisaburō whimpered between anguished gasps. Sweat glistened on his skin; the reek of his terror filled the room, but he spoke up bravely. "I accept—the pain. Even if you—don't want my love—I'm yours forever. I'll—do anything for you!"

Before the violent fusion of pleasure and anger and need could overwhelm him, Chamberlain Yanagisawa realized what he had to do. He must end his liaison with Shichisaburō—or face the ruin of his power, of his entire self. Yet for now, the young actor was too useful to drop. He'd successfully carried out orders. The stage was set for the destruction of Sano, and Chamberlain Yanagisawa's other rival. But if the plot somehow failed, Yanagisawa might require Shichisaburō's services again before the end of the murder investigation.

16

Sano's last task of the day was hearing reports from his detective corps. In his office, the men related the progress of their hunt for the poison dealer and investigation of the Large Interior. Doctors and pharmacists had been canvassed, without results so far; interviews with the residents of the women's quarters and a search of the rooms had failed to uncover useful information or evidence either. Sano instructed the men to resume work the next day. He assigned a team to track the passage of the ink bottle and letter from the Miyagi estate to Lady Harume. Then the detectives filed out of the room, leaving Sano and Hirata to review their inquiries.

"Police headquarters gave me a possible lead on the drug peddler," Hirata said, "an old man selling aphrodisiacs around town. And I'm using one of my informants—the Rat."

Sano nodded his approval. The police's drug dealer might have supplied the Indian arrow toxin that had killed Harume, and he was familiar with the Rat's abilities. "Now, what about Lady Ichiteru?"

Hirata's gaze slid away. "I spoke with her. But . . . I don't have anything definite to report yet."

He seemed uncharacteristically distracted, and his eyes shone with a peculiar intensity. Sano was troubled by Hirata's evasiveness, as well as his failure to obtain information on an important suspect. Nonetheless, he hated to reprimand Hirata.

"I suppose tomorrow is soon enough to finish investigating Lady Ichiteru," he said.

His voice must have conveyed doubt, because Hirata said defensively, "You know it's not always possible to get the whole story from someone on the first try." Squirming, he clasped and unclasped his hands. "Would you rather interrogate Lady Ichiteru yourself? Don't you trust me? After Nagasaki?"

Sano recalled how his inclination to meet all challenges alone there had almost destroyed him, and how Hirata's competence and loyalty had saved his life. "Of course I trust you," Sano said. Changing the subject, he described the examination of Lady Harume's corpse and his interviews with Lieutenant Kushida and the Miyagi. "We'll keep the pregnancy a secret until I inform the shogun. Meanwhile, try to discreetly find out who knew or guessed that Harume was with child."

"Do you think she knew herself?" Hirata asked.

Sano pondered. "It seems as though she must have at least suspected. My theory is that she didn't report the pregnancy because she wasn't sure who the father was, or whether the shogun would claim the child as his." Sano noticed Hirata staring off into space instead of listening. "Hirata?"

Starting nervously, Hirata reddened. "Yes, *sōsakan-sama*! Is there something else?"

If Hirata's behavior didn't return to normal soon, Sano thought, they must have a serious talk. But right now, Sano was eager to see Reiko. "No. There's nothing else. I'll see you tomorrow."

"What do you mean, she's not here?" Sano asked the manservant who'd greeted him in the mansion's private living quarters with the news that Reiko had left the house that morning and not yet returned. "Where did she go?"

"She wouldn't say, master. Her escorts sent word that they were taking her to various places in Nihonbashi and Ginza. But it's not clear what she was doing there."

An unpleasant suspicion formed in Sano's mind. "When will she be back?"

"No one knows. I'm sorry, master."

Annoyed by the postponement of a romantic evening, Sano realized that he was hungry—he hadn't eaten since noon, a bowl of noodles at his mother's house after the interview with Lieutenant Kushida. And he needed to wash away the taint of the illegal dissection. "Have my bath prepared and my evening meal brought," he told the servant.

Once bathed, dressed in clean robes, and settled in the warm, lamp-lit sitting room, Sano tried to eat his dinner of rice, steamed fish, vegetables, and tea. But his irritation with Reiko soon turned to concern. Had something bad happened to her?

Had she left him?

His appetite lost, Sano paced the sitting room. It occurred to him that this was what marriage must be like for women: waiting at home for their spouses to return, wondering and fretting. Suddenly he understood Reiko's rebellion against her lot in life. But anger precluded sympathy. He didn't like this one bit. How dare she treat him so? For the next hour, his rage alternated with growing worry. He imagined Reiko caught in a burning building, or assaulted by outlaws. In his mind he rehearsed the scolding he would give her when she got home.

Then he heard hoofbeats outside. His heart jumped with simultaneous relief and fury. At last! Sano rushed to the front door. In walked Reiko, followed by her entourage. The cold wind had put a vivid sparkle in her eyes and loosened strands of long hair from her coiffure. She looked utterly lovely—and satisfied with herself.

"Where have you been?" Sano demanded. "You shouldn't have gone without my permission, and without leaving word of your whereabouts. Explain what you were doing out so late!"

The servants, foreseeing a marital dispute, faded away. Reiko squared her shoulders, delicate chin jutting forward. "I was investigating Lady Harume's murder."

"After I ordered you not to?"

"Yes!"

Despite his anger, Sano admired Reiko's nerve. A weaker woman might have lied to avoid censure instead of standing up to him. His attraction to her charged the air of the dim corridor with invisible sparks. And he could tell that she felt it, too. Self-consciousness broke her gaze; her hand went up to straighten her disheveled hair; her tongue touched the chipped tooth. He felt himself becoming aroused against his will. He forced a sarcastic laugh.

"Investigating how? What could you possibly do?"

Hands clasped, jaws set in rigid self-control, Reiko said, "Don't be so quick to mock me, Honorable Husband." Icy scorn frosted her voice. "I went to Nihonbashi to see my cousin Eri. She's a palace official in the Large Interior. She told me that Lieutenant Kushida was caught in Lady Harume's room two days before the murder. Lady Ichiteru threatened to kill Harume during a fight they had at Kannei Temple."

She laughed at Sano's surprised look. "You didn't know, did you? Without me, you never would have, because both incidents were hushed up. And Eri thinks someone threw a dagger at Harume and tried to poison her last summer." Reiko described the events, then said, "How long might it have taken you to find out? You need my help. Admit it!"

This evidence placed Lieutenant Kushida in Lady Harume's room on the day Lord and Lady Miyagi had sent the ink bottle. Kushida might have read the letter and seen the perfect opportunity to administer the poison with which he'd already planned to kill her. Reiko had also confirmed Lady Ichiteru's hatred for Harume. Sano was impressed by Reiko's ability, then furious at her lack of remorse.

"A few stray facts don't solve a case," he blustered, although he knew they sometimes did. "And how can I be sure your cousin is a reliable witness, or that her theories are correct? You defied me and risked danger for nothing."

"Danger?" Reiko frowned in confusion. "What harm could come from just talking and listening?"

Further incensed by his wife's challenge, Sano spared no mercy for her feminine sensibilities. "When I was a police commander, I had a secretary, a man even younger than you." Sano's voice hoarsened at the memory of Tsunehiko's childlike innocence. "He died at a highway inn, his throat cut, in a pool of his own blood. He did nothing to deserve death. His only mistake was accompanying me on a murder investigation."

Reiko's eyes widened in shock. "But . . . you're still all right." Her bold voice became a tentative murmur.

"Only by the grace of the gods," Sano retorted. "I've been attacked—cut, shot at, ambushed, beaten—more times than I care to think about. So believe me when I say that detective work is dangerous. It could get you killed!"

Reiko stared. "All those things happened while you were investigating crimes and catching murderers?" she said slowly. The scorn had left her voice. "You risked death to do what was right, even when you knew people would kill to stop you?"

The new admiration in her eyes left Sano more shaken than her defiance had. Speechless, he nodded.

"I didn't know." Reiko took a hesitant step toward him. "I'm sorry."

Sano stood paralyzed, unable even to breathe. He sensed in this young woman a dedication to truth and justice that matched his own, a willingness to sacrifice herself for abstract principles, for honor. This similarity of spirit was an undeniable basis for love. The knowledge thrilled, and horrified, Sano.

But Reiko's face shone with joyful recognition of the same fact. Eagerly she reached out a slim hand to him. "You understand how I feel," she said, responding to their unspoken exchange. Passion heightened her beauty. "Let's work and serve honor together. Together we can solve the mystery of Lady Harume's murder!"

What would it be like, Sano wondered, to have that passion directed at me in the bedchamber? The thought dizzied him. The prospect of having a partner to share his mission was almost irresistible. He longed to take the hand she offered.

But he could not draw his wife into the perilous web of his profession. And he knew his own faults, which he didn't want to encourage in her. How could he live with someone as stubborn, reckless, and single-minded as himself? He still cherished the dream of a submissive wife, a peaceful home.

Sano said, "You've heard my reasons for wanting you to stay out of business that doesn't concern you. I've made my decision, and it's final."

Reiko's hand dropped. Hurt extinguished her radiance

like a shroud thrown over a lamp, but her resolve didn't waver. "Why should my life not be mine to risk if I choose, or my honor mean less than yours because I'm a woman?" she demanded. "I, too, have samurai blood. In centuries past, I would have ridden into battle at your side. Why not now?"

"Because that's just the way things are. Your duty is to me, and I expect you to serve it here at home." Sano knew he sounded pompous, but he believed every word. "For you to do otherwise would be pure selfish, willful disregard of your family responsibilities."

The irony of the situation struck him. That he, who had often jeopardized family duty for the sake of personal causes, should criticize Reiko for doing the same! Faltering, he grasped for the thread of the argument. "Now tell me why you went to Ginza. For more women's gossip?"

"If you're going to belittle my work, you don't deserve to know." Reiko's melodic voice coated a core of steel; her expression was no less cold or hard. "And if you don't want my help with the investigation, then it can hardly matter. Now please excuse me."

As she swept past him, Sano felt an immediate sense of loss. And he couldn't let her have the last word. "Reiko. Wait." He grabbed her arm.

Glaring, she pulled away. Her sleeve tore with a loud, ripping sound. Then she was gone, leaving Sano holding a long piece of silk in his hand.

Sano stared after her for a moment. Then he hurled the fragment of sleeve to the floor. His marriage was going from bad to worse. Stalking to his own chamber, he dressed in outdoor wear, hung his swords at his waist, and summoned a servant. "Have my horse saddled," he said.

He couldn't solve his problems alone. Therefore, he would consult the one person who might be able to help him with Reiko—and who might also have vital information relating to the murder investigation.

"Good evening, Sano-*san*. Please come in." Magistrate Ueda, seated in his office, did not seem surprised by Sano's unannounced arrival. Lamps burned on his desk amid writing supplies, official documents, and scattered papers: evidently he was catching up on work. To the servant who had escorted Sano into the mansion, he said, "Bring tea for my honorable son-in-law." Then he gestured for Sano to kneel opposite him.

As Sano complied, nervousness and shame tightened his stomach. He was unaccustomed to asking for help with personal problems. His trouble with Reiko signified a most embarrassing incompetence; a high-ranking samurai should be able to handle a mere woman. Seeking advice reflected a weakness that he didn't want to reveal to his father-in-law, whom he respected but hardly knew at all. Now Sano sought the words to obtain assistance while saving face.

Magistrate Ueda spared him the effort. "It's my daughter, isn't it?" At Sano's nod, an expression of grim sympathy came over his features. "I thought so. What's she done now?"

Encouraged by the magistrate's frankness, Sano poured out the entire story. "You've known Reiko all her life. Please tell me what to do."

The servant brought tea. Magistrate Ueda frowned and said in the authoritative tone he used in the Court of Justice, "My daughter is too intelligent and strong-willed for everyone's good. You must control her with a firm hand and show her who's in charge, hmm?"

Then he sighed and lapsed back into his ordinary voice. "Who am I to talk? I, who have always given in to Reiko's wishes. Sano-*san,* I fear you've come to the wrong person for advice."

They gazed at each other in rueful understanding: magistrate of Edo and most honorable investigator, confounded by the woman who united them. Suddenly they were friends.

"By putting our heads together, we should be able to find an answer to the problem," Magistrate Ueda said, sipping tea. "I've always compromised with Reiko because I didn't want to break her spirit, which I admire in spite of myself." A humorous twinkle lit his eyes when he saw Sano's wry grin. "Ah, I see that you do, too. Perhaps it's your turn to bend. Why not assign her an easy, safe part of your work, like keeping records?"

"That won't satisfy her," Sano said with conviction. "She wants to be a detective." Grudgingly, he admitted, "And she's not bad at it."

As he related Reiko's discoveries, Magistrate Ueda beamed with paternal pride. "Then there must be something else she can do. More covert inquiries, such as she carried out today, might prove very helpful, hmm?"

Every instinct in Sano clamored in rebellion against this alternative. "What if the killer thinks she's a threat and attacks her when I'm not around to protect her?" Despite his anger at his wife, the thought of losing Reiko shot terror through him. He was falling in love with her, he realized unhappily, with little chance of reciprocation. Yet he refused to relinquish control over his household.

"Your stubborn nature is a barrier in the path to a happy marriage," Magistrate Ueda said. "Reiko will have to submit if you force her obedience, but she would never love or respect you. Therefore I fear that a compromise on your part is necessary."

Sano sighed. "All right. I'll try to think of something for Reiko to do."

Now he recalled the other reason he'd come to see his father-in-law. "I was hoping you might be able to give me some background information on the murder suspects." Any crimes in their pasts or complaints against them would be recorded in the official court documents. Despite the problems in Sano's marriage, it had brought him one clear benefit: a connection with Magistrate Ueda. "Have Lieutenant Kushida, Lady Ichiteru, or Lord and Lady Miyagi been in trouble before?"

"I checked the records on Kushida and Ichiteru this morning, when I heard they were suspects," Magistrate Ueda replied. "There was nothing on them. The Miyagi, however, are a different matter. I recall an incident that occurred four years ago. The daughter of a guard disappeared from the estate next door to the Miyagi's. The girl's parents claimed that Lord Miyagi was responsible. He enticed her into his house and tried to seduce her, they said, then killed her when she resisted."

A tingle of excitement began in Sano's chest. Perhaps the daimyo did follow the ways of his cruel ancestors. Perhaps he'd poisoned the girl—and later Lady Harume, for refusing to perform acts he requested. "What happened?"

"The girl's body was recovered from a canal a few days later. The police couldn't tell how she died. No charge was brought against Lord Miyagi. The case remains unsolved." Magistrate Ueda's shrug conveyed a deep cynicism. "That is the way of the law."

"Yes," Sano said. "The word of a mere soldier wouldn't stand a chance against Lord Miyagi's influence."

"Influence is a formidable threat, Sano-*san*." The magistrate bent a penetrating gaze upon him. "Shortly after the daughter's death, that guard was run out of town by Lord Miyagi's retainers. He couldn't get another post. He and his wife died paupers. The *bakufu* neither protected them nor punished Lord Miyagi."

Sano made a decision. "There's something I want to tell you about the murder—something very sensitive. Will you promise to keep it in the strictest confidence?" At Magistrate Ueda's assent, Sano told him about the pregnancy.

Frowning in contemplation, Magistrate Ueda hesitated, then said, "Because of Lady Harume's pregnancy, the murder case now potentially involves the succession of power. Your investigation could implicate powerful citizens who wish to weaken Tokugawa rule by breaking the hereditary line. The outside lords, for example. Or the man responsible for many of your past troubles, hmm?"

Chamberlain Yanagisawa. Recalling his odd behavior at their last meeting, Sano wondered uneasily whether it signified the chamberlain's involvement in the murder. At first this case had seemed straightforward. Now the prospect of unraveling a high-reaching conspiracy daunted Sano.

"I respect your ability and your principles," Magistrate Ueda said. "But beware of making serious accusations against influential suspects. If you anger the wrong people, even your rank may not protect you." Another weighty pause, then: "I'm concerned for my daughter's sake as well as yours. You will promise not to endanger her recklessly, hmm?"

In warfare and politics, enemies often attacked one another's kin. "I promise," Sano said, feeling the contrary pull of honor and professional integrity, prudence and family considerations. Bowing, he said, "Thank you for your advice, Honorable Father-in-law. My apologies for disturbing you so late. I'd better go home and let you get back to work."

"Good night, Sano-*san*." Magistrate Ueda bowed. "I shall do everything in my power to help you resolve the murder case with minimum damage to our families." Then he smiled wryly. "And good luck with Reiko. If you can tame her, you're a better man than I."

It was a scant two hours until midnight by the time Sano returned to Edo Castle. From across the hills blew a frost-edged autumn wind. Acrid charcoal smoke rose from thousands of braziers. The sky's starry black canopy arched above the sleeping city. Sano, huddled in his heavy cloak as he rode through the castle's maze of walled passages, felt more than ready for sleep himself. This had been a long, tiring day, with the promise of another one tomorrow. Craving a warm bed, Sano entered his street in Edo Castle's Official Quarter.

He experienced a premonition of danger the moment before his vision registered its cause. The area was completely dark, though there should have been lights above the gates of every estate. The district seemed unnaturally quiet and deserted. Where were the sentries and patrol guards?

Hand on his sword hilt, Sano rode slowly toward his own house, keeping close to the rows of barracks that surrounded the mansions of his neighbors. By the light of the moon he saw two lanterns hanging from the roof of a gate, their flames extinguished. And below, a dark heap lying in the street. Sano dismounted, the sense of danger flowing over him like a malignant wind current. Crouching, he examined the heap. His heart thumped when he discerned the still bodies of two armored sentries, breathing but unconscious. Leaving his horse behind, Sano ran to the next gate, where he discovered more unconscious guards. Bloody wounds, made by a blunt weapon, marked their heads.

Alarm surged in Sano as he recalled past attempts on his life. Was this an ambush, set by Chamberlain Yanagisawa, who had tried to assassinate him many times before? Or by someone else who knew he'd left the district alone tonight? The great fortress of Edo Castle was, he knew from personal experience, no safe haven for a man with powerful enemies. Had an assassin disabled everyone who might have interfered with an attack? The guards, not expecting invasion during peacetime, had been easy targets. Was someone lying in wait for Sano now?

At his home, where Reiko, Hirata, the detective corps, and the servants slept, unaware of the danger?

Breathless with anxiety, Sano ran to his own estate. The wounded sentries lay unconscious across the threshold.

"Tokubei! Gorō!" Kneeling, Sano shook them. "Are you all right? What happened?"

The men stirred, groaning. ". . . got past us," Gorō muttered. "Sorry . . ." Dragging himself to his feet, he swayed dizzily, clutching his head.

"Who was it?" Sano asked.

"Didn't see. Happened too fast."

The ironclad gate was open. Sword drawn, Sano leaned into the courtyard. Nothing moved in the darkness. Beckoning for Gorō to follow, he entered cautiously—and stumbled over the inert bodies of his patrol guards. The door to the fenced inner enclosure stood ajar.

"Go in the barracks and wake the detectives," Sano told Gorō. "Tell them there's an intruder in the house."

The guard hurried off to obey. Sano approached the enclosure. Though aware that he could be walking into a trap, he must protect his household. He couldn't wait for help. Before him loomed the dark mansion. Sano crept up the wooden steps. He paused in the shadows beneath the deep eaves above the veranda, listening. Somewhere on the hill, a horse neighed but no sound came from inside the house. Sano tiptoed through the open front door and crossed the entry porch. Weapon raised, he moved stealthily down the corridor. Reaching his office, he halted. His whole body went still and tense.

Dim lamplight spread a yellow glow across the mullioned paper wall. The door was closed. Now Sano heard footsteps creaking the floor inside, a drawer sliding open, the rustle of paper. The intruder was apparently going through his possessions. Sano placed two fingers in the recessed door handle and pushed. The wooden panel slid quietly aside in its oiled frame. In the alcove that housed Sano's desk stood a figure dressed in a black cloak with a close-fitting hood. It was rummaging through a cabinet, facing away from the door.

Bursting into the room, Sano shouted, "Stop! Turn around!"

The intruder whirled. It was Lieutenant Kushida. Around him Sano's books and papers lay in a scattered mess. Having already swept the shelves clear, he'd been ransacking the cabinet. His wrinkled monkey-face went slack with dismay. For a moment he stood frozen. His panicky gaze skipped from Sano to the barred windows, then lit on his *naginata,* which leaned against the wall nearby.

"Don't move!" Sano ordered.

In a motion so fast that it seemed to leap into his hand, Kushida grabbed the spear. He rocketed over the desk, leapt from the alcove's raised platform, and advanced on Sano. His eyes were black pools of desperation. The weapon's sharp, curved blade gleamed in the dim lamplight.

"Don't even try," Sano warned, assuming a defensive crouch and raising his sword. "My men will be here any moment." From the front of the mansion came the sound of hurrying footsteps, voices calling. "Even if you kill me, you won't escape. Drop your weapon. Surrender."

Lieutenant Kushida charged. Sano jumped aside, and the blade narrowly missed his chest. He circled, preparing to strike back. The lieutenant jabbed the spear at his throat. Sano parried. The impact of the blades knocked him sideways. A stunning blow struck his hip: Kushida had deployed the spear's handle, as he must have done with the sentries. Sano stumbled, gasping from the pain. Regaining his balance, he lashed out with his sword.

But Kushida deftly evaded each slice. Teeth bared in a fierce grimace, he was everywhere and nowhere, like a ghost fighter who moved through space with unnatural speed. The *naginata*'s blade battered Sano's sword. Its metal-tipped end jabbed his legs and back. With his shorter reach, Sano couldn't get close enough to score a cut. Slashing and thrusting, Kushida chased him around the room. Sano vaulted backward over an iron chest. He slammed into a painted screen, then feinted a backhand slice. Kushida angled his spear to parry. Sano quickly brought his sword around. The blade cut Kushida's arm, but the lieutenant maintained his relentless assault, driving Sano back toward the wall.

Male voices outside the room grew louder, nearer. Running footsteps pounded the corridor.

"In here!" Sano shouted, losing more ground to Kushida.

A figure dashed through the door. Finally, help at last! Sano glanced around. Relief turned to horror.

Dressed in a pale pink-and-white-flowered night robe, long hair flowing down to her knees, Reiko held a sword in both hands. Her beautiful eyes shone with excitement.

"Reiko! What do you think you're doing?" Sano demanded, dodging the *naginata*'s lethal blade.

"Defending my home!" Reiko shot back.

With surprising agility, she lunged at Kushida, hair and skirts streaming. She whipped her sword around and delivered a resounding whack to the spear's handle, striking one of its metal reinforcing rings.

Sano gaped in shock. One finger's breadth in either direction, and she would have severed the shaft. It was a stroke worthy of an expert. But Reiko was so small, so delicate. Panic filled Sano. He inserted himself between Reiko and Lieutenant Kushida, flailing his sword.

"This is no game, Reiko. Get out of here before you get hurt!"

"Move! Let me at him!"

Reiko's face wore the sublime expression Sano had seen on battling samurai. Again she attacked Kushida. Their blades clashed. She gracefully avoided a counterstrike and launched a series of cuts that forced the lieutenant to retreat. Yet she couldn't possibly stand against such a formidable adversary. Then and there, Sano decided that he must never give her any part of his work. She had no sense. She wouldn't know when to stop.

Sano positioned himself beside his wife. Fighting off

Lieutenant Kushida, he reached out his free hand and shoved Reiko with all his strength.

With an indignant cry, she went flying out the door. Sano heard a crash as her body hit the corridor wall opposite. She was safe, but the moment of lapsed attention cost Sano. Kushida's spear came slashing toward his heart. He leapt away just in time; the blade grazed his ribcage. An evil grin stretched the lieutenant's face as he continued wielding the *naginata*. Sano inflicted more cuts on him, but he wouldn't stop.

Then an army of samurai burst into the room. Swords drawn, they surrounded Lieutenant Kushida. "Drop the spear!" ordered Hirata.

Cornered, Kushida tensed. His fierce gaze swept the faces of Sano's men. He took a step backward, his spear lowered ever so slightly.

And then chaos erupted as Kushida began battling the detectives. Blades clashed with the ear-splitting ring of steel. Whirling, darting figures trampled Sano's possessions. Shouts arose. Sano plunged into the melee, shouting, "Don't kill him! Capture him alive!" He had to find out why Lieutenant Kushida had come here.

Though outnumbered ten to one, Kushida fought bravely, ignoring repeated orders to surrender. In the course of the battle, paper walls tore, wooden mullions splintered. Inevitably blades met flesh, and blood spattered the tatami. At last, two detectives grabbed Kushida from behind. Hirata and three others pried the spear out of his hands. They wrestled him to the floor, where he kicked and thrashed.

"Get your hands off me! Let go!" These were the first words Kushida had spoken.

Sano sheathed his sword, gasping for breath. "Tie him up and dress his wounds. Then bring him to the parlor. I'll talk to him there."

Walking down the corridor, Sano met Reiko, who stood alone, sword dangling from her hand. She gave him a look of pure hostility. Then she turned away and swept toward her chambers.

* * *

Lieutenant Kushida knelt on the parlor floor, his wrists and ankles tied behind him. Naked except for his loincloth and the bloodstained bandages that covered sword wounds on his arms and legs, he struggled to free himself. His ugly face twisted with rage; angry grunts issued from him. His sweat filled the room with a rank, sour odor. Hirata and two detectives crouched near Kushida, lest he somehow break loose. A lantern above his head bathed him in stark light.

Sano paced the floor, gazing down at the captive lieutenant. His own injury was slight, but he felt a raw, aching need to lie with a woman, to purge himself of battle trauma and reaffirm life through the act of sex. He regretted that the sad state of his marriage wouldn't permit this release. Tonight's incident had further damaged relations between him and Reiko, perhaps permanently.

"Did you attack the guards outside my house and the other estates?" he asked Kushida.

The lieutenant fixed him with a hateful stare. "So what if I did?" he spat out. "They're all alive. I know how to wound without killing."

So much for remorse, Sano thought. "What were you doing in my office?"

"Nothing!" Lieutenant Kushida strained at his bonds, face reddening with the effort. Hirata and the detectives eyed him warily.

"You'll have to do better than that, Kushida," said Sano. "One doesn't knock out ten guards, enter another man's house without permission, and ransack his possessions for no reason. Now answer me: Why did you come here?"

"What difference does it make? You'll invent lies about me and draw your own conclusions, no matter what I say." Kushida's body heaved in an awkward lunge toward Sano. Hirata grabbed him, dragging him back. "May the gods curse you and all your clan!" Kushida spewed a stream of bitter invective.

"You're in a lot of trouble," Sano said, keeping his voice level despite rising impatience. "Even with your good record, you face execution for using a weapon inside Edo Castle, breaking into my house, and trying to spear my wife, my men, and myself. But I'm ready to listen to your story and recommend a lesser punishment if your reasons are good enough. So talk, and be quick about it. I haven't got all night."

Lieutenant Kushida glared at Sano, Hirata, and the detectives. He gave one last, strenuous tug at the ropes. Then resistance seeped out of him. Body limp, head bowed, Kushida said, "I was looking for Lady Harume's pillow book."

"How did you know about it?" Sano asked.

A sort of dignified misery settled upon Kushida's features. "I found it in her cabinet."

"And when was this?"

"Three days before she died."

"So you lied when you said you never went into Lady Harume's room." Sano felt extreme chagrin as he remembered Reiko telling him that her cousin had placed the lieutenant in Harume's private quarters at that very same time. Reiko's information had proved accurate. He had insulted her by questioning it.

"All right, I lied," Lieutenant Kushida said dully, "because I wasn't in her room to poison her, like you thought. And I didn't come here to hurt anyone. I had to get the diary. When I reported for duty tonight, I meant to steal it from Lady Harume's room. But the guard captain said you'd postponed my return to work." Kushida flashed a bitter look at Sano. "Then I found out from a soldier that you'd confiscated the diary as evidence. So I came here after it."

Sano wished he'd barred the dangerous, unbalanced guard from the castle entirely. Still, he might gain some useful information now. "Why do you want the diary?"

"I only managed to read a few pages the first time." Kushida's voice sounded weary, desolate. "I wanted to find out who her lover was, and I thought she might have written his name somewhere in the diary."

"How did you know Harume had a lover?" Sano exchanged a significant glance with Hirata: the lieutenant had not only admitted entering Harume's room, but also given himself an additional motive for her murder.

With the fight gone out of him, Kushida looked like a small, tragic ape. "When I escorted Lady Harume and the other women on their outings, she would sneak away from the group. Three times I followed her, and lost her. The fourth time, I tracked her to an inn in Asakusa. But I couldn't get past the gate because there were soldiers guarding it. They weren't wearing any crests, and they wouldn't tell me who they were."

Lord Miyagi's men, thought Sano, protecting their master's privacy during his tryst with Harume.

"I never saw the man she chose instead of me," Kushida continued. "But I know there was one. Why else would she sneak around? I lie awake at nights, wondering who he is and envying him the joy of her. I can't stand not knowing. It's killing me!" His eyes burned with an obsession that hadn't faded, even now that its object was dead. "Do you still have the diary?" Tense with hope, he beseeched Sano, "Please, may I see it?"

Sano wondered if the lieutenant had another, more practical reason for trying to steal the diary. Maybe he believed it contained incriminating evidence against him, which he wanted to destroy.

"When you were in Lady Harume's room, did you also find a jar of ink and a love letter asking her to tattoo herself?" Sano asked.

Kushida shook his head impatiently. "I've already told you, I never saw that ink jar. Or a letter. I wasn't looking for any such things. All I wanted was a—personal keepsake from Harume." Lowering his eyes in shame, he mumbled, "That's how I found the diary. It was with her underclothes. I told you I didn't know about the tattoo. I didn't poison her."

"I understand that Lady Harume became violently ill last summer," Sano said, "and that someone threw a dagger at her. Did you know? Were you responsible?" Seeking to verify Reiko's story, Sano also wondered whether Lieutenant Kushida feared that Harume's diary implicated him.

"I knew. But if you think I had anything to do with what happened, you're wrong." Kushida glared at Sano in contemptuous defiance. "I never would have hurt Harume. I loved her. *I did not kill her!*"

Ahead, shining like a sunlit path through a dark forest, Sano saw a way out of his own dilemma. Lieutenant Kushida's attempted burglary made him the prime suspect. His earlier lies rendered his denials unconvincing. If Sano charged Kushida with murder, his conviction was virtually assured: most trials ended in a verdict of guilty. Sano could avoid the political perils of continuing the investigation, and the disgrace of execution if he failed. And with a major source of conflict between him and Reiko gone, they could get a fresh start on their marriage. But Sano wasn't ready to close the case.

"Lieutenant Kushida," he said, "I'm placing you under house arrest until the investigation of Lady Harume's murder is complete. At that time, your fate will be decided. Meanwhile, you shall remain inside your family home, under constant guard; you are not permitted to leave for any reason except fire or earthquake." These were the standard terms of house arrest, the samurai alternative to jail, a privilege of rank. To the detectives, Sano said, "Escort him to the *banchō*." This was the district west of Edo Castle where hereditary Tokugawa vassals lived.

Hirata regarded Sano with dismay. "Wait, *sōsakan-sama*. May I have a word with you first?"

They went out to the corridor, leaving the detectives to guard Lieutenant Kushida. Hirata whispered, "*Sumimasen*—excuse me, but I think you're making a mistake. Kushida is guilty, and lying to cover it up. He killed Harume because she had a lover and he was jealous. He should be charged and sent to trial. Why are you being so easy on him?"

"And why are you so eager to accept the easy solution, so early in the investigation?" Sano countered. "This isn't like you, Hirata-*san*."

Flushing, Hirata said stubbornly, "I think he killed her."

Sano decided that this wasn't the right time to address his chief retainer's problems, whatever they were. "The weaknesses in the case against Kushida are obvious. First of all, the break-in is evidence of something wrong with him, but not necessarily that he's guilty of murder. Second, just because he lied about certain things doesn't mean we should disregard everything he says.

"Third: If we close the case too soon, the real killer may go free, while an innocent man is executed. More murders could follow." Sano told Hirata about Magistrate Ueda's conspiracy theory. "If there's a plot against the shogun, we must identify all the criminals, or the threat to the Tokugawa line will persist."

Hirata nodded in reluctant agreement. Sano leaned through the doorway and said to the detectives, "Proceed." Then he turned back to Hirata. "Besides, I'm not ready to dismiss my questions about the other suspects."

Although Hirata's unhappy silence troubled him, Sano didn't intend to drop his investigation of the Miyagi—or Lady Ichiteru.

Standing in the doorway to the shogun's bedchamber, *Otoshiyori* Madam Chizuru announced, "Your Excellency, I present your companion for the night: the Honorable Lady Ichiteru." She beat three ritual strokes on a small gong, then bowed and withdrew.

Slowly, regally, Lady Ichiteru marched into the chamber. She carried a large book bound in yellow silk and wore a man's kimono, striped in black and brown, with thick padding to widen her shoulders. Beneath it, cloth bands flattened her breasts. Her face was devoid of powder, lips unpainted, hair knotted in a severe, masculine style. After thirteen years as Tokugawa Tsunayoshi's concubine, she knew how to appeal to his tastes. Now, with retirement only three months away, her life was dominated by the increasingly urgent need to conceive his child before time ran out. She must take advantage of every opportunity to seduce him.

"Ahh, my dearest Ichiteru. Welcome." Tokugawa Tsunayoshi lay abed in a futon piled with colorful quilts, in a lair furnished with gilded lacquer cabinets and the finest tatami. Brilliant wall murals depicted a mountain landscape. Screens decorated with flowers kept out drafts and contained the warmth radiating from sunken charcoal braziers. A standing lamp cast a warm, inviting pool of light upon the shogun, who wore a mauve silk dressing gown and cylindrical black cap. Lavender incense perfumed the air. They were alone except for the bodyguards stationed outside the room and Madam Chizuru listening next door. Yet the shogun's mood was anything but romantic.

"It has been a most, ahh, irritating day," he said. Fatigue lined his pallid face. "So many decisions to make! Then there is the distressing business of, ahh, Lady Harume's murder. I hardly know what to do."

Sighing, he looked up at Lady Ichiteru for sympathy. She sat, laid aside the book, and cradled his head in her lap. He elaborated upon his troubles while she murmured comforting words: "Don't worry, my lord. Everything will be fine." After so many years together, they were like an old married couple, with her as his friend, mother, nursemaid, and—least often—his lover. As she stroked his forehead, impatience simmered beneath Ichiteru's tranquil demeanor. A distant temple bell tolled, signaling the relentless passage of time toward her dreaded thirtieth birthday. But she must let Tokugawa Tsunayoshi talk himself out before they could begin sex. While his doleful voice droned on, her thoughts drifted back to the one truly happy period of her life. . . .

Kyōto, the capital of Japan's emperors for a thousand years. In the heart of the city stood the great, walled complex of the Imperial Palace. Ichiteru's family were cousins of the current emperor. They lived in a villa within the palace grounds. Ichiteru had grown up in sheltered isolation there, but her childhood hadn't been lonely. The emperor's court numbered in the thousands. Ichiteru recalled idyllic days spent playing with her sisters, cousins, and friends. But outside the golden halo of her existence, the dark shadow of her future lurked.

As a constant background noise ran the complaints of the adults. They deplored the plain food, the outmoded garments everyone wore, the lack of entertainment, the shortage of servants, and the government. Gradually Ichiteru came to understand the reason for their genteel poverty and her elders' resentment toward the Tokugawa regime: The *bakufu,* fearing that the imperial family would try to reclaim its former power, maintained it on a limited income so it couldn't afford to raise troops and launch a rebellion. But not until she reached adulthood did Ichiteru become aware of how politics had charted her life from the very beginning.

"Ahh, Ichiteru." Tokugawa Tsunayoshi's voice drew her

back to the present. "Sometimes I think you're the only person who understands me."

Looking down at him, Ichiteru saw that his face had relaxed. At last he was ready for the business of the evening. "Yes, I do understand you, my lord," she said with a provocative smile. "And I've brought you a gift."

"What is it?" Like an eager child, the shogun sat up, pleasure lighting his eyes.

Lady Ichiteru placed the book before him. "It's a spring book, my lord"—a collection of *shunga,* erotic prints—"created by a famous artist, just for you."

She opened the cover and turned to the first page. In lovely, subtle colors, this showed two naked samurai lying side by side beneath trailing willow boughs. Their swords lay atop piles of discarded clothing as they fondled each other's erect organs. In the corner was a poem written in elegant calligraphy:

Warriors in peacetime:
Ah! Their jade shafts may prevail
Over blades of steel.

"Exquisite," breathed Tokugawa Tsunayoshi. "You know what I like, Ichiteru." From the other side of the wall came the soft rustle of Madam Chizuru stirring, alert to the beginning of the sexual play. Now the shogun noticed Ichiteru's mannish appearance. His eyebrows raised in happy interest. "And how nice you look tonight."

"Thank you, my lord," said Ichiteru, pleased that her scheme for his seduction was working. She let him admire the picture awhile longer, then turned to the second page of the book. The scene featured a bald Buddhist priest, standing in a temple worship hall with his saffron robe hiked above his waist. A young novice knelt at his feet, sucking his swollen member. The poem read:

As the lone raindrop is to a summer storm,
So does spiritual enlightenment compare
With the ecstasies of the flesh!

"Ahh, how blasphemous and disgusting!" Giggling, Tokugawa Tsunayoshi leaned against Ichiteru. Down the corridor came the rhythmic footsteps of patrolling guards. Next door, Madam Chizuru coughed softly. But the shogun seemed oblivious to these distractions as he batted his eyes flirtatiously at Ichiteru.

Smiling in encouragement, Ichiteru suppressed a shudder. She'd always felt extreme revulsion for the shogun's foolish personality and sickly body. Were she able to choose a lover, she would pick someone like Detective Hirata, whom she had so enjoyed teasing at the puppet theater. Now there was a man who could truly appreciate her! But ambition must prevail over emotion. Ichiteru must fulfill the destiny laid out for her long ago.

During her childhood music, calligraphy, and tea ceremony lessons, adult members of the imperial family would often drop by to observe. "Ichiteru shows great promise," they would say. A bright but naïve girl, ever compliant and respectful toward her elders, Ichiteru had basked in the praise. Soon came other lessons, given only to her.

A beautiful courtesan from Kyōto's pleasure quarter had come to the palace. Her name was Ebony, and she taught Ichiteru the art of pleasing a man: how to dress and flirt; how to make amusing conversation; how to flatter the male ego. On a wooden statue, Ebony demonstrated hand and mouth techniques for arousing a lover. Later she taught Ichiteru the use of erotica, toys, and games to maintain a man's interest. She undressed Ichiteru and introduced her to the pleasures of her own body. Fingers caressing the downy cleft of Ichiteru's young womanhood, Ebony had brought about her first sexual climax. When Ichiteru had gasped and arched and cried out in rapture, Ebony had said, "That is what a man wishes to see and hear when he beds you."

Using a wooden rod, Ebony had shown her how to tighten her inner muscles around a male organ. She taught Ichiteru ways to seduce a man who didn't like women; how to satisfy unusual appetites. Later the court physician had instructed her on the use of drugs to heighten arousal and promote conception. Ever dutiful, Ichiteru neither objected to anything demanded of her, nor asked why she had been singled out for this special schooling. Hence, she didn't learn until her sixteenth birthday where the lessons were leading.

Envoys from Edo came to the palace. Ichiteru was dressed in her best clothes and presented to them. Afterward, the empress told her, "You have been selected to be a concubine to the next shogun. The fortune-tellers have prophesied that you shall bear his heir and unite the emperor's clan with the Tokugawa. Through you, wealth and power shall return to the imperial family. You leave for Edo tomorrow."

Later Ichiteru learned that her family had sold her to the shogun's envoys. In a daze of grief and confusion, she endured the month-long trip from Kyōto to Edo. One thought sustained her: The fate of the imperial family depended on her. She must win Tokugawa Tsunayoshi's favor and induce him to impregnate her. It was her duty to the emperor, her country, and the people she loved.

However, Ichiteru's attitude had soon changed. She hated the noise and crowded conditions of the Large Interior, the constant surveillance, the indignity of compulsory sex, the quarrels and rivalries among the women. Soon her brightness turned to cunning; love of family turned to resentment toward those who had condemned her to misery. Her sense of duty vanished. She began to crave wealth and power for herself. She hated Lady Keisho-in's stupidity and tiresome demands for attention with passionate jealousy. The vulgar old peasant woman symbolized what Ichiteru wanted to be: A woman of the highest, most secure rank, living in luxury, free to do as she pleased, while commanding everyone's respect.

Thus began Ichiteru's drive to bear Tokugawa Tsunayoshi's heir. Her beauty, talent, and lineage attracted his capricious fancy; her status as his favorite made her a leader within the hierarchy of the Large Interior, no matter that the shogun wanted her company only a few nights a month. Because he squandered his virility on boys, this was much better than any of the other women fared. Four years into her concubinage, Ichiteru was pregnant.

The shogun rejoiced. Blessings poured into Edo Castle from across the land. In Kyōto, the imperial family eagerly awaited its return to prominence. Everyone pampered Ichiteru; she reveled in the attention. A luxurious nursery was prepared.

Then, after eight months, she delivered a stillborn baby boy. The nation mourned. Yet neither the shogun nor Ichiteru gave up. As soon as she regained her health, she returned to Tokugawa Tsunayoshi's bedchamber. Finally, last year, she had gotten with child again. But when she miscarried it at seven months, the *bakufu* blamed Ichiteru. They advised the shogun against wasting any more precious seed on her. They brought in new concubines to tempt his meager appetite.

One of them was Lady Harume.

Ichiteru's hatred of her rival still burned inside her, even now, with Harume dead. Reminding herself that Harume was no longer a threat, she turned to the next page of the book. Tokugawa Tsunayoshi gasped with delight. In a moonlit garden pavilion, a naked young boy crouched on all fours. Behind him knelt an older man, also naked, except for a black cap identical to the shogun's. With one hand, the man inserted his erection into the boy's anus; with the other, he grasped the boy's organ. Lady Ichiteru read the accompanying poem aloud:

> *"Day becomes night,*
> *The tides rise and ebb;*
> *Frost melts beneath the sun—*
> *Royalty may take its pleasure however found."*

Seeing the gleam of lust in Tokugawa Tsunayoshi's eyes, Ichiteru said with a provocative smile, "Come, my lord, and take your pleasure from me."

She parted her kimono. Strapped to her groin by leather bands was a flesh-colored jade shaft carved in realistic likeness of an erect male member. The shogun stared in amazement. A tremulous sigh escaped him. "Ahhhh . . ."

"Close your eyes," Ichiteru crooned.

He obeyed. She took his hand and placed it on the carving. The shogun moaned, stroking it up and down. Ichiteru reached beneath his robes. The tiny, soft worm of his manhood stiffened under her caresses. When he was ready, she gently removed his hand from the carving and raised him to his knees. He groaned as she removed his garments, leaving on his cap. She bent over, balancing on her knees and elbows, kimono lifted above her waist, and rubbed her bare buttocks against his erection. The shogun grunted, heaving at her. Ichiteru reached back and guided him to her womanhood, which she'd moistened with fragrant oil. As he moaned and thrusted, trying to penetrate her, she looked back and caught a glimpse of him: flabby muscles straining, mouth open, eyes closed to preserve the illusion that she was a man.

Please, she prayed silently. Let me conceive this time! Make me the mother of the next shogun, and my sordid, degrading life worthwhile!

The shogun's erection entered Ichiteru. Groaning, he plunged in and out. Hope rose within her. By this time next year, she could be Tokugawa Tsunayoshi's official consort. She would persuade him to restore the Imperial Court to its former splendor, thereby achieving her family's goal and placing them in her debt forever. Holding this vision of the future, Ichiteru endured the shogun's assault. And to think how close she'd come to losing everything!

Harume, young and fresh and lovely. Harume, with her robust, peasant charm. Harume, full of the promise that Ichiteru had once offered. Soon it was Harume whom Tokugawa Tsunayoshi most often invited to his bedchamber. After twelve years of whoredom and the agony of two births, Ichiteru was forgotten—but unwilling to accept defeat. She began plotting Harume's downfall. At first she spread cruel rumors and snubbed the girl, encouraging her friends to do the same, hoping that Harume would become so miserable as to ruin her health and looks. But the ploy failed. Lady Keisho-in took a liking to Harume, and promoted her to the shogun as his best prospect for an heir. Hating her rival, wishing her dead, Ichiteru had resorted to more effective means. Still, nothing worked.

Then, two months ago, Ichiteru had noticed that Harume

wasn't eating; at mealtimes, she just picked at her food. The bloom faded from her skin. Three mornings in a row Ichiteru discovered her vomiting in the privy. Ichiteru's worst fear was realized: Her rival was pregnant. Ichiteru grew desperate. She had to prevent Harume from beating her to their mutual goal of becoming mother to the next dictator. She couldn't just wait and hope that the child would be female or not live. She didn't want to spend the rest of her life as an overworked palace official, and no man worth marrying would accept a failed concubine as a wife. Nor did she want to return to Kyōto in disgrace. With new determination, she sought a way to destroy her rival.

Unwittingly, Harume had abetted Ichiteru's purpose by not reporting her condition. Perhaps, in her youthful ignorance, she didn't recognize it as pregnancy. Ever watchful, Ichiteru spied Harume stealing from the basket where the women disposed of bloodstained cloths. Ichiteru realized she must be wearing them so Dr. Kitano wouldn't discover that her monthly bleeding had ceased. Maybe she thought she was ill and would be banished from the castle if anyone knew. But Ichiteru could think of a better explanation: The child wasn't Tokugawa Tsunayoshi's. Ichiteru had seen Harume sneak off during excursions away from Edo Castle. Did she fear punishment for consorting with another man? Snooping through her rival's room in search of clues to his identity, Ichiteru had discovered a package containing a fancy jar of ink and a letter from Lord Miyagi. But whatever the reason for Harume's secrecy, it gave Ichiteru opportunity to hope and scheme.

And now Harume was dead. Since none of the other concubines could arouse the shogun sufficiently, Ichiteru regained her position as his favorite female partner. She had another chance at conceiving his heir before retiring. One problem remained: She must convince the *sōsakan-sama* that she was not guilty of Harume's murder. She must live to enjoy the fruits of thirteen years' labor.

Abruptly Tokugawa Tsunayoshi went soft inside her. With a cry of dismay, he collapsed upon the futon. "Ahh, my dear, I am afraid I cannot proceed."

Ichiteru sat back on her heels, ready to weep with disappointment and frustration, but she hid her emotions. "I'm sorry, my lord," she said meekly. "Perhaps if I help you . . . ?"

He made a gesture of dismissal, then pulled the quilt over himself and closed his eyes. "Another time. I'm too tired to try again now."

"Yes, Your Excellency." Ichiteru rose and straightened her disheveled garments. As she crossed the chamber, her resolve strengthened within her like flint in the bones and heart. Next time she would succeed. And until her future was secure, she must make sure her crime was never exposed.

Lady Ichiteru slipped out the door, closing it behind her. Memory and need intersected with a sudden click in her mind. She smiled in wicked inspiration. She knew just how to avoid the calamity of a murder charge and advance her position.

After a few hours' sleep and a breakfast of fish and rice, Sano left his mansion early the next morning. Inside, Reiko still slept; servants cleaned up the mess in Sano's office. The detective corps had left word that Lieutenant Kushida was securely imprisoned in his family home. Hirata had already left Edo Castle to check some leads on the drug peddler before finishing his interview with Lady Ichiteru. And Sano was taking a journey back in time.

Overnight, an autumn fog had billowed in from the river. White mist veiled the city, rendering the distant hills and the upper tiers of Edo Castle invisible. The sun was a pale circle floating in a sea of milk. As Sano headed toward the palace, patrolling sentries emerged out of the mist, only to disappear again. Moisture dripped off the stone walls of passages and slickened the paths. The thin cries of airborne crows and the drums summoning spectators to a sumo wrestling tournament sounded muted, as if strained through cotton mesh. The smell of wet stone, leaves, and earth dampened the tang of charcoal smoke. On such days when the sharp edges of reality blurred, the spirit world had an almost palpable presence for Sano. The ghostly trail into the past beckoned. What better time than now to follow it to hidden truths about Lady Harume's murder?

Sano found Madam Chizuru in her office, a tiny room in the Large Interior. On the wall hung wooden plates bearing the names of officials and servants on duty. A window overlooked the laundry courtyard, where maids boiled dirty bedclothes in steaming pots. The harsh odor of lye drifted through the lattice. Chizuru, dressed in her gray uniform, knelt behind the desk, going over household account books.

"Madam Chizuru, may I speak with you a moment?" Sano asked from the doorway.

"Yes, of course." The *otoshiyori* set aside her work and motioned for Sano to sit before her. Then she folded her hands and sat waiting, her masculine face impassive.

"What can you tell me about Lady Harume's background?" Sano asked. Instinctively he believed that the concubine's life held valuable clues about her death. Where she had come from, and who she'd been, could enlighten him more than witnesses, suspects, or evidence had yet.

Chizuru hesitated, then said, "The dossiers of His Excellency's household are confidential. Special permission is required for me to release details."

"I can get permission from the shogun and come back later," Sano pointed out. Though annoyed by Chizuru's resistance, he respected her adherence to the rules: If more people obeyed them, there would be less crime. "You might as well save us both some trouble by telling me now. And what does confidentiality matter now that Harume is dead?"

"Very well." Madam Chizuru conceded with a brief lowering of her eyes. "Lady Harume was born in Fukagawa. Her mother's name is Blue Apple; she's a nighthawk."

This was the poetic euphemism for unlicensed prostitutes, who serviced customers who couldn't afford the expensive, legal Yoshiwara courtesans. No wonder Harume had felt out of place among the generally highborn women of the Large Interior. Confidential or not, personal information had a way of spreading. Had Lady Ichiteru, in particular, resented Harume's presence enough to kill her? Hopefully Hirata would find out today.

"How was Harume chosen as a concubine?" Sano asked.

"The *bakufu* decided that variety would benefit the Tokugawa succession," Chizuru said.

Meaning that when ladies of samurai or noble blood failed to produce an heir, a peasant girl was worth a try, Sano interpreted. And Harume had succeeded in becoming pregnant, though the child's paternity wasn't established.

"What about Harume's father?" Sano said.

"He is Jimba of Bakurochō. You may know him."

"Yes, I do." The man was a prominent horse dealer who

supplied the stables of the Tokugawa and many powerful daimyo clans, and Sano had purchased mounts from him.

"When the shogun's envoys were searching for new concubines, they came across Harume," Madam Chizuru continued. "She had good looks, a little education, and adequate manners. She seemed promising, and was brought to Edo Castle. That's all the records say about Harume."

Later Sano would visit the dead concubine's parents and learn more about her. But for now, perhaps the crime scene would reveal undiscovered secrets. "I want to look around Lady Harume's room again. Are her things still there?"

Madam Chizuru nodded. "Yes. The floor has been cleaned, but otherwise, everything is just as it was when she died—I've not yet had a chance to send her belongings to her family. And her former chambermates have moved to other quarters. The room is vacant. Come."

Rising, she led Sano through the Large Interior, which was gradually awakening. Palace officials and guards made morning rounds. Maids filed through the corridors, carrying tea trays and water basins. Behind the paper walls, bedclothes rustled and sleepy feminine voices murmured. A fusty odor of sleep and stale perfume soured the atmosphere. But the hallway outside Lady Harume's room was deserted. Sano thanked Madam Chizuru, slid open the door, and shut himself inside the cell. He stood still for a moment, looking around, absorbing impressions.

The slatted window shutters admitted misty daylight. New tatami covered the floor. Furniture stood undisturbed. But under the clean smell of soap, Sano detected the lingering taint of blood and vomit. In his mind he saw Harume lying on the floor, hideous in unnatural death. Her spirit seemed to infect the air. Although Sano hadn't known her, he got a sudden, vivid image of the living girl: bright-eyed, vivacious, with a merry laugh that echoed across the distance from the netherworld. A cold shiver rippled over him, as if he'd seen a ghost.

Shrugging off his fancy, Sano began a systematic search through the chests and cabinets. On his last visit, he'd been concerned mainly with finding the poison. Now, as he examined Lady Harume's belongings, he asked himself: Who was she? Who were her friends? What had mattered to her? What traits had she possessed, what things had she done that might have inspired murder?

Sano took a closer look at the kimonos he'd casually inspected before, laying them out on the floor. Two were cotton, much creased, with no sign of recent wear—she'd probably brought them to the castle with her, then rejected them in favor of the six expensive silk ones, which she must have received as a concubine. All the fabrics shared an extravagance of color and design, a lack of fashionable elegance. Sano contemplated the most striking example of Harume's taste: a summer garment whose garish yellow lilies and green ivy seemed to vibrate against a brilliant orange background.

The iron chest yielded a stack of papers tied with frayed string. Sano leafed through them, hoping to find personal letters, but they were merely old Kabuki theater programs and illustrated broadsheets hawked by Edo newssellers. There was also a good-luck charm from the Hakka Temple in Asakusa—a prayer printed on cheap paper. Harume must have collected these things as souvenirs of holidays away from the castle. In drawers Sano discovered jars of face powder, rouge, and perfume, gaudy sashes, and floral hair ornaments; playing cards; cheap knickknacks; an old wooden doll with rope hair—probably a childhood toy. Sano sighed in frustration. There was nothing here to indicate that Harume had been anything but a common young woman with no intellectual interests or special relationships. Why would anyone have wanted to kill such a nonentity?

Perhaps Magistrate Ueda's theory was correct, and the murderer's real target had been her unborn child and the Tokugawa line. Unless Harume's parents supplied new leads, the investigation into her background was a dead end.

Then, as Sano replaced items in the cabinet, he picked up a blue silk purse with embroidered white peonies and a red drawstring. There was a bulge inside. Opening the purse, Sano removed a folded square of unbleached muslin. Curious, he unfolded it. Inside was a wad of black hair and three fingernails, apparently pried off the flesh, with dead skin around the edges. Revulsion twisted Sano's mouth. He didn't remember Harume's corpse missing any nails, and surely Dr. Ito would have noticed during the examination. Where had Harume gotten the grisly relics, and for what purpose?

A possible answer occurred to Sano, but it seemed incongruous, and he didn't see how his discovery related to the murder. Rewrapping the muslin around the nails and hair, he replaced them in the purse, which he tucked inside the drawstring pouch at his waist for later contemplation. Then he began a meticulous reinspection of Lady Harume's other possessions. What other evidence might he have missed?

When he was refolding the orange lilies-and-ivy kimono, its right sleeve crackled under his touch. Part of the sleeve's hem felt stiffer than the rest. Folding it back, Sano saw loose threads where the stitching had been cut away. Excitement stirred in him. He inserted his hand into the hem and removed a folded sheet of thin paper. Tiny pink petals embedded in the paper gave it a feminine air, as did the faint scent of perfume and the spidery calligraphy that covered one side. Sano carried the letter over to the window and read:

> You do not love me. Much as I try to believe otherwise, I cannot blind myself to the truth any longer. You smile and say all the right things because I command your obedience. But when I touch you, your body stiffens with distaste. When we are together, your eyes get a distant look, as if you would rather be elsewhere. When I speak, you do not really listen.
>
> Is there someone you care for more than me? Alas! My spirit sickens with jealousy. But I must know: Who is it that has captured your affection?
>
> Sometimes I feel like throwing myself at your feet and begging for your love. Other times I want to strike you for denying my soul's desire. Woe is me! If I committed seppuku, I would not have to endure this misery!
>
> But I do not want to die. What I really want is to

see you suffer as I do. I could stab you and watch the blood run out. I could poison you and delight in your agony. As you plead for mercy, I will only laugh and say: "This is how it feels!"

If you won't love me, I will kill you!

The letter bore neither date nor salutation, but the signature seemed to rise up off the page and fill Sano's vision. Dread settled upon him like the dense, cold weight of a heavy snow that had fallen on Edo several winters ago, collapsing roofs and blocking streets. The writer of the letter was Lady Keisho-in.

This new clue turned the murder case in a different, perilous direction. Sano saw how wrong he'd been to think he'd accurately assessed the scope of the investigation. Here was proof that the shogun's mother's relationship with Harume had been more than just one of mistress and attendant. During the interview with Keisho-in, her expressions of maternal fondness for Harume had been pure deception. Sano had thought the old woman stupid, yet she'd tricked him by concealing her destructive rage toward Lady Harume. Now Keisho-in joined the array of murder suspects.

The letter established her motive, in her own, handwritten words. As ruler of the Large Interior, she had access to all the women's rooms, and spies to keep her informed on every aspect of their lives. She could have seen the ink jar when it arrived at Edo Castle, read the accompanying letter, and recognized a perfect opportunity to kill Harume and have someone else blamed for the murder. She had servants to seek out rare poisons, and the wealth to purchase them. Between these factors and the letter, Sano had enough evidence to warrant a serious investigation of Lady Keisho-in—and perhaps even a murder charge against her.

Sano could see an additional reason why Lady Keisho-in might have wanted Harume dead—a motive even stronger than embittered love. Keisho-in must have known about Harume's pregnancy, which held special ramifications for her. Now the case against Lieutenant Kushida, the Miyagi, and Lady Ichiteru diminished in comparative significance. But the evidence in Sano's hand possessed the dangerous power of a double-edged blade. It opened a whole new line of inquiry, which might provide the truth about Lady Harume's murder and spare Sano the death penalty for failing to solve the case. But following the lead could ruin him anyway.

Sano didn't even want to think about what could happen, and he wished he'd never found the letter. If only he'd limited his attention to the previous suspects and evidence, and never learned about Keisho-in's unhappy love affair with Harume! Perhaps she was innocent. By omitting her from his investigation, Sano could save himself. Slowly he began to tear the letter in two.

Yet honor would not let him evade the truth. Justice must be served, even at the cost of his own life. Reluctantly Sano folded the letter and tucked it inside his pouch with the purse of fingernails and hair clippings. He would postpone dealing with the document for as long as possible. But sooner or later, unless he found conclusive evidence against Lieutenant Kushida, Lady Ichiteru, the Miyagi, or someone else, deal with it he must.

20

A squadron of mounted samurai rode sedately along the highway on Edo's western outskirts. The Tokugawa triple-hollyhock crest decorated the horses' equipage, banners mounted on poles attached to the riders' backs, and the huge black palanquin that followed. The open windows of the palanquin framed two faces.

Lady Keisho-in, her double chin bobbing in time with the bearers' steps, gazed out at the landscape. "Beautiful!" she exclaimed, admiring the scarlet-and-gold foliage of the woods and the misty hills beyond. Her powdered and rouged face wore a gap-toothed smile. "I can't wait to see the site of the future Tokugawa Dog Kennels. Are we almost there?"

The man seated opposite in the sedan chair watched Lady Keisho-in. He had a handsome profile, with a high brow, long nose, heavy-lidded eyes, and the full, curved lips of a Buddha statue. His shaven scalp accentuated the sculpted bones of his head. At age forty-two, Priest Ryuko had been Lady Keisho-in's companion and spiritual leader for ten years. His association with her made him the highest-ranking cleric in Japan, as well as indirect adviser to Tokugawa Tsunayoshi. Ryuko had suggested this outing, as he had many other past schemes. Despite the cold, damp weather, Keisho-in had acquiesced, as she usually did. He'd convinced her that it was necessary for her to inspect the building of the kennels, a special project of theirs.

Yet Ryuko harbored another, more personal motive. The kennels wouldn't be completed for several years, and in any case, their construction didn't require Lady Keisho-in's help. Ryuko had important business to discuss with her, away from Edo Castle and its many spies. Her future—and, therefore, his—might depend on the outcome of the investigation into Lady Harume's murder. They must protect their mutual interests.

"We shall arrive soon," Ryuko said, tucking the quilts more comfortably around Lady Keisho-in. He warmed her gnarled old hands in his strong ones, murmuring, "Patience," as much to himself as to her.

Keisho-in preened under Ryuko's attentions. Presently the palanquin rounded a curve in the road, and Ryuko ordered the bearers to stop. He helped Lady Keisho-in out, throwing a padded cloak over her shoulders. To the east, fields led to a village of thatched huts; beyond, the city, invisible beneath a heavy pall of fog, extended to the Sumida River. On the west side of the road, a huge expanse of forest had been reduced to a wasteland of jagged stumps. Woodcutters hacked down more trees, the ring of their axes echoing over the hills. Peasants sawed logs and hauled away branches, while samurai foremen directed the work. A team of architects consulted plans drawn on huge sheets of paper. The sweet, pungent smell of wet sawdust filled the air. Lady Keisho-in gasped with awe.

"Wonderful!" Leaning on Ryuko's arm, she stepped off the road and minced toward the construction site.

As laborers knelt and bowed at her approach and the architects came to pay their respects, Ryuko signaled everyone to return to work. He wanted noise to mask his conversation with Lady Keisho-in. But first the guided tour, to fulfill the ostensible purpose of the expedition.

"Here will be the main entrance, with statues of dogs at the door," Ryuko said, leading Lady Keisho-in to the eastern edge of the clearing. Slowly he walked her around the site. "Here will be rooms to house cages for twenty thousand dogs. The walls will be decorated with paintings of woods and fields, so that the animals can feel that they are outdoors."

"Perfect!" exclaimed Lady Keisho-in, her eyes goggling. "I can see it all now."

As the tour proceeded, Ryuko divided his concentration in two parts, according to long-standing habit. With the larger part he focused on Lady Keisho-in, watching for signs that she might be getting cold or tired, anticipating her need for flattery. Since his fortune depended on their relationship, he couldn't afford to displease her. With the remainder of his mind he watched himself, monitoring his performance. He saw a slender holy man shod in modest wooden sandals, wearing a padded brown silk cloak over his saffron robe. His gaze had a wise, penetrating intensity that he'd practiced in the mirror until it became natural. His manner was dignified, his voice suavely cultivated. No trace remained of his humble origin.

Orphaned at age eight, Ryuko had come to Edo to seek his fortune. He'd found refuge at Zōjō Temple, where the priests had fed, sheltered, clothed, and educated him. At fifteen, he'd taken religious vows. However, his tragic youthful experiences had endowed him with two contradictory traits, which prevented him from finding fulfillment in his vocation.

Ryuko hated poverty with a soul-searing passion. He would never forget the hardship of peasant life, slaving in the fields, with never enough to eat and no hope of a better existence. As a young priest, Ryuko had worked tirelessly to alleviate the suffering of Edo's poor. He solicited donations and distributed them to needy citizens. His work financed the care of orphans at Zōjō Temple. Soon he gained a reputation as a man of selfless, merciful character. The poor worshipped him; his superiors praised him for enhancing the image of their sect. Yet another urge compelled Ryuko.

He also remembered prostrating himself on the ground as the local daimyo passed by. Lord Kuroda and his retainers rode splendidly caparisoned horses. Their faces were plump from the food produced by the peasants' labor. They beat anyone who failed to meet the crop quota. How Ryuko had hated them! And how he'd envied their wealth and power. He wanted to be like them, instead of a poor peasant boy.

The desire grew stronger during Ryuko's early years as a priest. At Zōjō—home temple of the Tokugawa clan—he had plenty of opportunity to observe the splendor that money could buy. A devout Buddhist, Ryuko desired the spiritual enlightenment that would release him from such worldly concerns. He prayed ever longer; he toiled even harder at charitable work. Using his natural flair for politics, he rose in the temple hierarchy. Yet still he craved wealth and power.

Then he'd met Lady Keisho-in.

Now Ryuko told his patroness, "And this will be a reception room for His Excellency when he visits the kennels."

"Marvelous!" Lady Keisho-in let out a cackle of glee, whirling in girlish excitement. "Surely my son's benevolence will convince fortune to bring him an heir. My dearest Ryuko, you were so wise to recommend building the kennels!"

When, after too many years, Tsunayoshi was still without a son, he'd grown concerned for the Tokugawa succession. Neither he nor his advisers welcomed the idea of designating a relative as the next dictator and ceding power to a different branch of the clan. Hence, Lady Keisho-in had turned to Ryuko for help. Through prayer and meditation, he'd found a mystical solution to the problem. Tokugawa Tsunayoshi must earn the right to an heir by atoning for the sins of his ancestors via some act of generosity. Since he'd been born in the year of the dog, what better gesture than to bestow his patronage upon dogs?

On Ryuko's advice, Lady Keisho-in had persuaded Tokugawa Tsunayoshi to issue the Dog Protection Edicts, which furthered Ryuko's goal of promoting animal welfare according to Buddhist tradition. When this didn't produce the shogun's desired results, Ryuko had proposed a more drastic action: the establishment of the kennels. Funds were levied from various daimyo; Edo's best carpenters would build the structure. Ryuko was certain that the successful birth of a Tokugawa heir would follow, strengthening Keisho-in's influence with Tsunayoshi—and thus his own. But that time lay in the future. Now Ryuko wanted to make sure they lived to see it.

"Come and rest, my lady." He seated his patroness on a tree stump, far from their waiting escorts. "We can watch the work on the site and enjoy a bit of conversation before we return to Edo Castle."

With a puff of relief, Lady Keisho-in settled herself. "Ah, that feels good. You are so thoughtful, my dearest. Now, what shall we talk about?"

Ryuko studied her familiar features, breathed her familiar smell of perfume, tobacco smoke, and old age. They'd been together so long. He'd memorized her needs, her habits, her preferences—all the information essential to keeping her favor. Yet how well did he really know the most powerful woman in Japan? With a nostalgia sharpened by the present danger, he recalled the day they'd met.

Tokugawa Tsunayoshi had just succeeded to the rank of shogun, and Lady Keisho-in had come to Zōjō Temple to pray for a long, prosperous reign for her son. She'd caught sight of Ryuko among the priests gathered to pay homage to their lord's mother. Her ugly old face acquired an expression of bemused delight, a reaction that Ryuko often elicited from female worshippers who admired handsome priests. Halting her procession to the temple hall, she'd made his acquaintance. She'd taken a strong fancy to him, as she did to other young men who satisfied her need for companionship and sex. He had become her private spiritual leader, moving from Zōjō Temple to chambers in Edo Castle so that she could have his counsel whenever required. Lady Keisho-in lavished gifts upon him and his religious order. The temple complex grew in magnificence; its residents prospered. Keisho-in slavishly followed Ryuko's advice, often influencing the shogun to do the same. Money poured out of the Tokugawa treasury, funding subsidiary temples and charitable work. To Ryuko, a relationship with an unattractive woman twenty years his senior seemed a small price to pay.

He neither loved nor desired his patroness, but encouraged her infatuation with him. Forsaking his monastic life, he became her lover. He tolerated her moods and demands; he flattered her vanity. Under his contempt for her silliness, he felt a poignant sense of comradeship with Lady Keisho-in. They were both commoners who had risen to unexpected heights. And he was truly grateful to her for giving him everything he needed: wealth and power; spiritual fulfillment and the chance to do good.

In this mutually satisfactory manner they'd spent a decade together. Ryuko had expected the arrangement to last indefinitely. Keisho-in, healthy for an old woman, seemed in no danger of dying anytime soon. Tokugawa Tsunayoshi was young enough to serve many more years as shogun—and probably would, if an heir didn't appear. But after the murder of Lady Harume, the future seemed uncertain. Ryuko knew how fast fortunes could rise or fall in the *bakufu*; sometimes, a mere rumor could destroy a life. *Sōsakan* Sano's inquiry posed a dire threat to Lady Keisho-in. And the threat had tentacles, like an octopus, which could reach out and strangle everyone within her close circle—including Ryuko.

"My sources tell me that *Sōsakan* Sano is doing an extremely thorough job investigating Lady Harume's murder," Ryuko said, easing into his subject of concern. He must be very careful about handling Lady Keisho-in. "Detectives are all over the Large Interior. Hirata has leads on the source of the poison. Lieutenant Kushida is under arrest, but not yet charged with murder. It appears that Sano isn't seeking an easy way out. Instead he's living up to his reputation for pursuing the truth, regardless of the consequences."

Ryuko paused. Then, because Keisho-in rarely responded to subtle hints, he added a clearer warning: "One might wish to exercise caution under these circumstances."

"Oh, yes, Sano is a fine detective," Lady Keisho-in said, missing the point. "And I like young Hirata." She giggled. "I think he likes me, too."

She could be so frivolous, even at a time like this! Hiding his impatience, Ryuko said, "My lady, Sano's investigation may turn up information that is detrimental to . . . any number of persons. No one is safe from scrutiny."

"You say things in a way that I can't understand," Keisho-in complained. "Whatever are you talking about? Who's in danger?"

Her denseness forced blunt speech. "You, my lady," Ryuko said reluctantly.

"Me?" Keisho-in's rheumy eyes widened in surprise. Evidently she'd given no thought to how the murder investigation might affect her. Then she smiled, reaching up to pat Ryuko's arm. "I appreciate your concern, dearest, but I have nothing to fear from Sano or anyone else."

Ryuko studied her guileless face with confusion. He'd thought himself adept at reading her after all these years, but now he couldn't tell whether she spoke the truth. "Your relationship with Lady Harume was . . . shall we say . . . less than innocent," Ryuko reminded Keisho-in.

She let out a merry guffaw that turned into a fit of coughing, and Ryuko had to pound her back before she could continue. "Oh, my dearest, you are such a prude! What can it matter that Harume and I sometimes enjoyed a little bed sport? Surely no one could think it has anything to do with her murder!"

Sōsakan Sano might consider it relevant, if he found out about them. Gossip spread like fire in the Large Interior, and Ryuko feared that someone might let slip a careless word to Sano's detectives.

"There's nothing to worry about, dearest," Keisho-in said.

Did she mean she'd fixed things so well that Sano would never learn anything that could hurt her? Ryuko didn't trust his patroness to have managed this: Usually she depended on him to handle sensitive business for her. He longed to ask Lady Keisho-in a few straight questions about Harume, yet the cautious politician in him didn't really want to hear the answers. If *Sōsakan* Sano accused Lady Keisho-in of murder, then Ryuko's only defense against a conspiracy charge was a lack of compromising knowledge. So he confined himself to addressing the issue of mutual self-preservation.

"You allowed *Sōsakan* Sano access to the Large Interior without consulting me," Ryuko said. "A bit unwise, perhaps. I recommend taking steps to block his inquiries."

With a grimace of annoyance, Keisho-in waved away the suggestion. She had occasional contrary moods; unfortunately, this was one of them. "Stop talking in riddles, my dearest. Let Sano inquire all he likes. What difference does it make to me?" She puffed out her chest in self-righteous dignity. "I'm no murderer. I'm innocent."

Really? thought Ryuko. Keisho-in had a history of falling madly in love with younger men and women—like Harume. Inevitably they failed to satisfy her vast need for adoration. When the affairs ended, Lady Keisho-in would fly into a hysterical fury. Usually Ryuko could cajole her out of it, or a new romantic interest would distract her. But sometimes Keisho-in turned vindictive. Two particular incidents haunted Ryuko.

One had involved a concubine named Peach; the other, a palace guard. Both had suddenly vanished from Edo Castle after disappointing Lady Keisho-in. Ryuko's informants had told him that Keisho-in had complained about her lovers to the Tokugawa high military command. However, no one seemed to know where Peach and the guard had gone, or whether they were still alive. Ryuko guessed that Lady Keisho-in had ordered the pair's murders. If Sano ever learned of this, he would think she'd arranged a similar revenge against Lady Harume. Ryuko had to make her see the danger she courted by abetting Sano's investigation.

"Harume spent considerable time in His Excellency's bedchamber," Ryuko said. "What if she had become pregnant?"

Looking puzzled, Lady Keisho-in said, "That's what my son wanted, and what I wanted, too. Why else would I have urged him to do all this?" She looked around the clearing, where the architects busily conferred and the woodsmen sawed.

Ryuko could think of another reason why she'd championed the kennels. Showing mercy toward dogs would bring Tokugawa Tsunayoshi good luck, but the shogun must do his part to beget a son. Was Lady Keisho-in encouraging spiritual actions in the hope that he would neglect the physical ones?

"Let me put it another way." Pacing the ground, Ryuko mustered his fading patience. "What do you think will happen to you if an heir is born?"

Lady Keisho-in laughed. "I'll be the happiest grandmother in the world." Cradling her arms around an imaginary infant, she made cooing noises.

Was she as naïve as she seemed? All marriages harbored secrets, and their union, Ryuko realized, was no exception. Forced to speak crudely, he said, "If Lady Harume had borne His Excellency an heir, she would have become his official consort. She would have supplanted you as the highest-ranking woman in Japan."

"That would be just a formality." Lady Keisho-in folded her arms, haughty with annoyance now. "I am Tsunayoshi's mother. No other woman could ever replace me in his affections. He depends on my counsel. Why, he couldn't lead the country without me!"

"Your son does not enjoy the responsibilities of being shogun," Ryuko said, avoiding the issue of whether or not Tokugawa Tsunayoshi led the country at all. "He would rather occupy himself with religion or the theater." *Or boys*, Ryuko thought, but did not add. Lady Keisho-in refused to admit her son's preference for manly love. "With the arrival of an heir, the succession would have been secure. His Excellency might have used this as an excuse to abdicate his position and appoint a council of regents to head the government until the boy came of age."

This prediction of the shogun's behavior was shared by many astute *bakufu* members, but Lady Keisho-in's features bunched in a stubborn pout. "Ridiculous! My son is a dedicated leader. He won't retire until death takes him from this world. And he doesn't need a council to run the government while he has his mother to advise him. He loves and trusts me."

However, Tokugawa Tsunayoshi also trusted Sano; Ryuko had watched the *sōsakan*'s influence grow daily. Even a hint of suspicion might jeopardize Keisho-in's relationship with the shogun, who feared and abhorred violence. If he thought she might be a murderer, he might turn away from her and seek another woman to act as mother-confidant—probably Lady Ichiteru. The devious concubine had regained his favor since Harume's death, had already borne him two sons, albeit stillborn, and would seize the chance to improve her position.

And then what would happen to Ryuko?

"Please, my lady," he said. "Just suppose there was an heir, and your son did retire. Who would have more influence over the regent council? You, the mother of a past, retired shogun? Or the mother of the future one?"

Ryuko's suave voice harshened with agitation, and he bent over Keisho-in, grasping her hands. "If Harume had lived, you might have lost your position as ruler of the Large Interior, your privileges, your power. *Sōsakan* Sano will realize this eventually, if he hasn't already. You stand to become his prime murder suspect!"

Across the clearing, a huge oak crashed to the ground. Its branches swayed and rustled: the death throes of a giant. Peasants began sawing up and hauling away the tree's corpse. As Lady Keisho-in watched, her face took on a crafty, calculating expression that Ryuko had never seen before. She looked positively intelligent. A chill finger of dismay touched Ryuko. Was she finally becoming aware of her precarious position?

Or had she known all along?

Slowly Lady Keisho-in turned to Ryuko. She pulled him to his knees so that their faces were almost touching. All traces of good-natured silliness had disappeared from hers. "Tell me, my dearest," she said. Her gaze bored into Ryuko. "Are you so concerned about the murder investigation for my sake, or your own? Have you been up to something?"

The words, spoken on a vapor of breath that stank of tobacco and rotten teeth, wafted over Ryuko. Shock disoriented him. He envisioned battlefields after a war, with the wind carrying the odor of carnage. Despite all his efforts in the cause of charity and spiritual enlightenment, there had been incidents in his life that illustrated his greed, ambition, and ruthlessness. What if Sano found out? Surely he would suspect Ryuko of murdering Harume on Keisho-in's behalf in order to protect her and, simultaneously, his own position. Yet even as he imagined himself at the execution ground, the wily politician in Ryuko saw a way to use the situation to his advantage.

"Yes, my lady," he said, bowing his head as if in shameful confession. It wasn't a lie. He'd devised and carried out plots designed to further his interests and Keisho-in's, with and without her approval. He wondered how much she knew or guessed about him—and how much her poor memory had allowed her to forget about things they'd done together. If he was charged with Lady Harume's murder, would Keisho-in sacrifice him to save herself? "I'm afraid *Sōsakan* Sano will discover what I've done."

To his joy, Keisho-in responded just as Ryuko had hoped. She enfolded him in a suffocating embrace and declared, "I don't care if you've done anything wrong, especially if you did it for me. I love you, and I'll stand by you." Ryuko hid a smile against Keisho-in's breast. Let her believe—or pretend to believe—he'd killed Harume, if that was what it took to secure her complicity. Now they both would be safe from accusations of murder and treason. "As long as I live, no one shall harm a hair on your head!"

Patting Ryuko's shaven scalp, Lady Keisho-in giggled at her own joke, then said, "I'm cold, and this tree stump is hurting my bottom. Let's go back to Edo Castle. When we get there, I'll fix *Sōsakan* Sano. Just tell me what to do. You needn't worry about anything, my dearest."

21

Sano disembarked from the ferry that had transported him across the Sumida River to Fukagawa, birthplace of Lady Harume. Located at the mouth of the river where it emptied into Edo Bay, this suburb stood on former swamps filled in with vast heaps of city garbage and earth excavated during the construction of canals. After the Great Fire, many citizens had moved here for a fresh start. However, Fukagawa retained the hazards of its geographic situation. Floods, typhoons, and high tides wrought mass destruction. The area was rightfully considered unlucky. Here Lady Harume had made an inauspicious start on a life that would end with her murder eighteen years later.

The approach to the town center led Sano past warehouses that smelled of pine timber, sesame oil, and *hoshika,* a fertilizer made from sardines. Smoke from salt furnaces on the southern tidal flats obscured the view of Edo on the opposite shore. The cold air had a lung-saturating dampness. A busy commercial district lined the main avenue leading to the Tomioka Hachiman Shrine. This contained the Oka Basho, a notorious unlicensed quarter where nighthawk prostitutes operated. Teahouses and inns abounded, as well as Fukagawa's excellent seafood restaurants.

Hearing temple bells ring the noon hour, Sano realized he was hungry. He entered the Hirasei, a famous restaurant located just outside the shrine's torii gate. There he ate mixed sushi with vegetables, rice, and grilled trout. Then he said to the proprietor, "I'm looking for a nighthawk named Blue Apple. Can you tell me where to find her?"

The proprietor shook his head. "I don't know of anyone by that name. You might try the teahouses."

Sano did, with disappointing results: No one had ever

heard of Blue Apple; no one knew Lady Harume, except as the victim of a widely publicized murder. Sano headed toward the Hachiman Shrine. Its great copper-tiled roof rose above the streets like a giant samurai helmet; its high stone walls sheltered the Etai Temple, whose priests kept census records on everyone living in the district. They, if anyone, could direct Sano to Blue Apple.

"Her real name was Yasuko," said the old priest.

He and Sano stood in the Etai Temple cemetery, where Sano had finally located Lady Harume's mother. Her moss-covered stone memorial tablet lay in the area reserved for paupers. No flowers adorned these graves. Tall grass obscured paths down which visitors rarely came. The place had an air of bleak, chill desolation. Shivering under his cloak, Sano listened to the priest's recollections of Blue Apple, dead for twelve years.

"She came here for shelter during the floods, and I remember her because of her unique situation. Most nighthawks have no one to care for them. Their clients are usually poor, and mostly strangers rather than regular customers. But Yasuko was beautiful and much sought after. Her professional name came from the bluish, apple-shaped birthmark on her wrist. She was a trusting creature who often took lovers and tattooed herself with their names. When I prepared her body for cremation, I found characters inked between all her fingers and toes."

And following her example had led her daughter Harume to her death.

"Yasuko won the affection of Jimba of Bakurochō when he came to Fukagawa on business," the priest said. "After the child was born, he regularly sent money. Then Blue Apple became ill. She lost her looks—and her better clients. She serviced former criminals, and even *eta* to earn her rice. When she died, I brought the child, who was six years old, to our orphanage. Then I contacted Jimba. He took her home with him to Bakurochō."

The priest sighed. "I've often wondered what became of her." When Sano explained, distress shadowed his kind face. "How tragic." Then he said, "Still, perhaps Harume enjoyed a better, longer life than if she'd stayed in Fukagawa and become a nighthawk like her mother."

Sano had never given much thought to how few occupations were available for women. Now, with disturbing clarity, he saw the narrow scope of their lives: wife, servant, nun, concubine, prostitute, beggar. There was honor—and possibly happiness—in marriage and motherhood, but not even those alternatives offered the chance for independence, or scholarship, martial arts, adventure, or accomplishments that made life worthwhile for men. Uneasily Sano thought of Reiko, struggling to escape the confines of Japanese culture, and his own efforts to contain her. Men made the rules. He, himself, was part of a system that had decreed his wife's limited existence.

And Lady Harume's.

Such contemplation wasn't exactly enjoyable. Sano thanked the priest, then left the temple. Yet even as he regretted the time wasted on this trip, he couldn't help feeling that he'd learned something of importance to the murder case, and to his troubled marriage.

Bakurochō district lay northwest of Edo Castle, between the Nihonbashi merchant quarter and the Kanda River. A marketplace for horses even before the founding of the Tokugawa capital, it supplied Edo's thirty thousand samurai with mounts. Sano rode through muddy streets, past horse breeders herding their merchandise. These shaggy, varicolored beasts had journeyed from far northern pasturelands to be sold to the stables of Bakurochō's dealers. In a stately mansion resided the Tokugawa bailiffs, who administered the shogun's lands. Rustic inns housed provincial officials in town to buy horses or do business with the bailiffs. The famous archery range served as a front for an illegal brothel. Low wooden buildings housed food stalls, teahouses, a saddle maker's store, a blacksmith's workshop where burly men hammered out horseshoes. Porters hauled bales of hay, while *eta* street cleaners collected manure. Sano turned past the shop of an equestrian armorer and dismounted outside the Jimba Stables, where the crest of a galloping horse adorned the gate.

An assistant hurried out and bowed. "Good day, *sōsakan-sama*. Are you seeking a new mount?"

"I'm here to see Jimba," Sano said.

"Certainly. Come in."

Taking the reins of Sano's horse, the assistant led the way into the largest stable compound in Bakurochō. Gabled tile roofs crowned the fine Jimba family mansion, two stories of pristine white plaster walls, latticed windows, and railed balconies, with servants' quarters at the rear. A far cry from the Fukagawa slum of Harume's birth, Sano decided. Had the adjustment been difficult for her?

Opposite the mansion stretched the corral. Around this, poles supported straw dummies. The barn's open doors revealed stablehands grooming horses. The assistant led Sano to a stall where three samurai stood around a dappled gray stallion. A big man dressed in dark brown kimono and wide trousers held the animal by the head.

"You can tell he's healthy by the condition of his mouth," Jimba said, prying the lips apart to expose huge teeth. His thick fingers moved with practiced skill. At Sano's approach, he looked up; his face lit in pleased recognition. "Ah, *sōsakan-sama*. Good to see you again."

In his mid-forties, Jimba looked as vigorous as his livestock. A thick, sinewy column of neck supported his squarish head. His hair, pulled back from a receding hairline and knotted at the nape, showed only a few white threads. In his coarse features and swarthy complexion Sano could discern no resemblance to Lady Harume.

Jimba grinned, revealing three broken front teeth: a permanent reminder of the one time a horse had gotten the better of him. "Congratulations on your marriage. Ready to enlarge your clan? Ha-ha. What can I do for you today?" Leaving the assistant to complete the sale, he led Sano down the row of stalls. "A good racehorse, perhaps? Impress your friends at Edo Castle. Ha-ha."

Sano had never liked the ingratiating, overly familiar dealer, but he patronized Jimba's stable for the same reason other affluent samurai did: The dealer knew horses. He always picked strong, healthy animals and trained them to be fast, reliable mounts. He gave good value for the price, and never tried to pass off inferior mounts as top quality.

"I'm here about your daughter," Sano said. "As head of the investigation into her death, I must ask you some questions. But first, please allow me to express my sympathy for your loss."

Stalking over to the fence that bordered the corral, Jimba punched it with his fist, muttering a curse. A scowl obliterated his customary genial expression as he stared at a trio of stablehands preparing a horse for a test ride in full battle regalia. They affixed a wooden saddle to its back, then attached the bridle. Sano, having witnessed angry grief in the parents of murder victims before, said, "I'll do everything possible to deliver Harume's killer to justice."

Jimba waved away Sano's words. "Lot of good that will do. She's gone; nothing can bring her back. Ten years of money and hard work I poured into that girl. When her mother died, I took her away from Fukagawa and raised her myself. Put nice clothes on her; hired tutors to teach her music, writing, and manners. I recognized her potential, you see—I know females, horses and women both. Ha-ha." Jimba grinned proudly. "Harume was the prettiest of my three girls. She grew up to have what men like, if you know what I mean." He gave Sano a sly look. "Took after her mother. She was my best chance of making a connection with the Tokugawa."

Sano listened in dismay to the dealer's callous reference to his daughter. He'd obviously considered her less a cherished legacy from a doomed love affair than another piece of livestock to train and trade.

In the corral, the stablehands covered the horse with body armor and a steel helmet shaped like a snarling dragon's head. Two samurai helped the customer don armor tunic, leg guards, and helmet. Jimba continued, "Last winter, two of the shogun's personal attendants came here to buy horses. They mentioned that they were seeking new concubines for His Excellency. I put Harume through her paces, showing them how well she could speak and sing and play the samisen. They took her to Edo Castle and paid me five thousand *koban*!

"I held a party to celebrate. Harume had good breeding

capacity, and if she turned out to be anything like her mother was in the bedchamber, she could have borne His Excellency an heir. Even if he does prefer boys, ha-ha. I was all set to be the grandfather of the next shogun."

With all the associated wealth, power, and privilege, Sano thought. Jimba's greed disgusted him. Yet the horse dealer had only followed the example of many other Japanese, seeking to improve his position through a connection with the Tokugawa. Hadn't Magistrate Ueda married Reiko to Sano with the same goal in mind? In this society, women were chattel to men's ambition. Reiko was intelligent and courageous, yet people would always measure her worth by rank and childbearing ability. Now Sano began to understand her frustration. But after last night, he hoped more than ever that Reiko would obey his orders and stay safe at home.

"Now Harume is dead. I'll never earn back my investment." Jimba's expression was morose; he sagged against the fence. Then he turned to Sano with a speculative glint in his close-set eyes. "On second thought, maybe it will do me some good if you find out who killed my daughter. I'll make him compensate me for my loss!"

Hiding his aversion toward the horse dealer's mercenary attitude, Sano said, "Perhaps you can help me catch the murderer," then explained why he'd come. "What was Harume like?" When Jimba began describing her looks, Sano clarified, "No, I mean what sort of person was she?"

"Just like any other girl, I guess." Jimba looked surprised at the notion that Harume had possessed other attributes besides physical ones. Then, as he watched the stablehands boost the armored rider onto the horse's back, he smiled in reminiscence. "She was a tiny, sad little thing when I brought her here. She didn't understand that her mother was gone, or why I was taking her away from everything she knew. And she missed her friends—the little slum children from Fukagawa. She never really fit in here."

With a wry chuckle, Jimba said, "I'd never told my wife about Blue Apple, you see. Then suddenly, here was this child. She was furious. And my other children resented the attention Harume got. They mocked her for being the daughter of a whore. Her only friends were the maids. Considered them her own kind, I guess. But I put a stop to that. I wanted to separate her from low-class folk who would keep her down at their level. And when she got to be around eleven, the boys started coming around. She drew them like a mare in heat, ha-ha. She was the image of her mother."

Nostalgia softened Jimba's features: perhaps he had in his own way loved Blue Apple. After all, he'd supported their daughter, then adopted her when another man might have turned his back. "Harume started sneaking out of the house at night. I had to hire a chaperone so she wouldn't go and get pregnant by some peasant boy. By the time she was fourteen, she was getting marriage proposals from rich merchants. But I knew I could do better with her."

Imagining Harume's lonely childhood, Sano pitied the concubine. She'd gone from being an outcast in Bakurochō to a similar situation in the Large Interior. As a young girl she'd found solace in the company of male admirers. Apparently she'd followed the same pattern during her months at Edo Castle. Had her past overlapped her recent life in any other way?

"Those peasants Harume knew," Sano said. "Did she keep in touch with any of them after she moved to Edo Castle?" Sano wanted to know if she'd confided secrets to old companions. He also wanted new motives and suspects for her murder—preferably ones not associated with the Tokugawa.

"I don't see how she could have, locked up day after day. Even when she went out, the shogun's men keep a pretty close watch over the concubines."

Yet Harume had managed to slip away and meet Lord Miyagi. Still, a peasant wouldn't have had access to the ink bottle. This line of inquiry seemed a dead end. "Had you seen or heard from your daughter recently?" Sano asked.

An uneasy expression came over the horse dealer's face. ". . . Yes. I got a message from Harume about three months ago. She begged me to get her out of Edo. Said she was afraid. Seems she'd run afoul of someone—I don't remember her exact words. Anyway, she thought something bad would happen to her if she didn't leave right away."

Sano's heart beat faster in anticipation and dread. "Did Harume say whom she was afraid of?"

Jimba blinked rapidly; his throat muscles spasmed. So he did have feelings toward the daughter he'd used to further his ambitions. To give him time to regain his composure, Sano looked over at the mounted samurai, who was circling the corral at a trot. Watching him wave a spear, Sano thought of Lieutenant Kushida. By blaming Kushida for Lady Harume's murder, Sano could please the shogun and end the investigation. Yet by following Harume's elusive ghost into the past, Sano had already moved beyond the point of easy solutions.

"No," Jimba replied at last, with a grimace of regret. "Harume didn't give the name of the person who was threatening her. I thought she was homesick, or didn't like bedding the shogun, and had made up a story so I would rescue her. Sometimes it takes awhile for a filly to get used to a new stable. Ha-ha." His laugh was a gloomy chortle. "I didn't want to return the money, or ask the shogun to let Harume go. That would have offended His Excellency. I would never get any Tokugawa business again! And people would know it was Harume's fault. How would I ever find a husband for her? She would have been a burden to me forever!"

The horse dealer's voice rose in a defensive whine. "So I didn't answer the message. I didn't bother trying to find out whether someone was really trying to hurt Harume. Thought that if I ignored her, she would do her duty without complaining."

"Did you save the message? May I look at it?"

"It wasn't written. It was delivered by a castle messenger, by word of mouth." When questioned about the messenger, Jimba said, "Didn't get his name. Don't remember what he looked like."

Edo Castle had several hundred messengers, Sano knew. Tracing this one might prove difficult, especially if Harume, desiring secrecy, had persuaded a messenger to convey her words verbally as a favor, rather than writing a letter and employing him through official channels, which would leave a record.

"Was anyone else present when the message came?" Sano asked.

"No. And I didn't tell anyone about it, either, because I didn't want people to think Harume was making trouble. Then, after she died, I was too ashamed to let anyone know she'd been in danger and I'd refused to listen."

Although Sano would have his detectives look for the messenger in question, he could only hope that the man's recall was better than Jimba's.

"I am responsible for my daughter's death," Jimba lamented, folding his arms on top of the fence and burying his head in them. "If only I'd taken her fears seriously, I might have saved her." A sob strangled his voice.

Suppressing the urge to castigate the horse dealer for ignoring his daughter's plea for help, Sano said soothingly, "You couldn't have known what would happen."

Jimba raised a face bloated with tears and rage. "What a fool I am!" He cuffed himself on the head. "I could kill myself! I trained and groomed that girl. She was a prime piece of flesh. Through her, I could have joined the Tokugawa clan. I should have gone to the *bakufu* and asked them to find out what was wrong in the Large Interior, and to take care of the problem. But no, I failed to protect my investment. Stupid, stupid!"

Sano let him rage without offering further sympathy. Jimba had earned his own fate. And Sano had grave problems of his own.

Around the corral galloped the mounted samurai. He wove between the rows of targets, stabbing at them with his spear. Straw particles dusted the air. At last the rider grasped the reins and brought the horse to a stop beside his waiting spectators.

"This is a fine beast," he said. "I'll take her."

Suddenly the horse bucked. The rider sailed over its head and crashed to the ground. While his comrades rushed to his aid, the stablehands grabbed the reins. The horse kicked and strained, biting at their hands. Jimba vaulted the fence and hurried over to his fallen customer.

"The horse is just a bit skittish today," he explained. "Once she knows you're her master, she'll behave!"

Even a tame creature sometimes rebels against a lifetime of discipline, Sano thought. Jimba had trained the wildness out of Harume; yet she hadn't been completely controllable. Sano believed that her message to Jimba hadn't been a mere ruse. She'd made an enemy who had the power, opportunity, and temperament to harm a concubine of the shogun. Of all the murder suspects, who best fit the profile?

Beneath Sano's sash, Lady Keisho-in's letter burned him like a sheet of flame. She ruled the Large Interior and commanded the shogun's love. With the help of allies within the Tokugawa regime, she could have easily managed the murder, as well as an earlier poisoning attempt, and a dagger thrown by a hired assassin in a crowded street.

Now Jimba's evidence strengthened the case against her. Must Sano accuse Lady Keisho-in of murder—and bring grave peril upon himself?

The paper in Hirata's hand read:

INTERROGATION PLAN

1. Determine Lady Ichiteru's true feelings toward Harume.
2. Find out where Lady Ichiteru was during the dagger attack and possible earlier poisoning attempt on Harume.
3. Has Lady Ichiteru ever bought poison?
4. Had Lady Ichiteru been in Harume's room after the ink bottle and Lord Miyagi's letter arrived?
5. Check Lady Ichiteru's statement by asking Midori the same questions.

As Hirata rode across the Ryōgoku Bridge, he divided his attention between steering his horse past a band of porters hauling wood from the Honjo lumber yards and studying the plan for his second interview with Lady Ichiteru. He mumbled the directions scribbled in the margins. "Interview suspect at Edo Castle, not at the theater." "Do not let suspect evade questions." "If suspect makes lewd remarks, order her to stop." "Do not think about sex while interviewing suspect." "Above all, do *not* let suspect touch you!"

To fill a big hole in the fabric of the murder investigation, he must extract the relevant information from Lady Ichiteru. He had to correct his slip-up before Sano found out and lost trust in him. He wanted to rebuild his former image of himself as a good detective. And he desperately needed something to make up for the disappointing results of his other inquiries.

Yesterday the detective corps had failed to locate either the Indian arrow toxin or the elusive drug peddler, Choyei. This morning Hirata had sent them out to interrogate contacts within Edo's criminal underworld. He'd just revisited police headquarters, to no avail. There seemed little hope of solving the case by tracing the poison. Sano didn't believe Lieutenant Kushida was guilty. Failure would bring severe punishment. Everything might depend on Hirata's handling of the interview with Lady Ichiteru.

He'd spent a restless night, alternating between vivid, erotic dreams of her and wakeful bouts of self-recrimination. What a fool he was to let her trick him! After the capture of Lieutenant Kushida, he'd given up on sleep and formulated his plan for the interview. Now he would continue the search for Choyei while memorizing the plan and strengthening his resolve to withstand Lady Ichiteru's charms.

Yet even as Hirata tucked the paper under his sash for later reference, he yearned for Lady Ichiteru. In his memory, he heard her soft, husky voice, felt the warmth of her seductive gaze and the thrilling touch of her hand. Immediately a wave of heat swept his body. And beneath the excitement, he experienced the humiliating knowledge of his social inferiority, the helplessness of his desire.

"Watch out, master!"

The warning, called out by a passing stranger, snapped Hirata out of his thoughts. He looked up and saw that he'd passed the end of the bridge. His horse was meandering down the street, trampling wares set out for sale by itinerant vendors. Quickly Hirata reined in his mount. "My apologies," he said, increasingly worried about the upcoming interview. How would he get the truth from Lady Ichiteru if even the mere thought of her ruined his concentration?

Reaching the Honjo Mukō Ryōgoku entertainment district, he found the revelry undiminished by the dreary weather. A theater troupe improvised comedies in the street, before a large, noisy audience; business flourished in the teahouses and restaurants. But the freak show was closed, its platform empty and sliding doors pulled over the entrance. A sign outside read, NO PERFORMANCE TODAY. Hirata's spirits fell. If the Rat was out roaming the town, he could be gone for hours, even days. So much for leads on the poison dealer.

Then, as Hirata turned his horse back toward the bridge, he spotted a familiar figure amid the pleasure seekers. It was the bald giant who served as the Rat's bodyguard and collected admission fees at the shows. He headed down the firebreak, past the gambling dens and curiosity shows. Hirata followed. Maybe the giant could tell him where the Rat was.

The giant vanished into a gap between the wild animal menagerie and a noodle stall. A mob of drunks reeled in front of Hirata, blocking his way, and by the time he reached the gap, the giant was nowhere in sight. Hirata dismounted and secured his horse to a post. He walked down the narrow passage, which smelled of urine and led to an alley that ran behind the buildings. Roars emanated from the menagerie; steam wafted from restaurant kitchens; stray dogs foraged in malodorous garbage bins. Otherwise, the alley was deserted.

Hirata hurried past the closed rear doors of businesses. Then he heard voices: the Rat's rustic accent, and someone else's muffled tones. They came from the back room of a teahouse. Hirata peered through the barred window.

Ceramic sake urns lined the room. The Rat knelt on the floor, his back to Hirata, his shaggy head nodding as he listened to the woman seated opposite him. A cloak veiled her hair and body. In the faint daylight from the window, Hirata could just make out her face: plain and not young, with blackened teeth.

"The deal will benefit both of us," she said in a low, pleading voice. "My family will have peace, and your business will prosper."

"All right. Five hundred *koban,* and that's my final price," answered the Rat.

The woman bowed her head. "Very well. If you'll come with me, we'll get it now."

Having seen the Rat conduct this type of negotiation before, Hirata guessed what was going on. He raised a hand to knock on the door. Then a change in the atmosphere warned him of another human presence in the alley. He whirled. Strong hands grabbed his shoulders, lifting him off the ground. He found himself face to face with the Rat's giant.

"I'm here to see your master," Hirata explained, struggling in the man's iron grip. "Put me down!"

An evil grin split the giant's face. With dismay Hirata remembered that he was a deaf mute. He threw Hirata against the wall with a jarring crash. Hirata drew his sword. Then the door screeched open.

"What's going on?" demanded the Rat. Seeing Hirata facing off against his servant, he rushed outside, ordering, "Stop, Kyojin!"

The giant made gurgling sounds while pointing at the window, trying to say he'd caught Hirata spying.

"This man is police." Speaking with exaggerated lip movements, the Rat gestured in what seemed a private form of sign language. "Lay off before he kills you and arrests me!"

Glowering, the giant retreated. Hirata relaxed and sheathed his sword. "How nice to see you again so soon," said the Rat, with an insincere grin. "What can I do for you today?"

"Have you found Choyei, the drug peddler?"

Glancing nervously toward the open door, the Rat pawed at his whiskers. "I don't have time to talk now; I'm right in the middle of some business." He did a double take and rushed into the teahouse's back room, then came out muttering curses. "She's gone—must have slipped out the other way." Then he shrugged. "Oh, well. She'll be back. She's selling her deformed child to my freak show," he explained, confirming Hirata's guess. "Poor thing was born with no feet. Who else would want it except me? Now what were you saying?"

"The drug peddler," Hirata prompted.

"Ah." The Rat's sly little eyes gleamed through strands of long, untidy hair. "I'm afraid I couldn't find him. Sorry."

"But it's only been one day," Hirata said. "How far could you have looked in that time?"

"The Rat has eyes and ears all over Edo. If they haven't

picked up on Choyei by now, then either he's left town or was never here in the first place."

If his best informant couldn't find the possible source of the poison, then this lead was a dead end, Hirata thought. Disappointment turned to anger. "I paid you good money," he said, grabbing the Rat's collar. The giant moved toward him. "Are you reneging on our deal?"

"Stay, Kyojin! Oh, no. Not at all!" The Rat quickly reached into the pouch at his waist and extracted a handful of coins, which he gave Hirata. "Here you go. A full refund, with my apologies."

Suspicion deepened Hirata's anger as he stuffed the coins in his own pouch. Since when had the Rat ever voluntarily relinquished money? "Are you trying to trick me?" He shook the freak-show proprietor until his head bobbled. "Did Choyei pay you off?"

"No, no! Honest!"

The Rat struggled. The giant grabbed Hirata. A three-way tussle ensued. Finally Hirata gave up and let go. "If I find out you lied to me, you'll be arrested. And jailed. And beaten!" He underscored each threat by jabbing the Rat's chest with his fist. Then he stalked down the alley to retrieve his horse.

It was time to confront Lady Ichiteru.

By the time Hirata arrived back at Edo Castle, he was almost ill with eagerness to see Lady Ichiteru again. His skin felt feverish; his hands trembled as he rode through the main gate; anticipation evoked arousal. Realizing that he shouldn't face Lady Ichiteru alone in his condition, he stopped at Sano's mansion and fetched two detectives to accompany him. Their presence would ensure that he stuck to his plan and Lady Ichiteru behaved properly. But just as Hirata and the detectives were leaving the barracks, a servant hurried up.

"This came while you were gone, master," he said, proffering a small lacquer scroll case.

Hirata took it and withdrew a letter. As he read, his heart began to pound.

I have vitally important information relating to Lady Harume's murder. It is imperative that I speak to you—but not today, and not here at Edo Castle. For the wrong people to overhear what I must impart would endanger my life. Please meet me tomorrow at the hour of the sheep, at the location described below.

And please come alone.

It is with more than ordinary pleasure that I look forward to seeing you again.

Lady Ichiteru

A map followed, with directions written in the same elegant, feminine hand as the message. The creamy white rice paper had the softness of living flesh. Moistened by Hirata's suddenly sweaty hands, it gave off the scent of Lady Ichiteru's perfume. Impulsively he pressed it against his face. As the smell evoked erotic memories, he forgot the day's disappointments. Lady Ichiteru wanted to see him again! Did not her closing words imply that she shared his feelings? His spirits soared. He laughed aloud.

"Hirata-*san*? What are you doing?"

Hirata looked up to see the detectives watching him with concern. "Nothing," he said, hastily cramming the letter into the scroll case.

"Are we going to visit Lady Ichiteru now?" asked one of the men.

All Hirata's police instincts told him to stick to the plan he'd devised and avoid letting a murder suspect manipulate him. *She's up to no good*, said his inner voice. Yet Hirata couldn't endanger Lady Ichiteru by forcing her to give evidence within hearing of spies. And he yearned to explore the full potential of an acquaintance with her—outside Edo Castle's confines, free from the constraints of duty and prudence.

"No," he said at last. "I'm postponing the interview until tomorrow." Then he would decide whether to accept Lady Ichiteru's invitation. Deep inside Hirata, seven years of detective experience clamored in warning. "Dismissed."

The inner palace precinct was strangely vacant even for a cold autumn evening when Sano and Hirata traversed the garden. Cherry trees raised bare, black branches to a soot-colored sky; moisture gleamed on the surfaces of boulders; fallen leaves matted the grass. A lone patrol guard made his rounds. Taking advantage of their momentary privacy before reporting to the shogun, Sano shared the results of his inquiries and passed Hirata the letter from Lady Harume's room.

Hirata read, and whistled through his teeth. "Will you show this to the shogun?"

"Have I got a choice?" Sano said grimly, replacing the letter under his sash.

At the palace door, the guard said, "His Excellency is in a special emergency session with the Council of Elders. They await your report in the Grand Audience Hall."

Dismay washed through Sano like an icy tide. Council meetings invariably meant trouble for him. He wished he could postpone his report and the inevitable repercussions, but there seemed no chance of reprieve. With Hirata beside him, he proceeded down the palace corridors. Sentries opened massive double doors carved with scowling guardian deities. Sano took a deep breath. He and Hirata entered.

Glowing lanterns hung from the coffered ceiling. Tokugawa Tsunayoshi knelt upon the dais. A gilded landscape mural set off his black ceremonial robes. Chamberlain Yanagisawa occupied his usual place at the shogun's right, on the higher of the floor's two levels. Near him on the same level, the five elders knelt in two facing rows, at right angles to their lord. However, the secretaries were absent. Only the shogun's chief attendant served tea and brought tobacco and metal baskets of lit coals for pipes. The law barred all unnecessary personnel from special emergency sessions.

As Sano and Hirata knelt at the back of the room, Senior Elder Makino Narisada said, "Your Excellency, we apologize for requesting a meeting on such short notice, but the murder of Lady Harume has caused some disturbing incidents. The chief commander of the Large Interior has committed *seppuku* to atone for allowing a murder to take place during his watch. Rumors and accusations are rampant. One concerns Kato Yuichi, junior member of the judicial council. His fellow member and rival, Sagara Fumio, spread a story that Kato killed Lady Harume as practice for a mass poisoning of high officials. Kato confronted Sagara. They dueled. Now both men are dead, and the judicial council is in turmoil, with scores of men vying for the vacant positions."

It was just as Sano had feared: The murder had ignited emotions within the *bakufu,* a gunpowder arsenal waiting to explode. The dreaded nightmare of past investigations had returned—because he hadn't solved the case soon enough, more deaths had occurred.

"Other minor problems have caused inconvenience," Makino said. "Many people refuse to believe that a mere concubine was the murderer's only target. No one wants to eat or drink here." He eyed the untouched tea bowls in front of his colleagues. "Servants have abandoned their posts. Officials have fled Edo, ostensibly on business in the provinces." So that was why the palace seemed empty, Sano realized. "At this rate, there will soon be no one left to run the capital. Your Excellency, I recommend strong action to avert disaster."

Tokugawa Tsunayoshi, who had been shrinking farther and farther into himself as the senior elder spoke, threw up his hands in despair. "Why, ahh, I hardly know what to do," he said. Looking around for help, he caught sight of Sano. "Ahh!" he exclaimed, beckoning. "Here is the man who can restore matters to normal. *Sōsakan* Sano, please tell us you've identified Lady Harume's killer!"

Accompanied by Hirata, Sano reluctantly approached

the dais. They knelt before the upper floor level, bowing to the assembly. "I regret to say that the murder investigation is not yet complete, Your Excellency," Sano said. He glanced uncomfortably at Chamberlain Yanagisawa, who would surely seize this opportunity to denigrate him. However, Yanagisawa seemed preoccupied, his dark gaze turned inward. Feeling more confident, Sano began relating the progress of the case.

Senior Elder Makino assumed Chamberlain Yanagisawa's usual role of detractor. "So you haven't traced the poison yet. Lieutenant Kushida is under arrest for attacking you and trying to steal evidence, but you're not convinced he's the killer. That strikes me as extremely indecisive. What about Lady Ichiteru?"

Hirata cleared his throat and said, "*Sumimasen*—excuse me. We have no evidence against her."

Sano eyed him with consternation. Hirata never spoke at these meetings unless addressed directly, and as far as Sano knew, there was no evidence proving Lady Ichiteru's innocence, either. He couldn't contradict Hirata in front of the assembly, but as soon as they were alone, Sano intended to find out exactly what had happened during Hirata's interview with Lady Ichiteru—and what was causing his strange behavior.

"Well, if the killer is neither Lieutenant Kushida nor Lady Ichiteru," Makino said, "then you now have two fewer suspects than you did yesterday." He turned to Chamberlain Yanagisawa. "A step backward, wouldn't you agree?"

Stirred out of his private contemplation, Yanagisawa rebuked Makino: "A difficult case like this requires more than two days to close. What do you expect, miracles? Give the *sōsakan* time, and he'll succeed, as usual."

The senior elder's mouth dropped. Sano stared in amazement. Chamberlain Yanagisawa standing up for him at a council meeting? Sano's suspicion of his enemy increased. Was Yanagisawa encouraging Sano to follow the present course of the investigation because it led away from something he wished to hide? However, none of the findings had implicated Yanagisawa in the murder. None of Sano's informants had reported a new plot against him.

"I've found the source of the ink," Sano said. "Lord Miyagi admits sending it to Harume, along with a letter instructing her to tattoo his name on her body." He described the daimyo's liaison with the concubine, and Lady Miyagi's complicity.

Tokugawa Tsunayoshi sputtered in outrage. "Miyagi violated my concubine, then killed her? Disgraceful! Arrest him at once!"

"There's no proof that he poisoned the ink," Sano said. "It could have been done by someone else, either at the Miyagi estate, here in Edo Castle, or somewhere along the way. For now, Lord and Lady Miyagi remain under scrutiny. And I've started checking into Harume's background, because it's possible that the roots of her murder lie there. I've interviewed her father . . . and searched her room."

Sano heard Hirata's sharp intake of breath. Lady Keisho-in's letter felt like a metal blade cutting into his flesh. Duty required that Sano report all facts to the shogun, yet he hesitated. A Japanese citizen incriminated a member of the Tokugawa clan at his own peril. Any offensive word or action could be perceived as an attack against the shogun himself. Whether or not Lady Keisho-in had killed Harume didn't change this. For accusing the shogun's mother, rightly or wrongly, Sano could be charged with treason, then executed as punishment.

"A brilliant strategy," Chamberlain Yanagisawa said, his eyes sparkling with enthusiasm. "What have you learned?"

Now was the time to present Lady Keisho-in's letter and Jimba's statement. Now was the time for samurai courage. Sano struggled with himself. His spirit quailed; his stomach roiled. "I have a better sense of Lady Harume's character, which will help me understand how she might have provoked murder," he stalled. He didn't mention the hair and fingernails he'd found in Lady Harume's clothing because he didn't know whether they had any bearing on the case. "And I've turned up some new leads to pursue." Deciding to wait until later in the meeting to reveal the letter, Sano cursed himself for a coward.

Hirata breathed a tentative sigh of relief at the reprieve.

Sano thought he saw disappointment on Yanagisawa's face. Senior Elder Makino was eyeing the chamberlain with a puzzled frown, obviously wondering what had become of their pact to discredit Sano. Then he continued, "So what you are telling us, *sōsakan-sama,* is that you have wasted a lot of time on studying Lady Harume, and learned nothing of significance."

For once Sano had a spectacular comeback to Makino's baiting, yet he didn't relish using it. "Nothing could be farther from the truth," he said. "Your Excellency, please prepare yourself for bad news." As an expectant hush fell over the room, Sano braced himself for the reaction. "Lady Harume was with child when she died."

A collective gasp. Then perfect silence. Though the Elders quickly hid their shock, Sano could almost hear the hum of their minds formulating theories, calculating ramifications. Tokugawa Tsunayoshi rose awkwardly, then fell to his knees again.

"My son!" he exclaimed, his eyes sunken with horror. "My long-awaited heir! Murdered in his mother's womb!"

"This is the first I've heard of the pregnancy," Makino said. "Dr. Kitano regularly examines all the concubines, but he didn't discover it." The other elders echoed their senior's skepticism. "How did you come into possession of the knowledge, *Sōsakan* Sano? Why should we believe you?"

Cold sweat ran down Sano's back. After almost two years of concealing the illicit dissections at Edo Morgue, would the secret now come out and condemn him to exile? Nausea rose in his throat as he tried to frame a convincing lie. Beside him, Hirata, who knew of Sano's transgressions, sat with head bowed, waiting for the blow to fall.

Then Chamberlain Yanagisawa said, "The fact of Lady Harume's condition is more important than *Sōsakan* Sano's method of ascertaining it. He wouldn't make a mistake on such a serious matter."

"Yes, Honorable Chamberlain." Sounding increasingly puzzled, Makino conceded defeat.

Saved, by the enemy who had tried time and again to destroy him! For a moment Sano was too grateful to question Yanagisawa's motives. Then he noticed that a peculiar change had come over the chamberlain. Yanagisawa's eyes shone with alertness; he seemed energized by the news of the unborn child's death. Sano understood that Yanagisawa might have wished it for the same reason as Lady Keisho-in. But if he hadn't known about the pregnancy, why would he have murdered Harume?

The shogun raised his fists skyward and keened, "This is an outrage!" His sobs echoed throughout the hall. And Sano had still another unpleasant topic to broach.

Choosing his words carefully, he said, "Your Excellency, there is some . . . question about the . . . parentage of Lady Harume's child. After all, she did have . . . relations with Lord Miyagi, and possibly Lieutenant Kushida. We must consider the possibility that . . ."

Turning on Sano, the shogun glared through his tears. "Nonsense! Harume was, ahh, devoted to me. She would never have let another man touch her. The child was mine. He would have succeeded me as, ahh, dictator of Japan."

The elders avoided one another's gazes. Yanagisawa remained silent in his air of contained energy. Everyone knew Tokugawa Tsunayoshi's habits, but no one dared question his virility, and the shogun himself would never admit that another man had succeeded where he'd failed.

"The murder of my heir is treason of the most, ahh, heinous kind. I must have revenge!" Scowling, Tokugawa Tsunayoshi drew his sword. For once he seemed a true descendant of the great Ieyasu, who had defeated rival warlords and unified Japan. Then the shogun dropped the sword and wept. "Alas, who would commit such a terrible crime?"

The door banged open. The assembly turned to see who dared interrupt the special emergency session. In minced Lady Keisho-in.

Aghast, Sano fought the urge to release his tension in wild laughter as he looked around the room. Did anyone else realize that here was an answer to the shogun's question? But, of course, the other men hadn't read her letter.

The elders and Chamberlain Yanagisawa bowed courteously to Lady Keisho-in, recognizing her right to do as she pleased. Simpering like a courtesan in the Yoshiwara spring parades, she bowed back. The shogun greeted his mother with a cry of gladness.

"Honorable Mother! I have just had the most, ahh, terrible shock. Come, I need your counsel!"

Lady Keisho-in crossed the room and settled upon the dais beside her son. She held his hand while he repeated Sano's news. "Tragic!" she exclaimed, pulling a fan out of her sleeve and vigorously fanning her face. "Your chance for a direct heir; mine for a grandson—ruined. Mah, mah!" she wailed. "And I didn't even know Harume was with child."

Was she feigning grief and ignorance? The letter had altered Sano's view of Lady Keisho-in as a simpleminded old woman. And he guessed that the women of the Large Interior knew more about one another than Dr. Kitano did. Keisho-in wasn't as stupid as she seemed. Had she discovered Harume's pregnancy, perceived the threat to herself, and taken action to avert it?

Sano was sure of only one thing: Keisho-in's arrival forestalled his mention of the letter. To reveal it before her and the Council of Elders would constitute the official accusation he wasn't ready to make. He needed more evidence against Lady Keisho-in first. Therefore, he must continue to bear the burden of his secret, regardless of his duty to keep Tokugawa Tsunayoshi informed. Hope lightened Sano's guilt. Perhaps further inquiries would lead him away from Lady Keisho-in.

"We were just discussing the, ahh, problems caused by the murder," Tokugawa Tsunayoshi explained to Keisho-in, "and the progress of *Sōsakan* Sano's investigation. Honorable Mother, please give us the benefit of your wisdom."

Keisho-in patted his hand. "That is just what I have come here to do. Son, you must halt the investigation and order *Sōsakan* Sano to remove his detectives from the Large Interior at once!"

Alarmed, Sano said, "But Lady Keisho-in, you yourself granted us permission to interview the residents and staff and search for evidence. And we haven't finished yet."

Among the council, eyebrows lifted; covert glances were exchanged. "With all due respect, Honorable Lady, but the

Large Interior is the scene of the crime," Senior Elder Makino said, though obviously reluctant to support Sano.

"And hence, the rightful focus of the investigation," Chamberlain Yanagisawa added. As the elders nodded assent, he watched Sano and Lady Keisho-in. A strange smile lifted one corner of his mouth.

Even the shogun looked surprised. "Honorable Mother, it is, ahh, imperative that the killer of my heir be caught and punished. How can you deny *Sōsakan* Sano any opportunity to, ahh, fulfill his mission?"

"I want the killer brought to justice as much as anyone else," Keisho-in said, "but not at the expense of peace in the Large Interior. Alas!" She wiped tears on her sleeve; her voice thickened with emotion. "Nothing can bring back the child that died with Harume. We must say good-bye to the past and plan for the future." Smiling tenderly at her son, she said, "For the sake of the succession, you must forget about revenge and concentrate on begetting a new child." She turned to the assembly. "Now permit an old woman to offer you men some advice."

With the condescending air of a nursemaid instructing a child, Keisho-in addressed Japan's supreme governing council. "The female body is very sensitive to outside influences. The weather, the phases of the moon, a quarrel, disagreeable noises, a bit of bad food—anything can upset a woman's humor. And bad humor can interfere with the flowering of a man's seed inside her womb."

Lady Keisho-in ran her hands down her stout body, then spread them against her abdomen. The elders looked down at the floor, repelled by such frank discussion of delicate matters. Chamberlain Yanagisawa gazed at Keisho-in as if fascinated. The shogun hung on his mother's words. Hirata cringed with embarrassment, but Sano felt only dread, because he guessed what Lady Keisho-in was doing.

"Conception requires tranquillity," Keisho-in continued. "With detectives trooping in and out of the Large Interior, asking questions and prying everywhere, how do you expect the concubines to get with child? Impossible!"

She rapped Tokugawa Tsunayoshi's hand with her fan. "That is why you must get rid of the detectives." Folding her arms, she gazed around the assembly, daring anyone to challenge her.

The elders frowned, but said nothing: several predecessors had lost their seats on the council for disagreeing with Lady Keisho-in. While Sano summoned the courage to do what honor and conscience required, Chamberlain Yanagisawa broke the uncomfortable silence.

"Your Excellency, I understand your honorable mother's concerns," he said carefully. Even the shogun's second-in-command must respect Lady Keisho-in. "But we must balance our wish for an heir against the need to uphold the strength of the Tokugawa regime. By letting a traitor get away with murder, we demonstrate weakness, and vulnerability to further attack. Wouldn't you agree, *Sōsakan* Sano?"

"Yes," Sano said unhappily. "The investigation must proceed without restriction." Lady Keisho-in was blocking his access to the Large Interior and its occupants, but surely not for the reason she'd given. She sought to prevent him from discovering anything that would implicate her in the murder. She feared that someone would reveal her affair with Lady Harume, and she wanted to find the letter before he did. Her interference was additional evidence in favor of an open accusation against Lady Keisho-in.

"Don't listen to them," Keisho-in ordered her son. "I have the wisdom of age. My Buddhist faith has given me knowledge of mystical forces of destiny. I know what's best."

A picture of helpless uncertainty, the shogun looked from Keisho-in to Yanagisawa, then to Sano. Sano's ears thrummed with the pounding of his heart. The faces of the assembly blurred before him. His lips felt cold and numb under the pressure of the words he must speak to save the investigation and focus it on Lady Keisho-in. But the demands of honor and justice fueled his courage. His hand went to his sash, ready to produce the letter. In Bushido, the life of one lone samurai mattered less than the capture of a murderer and traitor.

Then, in a searing blaze of awareness, Sano remembered that he was no longer alone. Should he be condemned to death for treason, then Reiko and Magistrate Ueda would join him at the execution ground. He was willing to sacrifice himself to his principles, but how could he endanger his new family?

A new sense of connection filled Sano's spirit with a sweet, painful warmth. He let his hand drop from his sash. Through years of solitude, how he'd longed for marriage! Then came a surge of resentment. Marriage encouraged cowardice at the expense of honor. Marriage had brought new obligations that conflicted with prior ones. Now Sano understood Reiko's dissatisfaction even better. Both had lost their independence through marriage. Was there a way to make the loss bearable?

Would that they lived to find it!

At last Tokugawa Tsunayoshi spoke. "*Sōsakan* Sano, you shall, ahh, continue the murder investigation. But you and your detectives must stay away from the Large Interior and the women. Use your ingenuity to catch the killer by other means. And when you do, we shall all, ahh, rejoice." Then he fell, weeping, upon his mother's bosom.

Looking straight at Sano, Lady Keisho-in grinned.

Out of the Large Interior filed the nine men Sano had assigned to the investigation there, ejected by the shogun's order. Sano and Hirata, waiting beside the palace door, fell into step with the detective in charge as the group trudged homeward through the night.

"Did you find anything?" Sano asked.

Detective Ozawa, a man with flat features and a past career as a *metsuke* spy, shook his head. "No poison or any other clues anywhere."

Along the castle's walled passages, burning torches smoked in the misty air. Owls hooted in the forest preserve; across the city, dogs bayed. Autumn's melancholy charm had always appealed to the poet in Sano, but now its connotations of death worsened his spirits. "What about the interviews?"

"Nobody knows anything," Ozawa said, "which could mean they're telling the truth, they're afraid to talk, or someone ordered them not to. I'd bet on the last."

"Did you search Lady Keisho-in's chambers?" Sano asked.

Ozawa looked at him in surprise. "No. I didn't know you wanted us to, and we would have needed special permission from her. Why?"

"Never mind," said Sano, "that's all right."

"It's probably just as well that we quit," Ozawa said. "We could have spent the rest of the year in the Large Interior without learning anything."

That was little consolation to Sano, because the shogun's edict had deprived him of access to not only Lady Keisho-in's quarters and five hundred potential witnesses, but also another important suspect: Lady Ichiteru. Now the thought of her reminded Sano of an unpleasant task he must perform tonight.

When they reached Sano's mansion, the detectives headed for the barracks. Sano said to Hirata, "Let's go to my office."

There, warmed by charcoal braziers and cups of hot sake, they knelt facing each other. Hirata looked miserable, his head bowed in anticipation of punishment. Sano hardened his heart against pity. He'd let Hirata's dubious behavior slide for too long. Now it had compromised their work, perhaps irretrievably. Sano hated to risk damaging the friendship he valued above any other, but this time he meant to get some answers.

"What happened during your interview with Lady Ichiteru, and why did you let our superiors think we believe she's innocent?" Sano said.

"I'm sorry, *sōsakan-sama*." Hirata's voice quavered. "There's no excuse for what I did. I—Lady Ichiteru—" He gulped, then said, "I couldn't get her to answer my questions, so I don't really know if she killed Lady Harume. She—she got me all mixed up . . ." His gaze turned luminescent with memory. Then he looked down, as if caught in a shameful act. "I shouldn't have spoken at the meeting. I made a bad mistake. You should dismiss me. I deserve it."

The news shook Sano. Accustomed to relying on his chief retainer, he felt as though an essential support beam had been yanked from the structure of his detective corps. But Sano's anger dissolved at the sight of Hirata's humility.

"After all we've been through together, I won't dismiss you for one mistake," he said. Overcome with relief, Hirata blinked moist eyes. Tactfully Sano busied himself with pouring them each another drink. "Now let's concentrate on the case. We've lost our chance for an official interview with Lady Ichiteru, but there must be other methods of getting information on her."

They drank, then Hirata said hesitantly, "We might still be able to talk to Ichiteru." From under his kimono he removed a letter and handed it over.

As Sano read, excitement eclipsed his depression. "She

has information about the murder? Maybe this is the break we need."

"You mean you think I should go?" A wild joy flared in Hirata's eyes before consternation clouded them. "To see Lady Ichiteru, alone, at this place she describes?"

"It's you she's asking for," Sano answered. "She might not be willing to speak to anyone else. And we can't endanger her—or defy the shogun's orders—by meeting in the castle."

"You trust me with such a critical interview? After what I've done?" Hirata sounded incredulous.

"Yes," Sano said, "I do." His purpose for sending Hirata to the rendezvous was twofold: he wanted Lady Ichiteru's information, but he also wanted Hirata to regain his self-confidence.

"Thank you, *sōsakan-sama.* Thank you!" Fervent with gratitude, Hirata bowed. "I promise I won't let you down. We'll solve this case."

After Hirata had gone, Sano went to his desk. Reading reports from his detectives, he wished he could share Hirata's faith. His men had questioned every member of the Miyagi household; no one admitted to tampering with the ink, or seeing anyone do so. They'd traced the bottle's path to Lady Harume. The messenger who had delivered it claimed he'd neither opened the sealed package nor made any stops along the way. Interviews with the castle guard who'd taken in the package, the servant who'd carried it to the Large Interior, and numerous individuals with possible access to the bottle while in transit had proved inconclusive.

Sano rubbed his temples, where a dull headache throbbed—he shouldn't have imbibed liquor on an empty stomach. His journey into Lady Harume's past had made the case more perplexing instead of less; he still believed that the facts of her life related to the murder, but couldn't make the connection. Sano felt drained of energy, in need of solace. Where was the comfort he'd expected to find in marriage?

Then Sano felt Reiko's presence: a mental sensation vaguely akin to the ripple of a distant stream. He realized he'd been feeling it ever since arriving home, like an undercurrent beneath his thoughts. In the space of a mere three days, he had become attuned to his bride. He would always know when she was near. Marriage had worked this strange magic despite the conflicts that divided them. Did Reiko feel it, too? The thought gave Sano hope for a chance of mutual understanding and harmony. Now, as the sensation grew stronger and he heard the creak of the floorboards under her soft footsteps, he forgot the cares of the day. She was coming to him. His heart pounded; his mouth went dry in anticipation.

A knock at the door: three quiet, firm raps. "Come in." Sano's voice hoarsened with nervousness, and he had to clear his throat.

The door slid open. Reiko entered the room. She wore a red dressing gown printed with gold medallions, its lush folds emphasizing the delicate yet seductive curves of her figure. Her knee-length hair swathed her like a shimmering black cape. She looked utterly beautiful and unapproachable. In her proud posture, Sano could see generations of samurai ancestors. Reiko's gaze was cool as she knelt a good distance away from Sano and bowed, her voice level when she said, "Good evening, Honorable Husband."

"Good evening," Sano said, chilled by her formality. "Did you have a good day?"

"Yes, thank you."

Where did you go? Sano wanted to ask. What did you do? But those questions would sound like an interrogation, and probably cause another quarrel. Sano controlled his tendency to batter against any obstacle that stood between him and the truth. Marriage was teaching him patience. He felt as though he'd aged years since his wedding, slowly, painfully maturing into the role of husband. Instead he waited for Reiko to speak. Didn't her visit indicate a desire for his company?

"My father paid a call while you were out," Reiko said. "He wishes to see you tomorrow morning at the hour of the dragon, in the Court of Justice."

Realizing that she'd come only to deliver this message, Sano experienced the heavy letdown of disappointment. "Did he say why?"

"Only that there's a trial that he believes will interest you. I asked if it had anything to do with your investigation, but he refused to say." A bitter smile twisted Reiko's mouth. "Like you, he thinks it's none of my business."

With difficulty, Sano resisted the bait. "Thank you for bringing me the message."

How he ached to touch her! He could imagine the silken sheen of her hair on his fingers, the soft pliancy of her body against his. The tantalizing scent of jasmine wafted across the distance between them. Oddly, her strength of will only increased the attraction she held for him. To win the love of this proud wife would be a greater conquest than domination of a weaker woman. The battle would require less brute muscle than intelligent strategy—the skill on which he prided himself in his detective work. His warrior spirit rose to the challenge.

Reiko bowed, signaling her intention to leave. Seeking a way to keep her with him, Sano said the first thing that came into his head. "About last night—I'm sorry if I hurt you when I pushed you out of Lieutenant Kushida's way."

"You didn't hurt me." Reiko's voice remained cool, her expression implacable. "And you needed my help more than I needed your protection. Why don't you just admit it?"

This was getting them nowhere, except further apart. In desperation, Sano blurted, "I admired that stroke you used against Kushida."

Now Reiko's eyes rounded in surprise at the compliment. "Thank you, but it was nothing, really." A becoming flush of pleasure bloomed in her cheeks. "It's just something I learned from a martial arts treatise by Kumashiro."

"You've read Kumashiro's works?" Now it was Sano's turn to be surprised. The great swordsman, who had lived two hundred years ago, was a hero of his own. Now his love of the history of martial arts prevailed over his belief that a wife shouldn't practice them. He found himself and Reiko discussing *kenjutsu*. Because she'd read as widely as he, this was one of the most satisfying conversations he'd ever had on the subject. Reiko's intelligence impressed him, and he enjoyed watching her glow with enthusiasm. She moved closer; her posture relaxed; her smile mirrored his pleasure in their mutual interest. Sano believed that she'd come here because she'd wanted to see him: after all, she could have sent a maid to deliver her father's message. She, too, felt the attraction that sparked between them.

Then, in the middle of a passionate argument about the merits of a particular style of swordsmanship, Sano realized he was making the same mistake that Magistrate Ueda rued: encouraging Reiko's interest in unfeminine pursuits.

His expression must have shown his dismay, because Reiko stopped talking in the middle of a sentence. Sadness quenched the sparkle in her eyes; she'd read his thoughts. "It's late," she said regretfully. "I shan't interrupt your work any longer." As their camaraderie died, the room seemed to grow suddenly colder. "Good night, Honorable Husband." Reiko bowed and rose.

"Wait," Sano said. When she paused at the door, a question in her eyes, he wanted to say: Investigating Lady Harume's life has opened my eyes. I understand what it's like to be female in a world ruled by men. I realize the cruelty of a society that limits a woman's existence. *I know how you feel!*

Yet how could he claim to understand Reiko's position, while still maintaining his own? He didn't want her involved in a murder investigation that had grown even more perilous with Lady Keisho-in's emergence as a suspect. He still doubted her ability to accomplish anything worth the risk of her life. Knowing this, Reiko would surely repudiate his sympathy as a mere ploy to win her affection against her will. Sano cast about for a neutral topic of conversation, but anything he might say could lead to the central issue of her independence—his authority—and another quarrel.

"Good night," Sano said at last.

With a swish of silk garments and a whiff of jasmine, Reiko slipped out the door, closing it softly behind her. More despondent than ever, Sano sat alone at his desk. Her presence still lingered: a clear, rippling stream slowly carving its path through the bedrock of his soul. Yet unless they could somehow get beyond this terrible impasse, they were doomed to live like strangers, together yet apart. Love seemed a hopeless dream.

Against his better judgment, Sano poured himself another cup of sake. Then, sipping the lukewarm liquor, he turned his thoughts to another unhappy lover, Lieutenant Kushida. The palace guard represented Sano's best chance to conclude the murder investigation quickly, and with his life intact. However, as he scanned the detectives' report on Kushida, his spirits waned further. No incriminating evidence had been found in his background or his quarters. That left Sano right where he'd started: with Kushida's statement, and the attempted burglary.

Sano reached over to the built-in shelves of his study niche and removed Lady Harume's diary. Riffling through the pages, he again wondered why Lieutenant Kushida had wanted to steal them. Then Sano noticed something he'd missed before. He held the open diary near the lamp for closer scrutiny.

Tiny ink marks filled the inner margins of the pages, where the silk cord joined them. Sano untied the cord and separated the sheets. The marks were the fine outer brushstrokes of characters that Lady Harume had written along the edge of the middle pages, then hidden beneath the binding. Arranged sequentially, they read:

> *Lying together in the shadows between two existences,*
> *Skin touching bare skin,*
> *Your breath joins mine; your sighs fill my depths*
> *And our blood sings to the rhythm of a single heartbeat.*
> *As you explore the secret places of my body*
> *I open myself to your touch—*
> *Ah, if only I could take all of you inside me*
> *So that we might never part.*
> *But alas! Your rank and fame endanger us.*
> *We can never walk together in daylight.*
> *Yet love is eternal; you are mine forever, as I am yours,*
> *In spirit, though not in marriage.*

Sano reread the lines with repressed jubilation. Harume's expression of eternal love didn't reflect Lady Keisho-in's complaints of betrayal. She must have been involved with someone else, whom she'd loved so much that she couldn't resist committing her emotions to paper despite the fear of discovery.

But who was this lover of public reputation and unspecified name? Any man would be condemned to death for bedding the shogun's favorite concubine; even a woman could earn the same fate by usurping Lady Harume's affection. How had this particular individual's position worsened the danger? Had the affair occasioned the earlier attempts on her life?

Sano cautioned himself against hoping too much for a lead that pointed away from Lady Keisho-in. Perhaps Harume had been writing about the shogun's mother during a happier phase of their relationship. Though Sano knew that love often surmounts the barriers of age, he wanted to believe that Harume had accepted old, homely Keisho-in's advances only to gain privileges. He wanted to believe that the hidden verse implicated someone else.

Lieutenant Kushida had denied sexual contact with Harume, but what if he'd lied? Maybe he'd tried to steal the diary because he feared Harume had named him as her lover. The impassioned tone of the verse and the sexual acts suggested didn't fit Harume's arrangement with Lord Miyagi, but their liaison could have later evolved beyond his spying at her through windows, despite his denials. It wasn't uncommon for a worldly older man to win a young girl's affection. Either the daimyo or Lieutenant Kushida might have killed Harume to prevent the affair from being exposed, or the shogun from finding out that the suspect had impregnated her.

Or perhaps there was another, yet unknown lover in Harume's past.

Sano must investigate the possibility. But for now he invested his hopes in Lieutenant Kushida and Lord Miyagi as the prime suspects.

25

The bathchamber of the Miyagi mansion was similar to those in any of Edo's great daimyo estates. A sunken wooden tub full of hot water steamed in the center of the spacious room. Shelves held rinse buckets, drying cloths, rice-bran soap, and jars of scented oil. A slatted floor allowed spilled water to flow into drains below. Charcoal braziers heated the air. But this particular bathchamber also had two unusual features.

A bamboo screen enclosed one corner, and in the wall, a tiny sliding door was inset at eye level. Lady Miyagi knelt on a cushion in the enclosure. Hearing footsteps, she tensed, alert to her husband's arrival. The spyhole door slid open, and she sensed his anticipation as he looked into the bathchamber, awaiting the entertainment she'd arranged for him. She clapped, the signal for the ritual to begin.

The door opened. In walked Lord Miyagi's concubines, Snowflake and Wren. Both wore dressing gowns, their long hair pinned up. Chattering together, they did not appear aware of their lord watching through the spyhole. Nor did they seem to notice Lady Miyagi, although the screen only hid her from the daimyo and she was clearly visible to them. At the Zōjō Temple orphanage four years ago, she'd inspected all the girls, seeking the right combination of cleverness and docility, before taking these two home with her. She'd trained Snowflake and Wren in the art of pleasing her husband. Now they were superb actresses. As if oblivious to the presence of master and mistress, they slipped off their robes.

From behind the spyhole, Lord Miyagi sighed. Lady Miyagi smiled, vicariously enjoying his pleasure at the sight of his concubines' naked bodies. Snowflake had large breasts with prominent nipples. Wren, small of bosom, had wide, curving hips. They complemented each other perfectly, and Lady Miyagi could feel the heat of her husband's excitement, like flames licking the wall. Snowflake picked up a bucket and doused herself with water. Squatting, she scrubbed her arms with soap. To Wren, she said coyly, "Will you wash my back?"

Giggling, Wren complied, then lathered Snowflake's bosom. Snowflake cooed with apparent delight. She closed her eyes and sighed as Wren fondled her breasts, pinching and sucking the nipples.

Lady Miyagi heard her husband moan. She knew he was taking his manhood out of his loincloth, stroking it. Wren cast an oblique glance at Lady Miyagi, who gestured for her to continue touching Snowflake. Lord Miyagi enjoyed this drawn-out erotic play. Lady Miyagi didn't know—or care—whether the concubines did, or if they only feigned pleasure out of duty to the master who fed and sheltered them, or fear of their mistress's anger lest they disobey. But she herself felt no physical response. An early experience had destroyed her capacity for sexual pleasure.

As a child of a secondary branch of the Miyagi clan, she'd grown up on this estate. Back then the house had always been full of people. The former daimyo—her husband's father—had loved hosting lavish parties. At one of these, eleven-year-old Miyagi Akiko had met an uncle newly arrived from Tosa Province. Ten years her senior, Uncle Kaoru had charmed her with his good looks and friendliness. She'd begun tagging after him, bringing him little gifts of flowers and sweets. In a childish way, she fell in love.

Then one night, her bedchamber door slid open. Kaoru whispered, "Come with me, Akiko. I have a surprise for you."

Eagerly she accompanied him out into the warm summer night. With Kaoru's strong hand holding hers, Akiko felt a mounting excitement that she didn't understand. He led her into the stables. Horses stirred at their approach. Akiko's heart thumped as Kaoru drew her into a vacant stall, where moonlight streamed through the open window and fresh straw covered the floor.

Kaoru's eyes gleamed with a strange intensity. "Do you love me, Akiko-*chan*?"

". . . Yes." Uneasily she backed away.

Blocking the door, Kaoru smiled and stroked her hair. "Don't be afraid." He ran his hands down her slight body. "So young. So nice." A guttural moan escaped him.

"I—I want to go back in the house," Akiko said, shrinking from his touch.

He untied her sash and tore off her kimono. He flung himself upon her, panting like a dog.

"What are you doing, *oji-san*? Stop, please!"

Pinned beneath him on the straw, Akiko smelled his sweat mingling with the pungent odor of horse manure. His breath stank of liquor. She struggled, and he slapped her face. "Don't fight me," he rasped. "You've been asking for this, and now you're going to get it!"

The hardness at his loins bludgeoned Akiko as he forced her legs apart. She screamed in terror. The straw scraped her skin; his weight crushed her. She'd heard tales of peasant girls, and even female relatives, violated by men of her clan, but had never imagined that it could happen to her. Again she screamed: "Help!"

Kaoru hit her again, harder. "Quiet, or I'll kill you." Then he entered her.

Akiko felt a searing pain between her legs, as though he'd driven a sword through her. With Kaoru's repeated thrusts, the sword plunged deeper. Agony blinded Akiko; she wept silently. Horses stomped and whinnied. The torture went on and on. Then Kaoru cried out. He withdrew, and the pain eased. Through her tears, Akiko watched him rise from her.

"Oh, no," he said, looking down at his hands, his clothing, the straw. A dark substance covered everything. Dimly, Akiko realized that it was blood—hers. Kaoru said, "If you tell anyone about this, I'll kill you." Panic tinged his voice. "Do you understand? I'll kill you!"

Later Akiko had vague memories of lying half-conscious in the straw until morning came and someone found her;

of doctors forcing bitter medicine down her throat. After a while she recovered, but not completely. Between her legs and in her lower abdomen, where she had once felt pleasant stirrings during romantic fantasies, scar tissue obliterated sensation.

Uncle Kaoru remained at the estate. Akiko never reported what he'd done to her. If anyone guessed, no one ever punished him. Akiko spent her days hiding alone in her bedchamber with the shutters closed. Then Kaoru suddenly departed for Tosa Province. Relief lightened the weight of terror that imprisoned Akiko. She ventured into the garden for the first time in two months. As she stood blinking in the sunshine, someone came up beside her.

"Hello, Cousin."

Instinctively she flinched at the male voice. Then she recognized her sixteen-year-old cousin Shigeru, first son of the daimyo. Though they'd both lived on the estate all their lives, she barely knew him: The future lord of Tosa Province was too busy to bother with girls. Now Akiko saw that this slender youth of slouching posture and soft, moist eyes and mouth possessed none of the masculine brutality that she feared, but his rank intimidated her.

"I saw what happened in the stable," Shigeru said. "I told my father, and he sent Uncle Kaoru away." The future daimyo gave her a sly, ingratiating smile. "I just thought you'd like to know."

Gratitude overwhelmed Akiko. Unbidden, he'd helped her when no one else cared. From that moment, she dedicated her life to Shigeru. She needed someone to worship; he needed slavish devotion. They became inseparable companions, and he the beneficiary of her love. Under his protection, she was safe from other men. He confided his private thoughts to her: his dislike of responsibility; his dreams of a quiet life devoted to pleasure. And he never tried to touch her. Soon she learned his favorite pastime: spying on women.

Ever anxious to please, Akiko helped Shigeru sneak into the women's quarters so he could watch the women undress and bathe. He would stimulate himself while she acted as lookout. On some level, she understood that he must have noticed her attachment to Kaoru, followed them to the stable that night, and enjoyed watching the attack instead of stopping it. She also understood that he'd seen the advantages of transferring her devotion to himself. Yet she never admitted that Shigeru was using her. She loved him; she needed him. Therefore she must do whatever was necessary to preserve their friendship.

Eight years passed. As Akiko matured, the terrifying prospect of marriage loomed. She couldn't bear the thought of leaving Shigeru, of living with a strange man who would touch her body. The attack had inflicted permanent physical damage: Her monthly bleeding brought on excruciating cramps; perhaps she could never bear children. However, this possible defect wouldn't save her. Not a whisper about her injury had passed beyond the immediate family; her parents didn't want to ruin her chances of an advantageous match.

Then Shigeru's father died, and he became daimyo. The clan had delayed his marriage in the hope of a union with some powerful samurai clan, but the Miyagi's minor status attracted no worthy prospects; hence, the clan decided to consolidate its assets by wedding Shigeru to a relative. Akiko's branch of the family was next in the line of succession, and she its eldest daughter. Shigeru married her.

Akiko was overjoyed. Now she could live forever under the protection of a husband who wouldn't force any physical attentions on her. "Marriage doesn't have to change things between us," Shigeru said. "Let's just go on like always."

They altered the household to suit their mutual taste. Shigeru sent most of the relatives and retainers to his estate in Tosa Province. Akiko dismissed most of the servants. When not pursuing Shigeru's sexual gratification, they preferred poetry and music to entertaining company. During the months he spent in Tosa every year, Akiko pined for him. As wife of a daimyo, she lost some of her fear of men and gained an air of authority, but only when Shigeru was with her did she feel truly safe, or happy.

Now Lady Miyagi heard her husband's breaths quicken; she pictured his hands stroking himself faster and harder.

When Snowflake glanced at her, she signaled for the love play to proceed. Snowflake lay on the floor, legs spread wide. Wren got down on hands and knees, crawling backward over her. She buried her face in Snowflake's crotch, licking and sucking with exaggerated noise. Snowflake moaned and writhed. Grasping Wren's buttocks, she pulled her partner's womanhood down upon her own mouth. Lord Miyagi grunted and gasped. Lady Miyagi knew that his ecstasy was near. Gladness filled her heart.

Though she'd never experienced physical joy herself, she could share her husband's. Mutual need had wrought a spiritual bond between them. Even without sex, she found the deepest personal fulfillment in their marriage; she felt no need for children. Let Shigeru's nephew succeed him as daimyo. They were mated souls, like the two swans in the family crest, a self-sufficient pair . . . or so she tried to tell herself. Once she had thought this union eternal, invincible. Then Harume had entered their lives, that evening last spring.

Lord and Lady Miyagi had been standing on a pier, watching fireworks burst over the Sumida River, amid noisy crowds celebrating the opening of the boating season. Shigeru had pointed out Harume among the shogun's entourage. Imagining the girl as just another harmless diversion, Lady Miyagi had procured a meeting. How could she have foreseen that Harume would pierce the weakness in their marriage? Discovering that the affair had taken a turn that could divide her from Shigeru had actually made her ill; she'd vomited in the street. Harume had threatened not only her happiness, but her very existence. Lady Miyagi rejoiced in Harume's death. She was safe once again. Shigeru need never know what had almost happened.

However, the threat had not completely died with Lady Harume. Its specter haunted Lady Miyagi, ready to rise again. And a new menace, in the form of the murder investigation, shadowed her life. Even the news of Lieutenant Kushida's arrest had not eased her mind.

Now Shigeru's moans grew louder with the urgency of his need. Lady Miyagi gave another signal to the concubines. Snowflake thrust her pelvis against Wren's face and screamed. Wren arched her back, closed her eyes, and let out a series of blissful cries. Through the wall came a hoarse shout. Tears of joy stung Lady Miyagi's eyes. Once again she had served her lord's desire.

Hearing his footsteps retreat, she rose. Snowflake and Wren disentangled themselves and bowed. "That was excellent," Lady Miyagi said, then walked down the corridor to Shigeru's bedchamber.

In the light of a lamp on the table, he lay upon his futon, covered with a quilt, his head pillowed on a wooden neck rest. This was Lady Miyagi's favorite part of the ritual: when she and Shigeru came together again. She lay on the futon next to his. They never touched. Shigeru was usually half asleep by this time. Lady Miyagi would wait awhile to see if he needed anything, then snuff out the lamp. Eventually she, too, would sleep, secure in their unique love.

But tonight Shigeru was wide awake, his gaze pensive as he stared at the ceiling. Lady Miyagi said, "What's wrong, Cousin?"

He turned to her. "It's this murder investigation." The worry on his face made him look simultaneously older and younger; in his soft, drooping features, Lady Miyagi could see both her girlhood companion and the elderly man he would become. "Ever since *Sōsakan* Sano came here, I have been suffering from the most terrible feeling of doom."

"But why? What have you to be afraid of?" Though she kept her voice calm, Lady Miyagi was disturbed. Why hadn't she sensed his fear? Why hadn't he confided in her sooner? Were they losing their precious spiritual connection? Anger filled Lady Miyagi like hot, suffocating flame. Harume had done this! And beneath her anger, a shard of fright lodged in her breast.

How much did Shigeru know? What would happen to them? Suddenly Lady Miyagi didn't want to hear what he was going to say. Lying rigid beneath her quilt, the fear growing into a jagged crystal in her heart, she braced herself for disaster.

"I've heard that *Sōsakan* Sano is a man who will stop at nothing to discover the truth," Shigeru said. "Suppose he finds out what happened between Lady Harume and me? I could be charged with murder."

"He already knows about the affair," Lady Miyagi said reasonably, though horror sickened her. Shigeru, arrested—perhaps even convicted and executed? How would she live without him? "You've admitted sending the ink, but *Sōsakan* Sano can't prove that you had anything to do with the murder." She had to force herself to speak the next words: "And what more is there for him to find out?"

Even in her terror of losing Shigeru, Lady Miyagi tasted bitter jealousy. She didn't want to learn anything about him and Harume that she didn't already know; she didn't want to be hurt again.

"Harume said that unless I gave her ten thousand *koban*, she would tell the shogun I had forced myself on her," Shigeru said unhappily. "I thought she was bluffing, but I couldn't be sure. So I paid her, a little at a time, so you wouldn't notice money missing from the household accounts. I didn't want you to worry."

Shigeru seemed to deflate, as if drained by the confession. "Harume's blackmail gives me a strong motive for murder. If *Sōsakan* Sano learns of it, I'll be the prime suspect. Now do you understand why I'm afraid?"

Relief flooded Lady Miyagi. Forgetting her doubts and fears, she wanted to laugh with joy. Blackmail—that's all it was, not another cruel betrayal. And how kind of her husband to consider her feelings. New confidence flowed through Lady Miyagi, washing away her suspicion that he'd hidden the truth from her for some less noble reason. She was the strong, sensible one who always took care of problems. She could avert any threat, triumph over any adversary who threatened them.

"Don't worry, Cousin," she said. "I'll fix things so that you'll be safe from *Sōsakan* Sano. Rest now, and leave everything to me."

Shigeru's eyes were tearful with relief and gratitude. "Thank you, Cousin. What would I ever do without you?"

Rolling over, he snuggled under the quilt. Lady Miyagi extinguished the lamp. Soon Shigeru was snoring quietly, but she lay awake, scheming. Lieutenant Kushida was the logical prime suspect, and Lady Miyagi expected him to be convicted of the crime. Yet she didn't dare count on it. From the beginning she'd anticipated and prepared for trouble. Already she'd acted in their mutual defense. Now she must take further steps to protect her beloved husband. Their special marriage.

Her life.

26

As midnight approached, the fog dispersed over the *ban-chō*, the district west of Edo Castle where Tokugawa hereditary vassals lived. Stars glittered in ragged patches of indigo sky. The moon's radiance turned the fleeing mist to a silvery haze that lit the labyrinth of deserted streets. In the dense bamboo thickets surrounding hundreds of tiny, rundown *yashiki*, nocturnal life seethed. Foraging rats rustled the wet leaves; stray dogs fought; crickets chirped. But most of the human population slumbered within dark houses. Sentries dozed in gatehouses, enduring the tedium of a quiet watch. All was peaceful—except the Kushida estate: There torches burned above the gate and around the bamboo thicket. Tokugawa troops patrolled the perimeter and perched on the thatched roof, preventing the escape of the criminal under house arrest.

In a small, dark storage chamber converted to a jail cell, Lieutenant Kushida lay on his futon. The alchemy of sleep carried him out of imprisonment, into the Large Interior. Down empty corridors he followed the sound of Lady Harume's singing:

"Summer's green bamboo shoots grow tall and bold,
The lotus spreads its pink petals . . ."

Kushida's heart filled with joyous anticipation. This time she would accept his love. She would satisfy the terrible lust that gnawed at him.

"Rain showers the roofs,
A cuckoo calls—
Come to me, my love . . ."

At last Kushida arrived at Lady Harume's door. He pushed it open and saw Harume lying dead on the floor. Blood drenched her nude body and long, tangled hair. The fatal tattoo branded her shaven pubis like ink on ivory. As Kushida stared in horror, Lady Harume's eyes opened. Her hand beckoned. In a strangled croak, she sang:

"Come to me, my love!"

Jerking awake, Kushida lurched upright in bed. His chest heaved as though he'd been running. And his manhood was erect, painfully engorged with the lust he still felt for Lady Harume. She had haunted his dreams ever since they'd first met. After her death, the dreams had become nightmares. Yet love and desire persisted. And within his spirit, like underground steam seeking a fissure through which to explode, swelled his anger toward the woman who had humiliated and ruined him.

Clambering to his feet, Kushida cursed himself for succumbing to sleep and allowing the dreams to come. But he'd needed a reprieve from the harsh reality of his situation. Now he paced the floor, trying to bring his emotions under control.

At first he'd attempted to resign himself to his imprisonment with samurai stoicism. He'd spent the day in quiet meditation, eating the meals brought to him, depositing his urine and feces into the wastebucket. But soon he could hold his peace no more. The room had grown dark and steadily colder since nightfall because his captors would give him no lamp or charcoal brazier, lest he try to burn his way out. The shame of being caged like an animal tormented his spirit. And the internal pressure of anger and need expanded within him, fueling his desperate craving for freedom.

Ten steps along one blank wall, then Kushida turned the corner and marched eight steps along another, and ten more past the door outside which a soldier stood guard. Having memorized the room's dimensions, he needed no light to direct him. The fourth wall of the room boasted a high, barred window that had once overlooked the garden but now faced a corridor—the house had expanded over the years, with new wings added to accommodate the family's growth. Now the wavering glow of a candle moved across the window, casting dim light into Kushida's cell. An old, white-haired samurai appeared in the corridor.

"Can't sleep, young master?" It was Yohei, a retainer whose family had served Kushida's clan for generations. As he smiled, sorrow deepened the wrinkles in his round face. "Well, neither could I, so I came to keep you company."

The rest of the household, including Kushida's parents, had avoided him all day. They believed him guilty of murder and wanted no share of his disgrace. But Yohei had adored Kushida since his birth, always giving him special treats, caring for him like a doting uncle. He alone had braved social censure to visit Kushida periodically. Now he said, "Are you bearing up all right? Anything I can do for you?"

The old man's kindness brought tears to Kushida's eyes. "How did this happen, Yohei?" he lamented.

"Fate often does strange things. Perhaps it is punishing you for the sins of your ancestors."

After hours of soul-searching, Kushida could blame neither fate nor his ancestors for the ills that his own actions, his own history, had created. Across the distance of twenty-five years, he saw the school where he'd learned the art of the spear. He heard the voice of his teacher.

"All your energy must be channeled into the development of combat skill," *Sensei* Saigo lectured the class. "Don't dissipate your strength in wasteful self-indulgence. At meals, stop eating before you've had your fill; let hunger sharpen your awareness. Abstain from liquor and frivolous recreation, which dull the mind and weaken the body. Above all, resist the temptation to gratify your carnal desires. The spear is your manhood. Through it, you shall find true fulfillment."

Young Kushida had yearned to be a great spear fighter. Hence, he zealously followed Saigo's teachings. Then one day when Kushida was twelve, he discovered in his father's study a book of *shunga*. The frontispiece was a painting of a beautiful naked woman coupling with a samurai lover. A dark, unfamiliar excitement filled Kushida. Instinctively he reached under his kimono. His hands began a motion they'd never been taught. Excitement culminated in blinding ecstasy—followed by anguish and guilt. He'd committed the self-indulgence that Saigo had warned him against, sacrificing discipline to pleasure.

When he confessed his misdeed, the *sensei* had assigned him extra combat practice and meditation sessions. At first Kushida yielded to his physical urges often, but eventually he overcame his bad habit. He immersed himself in *naginatajutsu,* attaining impressive skill, and remained celibate. Even while working near the shogun's women, he could go days, even months, without thinking about sex.

Then Lady Harume came to Edo Castle.

He'd been on duty the day she arrived. When Madam Chizuru introduced her to Kushida, a jolt of recognition rocked him. With her pert face and voluptuous figure, she resembled the girl in the *shunga* that had provoked Kushida's first orgasm. Repressed desire exploded in him, and the desire focused on Lady Harume, who'd reawakened it.

Confused by lust, Kushida hadn't perceived the danger. He decided there was no harm in merely looking at a woman. Thus he'd begun spying on Harume. Soon he stopped combat practice. At night he would stimulate himself to climax while fantasizing about her. He became aware of the loneliness of a life dedicated solely to Bushido. True fulfillment, he discovered, also required union with a woman.

Gathering his courage, he'd confessed his feelings in letters to Lady Harume. When she ignored them and began avoiding him, he persuaded himself that she was just shy, or afraid. He had something precious to offer her: a heart that had never belonged to another woman; a body unsullied by past amorous adventures. How could she not welcome such a gift? So he took the drastic step of speaking his love. But Lady Harume had repulsed him. Her words still hurt like a deep, festering scratch across Kushida's mind.

"Why do you keep bothering me? When I didn't answer

your silly letters, it should have been clear that I don't want anything to do with you." Repugnance distorted Harume's pretty face. "You must be as stupid as you are ugly. You want me to run away with you? Die in a love suicide with you so we can spend eternity together?" Harume laughed. "You're not even fit to breathe the same air as me. Now go away and leave me alone. I never want to see you again!"

Humiliated and furious, Kushida hadn't just shaken Harume and threatened to kill her, as he'd admitted to the *sōsakan-sama*. He'd twisted her arm behind her, covered her mouth when she tried to scream for help, and thrust her into a vacant room. There he'd torn her kimono and forced her to the floor. He meant to kill her, then and there—but first he would have her.

Harume fought back. She bit his hand, and when he loosened his grip, she kicked him in the groin. While he doubled over in speechless agony, Harume laughed. As if to increase his pain, she said, "I already have a lover. I belong to him forever. Soon I shall wear a tattoo that proclaims my love for him, on this body that you want so much." Then she escaped.

In the terrible days that followed, Kushida realized what had happened. He'd thrown away everything—discipline, self-respect, and the serenity of the pure life of Bushido—for a cheap, shallow girl who didn't recognize his worth. A girl who would tattoo herself, like a common whore! Out of love grew hatred. Kushida blamed Harume for his misery. He plotted revenge. He would sneak into her room while she slept and drive his spear through her. He would strangle her with his bare hands, while having his pleasure from her. These violent fantasies aroused him as much as his dreams of love once had. But never had he foreseen that her death would fail to ease either his desire or his jealous anger. He hadn't expected to feel such awful guilt over hurting Harume. He'd tried to steal her diary because he feared she'd recorded his attack on her, but he hadn't anticipated his current sorry predicament.

Now a new sense of purpose grew in him. He didn't want to live without his beloved Harume, but he didn't want to die for her murder, either. The disgrace of a public execution would forever taint his clan's honor. Somehow he must appease Lady Harume's spirit and bring peace to his own, while restoring the honor of his family name.

However, he could accomplish nothing while locked in this cell. Restlessness tormented Kushida like spiders writhing in his muscles; the pressure inside him mounted.

Yohei said, "How about a game of go? It will soothe your mind, young master."

Let me out of here! Kushida almost screamed. He wanted to beat on the walls in rage, yet he forced himself to say calmly, "Thank you for coming, but how can we play go, with you out there and me in here?"

Yohei beamed. "Two boards and two sets of counters. We'll call out our moves and make them for each other."

Though he had no wish to play, a plan formed in Kushida's mind. "All right," he said.

The retainer fetched the equipment. Through the window bars he passed a lacquer container of flat, round black and white pebbles and a four-legged ebony board with a grid of perpendicular lines incised on its ivory surface.

"You may open the game, young master," Yohei said.

Kushida placed a black pebble at the intersection of two grid lines. "Eighteen horizontal, sixteen vertical."

"Four horizontal, seventeen vertical," Yohei responded.

The pressure grew within Kushida as he set a white pebble in place. Every fiber of him tensed; the need for freedom swelled the blood in his veins. He endured the slow, tedious game, making moves at random. From outside the door came loud snores: The guard had fallen asleep.

"Young master, you're not concentrating on the game," Yohei chided. "I've captured almost all your pieces, and you haven't taken any of mine."

Hating to deceive his friend, Kushida said, "You're wrong, Yohei. I'm winning."

Yohei's puzzled face appeared in the window; he squinted, trying to see Kushida's board. "One of us has gotten the moves mixed up."

"It must be me," Kushida said. "I can't keep my mind on the game." Moving close to the window and lowering his voice, he said, "It would be better if we sat together. You could make sure all the pieces are in the right spots."

Yohei shook his head. "I can't let you out, young master. You know that."

"But you can come in here with me." Seeing indecision pucker the old man's forehead, Kushida coaxed, "Come on. As long as you leave before the guard wakes up, he won't care."

"Well . . ."

Kushida's desperation inspired cunning. "You don't believe I killed Lady Harume, do you, Yohei?"

"Of course not," the loyal retainer said indignantly. Then his certainty wavered. "But you attacked the *sōsakan-sama* and his men."

"I didn't kill Harume," said Kushida. "I didn't even know she was going to tattoo herself, so why would I have poisoned her ink jar? But *Sōsakan* Sano needs to make an arrest, so he framed me. I never broke into his house; I never attacked anyone. It's all a lie!"

Sputtering with outrage, Yohei burst out, "How dare the *sōsakan-sama* falsely accuse my young master? I'll kill him!"

"And end up convicted for murder yourself? No, Yohei, you mustn't." Kushida sighed with feigned resignation. "All we can do is wait for the truth to come out. Then my name will be cleared." His skin felt tight, his skull ready to explode from the throbbing pressure. "Now open the door and come inside so we can finish our game. I promise I won't try to escape. You've known me all my life, Yohei. You can trust me." Kushida let his voice quaver: "Besides, I'm lonely. I—I need someone near me."

Yohei's eyes brimmed with love and pity. "All right." He put a finger to his lips and headed toward the door.

Hurriedly, Kushida replaced the go pieces in their container, and tucked it in his kimono. Then came the clank of the door's iron bar as Yohei pulled it out of the brackets. Kushida lifted the go board by its legs and stood to one side of the door, heart pounding. The guard snored on. Slowly the door slid open. Yohei entered the room on tiptoe, holding the candle.

"Young master . . . ?"

Kushida stuck out his foot. Yohei tripped over it and sprawled on the floor. "What—?!"

In the space of a blink, Kushida leapt over Yohei and into the corridor. "No, young master!" he heard his friend shout. The guard sat against the wall, spear in hand. Hearing the commotion, he stirred. Kushida swung the go board. With the sickening thump of solid wood and ivory against bone, it slammed against the guard's head; he fell unconscious. Kushida flung aside the board, plucked the spear out of the guard's limp hand, then ran down the corridor.

"Please come back, young master!" Yohei called, hobbling after him. "You'll never get away. The *yashiki* is surrounded. The soldiers will kill you!"

Doors screeched open and cries arose as the noise awakened the household. Troops appeared and began chasing Kushida. "The prisoner is loose!" they cried. "Catch him!"

Legs pumping furiously, Kushida raced for the back door. He glanced over his shoulder and saw two soldiers gaining on him. Pulling the container of go pieces out of his kimono, he tossed it into the soldiers' path. The container hit the floor and the lid popped off, scattering pebbles. Amid surprised yelps, the soldiers slipped, then crashed to the floor.

Kushida flung open the door and burst out into the lantern-lit courtyard, startling two sentries. Wielding his stolen spear with deadly efficiency, Kushida struck their heads with its shaft. They crumpled to the ground. More soldiers leapt off the roof to join the battle, but Kushida was already through the gate. Two slashes of his spear wounded the guards stationed outside. Patrolling troops rushed to the rescue; archers fired arrows. Running for his life, his love, and his honor, Kushida fled into the night.

"We observed all the correct procedures for house arrest, but the old man let him out," said the commander who had summoned Sano to the Kushida estate. "None of this is our fault."

He gestured angrily around the torch-lit courtyard. There lay four men wounded by Lieutenant Kushida during his escape. Kushida's parents and a few retainers huddled on the veranda of the house, a modest one-story building with half-timbered walls and barred windows. From outside in the street, curious spectators peered through the bamboo thicket.

Sano had been awakened by the arrival of the messenger who had delivered the bad news. Now he stood in the chilly courtyard with Hirata as troops milled around, spectators chattered, and the first azure luminescence of dawn paled the sky. Inwardly he berated himself for losing a suspect. He should have recognized Lieutenant Kushida as an escape risk and denied him the privileges of rank, placing him in Edo Jail instead of under house arrest. Though Sano considered Lady Keisho-in the more likely murderer of Harume, he still didn't believe that the lieutenant had told the complete truth about either his relationship with Harume or his reasons for breaking into Sano's estate. With difficulty, Sano resisted the temptation to vent his anger at himself on the troops for letting a single man overcome them.

"Let's forget about blame for the moment and concentrate on capturing Lieutenant Kushida," Sano said. "What's been done so far?"

"Men are out searching the *banchō,* but they've sent

back no word on Kushida yet. Unfortunately, he's a fast runner."

Kushida could be clear out of Edo by sunrise, Sano thought with a heavy heart. Yet he doubted that leaving town was the lieutenant's whole motive for escaping. Why had he broken house arrest? The answer could be crucial to locating Kushida. Sano told the commander to continue the search. Then, motioning for Hirata to follow, he walked over to the Kushida family and introduced himself.

"Did your son say anything that might tell us why he escaped, or where he was going?" he asked the lieutenant's father.

"I have not spoken to my son since he was suspended from his post." The elder Kushida glared, his simian features set in hard lines. "And his most recent bad behavior did nothing to reconcile us."

Now Sano could better understand Lieutenant Kushida's obsessive passion for Harume: with such an unloving, unforgiving parent, he must have been starved for affection.

Kushida's mother cast a frightened glance at her husband, then nodded toward an old samurai weeping by the door. "Yohei saw him last."

This, then, was the faithful retainer whom Kushida had tricked into opening the cell door.

"Nothing that my young master said or did warned me that he meant to escape," Yohei mourned. "I don't know why he did it."

Staggering forward, Yohei prostrated himself at Sano's feet. "Oh, *sōsakan-sama,* when you catch my young master, please don't kill him! I'm the one who's responsible for what happened tonight. Let me die in his place!"

"I won't kill him," Sano promised. He needed Kushida alive for further questioning. "And I won't punish you if you'll help me find him. Does he have any friends he might run to for help?"

"There's his old *sensei*—Master Saigo. He's retired now, and lives in Kanagawa."

This village was the fourth station along the Tōkaidō highway, about half a day's journey away. Sano bade farewell to the Kushida family. Then he and Hirata mounted their horses outside the gate.

"Dispatch messengers down the highway to warn the post station guards to be on the alert for Kushida," Sano told Hirata. "But I'm not convinced he'll leave town."

"Nor am I," Hirata said. "I'll have the police circulate Kushida's description around town and tell the neighborhood gate sentries to watch for him. Then . . ." Hirata sucked in a deep breath and blew it out. "Then I'll meet Lady Ichiteru."

They parted, and Sano headed back toward Edo Castle to launch troops on a citywide manhunt before attending the trial that Magistrate Ueda wanted him to see. Whether or not Kushida had killed Lady Harume, he was a danger to the citizens. Sano felt responsible for his capture, and any crimes the lieutenant might commit before then.

The trial was already in progress by the time Sano arrived at the Court of Justice. He slipped quietly into the long, dim hall. Magistrate Ueda occupied the dais, his somber face illuminated by lamps on the desk before him, with a secretary on either side. He caught Sano's eye and nodded a greeting. The female defendant wore a muslin shift. Wrists and ankles bound, she knelt before the dais on a straw mat on the *shirasu*. A small audience knelt in rows in the center of the room.

While a secretary read the date, time, and the names of the presiding officials into the court record, Sano recalled how Reiko had told him about observing proceedings in this court during her youth. He wondered if she was here now, watching from some hidden vantage point, still defying him. Would they ever come together as true husband and wife? Why had her father wanted him to witness this trial?

Then the secretary announced, "The defendant, Mariko of Kyobashi, is charged with the murder of her husband, Nakano the sandal maker. This court shall now hear the evidence. I call the first witness: her mother-in-law."

As the defendant wept, an old woman rose from the audience. Hobbling up to the dais, she knelt, bowed to

Magistrate Ueda, then said, "Two days ago, my son suddenly became ill after our evening meal. He gasped and coughed and said he couldn't breathe. He went to the window for some air, but he was so dizzy that he fell on the floor. Then he began vomiting—at first the food he'd eaten, then blood. I tried to help, but he thought I was a witch who wanted to kill him. I, his own mother!"

The old woman's voice cracked in anguish. "He began thrashing and screaming. I hurried out and fetched a doctor. When we got back to the house just a few moments later, my poor son was lying dead. He was as stiff as that pillar."

Excitement eased the weight of Sano's worry and fatigue. The sandal maker had died of the same symptoms as Lady Harume! Now Sano understood why Magistrate Ueda had summoned him.

"Mariko cooks and serves all our meals," the witness said, glaring at the defendant. "She was the only person to handle my son's bowl before he ate. She must have poisoned him. They never got along. At night she refused to do her wifely duty by him. She hates housekeeping and shopping and sewing, and helping in the store to earn her keep, and taking care of me. We starved and beat her, but even that wouldn't make her behave properly. She killed my son so she could go home to her parents. Honorable Magistrate, I beg you to grant my son justice and sentence that wicked girl to death!"

Then followed the testimony of more witnesses: the doctor; neighbors who confirmed the unhappy state of the defendant's marriage; the police who had found a bottle hidden under the defendant's kimono, tested the contents on a rat, observed its quick demise, and made the arrest. A solid case, Sano thought.

"What have you to say in your own defense, Mariko?" asked Magistrate Ueda.

Still weeping, the woman raised her head. "I didn't kill my husband!" she wailed.

The magistrate said, "There is much evidence of your guilt. You must either refute it, or confess."

"My mother-in-law hates me. She blames me for everything. When my husband died, she wanted to punish me, so she told everyone I poisoned him. But I didn't. Please, you must believe me!"

Stepping forward, Sano said, "Honorable Magistrate, I beg your permission to question the defendant."

Heads turned; a buzz of surprise swept the audience. It was rare for anyone except the presiding official to conduct interrogations during trials. "Permission granted," Magistrate Ueda said.

Sano knelt beside the *shirasu.* From behind a tangled mop of hair, the defendant eyed him fearfully, like a captive wild animal. She was emaciated, her face covered with bruises, both eyes blackened.

"Did your family do this to you?" Sano asked.

Trembling, she nodded. Her mother-in-law said righteously, "She was lazy and disobedient. She deserved every beating my son and I gave her."

Anger blazed in Sano. The fact that this situation occurred often made it no less reprehensible to him. "Honorable Magistrate," he said, "I need information from the defendant. If she provides it, I shall recommend that the charge against her be modified to murder in self-defense, and that she be returned to her parents' home."

Protests rose from the audience. A *doshin* said, "With all due respect, *sōsakan-sama,* but this sets a bad example for the citizens. They'll think they can kill, claim self-defense, and get away with it!"

"She murdered my son! She deserves to die!" shouted the mother-in-law.

"You and your son mistreated that girl," Sano retorted, though he wondered why he was interfering in business that had nothing to do with his own investigation. Dimly he realized that his rage stemmed from his new awareness of the plight of women, a need to somehow make amends to Reiko for society's cruel treatment of her sex. "Now you're paying the price."

"Silence," Magistrate Ueda thundered over the audience's clamor, which subsided after the guards dragged the cursing, shrieking mother-in-law out of the room. To Sano, he said, "Your recommendation shall be accepted if the defendant cooperates. Proceed."

Sano turned to the girl. "Where did you get the poison that killed your husband?"

"I—I didn't mean to kill him," she sobbed. "I only wanted to make him weak, so he couldn't hurt me anymore."

"You're safe now," Sano said, but he could only hope her parents wouldn't punish her for the failed marriage—or wed her to another cruel man. How little he could do to correct centuries of tradition! Especially when he wasn't willing to begin at home. "Now tell me where you got the poison."

The defendant sniffed mucus up her nose. "I bought it from an old traveling peddler."

Choyei! Sano's heart leapt. "Where did you meet him?"

"At Daikon Quay."

Canals gridded the district northwest of Nihonbashi. Flagstone quays fronted warehouses; along these, dockworkers carried firewood, bamboo poles, vegetables, coal, and grain to and from moored boats. Sano knew the area from his police days, because the *yoriki* barracks were located in adjacent Hatchobori, on the edge of the official district. He rode down Daikon Quay, past porters laden with bundles of the long white radish. Everyone's breath formed clouds of vapor in the bright, chill air; a stiff breeze rippled the waters of the canals, which reflected the sky's wintry blue. Shouts, crashes, and the clatter of wooden soles rang out with sharp clarity. Sano could smell the distinctive blend of charcoal smoke and distant mountain snows that for him poignantly heralded the year's final season.

The defendant had given him directions to the place where she'd met Choyei: "He has a room in a house in the third street off the quay."

Sano steered his mount into the street. Rows of two-story slum dwellings lined a space barely wide enough to accommodate Sano's horse. Overhanging balconies blocked the sunlight; from clotheslines stretched across the narrow gap, laundry flapped. Night-soil bins, overflowing trash containers, and a privy shed befouled the air. Oily smoke rose from chimneys. Closed doors hid whatever activities the one-room apartments sheltered. The street was empty, permeated with a dreary quiet.

Dismounting outside the fifth door, Sano knocked. When he received no answer, he tried the door, but it wouldn't budge. He peered through the cracks in the window shutters. "Choyei?" he called.

The door of the next apartment creaked open. A thin, unshaven man came out. "Who are you?" he demanded. When Sano identified himself and stated the purpose of his visit, the man bowed hastily. "Greetings, *sōsakan-sama.* I'm the landlord, and it just so happens that I need to see the peddler, too. He owes me rent. I know he's in there, with some man who came to see him. I heard them talking just a moment ago. The old rascal is just pretending he's not home." Pounding on the door, the landlord yelled, "Open up!"

Sudden intuition compelled Sano to action. He rammed his shoulder once, twice, three times against the door. The wooden panel gave way. From inside the room came wheezing, sucking noises, punctuated by groans. Alarm struck Sano's heart. "No," he said as comprehension spurted through him like ice water. "Please, no."

"What's wrong, *sōsakan-sama*?" the landlord cried. "What's that sound?"

Sano burst into the room. At first it was too dark for him to see more than shadowy silhouettes. Then, as his eyes grew accustomed to the dimness, the shadows became a chest, a cupboard, and a table. Bowls and jars covered every surface, including the floor. Pots steamed on a clay stove. The air was redolent with the medicinal odors of a pharmacist's shop. In a far corner lay a human figure, the source of the terrible noise.

Sano tripped over a mortar and pestle. He pushed aside a frame of the sort worn by traveling peddlers, a wooden contraption with baskets suspended from crosspieces. He knelt by the prone figure.

"Give me some light!" he ordered.

The landlord opened the shutters and lit a lamp. Choyei flashed into vivid focus. He was ancient, but vigorous of physique. Dirty white hair straggled around his bald crown.

Eyes bulging with terror stared up at Sano from a face as gray and creviced as sun-baked mud. Blood flowed out of his gaping mouth and poured from a wound in his chest, staining his ragged kimono. *Wheeze, suck, groan.* The noise continued as he arched in pain, fighting for breath.

"Oh, no, oh, no," moaned the landlord, wringing his hands. "Why did this have to happen on my property?"

"Get a doctor," Sano commanded. Then he examined the deep gash between Choyei's ribs, made with a sharp blade, that alternately sucked and burbled blood. "Never mind, it's no use." Sano had seen this type of injury before, and recognized it as fatal. "Call the police instead." Choyei's visitor must have stabbed him and fled just moments ago. "Hurry!"

The landlord rushed out. Sano pressed his hand over Choyei's wound, temporarily sealing the hole. The wheezing abated. Choyei inhaled and exhaled hungrily. Feeling the warm, wet suction of bloody flesh against his palm, Sano said, "Who did this to you?"

The peddler's mouth opened and closed several times before his voice emerged. "Customer . . . bought . . . *bish,*" he gasped out. Red froth bubbled from his nose. "Came back today . . . stab . . ."

Bish: the arrow toxin that had killed Lady Harume. Elation rushed through Sano. The customer must have been her murderer, who had returned to prevent Choyei from ever reporting the purchase to the authorities. Sano cast an impatient glance toward the door, wishing the police would hurry. The killer was still in the area. He longed to give chase, but he needed the testimony of his only witness.

"Who was it, Choyei?" Urgently Sano gripped the dying peddler's hand. "Tell me!"

Choyei emitted sickening gurgles. Blood continued to leak from the wound. His lips and tongue struggled around the syllables of a name that seemed caught in his throat.

"What did he look like, then?" Sano said.

"No . . . No!" Choyei's hand clutched Sano's. His mouth formed words, but no sound came.

"Easy. Relax," Sano soothed him.

While the peddler struggled to speak, Sano's mind raced

through possibilities. The brutal stabbing argued in favor of Lieutenant Kushida. Had he escaped house arrest to assault Choyei?

"Did he use a spear?" Sano said, hiding his impatience.

Choyei's body thrashed and his head rolled from side to side in a violent protest against impending death.

"What did he look like? Tell me so I can find him!"

Now the drug peddler seemed to accept his fate. His hold on Sano's hand weakened while involuntary tremors shook him. With a great effort, he gathered a deep, rattling breath and whispered: ". . . thin . . . wore dark cloak . . . hood . . ."

That description could fit Lord Miyagi as well as Kushida. Or what about Harume's secret lover? How Sano welcomed this evidence that pointed away from Lady Keisho-in!

Running footsteps clattered down the street. A *doshin* and two civilian assistants arrived at the door. Quickly Sano repeated Choyei's description of the killer, then added his own of Lieutenant Kushida and Lord Miyagi. "It might be either of them, or someone else, but he can't be far away. Go!" The police rushed off, and Sano turned back to the drug peddler. "Choyei. What else can you tell me? Choyei!"

Desperation tinged his voice as he felt the drug peddler go limp under his touch. The animation faded from Choyei's eyes. One more faint moan, a last drool of blood, then the source of the poison—and Sano's only witness to murder—was dead.

28

The house to which Lady Ichiteru's letter had directed Hirata was built on a willow-shaded canal near the river, in a wealthy merchant district. Usually Hirata took pride in his knowledge of Nihonbashi, gained from years of police work. However, as he walked over an arched bridge and through the gate leading into the street, he found himself in unfamiliar territory. Age and affluence lay like a rich patina upon the district. Moss furred high stone walls; a green film lustered the copper-tiled roofs. Because of their fortunate proximity to water, the mansions had survived many fires, making them some of the oldest buildings in town. But Hirata felt his own luck—and confidence—draining away with every step toward his rendezvous with Lady Ichiteru.

In his fist he clutched like a talisman the list of questions he must make Ichiteru answer. Folded inside was her letter. He'd spent hours guessing at possible meanings of the last line: "It is with more than ordinary pleasure that I look forward to seeing you." Now, as he unfolded his list to study it one final time, he saw with dismay that the sweat from his palm had run the ink of the two documents together. This interview might determine his fate and Sano's; yet Hirata felt terribly unprepared, despite all his planning. He hungered for Ichiteru, but wished he'd brought another detective along, or sent one in his place.

Now he had reached the designated house, a miniature estate set off from the others by a large garden. The mansion seemed to lurk beneath spreading pine boughs that almost hid its low roof. It hadn't escaped fire unscathed; smoke had darkened the walls. With his heart drumming the opposing rhythms of desire and doom, Hirata knocked on the gate.

It opened, and a young girl's pretty face appeared. Hirata recognized Midori, whom he'd all but forgotten. "Detective Hirata-*san*!" she exclaimed in delight. "I was so hoping to see you again." Eagerly she drew him into an overgrown jungle of weeds and unpruned shrubs, brown and lifeless with the waning season. An arbor draped with withered vines overhung the flagstone path to the veranda. Dressed in a kimono printed with red poppies, Midori was like a flower in a dead wilderness. She giggled in excitement. "What brings you here? How did you know where to find me?"

Her enthusiastic welcome flattered Hirata, easing his nervousness. At once he felt more like the competent professional he really was. Wishing to prolong the sensation, and reluctant to hurt Midori by correcting her assumption that she was the object of his visit, he said, "Oh, we detectives have ways of finding out things."

"Really?" Midori's eyes widened in awe.

"Sure," Hirata said. "Just try me. Come on. Give me a mystery to solve."

With her head tilted in thought, a finger to her cheek, Midori made a charming picture. Then she grinned mischievously. "I've lost my favorite comb. Where is it?"

She laughed at Hirata's disconcerted expression, and after a moment, he joined her. "I confess; I don't know," he said. "But I'll come over and help look for it if you want."

"Oh, would you?" Dimples sparkled in Midori's face.

Cheered by her frank admiration, Hirata chatted about inconsequential things with Midori. They didn't hear the door open, or notice Lady Ichiteru until she spoke.

"I am honored by your acceptance of my invitation, Hirata-*san*." Down the length of the arbored passage, her low voice issued like a warm draft from a furnace. "A thousand thanks for being so . . . prompt."

Cut off in midsentence, Hirata turned and saw Ichiteru standing on the shadowy veranda. Her pale skin, mauve silk kimono, and the ornaments in her upswept hair gleamed as if she somehow concentrated the meager light upon herself. Her enigmatic gaze transfixed Hirata. At once his dread returned.

"Midori, why do you detain my guest outside instead of bringing him to me?" Lady Ichiteru rebuked the girl.

Hurt filled the eyes Midori turned on Hirata. Crestfallen, she said, "Oh. You've come to see her. I guess I should have known. I'm sorry for keeping you." Bowing awkwardly, she added, "I'm sorry, my lady."

Hirata pitied her embarrassment. Vaguely he remembered that his plan called for questioning Midori.

"Detective Hirata-*san,* there's something I should probably tell you," Midori whispered, averting her face so Ichiteru wouldn't notice.

"Yes, sure," Hirata said. But Ichiteru's seductive beauty lured him like a physical force. "Later." Leaving Midori, he moved through the dark tunnel of vines. The crumpled list of questions fell from his hand. He climbed the steps of the veranda and accompanied Lady Ichiteru into the house.

The corridor was dim, and smelled of mildew and the dank canal. Drifting a few steps ahead, Lady Ichiteru shimmered like a ghostly vision. Panic and anticipation weakened Hirata's legs. Every sane, prudent instinct told him to conduct their conversation outside, in the safety of the public thoroughfare. But the powerful, bittersweet scent of her perfume tantalized him. He would have followed Ichiteru anywhere.

She ushered Hirata into a room at the end of the corridor, where a single lamp burned upon a low table which also held a sake decanter and two cups. Age and dampness had discolored the painted landscape murals on the walls, so that they looked like cliffs and clouds under water. Carved sea demons snarled upon ancient cabinets. Through the shuttered windows Hirata could hear the waters of the canal lapping at the stone embankment. A futon lay upon the tatami. At the sight of it, Hirata felt heat gather in his loins. Tearing his thoughts away from the bed's implicit invitation, he blurted the first thing that came into his mind: "Whose house is this?"

A fleeting smile crossed Ichiteru's face. "Does it matter?" Kneeling beside the table, she motioned for him to join her. She murmured, "The important thing is that you are here . . . and so am I."

"Uh, yes," Hirata said. Clumsily he trod on the hem of his trousers and almost fell as he knelt opposite Ichiteru. Shame flushed him. The room seemed too warm and too cold at the same time; his hands felt like ice, while sweat saturated his clothes. "So, uh, what did you want to tell me?"

"Come now, Hirata-*san*." Ichiteru shot him a coquettish glance. "There's no need to be . . . in such a hurry. Are you that eager to get away?" Her full lips pouted. "Do you dislike me so much?"

"Oh, no. That is, I like you just fine." A hot blush crept over Hirata's neck and ears.

"Then let us first . . . enjoy this time we have together." Ichiteru's kimono, worn fashionably off the shoulders, slipped lower, revealing the top of the areole around one nipple. "May I offer you refreshment?" She lifted the sake decanter, arching her painted brows in suggestive invitation.

Hirata usually preferred not to drink while on duty, but now he needed to calm his nerves and still his trembling hands. "Yes, please," he said.

Lady Ichiteru poured a cup of sake. When she passed it to Hirata, her smooth, warm fingers caressed his. Her eyes drew him into their fathomless depths. With difficulty, Hirata looked away and drained the cup in one swallow. The liquor had an odd, musty taste, but he was too grateful for its immediate calming effect to care. Ichiteru watched him, her hands clasped in her lap, a smile playing around her mouth.

"Now I believe we're ready," she said.

Leaning forward, she drew her fingertips down Hirata's cheek. Her touch left a trail of heat. Aroused but aghast, he shrank away.

"What—what are you doing?" he demanded. The rational part of his mind guessed that she was trying to distract him through seduction. For the sake of the investigation, he must not let it happen, no matter how much he wanted her. "Your letter said that you had important information about Lady Harume's murder. And I need answers to the questions you avoided at the puppet theater." Wishing he hadn't lost his plan, he tried to recall its instructions. "Where were you when Harume was almost killed by a flying dagger? How did you really feel about her?"

"Shhhh . . ." Tenderly Ichiteru's finger traced his lips.

"Stop that," Hirata said. He tried to stand, but a peculiar sensation came over him. His limbs were as heavy as bags of sand; his head felt disconnected from the rest of his body. His senses grew extraordinarily acute. Every pore seemed to open, every nerve to vibrate. The murky colors of the room glowed; the lapping of the canal sounded as loud as ocean waves; Lady Ichiteru's perfume filled his lungs like the fragrance from a million flowers. Hirata heard the rapid drumming of his heart, the rush of his blood. His manhood swelled into an erection bigger than any he'd ever known.

Ichiteru was helping him to his feet, half carrying him to the futon. "No," Hirata protested weakly. Through a dreamy haze that filmed his mind, he recalled the police clerk mentioning a drug that induced trances and heightened sexual pleasure. Hirata also recalled that Ichiteru hadn't imbibed any of the sake. She must have put the drug there.

Had she bought it from Choyei, along with the poison that had killed Lady Harume?

"Let me go. Please!" Hirata feared for his own life, but Lady Ichiteru's nearness sent shivers of delight through him; her touch burned all vestiges of reason from his mind. Surrendering, he collapsed on the futon. The coffered ceiling was decorated with painted waves that undulated before Hirata's dazed vision. Ichiteru hovered over him as if airborne, the folds of her mauve kimono swirling. Then she raised her arms and the garment fell away, leaving her naked. Hirata gasped. Ichiteru's breasts were full and lush, the nipples large as coins. Her hips curved voluptuously from a tiny waist; a tuft of silky black pubic hair nestled in her crotch. Sleek, creamy skin enhanced the elegant bone structure of her neck, shoulders, and long, graceful limbs. Beneath her perfume, Hirata smelled her natural odor: pungent and salty as the sea. A tide of desire rose in him, but mortal fear rode its crest.

"No. Please. We can't do this. If the shogun finds out, he'll have us both killed!"

Lady Ichiteru only smiled, untied his sash, and removed his garments. She unwound the bands of his loincloth, and his erection sprang free. As he exclaimed in horrified excitement, she said, "It is for the sake of His Excellency that I summoned you here. He is in great danger." Ichiteru's voice surrounded Hirata like a cloud of disembodied sound; her scent engulfed him. "The murder of Lady Harume was part of a plot against our lord."

"What plot? I—I don't understand." The drug was rapidly diminishing Hirata's mental capacity; his brain floated in a sea of intoxication. Lady Ichiteru leaned close. Gently her breasts brushed his chest. The exquisite sensation drew a moan from Hirata. He heard the waters of the canal crashing against its banks. He must escape. He must have Ichiteru. But he could manage neither; the drug immobilized his limbs.

Then Ichiteru cupped her breasts in both hands and pressed his manhood into the warm, smooth cleft between them. Up and down she moved, smiling. The friction was unbearably arousing. Hirata cried out as his pleasure mounted too fast, too high.

"Stop. Don't!" Enough of his self-consciousness remained that he didn't want to spurt all over Lady Ichiteru, but his protest went unheeded. She continued her movements. Hirata felt the rapid approach of inevitable release. Deftly Ichiteru applied pressure to several points at the base of his erection. Hirata's climax erupted in spasms of ecstasy. Even as he moaned and gasped, he made a feeble attempt to shield Ichiteru, but his hand refused to move. Ichiteru and the place where their bodies touched seemed impossibly far away, and he strained to focus his vision there. Then surprise silenced him.

No seed had spilled from his manhood, which was still

rock hard. And the climax hadn't diminished his arousal in the least.

"What did you do to me? What kind of magic is this?" he demanded.

Looming over him, Ichiteru put a finger to his lips. "Shhh . . ." Her musical laughter mocked his panic. As the drug's effects intensified, Hirata grew dizzier. The bed beneath him rocked, and the water sounds grew louder. Waves of heat licked him. He and Ichiteru were spinning, the patterns of the ceiling a blur of color above them. Only her beautiful face remained in clear focus. "Don't be afraid . . . it won't hurt you. Just enjoy yourself . . ." Each word resonated through Hirata's head. "And don't you want to know who killed Lady Harume?"

"No. I mean, yes!" Hirata fought the resurgence of desire rising in him.

"It was someone who was jealous of Harume. . . . A man who feared that the birth of the shogun's heir would thwart his ambitions . . ." Lady Ichiteru held a red lacquer cylinder as thick as her arm. "He seeks to rule Japan, and cannot afford to lose his one avenue to power."

The spinning accelerated; Hirata's mind reeled. Frantically he tried to remember the facts of the case, and the male suspects. "Who are you talking about? Lieutenant Kushida? Lord Miyagi? Lady Harume's secret lover?"

"None of them . . . of them . . . of them . . ." Lady Ichiteru's soft voice echoed over the sounds of water, the pulse of Hirata's own blood. She slipped the hollow cylinder over his organ. The oiled silk lining sheathed him in pure pleasure. As Ichiteru moved the cylinder, ridges under the lining alternately gripped and released him. Panting, Hirata began the ascent toward another orgasm.

"Priest Ryuko has spies everywhere . . . knew about Lord Miyagi's letter . . . He comes and goes freely within the Large Interior . . . One day I heard him tell Lady Keisho-in that Harume was with child and must die. . . . Together they decided that Ryuko would buy poison and put it in the ink."

Even while the new evidence against Keisho-in filled Hirata with horror, the spasms of climax convulsed him.

Again Ichiteru prevented the full release he craved. She removed the cylinder and tossed it away.

"Please. Please!" Sobbing with need, Hirata strained to reach her, but he couldn't move a muscle. Now Lady Ichiteru knelt above him, thighs straddling his torso. The magnificence of her body, the serene loveliness of her face, and her feral, bittersweet smell maddened him.

"I beg you to warn His Excellency that the Tokugawa succession is in grave danger," Ichiteru said. "There will never be a direct heir as long as Ryuko and Keisho-in remain at Edo Castle. They will murder any other woman who conceives the shogun's child. . . . They fancy themselves emperor and empress of Japan. . . . They will manipulate the shogun . . . and squander his money on their own whims. . . . The *bakufu* will weaken and insurrection arise. . . . You must expose these murderers and save the Tokugawa clan and the entire country from ruin."

Despite his agitation, Hirata could see the danger of doing so. "I can't. At least not without corroboration. If my master and I should falsely accuse the shogun's mother, that would be treason!"

"You must promise to take the chance." Ichiteru's hand, coated with gardenia-scented oil, caressed his organ until his moans turned to hoarse cries and he felt ready to burst—then she stopped. "Otherwise . . . I will leave now . . . and you shall never see me again."

Horror flooded Hirata at the thought of losing Lady Ichiteru, of never satisfying the urgent need that consumed him. From passion grew love, like a malignant flower blooming in his spirit. Ichiteru was wonderful; she would never speak anything but the truth. "All right," Hirata cried. "I'll do it. Just please, please—"

Lady Ichiteru's approving smile filled him with guilty delight. "You have made the right decision. Now you shall have your reward."

She lowered herself onto his erection. Hirata almost swooned as he slid into her moist, hot womanhood. Faster and faster the room spun; sound, sight, and smell merged into a single, overpowering sensation. Up and down moved Ichiteru, with accelerating speed. Her inner muscles held him in a fierce suction. Hirata's excitement climbed toward a peak higher than ever before. His heart thundered; his straining lungs couldn't get enough air; sweat bathed him. He would die of pleasure. Panic seized Hirata.

"No. Stop. I can't take any more!"

Then he exploded in a cataclysm of rapture. He felt the seed pumping from his body, heard his own shouts. Above him Ichiteru reigned in triumph. As he succumbed to her power, Hirata knew that the path he'd chosen was fraught with peril. Yet both duty and desire compelled him to travel it. He couldn't ignore a possible threat against the shogun, and he must have Lady Ichiteru. Hirata had no choice but to report her statement to Sano, who would proceed with the investigation from there.

Even at the risk of their own lives.

The vibrant, haunting tones of koto music told Reiko that she had at last found the witness she'd been seeking for two days. From the lofty hilltop behind Zōjō Temple, the ancient melody drifted down through forests, over worship halls, pavilions, and pagoda, each note sharply defined in the clear air.

"Let me out here," Reiko commanded her palanquin bearers.

Alighting at the foot of the hill, she hurried up a flight of stone steps that ascended through fragrant pines. Birds warbled an accompaniment to the music, which grew louder as she climbed higher. However, the tranquil beauty of the place made little impression upon Reiko. Everything—not just her personal ambitions or her marriage to Sano, but their very lives—might depend on what the witness knew about Lady Harume's murder. Anticipation quickened her steps; her billowing cloak flapped behind her like umber wings. Gasping for breath, heart pounding, Reiko arrived at the summit.

A vast panorama spread around her. Below, on the other side of the hill, stone bridges arched across Lotus Pond to the islet upon which stood a shrine to the goddess Sarasvati. The temple's tile roofs gleamed in the sunlight; fiery foliage blanketed the surrounding landscape. In the north, Edo lay beneath a haze of charcoal smoke, embraced by the Sumida River's shining curve. Reiko walked toward the many-armed statue of Kannon, goddess of mercy, and the pavilion beside it. An audience of peasants, samurai, and priests had gathered to hear the musician who knelt before the koto, under the pavilion's thatched roof.

He'd always seemed ancient to Reiko, and she guessed

he must be over seventy now. His head was as bald and speckled as an egg. Age had stooped his shoulders and pulled down the lines of his narrow face; bent over the long, horizontal instrument, he looked like an elderly crane. But his knotty hands played the koto with undiminished strength. He twisted the tuning pegs, deftly moved the stops, and struck the thirteen strings with an ivory plectrum. Eyes shut in concentration, he coaxed forth music that seemed to hold the entire world immobile with awe. The song's ethereal beauty brought involuntary tears to Reiko's eyes. Abandoning haste, she waited outside the pavilion for the performance to end.

The audience listened reverently as the music gained volume and complexity, layering improvisation upon theme. The final chord hung in the air for an endless moment. Head bowed, eyes still closed, the musician sat as if entranced. The audience faded away. Reiko approached.

"*Sensei* Fukuzawa? Might I please have a word with you?" She bowed, adding, "You may not remember me. It's been eight years since we last met."

The musician opened his eyes. Age hadn't dimmed their keen, bright clarity. His face lit with immediate recognition. "Of course I remember you, Miss Reiko—or, I should say, Honorable Lady Sano." His voice was weak and quavery; his soul spoke chiefly through the koto. "My congratulations on your marriage." Extending his hand in a gesture of welcome, he said, "Please join me."

"Thank you." Reiko climbed the steps into the pavilion and knelt opposite him. Warm sunlight streamed through the lattice walls; a folding screen provided shelter from the wind. "I've been looking all over for you—at your house in Ginza, and the theaters. Finally one of your colleagues told me you'd begun a pilgrimage to temples and shrines across the country. I'm so glad I caught you before you left Edo."

"Ah, yes. I want to visit the great holy places before I die. But what caused your sudden urge to see your old music teacher?" The old man's eyes twinkled. "Not, I presume, the desire for more lessons."

Reiko smiled ruefully. During the six years in which

Sensei Fukuzawa had taught her to play the koto, she'd been a reluctant pupil. When her lessons ended, she put away her instrument with great relief and never touched it again. Now she was old enough to regret the waste of her *sensei*'s effort and feel ashamed of the callous way she had rejected the art to which he'd devoted his life. Uncomfortably she remembered her father pointing out her naïveté and overconfidence, and Sano her headstrong contrariness. These, too, were faults she must admit and conquer.

"I want to apologize for my poor attitude," Reiko said, though humility didn't come easily to her. "And I've missed you," she added, realizing for the first time how much she had. Unlike her relatives, *Sensei* Fukuzawa had neither scolded nor punished her for misbehaving. Unlike other teachers, who raged, threatened, and even hit students when they made mistakes, he'd always inspired through patient kindness rather than fear. Thus he had coaxed Reiko's meager talent to its full potential, while providing a haven from the criticism she got from everyone else. Didn't the fact that she could now appreciate the value of such a rare person mean her character was improving?

"No apology is necessary; it is enough to see that your character has matured," the old man said, echoing her thoughts. "But I suspect that there is a serious reason for the honor of your attention?" He smiled gently.

"Yes," Reiko admitted, recalling his ability to see through people, as if studying music had given him special insight into the human spirit. "I'm investigating the murder of Lady Harume. I heard that you spent the past month in the castle, giving lessons to the women of the Large Interior." His age and reputation made him one of the few men allowed there. "I want to know whether you saw or heard anything that might help me figure out who killed her."

"Ah." *Sensei* Fukuzawa ran his gnarled fingers over the koto strings, contemplating Reiko. From the instrument came a wandering, abstract melody in a minor key. Though neither his expression nor his tone indicated anything except benign interest, Reiko read disapproval in the music. She hurried to justify herself to the old teacher because she craved his good opinion. After explaining why she wanted to investigate the murder, she delivered the news that had increased her determination to solve the case.

"My cousin Eri told me this morning about a rumor that's circulating around the castle. Apparently the shogun's mother had an affair with Harume that ended badly. Everyone says she wrote a letter to Harume, threatening to kill her, and therefore, Lady Keisho-in is the murderer. I don't know if there really is such a letter, or if it means she's guilty. But my husband's other prime suspect—Lieutenant Kushida—has disappeared. He's under a lot of pressure to solve the case. If he hears the rumor and finds the letter, he may decide to charge Lady Keisho-in with poisoning Harume. But what if he's wrong, and she's innocent?

"He'll be executed for treason. And I, as his wife, will die with him." Clenching her hands in her lap, Reiko tried to subdue her fear. "I can't depend on my husband to find the real killer, or to protect me. Haven't I the right to save my own life?"

The koto music took a brighter turn, and *Sensei* Fukuzawa nodded. "Knowing that a former pupil is in danger, I would gladly help. Let me see . . ." As he played, he contemplated a pleasure boat drifting on Lotus Pond. Then he sighed and shook his head.

"It is no use. When one is my age, recent events blur in one's memory, while those of thirty years ago are as clear as water. I could re-create every note of my first performance, but as for the month I spent at Edo Castle—" He shrugged in sad resignation. "The ladies and I had many conversations during their lessons. Quarrels often arose between them, and women do gossip constantly; however, I can't think of anything they said or did that seemed out of the ordinary. Nor do I recall meeting Lady Harume. Certainly I had no premonition of her death."

He added, "I am sorry. It seems you've gone to much trouble for nothing. Please forgive me."

"That's all right, it's not your fault," Reiko said, hiding her disappointment and knowing that she herself was to blame for it. In her youthful arrogance, she'd formed an exaggerated notion of her detective abilities and the value of her contacts. Now reality stripped her of delusion.

She'd used her last lead, to no avail. She would neither solve the murder case nor save her life. True, she'd discovered Lady Ichiteru's quarrel with Harume, and that Lieutenant Kushida had been in Harume's room shortly before the murder. Yet this evidence hadn't led to a conviction. Reiko's unhappiness turned to anger at herself and her sex. She was nothing but a worthless female who might as well go home and sew until the soldiers came to take her to the execution ground!

And beneath the anger seethed a disturbing mixture of contrary emotions. Though Reiko regretted that she couldn't prove her superiority to Sano by beating him at his own game, she realized that she'd also wanted to please him by finding Lady Harume's killer. She wanted him to like and respect her. Even as defeat shamed her, she rued the lost hope of love.

Suddenly the koto music ended on a dissonant chord. "Wait a moment," *Sensei* Fukuzawa said. "I do remember something after all. It was so peculiar; how could I have forgotten?" He clucked in irritation at his bad memory, and Reiko's spirits rose anew. "I saw someone in the Large Interior who shouldn't have been there. It happened . . . let me see . . . I believe it was two days ago."

"But Lady Harume was already dead by then," Reiko said. Again her hopes plummeted. "You couldn't have seen the murderer come to poison the ink. Unless—are you absolutely sure of the time?"

"For once I am, because it was a memorable occasion. I was finishing my last lesson before leaving Edo Castle and embarking on my pilgrimage, when I felt an attack of diarrhea and cramps coming on. I rushed to the privy. It was when I went back to the music room that I saw him in the corridor. Even if he had nothing to do with the murder, there is definitely something strange going on at the castle. I should have reported the incident, but didn't. Perhaps if I tell you what happened, and you think it's important, you could inform your husband so he can take appropriate action."

"Who was it that you saw?" Reiko said. Perhaps the killer had revisited the crime scene.

"The No actor Shichisaburō."

Reiko was disconcerted. "Chamberlain Yanagisawa's lover? But he is not a suspect. And how did he get inside the Large Interior? Even if he managed to slip past the sentries, wouldn't the palace guards have thrown him out?"

"I doubt whether anyone recognized him besides me," said the old musician, "because he was disguised as a young woman, wearing a lady's kimono and a long wig. Shichisaburō often plays females on stage—he's adept at imitating their manners. He looked like he belonged in the Large Interior. The corridors are dim, and he was careful to keep his face averted."

"Then how did you know it was him?"

Sensei Fukuzawa chuckled. "I have spent many years performing musical accompaniments for the theater. I've watched hundreds of actors. A man impersonating a woman always betrays his true sex in some small way that goes unnoticed by audiences. But my eye is sharp. Not even the best *onnagata* can fool me. In Shichisaburō's case, it was his stride. Because a male's body is denser than a female's, his steps were a bit too heavy for a woman of his size. I immediately said to myself, 'That's a boy, not a girl!' "

Alarm flared in Reiko as she glimpsed a possible explanation for this subterfuge. If what she suspected was true, then how fortunate that she'd found such an astute observer as *Sensei* Fukuzawa! Perhaps she could prove her worth as a detective and save her life at the same time. Through her excitement, she got a firm grip on her objectivity, wanting to make sure she was right before drawing conclusions.

"How can you be positive it was Shichisaburō and not some other man, if you didn't see his face?" she asked.

"Shichisaburō's family is an ancient, venerable clan of actors," *Sensei* Fukuzawa said. "Over generations, they've developed signature techniques for the stage—unobtrusive gestures and inflections that are recognized only by experts on No drama. I've watched Shichisaburō perform. When he turned the corner ahead of me, I saw him lift the hem of the robe off the floor in the manner invented by his grandfather, for whom I often played musical scores."

Sensei Fukuzawa demonstrated, gathering the skirt of his

own kimono between thumb and two fingers, with the others curled into the palm. "It was definitely Shichisaburō."

"What did he do?" Reiko forced the words through the anxiety that compressed her lungs.

"I was curious, so I followed him at a distance. He looked around to check if anyone was watching, but he didn't notice me—bad eyesight runs in his family, though they're all trained to act as if they can see just fine. He walked straight to Lady Keisho-in's chambers. There were no guards stationed outside, as there have been on occasions when I've played for the shogun's mother. No one else was around, either. Shichisaburō went inside without knocking, and stayed for some moments. I waited around the corner. When he came out again, he was hiding something inside his sleeve. I heard the rustle of paper."

Reiko thought of Shichisaburō's connection with Chamberlain Yanagisawa, her husband's enemy. She recalled Yanagisawa's rumored attempts to assassinate Sano, to destroy his reputation and undermine his influence with the shogun. Her suspicions gained substance. Had Yanagisawa bribed Lady Keisho-in's guards to desert their posts? In a turmoil of fear and anticipation, she said, "And then what?"

"Shichisaburō hurried through the women's quarters. I barely managed to keep up with him. He slipped into a chamber at the end of a passage."

Lady Harume's room, Reiko thought. Dread and elation dizzied her as she considered the political climate surrounding the murder: the imperiled succession; the jealousies and power struggles; the rumors about Lady Keisho-in. Shichisaburō's clandestine visit linked these elements of the case in a pattern that signaled catastrophe.

"I put my ear to the wall," *Sensei* Fukuzawa continued. "I heard Shichisaburō rummaging around inside. When he came out, he was empty-handed. I meant to confront him, but unfortunately, I felt the diarrhea coming on again. Shichisaburō vanished. My illness prevented me from immediately reporting what I'd seen, and later I was so busy finishing my lessons and bidding farewell to the ladies that I forgot all about it."

The last piece of the puzzle brought the whole pattern into deadly focus. Reiko leapt to her feet.

"Is something wrong, child?" The old music teacher's forehead wrinkled with confusion. "Where are you going?"

"I'm sorry, *Sensei* Fukuzawa, but I must leave at once. This is a matter of extreme urgency!"

Bowing, Reiko hastily made her farewell. She fled down the hill and jumped into the waiting palanquin. "Take me back to Edo Castle," she ordered the bearers. "And hurry!"

There was no doubt in her mind that Sano would investigate the rumors about Lady Keisho-in, and find supporting evidence. Honor and duty would compel him to charge her with murder, regardless of the consequences. Reiko alone knew that Sano was in grave danger. Only she could save him—and herself—from disgrace and death. She must warn him before he stepped into the trap. Yet as Reiko sat forward in the palanquin, willing it to move faster, a new fear penetrated her consciousness.

If she succeeded, would Sano appreciate what she'd done? Or would her defiance destroy any chance of love between them?

"With Lady Ichiteru's testimony, the letter, the diary, and Harume's father's statement, there's too much evidence against Lady Keisho-in to ignore," Sano told Hirata. "We can't delay interrogating her any longer. And Priest Ryuko is the right size and shape to match the description of the man who stabbed Choyei."

Sano had already described discovering the drug peddler and the unsuccessful search for his killer. He'd also told Hirata about taking the materials from Choyei's room to Dr. Ito, who had found the poison there. They walked through the twilight streets of Edo Castle's Official Quarter, bound for the palace. Roofs were peaked black silhouettes against a sky that deepened from fading blue overhead to salmon above the western hills. Wispy red clouds smeared the heavens like streaks of blood. The cold breathed from stone walls and settled into the bones. Sano carried Harume's diary, with Lady Keisho-in's letter folded inside.

He said, "This is just an interview, to get Keisho-in and Ryuko's side of the story. It's not a formal accusation of murder."

Yet they both knew that Keisho-in and Ryuko might interpret the confrontation as a murder charge and take offense, then countercharge Sano and Hirata with treason. It would be the couple's word against theirs—with the shogun the ultimate judge. What were the chances of Tokugawa Tsunayoshi siding with them instead of with his beloved mother?

Sano imagined the cold shadow of the executioner falling over him, the long blade outlined against the barren ground where traitors died. And Reiko would see it with him. . . . Nausea gripped his stomach. Hirata didn't appear to feel any better. His skin had an unhealthy pallor, and he kept blinking. Oddly, he'd been in bed asleep when Sano arrived home. Though groggy and disoriented when roused, Hirata had insisted he was fine. After relaying what he'd learned from Lady Ichiteru, he hadn't said a word, and tried to avoid Sano's gaze. Sano pitied Hirata; the concubine's news had been a bad shock, and he probably blamed himself for the evidence that had forced their hand.

"Everything will be all right," Sano said, as much to reassure himself as Hirata.

Upon entering Lady Keisho-in's chamber, Sano and Hirata found the shogun's mother and her priest settled on cushions in the lantern-lit parlor. They wore matching purple satin dressing gowns stamped with gold chrysanthemums. Both color and flower were normally reserved for the use of the imperial family. The empress and emperor of Japan, Sano thought, recalling what Lady Ichiteru had said about the couple's ambitions. A quilt covered their legs and the square frame of a charcoal brazier. Around them were spread dishes of soup, pickles, vegetables, quail eggs, fried prawns, dried fruit, and a whole steamed fish, a sake decanter, and a tea urn. Lady Keisho-in was munching a prawn. Ryuko had just dealt out a game of cards. He set down the pack as Sano and Hirata knelt and bowed, his eyes wary.

Licking her greasy fingers, Lady Keisho-in said, "How nice to see you again, *Sōsakan* Sano. And your assistant, too." She batted eyes at Hirata, who stared at the floor. "May I offer you some refreshment?"

"Thank you, but we've already eaten," Sano lied politely. The odors of fish and garlic sickened him; he could not have swallowed food.

"A drink, then?"

"I don't think the *sōsakan-sama* is here on a social visit, my lady," Ryuko said. He turned to Sano. "What can we do for you?"

Although Sano had met Ryuko during religious ceremonies, they'd never done more than exchange greetings, but he knew the priest's reputation. The cozy atmosphere confirmed the rumors about his intimate relationship with

Keisho-in. Meeting Ryuko's shrewd gaze, Sano understood that he was the motivating intelligence behind her power. The discovery didn't cheer Sano. His main argument in favor of Lady Keisho-in's innocence was her good-natured stupidity. However, with Ryuko as a confederate, she wouldn't have to be evil or smart to commit murder.

"Please forgive the intrusion, Honorable Lady, but I must speak to you about Harume."

"Haven't we already done that?" Lady Keisho-in frowned in confusion. "I don't know what more I can say."

She looked to Ryuko for help, but he was gazing at the diary in Sano's hand. An unnatural stillness of expression masked whatever he thought or felt.

"Some matters have recently come to my attention," Sano said. With the sense of crossing a line between safe ground and battlefield, he said, "What was your relationship with Harume?"

Shrugging, Keisho-in stuffed a radish pickle into her mouth. "I liked her very much."

"You were friends, then?" Sano asked.

"Why, yes, of course."

"More than friends?"

"Just what exactly are you asking?" Priest Ryuko interjected.

Ignoring him, Sano said, "This is Harume's diary." He untied the binding cord and read the hidden words of erotic love, emphasizing the final passage:

> *"But alas! Your rank and fame endanger us.*
> *We can never walk together in daylight.*
> *Yet love is eternal; you are mine forever, as I am*
> *yours,*
> *In spirit, though not in marriage."*

"Did Harume write that to you, Lady Keisho-in?" Sano asked.

Keisho-in's mouth fell open, revealing an ugly mush of chewed food. "Impossible!"

"The reference to rank and fame fits you," Sano said.

"But the passage doesn't mention Lady Keisho-in by

name," Ryuko cut in smoothly. "Did Harume say anywhere in the diary that they were lovers?"

"No," Sano admitted.

"Then she must have been writing about someone else." Ryuko's voice remained suavely calm, but he withdrew his legs from beneath the quilt, as if he was too warm.

"Shortly before Harume died," Sano said, "she begged her father to remove her from Edo Castle. She said she was afraid of someone. Was it you, Lady Keisho-in?"

"Preposterous!" Keisho-in chewed a rice ball angrily. Was her response genuine, or an act? "I showed Harume nothing but kindness and affection."

"My lady doesn't like what you're implying, *sōsakan-sama.*" A warning note edged Ryuko's voice. "If you have any sense, you will leave now, before she decides to express her displeasure through official channels."

The threat was no less of a blow for being expected. Had Sano been interviewing just Lady Keisho-in, he might have subtly ascertained her innocence or extracted a confession without open confrontation. But Ryuko was forcing the issue. He would never let his patroness admit to murder, because he would share her punishment. He would protect his own skin by attacking Sano . . . especially if he'd conspired to murder the shogun's unborn heir. Inwardly Sano cursed his truth-seeking nature, which doomed him to build his own funeral pyre. But he couldn't change the demands of duty and honor. Resigned, he took out the letter.

"Tell me if you recognize this, Lady Keisho-in," Sano said, and read:

> " 'You do not love me. Much as I try to believe otherwise, I cannot blind myself to the truth any longer.' "

As he voiced the pained recriminations, jealous passion, and pleas for Harume's love, Sano periodically checked his audience's reaction. Keisho-in's eyes grew wider and wider, her face haggard with shock. Ryuko's expression turned from incredulity to dismay. They looked the picture of criminals caught in the act. Sano felt little satisfaction.

A conviction of Lady Keisho-in would be hard to get from a judicial system controlled by her son; the price of trying could be Sano's life.

> " 'What I really want is to see you suffer as I do. I could stab you and watch the blood run out. I could poison you and delight in your agony. As you plead for mercy, I will only laugh and say: "This is how it feels!"
>
> " 'If you will not love me, I will kill you!' "

Silence. Lady Keisho-in and Priest Ryuko sat paralyzed. The charcoal fumes, the food odors, and the room's stifling heat enclosed Sano, Hirata, and the two conspirators in a nauseating pall.

Then Keisho-in began to cough, clutching her throat. "Help!" she gasped out.

Ryuko pounded her back. "Water!" he commanded. "She's choking on her food!"

Hirata leapt up. From a ceramic jar he poured water into a cup for the priest, who held it to Keisho-in's lips. "Drink, my lady," Ryuko urged.

Her face reddened; her eyes teared as she retched and wheezed. She gulped the water, drooling it onto her robe.

Ryuko glared at Sano. "Look what you've done."

Remaining in his place, Sano recalled how Keisho-in had swooned upon hearing that Harume had been murdered. Had that been an act intended to hide the fact that she already knew? Was this a clever diversion, or true distress?

Keisho-in lay back on the cushions, inhaling and exhaling with exaggerated relief. Ryuko fanned her face. Sano said, "You wrote this letter to Harume. You threatened to kill her."

"No, no." Lady Keisho-in flapped her hands in weak protest.

"Where did you get that?" Priest Ryuko demanded. "Let me see it."

Sano held the letter up, safely out of the priest's reach—

he didn't want the evidence to wind up in the charcoal brazier. "From Harume's room," he said.

The couple exclaimed simultaneously, "That cannot be!" Ryuko's face was ashen, his eyes filled with horror. Sitting up, Lady Keisho-in said, "I wrote that letter; yes, I admit it. But not to Harume. It was written to my dearest love, who is right here!" Feebly she clutched Ryuko's arm.

It was a crafty explanation, which Keisho-in's choking spell had no doubt given her time to concoct. Ryuko recovered quickly, too. "My lady is telling the truth," he said. "Whenever she feels that I'm not attentive enough, she gets angry and expresses her complaints in letters. Sometimes she threatens to kill me, though she doesn't really mean it. I received that letter some months ago. As usual, we made up, and I returned it to her."

"Yes, yes, that's right," Lady Keisho-in said.

The priest had himself under control now, yet Sano could see fear behind his level gaze. "There is nothing in that letter to prove it was written to Harume," Ryuko said. "You've made a mistake, *sōsakan-sama*."

"There's nothing to prove it was written to you, either," Sano countered. "And I found it hidden in the sleeve of Harume's kimono. How do you explain that?"

"She—she must have stolen it from my chambers," Keisho-in blurted. She was less adept at concealing emotion than Ryuko, her panic obvious in her audible, rapid breaths. "Yes, that must be what happened."

"Why would she do that?" Sano said, unconvinced. The couple stared at him in speechless confusion. The distinctive odor of fear—sweat laced with honey—permeated the room. Sano knew it came from himself and Hirata as well as Keisho-in and Ryuko. He delivered the final, damning piece of evidence. "We have a witness who overheard you conspiring to murder Harume and her unborn child so that His Excellency would remain shogun for the rest of his life and you would retain your influence over him."

"That's a lie!" Keisho-in exclaimed. "I could never do such a horrible thing, and neither could my dearest!"

"What witness?" demanded Ryuko. Then comprehension cleared the bewilderment from his face. Anger tightened his jaw. "It was Ichiteru, that scheming whore who seeks to replace my lady as the mother of Japan's dictator. She probably lied about us because she killed Harume herself." Glaring at Sano, he said, "And you want to frame us for murder so that you can control the shogun. You forged the so-called diary, planted the letter, and paid Harume's father to cast suspicion upon my lady."

Despair stole over Sano. This, then, would be Keisho-in and Ryuko's defense against his accusations. No doubt it would sound eminently reasonable to the undiscerning Tokugawa Tsunayoshi. "Granted, Harume had access to your quarters," Sano said, "but you also had access to hers. Did you poison the ink, Lady Keisho-in?"

"No. No!" The words came out in a squeaky whisper; Keisho-in's face blanched, and she clutched her chest.

"My lady, what's wrong?" Ryuko said.

"Where were you today between the hour of the snake and noon?" Sano asked him.

"In my quarters, meditating."

"Were you alone?"

Keisho-in emitted pained cries. The priest replied impatiently, "Yes, I was. What are you getting at now?"

"The peddler who supplied the poison that killed Harume was murdered today," Sano said.

"And you have the audacity to suggest I did it?" Ryuko's fury didn't hide his panic. Great patches of sweat darkened his gown; his hands shook as he eased the moaning, writhing Keisho-in down onto the cushions.

"Is there anyone who can prove you weren't at Daikon Quay this morning?"

"This is absurd. I don't know any drug peddler." Ryuko stroked his patroness's forehead. "My lady, what is it?"

"An attack," Lady Keisho-in shrilled. "Help—I'm having an attack!"

"Guards!" Priest Ryuko shouted to the men stationed outside the door. "Fetch Dr. Kitano." Then he turned on Sano, his face livid with rage and terror. "If she dies, it will be your fault!"

Sano didn't believe the old woman was really ill, and he wasn't going to let her fakery prevent him from observing that Ryuko had no alibi for Choyei's murder. The combined strength of motive and evidence forced Sano to step over a line he'd hoped never to cross. A feeling of doom resounded through him. "I've no choice but to charge you both with the murder of Harume and her unborn child," he said, "and conspiracy to commit treason against the Tokugawa state."

Then the shogun must decide what was truth or lies. Exchanging resigned glances, Sano and Hirata rose to leave.

"You're the criminals!" Priest Ryuko shouted at them, while Lady Keisho-in heaved and sobbed upon the cushions. "You conspired against my lady to advance your own positions, and now you've endangered her health. But you're not going to get away with it. When His Excellency hears about this, we shall see who retains his favor—and who dies traitors!"

The door opened, and Ryuko exclaimed gratefully, "At last, the doctor!"

However, it was one of Sano's detectives, escorted by palace guards. He held out a folded paper. "Sorry to interrupt, *sōsakan-sama,* but I have an urgent message from your wife. She insists that you read it before you leave here."

Surprised, Sano accepted the letter, wondering what Reiko had to say that couldn't wait until he got home. While Ryuko frantically ministered to Lady Keisho-in, Sano read:

Honorable Husband,

Though you have ordered me to stay out of the murder investigation, I have disobeyed again. But please withhold your anger and heed my words.

I've learned from a trustworthy witness that the actor Shichisaburō sneaked into the Large Interior, disguised as a woman, on the day after Lady Harume's death. He took something out of Lady Keisho-in's chambers and put it in Harume's room. I believe it was a letter implicating Lady Keisho-in in the murder. I also believe that Shichisaburō stole the letter on Chamberlain Yanagisawa's orders and planted it at the murder scene for you to find. The chamberlain must be trying to frame Lady Keisho-in for murder and force you to accuse her.

For your sake and mine, I beg you not to fall into his trap!

Reiko

Shock numbed Sano. Horror followed as he wordlessly passed Hirata the letter to read. Despite his earlier misgivings about Reiko's detective abilities, he couldn't refute her theory. He realized that Lady Keisho-in was even more of a rival to Chamberlain Yanagisawa than himself. And the ploy sounded just like Yanagisawa. It explained why he'd acted so pleasant lately: he anticipated being rid of Sano very soon, along with Lady Keisho-in, the other obstacle to his quest for power. His spies must have discovered the letter's existence during a routine search of the Large Interior. He'd offered to help Sano and opposed Keisho-in's move to obstruct the investigation because he wanted to be sure the letter was exposed. The news of Harume's pregnancy had thrilled him because it elevated a simple murder to high treason—a crime whose consequences would destroy his rivals.

Now Sano realized that the hidden diary passage and Harume's message to her father must refer to someone else besides Keisho-in. Lady Ichiteru must have lied. The whole case against Keisho-in and Ryuko fell apart without the letter. Sano beheld them through fresh eyes. He saw in Keisho-in's suffering the genuine anguish of a woman falsely accused, and in Ryuko the desperation of an innocent man defending his life. Reiko's message had arrived in time to prevent him from bringing official charges against them, but could he repair the damage already done?

"*Sōsakan-sama,* what are we going to do?" Hirata's face mirrored Sano's dismay.

Keisho-in was retching into a basin while Ryuko held her head. Kneeling before them, Sano bowed. "Honorable

Lady Keisho-in, Priest Ryuko. I owe you an apology. I've made a terrible mistake." Quickly he reported the contents of Reiko's letter, adding his own supporting observations. "I humbly beg your forgiveness."

Shocked out of her fit, Keisho-in sat up and gaped. Ryuko stared, shaking his head at this new outrage.

"*Aiiya,* such a handsome, charming man as Chamberlain Yanagisawa," Keisho-in fretted. "I can't believe he would do such a thing to us."

"Believe it, my lady," Ryuko said grimly. He, unlike his patroness, was cognizant of the realities of *bakufu* politics, and ready to accept Sano's explanation.

"Dreadful! Of course I forgive you, *Sōsakan* Sano."

Though Priest Ryuko's gaze remained cool—he would not easily forget Sano's affront—he nodded. "It seems we must mend our quarrel and unite against a greater evil."

Relief flooded Sano. "Done," he said.

Together he and Hirata, Lady Keisho-in, and Priest Ryuko formed a plan to oust Chamberlain Yanagisawa.

Alone in her bedchamber, Reiko waited for the news that would determine her fate. The maids had lit the bedside lamp, spread her futon, and laid out her night robes. Yet Reiko still wore the clothes in which she'd traveled to Zōjō Temple. Pacing the chamber, she halted tense and breathless every time she imagined she heard voices outside. The mansion was quiet, the servants and detectives asleep. Only Reiko remained alert.

If her message hadn't reached Sano in time, soldiers would soon come to evict the household and arrest her, the wife of the traitor who had attacked the shogun's mother. If Sano had gotten the message and heeded her warning, they would be spared a disgraceful death, but Reiko doubted whether he would forgive her latest defiance. Many a proud samurai would rather die than lose face. Sano would probably send her back to her father tonight. Either way, her marriage was over.

With painful hindsight, Reiko saw the mistakes she'd made. Why hadn't she placated Sano's male pride and negotiated a compromise, instead of alienating him from the start? It was her curse always to want what she couldn't have. Her impetuous nature had cost her the man who challenged, angered, and aroused her; the man she'd hated and wanted with an intensity she'd never before experienced.

The man she loved.

Reiko experienced the knowledge as a bittersweet ache in her heart. She yearned to know what had happened in Lady Keisho-in's chambers. When would someone come and end the terrible suspense?

The lamp flame wavered like a feeble beacon of hope in the night. In the charcoal braziers, hot embers crumbled softly into ash. Reiko's shadow climbed the furniture, the paper partitions, and the painted wall mural as she paced. Apprehension tightened her muscles into rigid steel cords.

Then, just before midnight, came the sound of quiet footsteps in the passage. The moment had arrived, with this stealthy approach that was more menacing than the clamor of armed soldiers Reiko had imagined. Perhaps the shogun intended to spirit the traitors away from Edo Castle, execute them in secrecy, and preserve the appearance of Tokugawa invincibility. Or maybe Sano had sent an envoy to remove her quietly from the house, thereby avoiding a scandal. But Reiko was not one to cower before danger. She hurried to the door and flung it open.

There stood Sano, alone in the corridor. Disconcerted, Reiko stepped backward. She hadn't expected him, and he looked strangely different. Weariness shadowed his handsome face. He wore no swords. His gaze was somber; the arrogance had vanished. For the first time, Reiko saw his essential humanity, instead of the product of a thousand years of samurai training and discipline. Confusion rendered her speechless.

Sano broke the silence. "May I come in?"

Though Reiko would have defied an order, she couldn't refuse the plea in his voice. She let Sano enter, then closed the door. With the household asleep, they were more alone together than they'd ever been before. Sano's new vulnerability magnified his physical presence; the barrier of anger was gone. Now Reiko was keenly aware of them as man and woman, not opposing arguments. A trembling began inside her. Something was going to happen, but perhaps none of the events she'd imagined.

To hide her nervousness, she blurted, "I wasn't expecting you." At the same time, Sano said, "I'm sorry to disturb you so late." After an awkward pause, Sano spoke again. "I got your message, and I wanted to thank you. You saved me from making a bad mistake."

He explained what had happened with Lady Keisho-in. Reiko experienced horror at how close they'd come to ruin, then relief at the outcome. But the question of their marriage remained. They couldn't continue as they'd begun; a perpetual war of wills would destroy them both. Though the attraction pulled Reiko toward Sano ever more strongly, she wasn't ready to surrender her dreams, especially after proving her worth. When he finished speaking, she averted her face, loath to betray her conflicting desires.

"Reiko-*san*." To her astonishment, Sano knelt at her feet. "I've misjudged your skill, and I beg you to accept my apology. If I were half as clever a detective as you, I might have discovered Chamberlain Yanagisawa's plot in time to avoid a lot of trouble." A self-deprecating smile quirked his mouth. "But I was stupid. And blind. And stubborn." The words came out haltingly, as if they caused him pain. "I should have listened to you in the beginning, and not been so quick to refuse your help."

Reiko stared down at him in wonder. A samurai abasing himself to a woman and admitting he'd been wrong? As much as she'd admired his bravery and his dedication to principles, Reiko now admired Sano's humility. She'd learned that it took more strength of character to acknowledge one's faults than to fight sword battles. The ice of her resistance toward Sano began to thaw.

"It's hard for me to trust people," Sano went on. "I always try to do everything myself—partly because I don't want to harm anyone else, but partly because I think I can do better than they can." Color rose in his cheeks, and he spoke faster, as though hurrying to finish before he lost courage. "You showed me the self-deluding fool that I am. You were right not to give up investigating the murder and leave your fate in my hands. I don't blame you if you'd rather go home to your father than live with me. If you want a divorce, I'll agree to it.

"But if you'll give me time to improve my character, a chance to learn how to be the kind of husband you deserve—" He drew a deep breath and blew it out. "What I'm trying to say is, I want you to stay. Because I'm in love with you, Reiko." His eyes shone with ardor. Then he looked away. "And I . . . I need you."

Behind the quiet words Reiko could almost hear the echo of a fortress crumbling. Now Sano faced her again, the hesitancy gone; his voice rang clear and true. "I need you, not only as a wife, or a mother for my children, or for my pleasure, but as the woman you are. A partner in my work. A comrade in honor."

Reiko struggled to absorb everything he'd said. Sano not only returned her love, but he was offering her a marriage on her terms! She could have him, without losing herself. Gladness swelled within her. Savoring the triumph of the moment, she stood perfectly still, not daring even to breathe. But Sano was waiting for her decision, anxiously trying to read her expression. Emotion choked Reiko's throat; words would not come, so she answered in the only way possible. She held out her hand to Sano.

Joy lit his face as his warm, strong fingers grasped and covered hers. Rising, he gazed down into her eyes. An eternity passed in wordless mutual discovery, the exchange of a million unspoken thoughts. In silence Reiko conveyed her love to Sano; he promised her freedom as well as protection. Between them shimmered a vision of the future, hazy but radiant. Then a troubled sigh gusted from Sano.

"This isn't going to be easy," he said. "We'll both have to change. It will take time—and patience. But I'm willing to try, if you are."

"I am," Reiko whispered.

Even as she gave her pledge, fear quaked under her happiness. Sano's maleness intimidated her. She felt his need in the grip of his hand around hers, the quickening of his breath. Her own vulnerability appalled her.

Now Sano drew her nearer, cupping her face in his hand. She realized that this was for her the first test of their marriage. They couldn't always be like two soldiers marching side by side into battle. The power balance between them would shift back and forth, one prevailing while the other yielded. In the arena of carnal love, he had the advantages of age, strength, and experience. It was her turn to submit to him first. Yet the force of Reiko's response to Sano weakened her instinctive resistance. Desire was a voracious hunger. Ardently she pressed herself against him.

His arms came around her. She saw lust darken his features, felt the insistent rhythm of his heart and the frightening hardness at his groin. Terror leapt inside Reiko. But

Sano caressed her hair, her neck, her shoulders with extreme gentleness: He was restraining himself because he understood her fear. Emboldened, Reiko touched the bare skin at the neckline of his kimono. His hands circled her waist. Gazes locked, they moved toward the futon, and Reiko couldn't tell whether Sano was leading the way, or she.

They sank onto the futon, and at Sano's touch, Reiko's hair tumbled free of its combs. Willingly she let him untie her sash, but when he tried to slip off the layered kimonos, she recoiled. No man had ever seen her naked, and she feared his scrutiny, especially if she must be exposed while he remained clothed.

Sano withdrew at once. "I'm sorry." As if reading her thoughts, he untied his own sash. He shrugged off his brown kimono and white under-robe. Reiko stared in amazement.

Scars seamed the tanned skin on the lean, sculpted muscles of his arms and chest, the flat planes of his stomach. The skin on his calves was pink and flaky, healing from burns. Naked except for his loincloth, Sano looked like a survivor of war and fire. A tender pain arced through Reiko. She touched a large, dark scab just below the outer right edge of Sano's collarbone.

"What happened to you?" she asked.

With a rueful smile, he said, "An arrow wound, while I was in Nagasaki."

"And the burns?"

"The man who shot a Dutch merchant tried to stop the murder investigation by setting my house on fire."

Reiko touched a long line of puckered flesh on his upper left arm. The wound had been serious. "What about this?"

"A souvenir from the Bundori Killer."

"And these?" Reiko traced other scars on her husband's left shoulder and right forearm.

"Sword fights with a traitor who attacked the shogun, and an assassin who tried to kill me."

Without his saying so, Reiko realized that Sano had defeated both men. His victories impressed her, as did his courage to risk his life in the line of duty.

Unexpectedly, Sano looked mortified, rather than proud of his deeds. "I'm sorry that the sight of me disgusts you."

"No! It doesn't at all!" Reiko hastened to assure him. The ugly scars were symbols of everything she valued in Sano, yet she knew that words wouldn't convince him. Forgetting her own shyness, she removed her garments, baring her slender figure and small, pointed breasts. She took Sano's hands and placed them on her waist.

Relief, gratitude, and desire mingled in his deep sigh, his somber smile. "You are beautiful," he said.

Pride gave Reiko daring. She tugged at Sano's loincloth. The band of white cotton defied her clumsy efforts, and he helped her. Then the last fold came away, and she gazed in fascination at her first sight of an aroused man. His size at once alarmed and profoundly stirred her. When she touched his organ, it pulsed in her hand, a shaft of rigid muscle beneath smooth, sensitive skin. She heard him moan. Then his embrace drew her down onto the futon.

The warmth of intimate contact startled Reiko, as did the difference between her body and Sano's. He was hard where she was soft, all large bones and steel sinews to her delicacy. Then he began fondling her breasts, teasing her nipples, stroking her thighs. Lifted to new heights of sensation, Reiko returned touch for touch; the strangeness disappeared as their harsh breaths mingled and pleasure made them equals. Sano's mouth on her throat, his manhood pressing against her elicited a moan from Reiko. Between her legs, his fingers caressed. Her inner flesh swelled and moistened. When he mounted her, she was more than ready.

Sano lowered his weight upon her slowly, so as not to crush her. He wet himself with saliva to ease their union. Gently he thrust against Reiko's womanhood. Despite his care, she felt a sharp pain as he entered. She stiffened, gasping.

"I'm sorry," Sano said quickly.

Yet through the pain bloomed a demanding need. Arching against him, Reiko whispered, "Oh. Oh, yes."

He began to move within her. Gradually the slick profusion of Reiko's desire lessened the rough, tearing friction.

Her body was melting inside, opening to Sano. She clasped him with fierce delight, reveling in the sight of his enjoyment: closed eyes, parted lips, the heaving of his chest. His embrace tightened; she felt the scars under her fingers. It was as if she held all her samurai heroes in her arms. Then rising excitement drowned conscious thought. Reiko was locked in a battle for satisfaction; she was climbing a mountain. Sano's thrusts drove her higher and higher. Then she reached the peak, where victory waited. Reiko cried out as her body convulsed with a rapture she had never known.

She was a miracle beyond Sano's dreams, a wondrous blend of strength and fragility, her body like resilient steel sheathed in silk. Lost in the feel and scent of Reiko, he thrust harder and faster as his need consumed him.

Unbeknown to her, this was a new experience for him, too: Never before had he been anyone's first lover. Thus, he'd feared hurting Reiko; he hadn't been sure he could make the initial act of sex enjoyable for his wife. Because he'd not had a woman for so long, he'd worried that he wouldn't be able to postpone his release long enough to satisfy Reiko. Now he felt a happiness that went beyond physical gratification. The sight of her beautiful face contorting in ecstasy and the sound of the cries that accompanied her climax lifted him to the verge of his own. This union confirmed their marriage as one in which both could give and receive satisfaction—in life's daily business, as well as in the bedchamber.

Arousal and tension rapidly concentrated in Sano's loins; he heard the surging of his blood, the wild clamor of his heart as he drove deeper into Reiko. She moaned and held him tighter. Then, with a shout that issued from the depths of his soul, he was launched into a timeless space of pure ecstasy. Emptying his seed, Sano shuddered in the throes of a release as much spiritual as carnal. The bitterness, anger, frustration, and sadness of the past fled him in a great rush. When the climax subsided, he felt exhausted, but exhilaratingly refreshed. He rested on his elbows and looked down at Reiko.

She smiled, lovely and serene. Through the emotion that

swelled his throat and stung his eyes with tears, Sano smiled back. After many years of lonely wandering, he was home. Their love had restored to him a lost sense of self and power. There was no limit to what he could do, what they could achieve together.

Sudden loud noise startled them: cheers, applause, the rat-a-tat of firecrackers. A volley of pebbles showered the roof; torchlight flared in the garden outside; the silhouettes of dancing figures cavorted across the paper windowpanes. The detectives, guards, and servants were celebrating the consummation of their master's marriage with a traditional wedding-night ceremony.

"Oh, no." Sano burst out laughing.

Reiko joined in. "How did they know?"

"The walls are thin. Someone heard us, and told everyone else."

Far from being annoyed, Sano was touched by the tribute—and glad for the interruption, which gave the new bride and groom something to talk about, filling any awkward silence. Beneath him, Reiko giggled with embarrassed glee. Then came a knock at the door. Hurriedly they disengaged and pulled on their kimonos. Sano answered the door and found Reiko's nurse, O-sugi, standing outside, holding a laden tray.

"Some refreshment, *sōsakan-sama*?" O-sugi beamed.

Sano realized that he was starving. "Thank you," he said, taking the tray and closing the door. He and Reiko performed the necessary ritual of wiping away spilled semen and blood. Then they ate.

"Here, this will replenish your virility," Reiko said mischievously, spooning raw fish roe into Sano's mouth.

He poured the heated sake. "A toast," he said, raising his cup, "to the beginning of our marriage."

Reiko lifted her cup. "And the success of our investigation."

An edge of apprehension cut into Sano's happiness. He still feared that Reiko would get hurt while pursuing Lady Harume's killer. As his love for her grew, how could he bear for anything bad to happen to her? Despite her intelligence and training, she was young, inexperienced. How far should he trust her with the difficult, sensitive job of detection?

However, he had promised Reiko a marriage of partners; he couldn't go back on his word. Lifting his cup, he drank the sake. Reiko followed suit. Then Sano summarized the progress of the case.

"I'm assigning Hirata to look into the earlier attempts on Harume's life," he added. "And I have some ideas about her mysterious lover."

"Well," said Reiko, "since Lieutenant Kushida is still missing, I guess that leaves Lady Ichiteru and the Miyagi for me. Tomorrow I can ask my cousin Eri to arrange a meeting with Ichiteru, and I'll visit the daimyo and his wife."

Her gaze challenged Sano. This, he realized, was the first test of his resolve. He hated the idea of Reiko going anywhere near a possible murderer. Fighting the impulse to dissuade her, he swallowed words that would turn his promise into a betrayal. He tried to convince himself that Lieutenant Kushida or Harume's unidentified lover was most likely the killer, while the other suspects posed no threat to his wife. At last he nodded.

"All right," he said, "but please be careful."

Morning brought milder weather, with a south wind blowing in from the sea. Puffy white clouds, like the stylized designs painted on Chinese porcelain, floated in the cerulean blue sky as Sano and Hirata rode along the Great North-South Road, Edo's main thoroughfare. Merchants slid open the wooden shutters of their shops, revealing fine furniture, paintings, lacquerware, and fabrics; servants mopped doorsteps. The street began to fill with peddlers and tea vendors, peasants calling cheerful greetings to one another, orange-robed priests with begging bowls, ladies riding in palanquins, mounted samurai.

Sano said, "We need to talk, Hirata-*san*."

Hirata felt a constriction of his veins, heart, and windpipe. "Yes, *sōsakan-sama*," he said heavily.

"The false case against Lady Keisho-in and Priest Ryuko was primarily Chamberlain Yanagisawa's doing," Sano said, "with coincidental supporting evidence from the diary, Harume's father, and Choyei's murder. But another person contributed to the fiasco that could have cost us our lives, if not for my wife's independent investigation: Lady Ichiteru."

His expression grave, Sano spoke with reluctance, obviously no more eager for this conversation than Hirata. "You were responsible for questioning Ichiteru, but somehow you managed to learn nothing at all during your first interview with her. When I asked you what the problem was, you avoided answering. It isn't like you to be evasive—or incompetent—but I let the matter go because I trusted you to work things out yourself. I trusted your detective instincts and accepted Ichiteru's statement without corroborating testimony, as you did. Now I see that I made a mistake."

Shame assailed Hirata. He'd betrayed his master's trust, an unforgivable sin. A long night spent in self-recrimination had increased his guilt. Now Sano's words tore his spirit. The beauty of the day, the sunlight that sparkled on the canals, seemed to mock his woe. He longed to die on the spot.

"Something's wrong," Sano said, "and I can't ignore it any longer. When Ichiteru told you about overhearing Keisho-in and Ryuko plotting to kill Harume, what made you so ready to believe her? You know that criminals often lie to incriminate other people and divert suspicion from themselves. What happened between you and Ichiteru?"

Hirata saw that Sano was less angry than concerned, more intent on understanding than chastising. Sano's sympathy made him feel even worse, because it required an explanation when he would have preferred a sound beating. Reluctantly he poured out the whole miserable tale of Ichiteru's seduction, his own gullibility. He forced himself to watch the dismay on Sano's face. When he finished, he said, "There's no excuse for what happened. I should have known better. Now I've disgraced myself and let you down."

Blinking away tears, Hirata drew a deep, tremulous breath. "I'll leave today." He would find a private place to commit *seppuku*, thereby redeeming his honor.

"Don't be ridiculous!" Alarm blared in Sano's voice and eyes: He knew what Hirata was thinking. "You've made a bad mistake, but it's the first since you entered my service. I'm not going to dismiss you, and I forbid you to leave!"

Then he said more calmly, "You're punishing yourself harder than I ever could. I forgive you; now, you do the same. We've no time to waste dwelling on what's past. I need you to go to Daikon Quay and see if you can pick up any leads on Choyei's murder. Then visit the scene of the dagger attack on Lady Harume—maybe something there will point us to her killer."

"Yes, *sōsakan-sama*." Relief eased the constriction inside Hirata; he could breathe again. Sano was giving him another chance! "Thank you."

Yet his guilt remained. Opposing purposes warred in him. He must make up for the trouble he'd caused. Lady Ichiteru had nearly ruined the most important thing in his life—his relationship with his master. He was furious at her for manipulating him, and craved revenge, but he still wanted her. And though her lies made her a stronger suspect than ever, he wanted to believe in her innocence, because if she turned out to be the killer he would doubt his own judgment forever. He would never again trust himself to decide whether someone was guilty; he would dread missing clues. He would anticipate failure, making it inevitable.

Forcing a semblance of rationality, Hirata said, "We know that it was a man who stabbed Choyei, so Lady Ichiteru is innocent of that crime." Hirata suppressed the thought that she could have hired someone to buy the poison, then assassinate the drug peddler. "Still, she probably knows something about Harume's murder. I request permission to confront Lady Ichiteru and get the truth out of her."

Instead of answering at once, Sano gazed into the distance, watching an oxcart toil up the road. Then he said, "I'm ordering you to stay away from Lady Ichiteru. You've already lost your objectivity toward her, and the penalty for consorting with the shogun's concubine is death; you can't let it happen again. Reiko will question Ichiteru. While you're investigating Choyei's murder and the attack on Harume, you can look for connections to Ichiteru, but leave her alone." He added, "I'm sorry."

A fresh wave of misery and shame overwhelmed Hirata. Sano didn't trust him anymore. Would that he'd never met Ichiteru! The need for revenge consumed him.

They'd reached the junction with the highway leading north out of Edo, and Sano said, "I'm off to Asakusa. I'll see you back at the house later." He peered at Hirata with concern. "Are you all right?"

"Yes, *sōsakan-sama*," Hirata said, then watched Sano ride away. But he wasn't all right, and he wouldn't be until he regained Sano's trust. As he headed toward Daikon Quay, he decided that the only way to do that was to uncover the evidence that would ultimately identify Lady Harume's killer.

Several hours of canvassing the area around the scene of Choyei's murder eroded Hirata's hopes for salvation. The rooms in the adjacent lodging houses belonged to single males—dockworkers and laborers—who were away at their jobs when Hirata called, and had probably been absent during the murder, too. Thus Choyei's killer had slipped through the alleys unobserved. In the nearby commercial district, Hirata had no better luck. He questioned people who recalled seeing many men dressed in cloaks and hoods for yesterday's cold weather. The killer had easily blended with the crowd. By noon, Hirata was tired, discouraged, and hungry. Above a row of storefronts off the quay, he noticed a sign advertising fresh eel. He went inside to fortify body and spirit.

The small dining room at the front was jammed with customers who sat on the floor, scooping food into their mouths with chopsticks. In the rear kitchen, huge rice pots simmered. Cooks flung wriggling eels on chopping blocks, split them from gill to tail, cut off the heads, and extracted the bones. The long strips of meat, skewered on bamboo sticks and basted with soy sauce and sweet sake, roasted over an open fire. Clouds of pungent smoke whetted Hirata's appetite and evoked a sharp pang of nostalgia. The restaurant reminded him of establishments he'd frequented during happier days as a *doshin*. He'd been so confident then; how could he have known his career would founder upon a woman's treachery?

Hirata sat, then ordered a meal from the proprietor, a stout man with missing finger joints on both hands. Customers and staff exchanged gossip. The place was clearly a popular local meeting place. Maybe this trip didn't have to be a waste of time after all.

The proprietor brought Hirata's food: chunks of grilled eel and pickled eggplant on rice, with a pot of tea. Hirata introduced himself, then said, "I'm investigating the murder of a peddler not far from here. Have you heard about it?"

Wiping his sweaty brow with a rag, the man nodded. "Lots of bad things happen nowadays, but it's still a shock when it's someone you know."

Hirata's interest stirred. "You knew him?" This was the first person to admit an acquaintance with Choyei, who seemed a recluse without friends or family.

"Not very well," the proprietor confessed. "He never talked much; kept to himself. But he ate here often. We had a deal: he let me buy things cheap, and I took messages from his customers. He roamed all over town, but word got around that he could be reached here." The proprietor glanced at the Tokugawa crests on Hirata's garments, then said, "Mind if I ask why a high-ranking official like you is interested in an old peddler?"

"He supplied the poison that killed the shogun's concubine," Hirata said.

"Hey. Wait. I don't know anything about poison." The proprietor raised his hands defensively. "As far as I knew, the old man sold only healing potions. Please, I don't want any trouble!"

"Don't worry," Hirata said, "I'm not after you. I just need your help. Did a man wearing a dark cloak and hood come looking for the peddler yesterday?"

"No. I can't recall that anyone asked for him then."

Disappointment descended upon Hirata: Perhaps this lead was a dead end after all. Reluctantly he said, "Were any of his customers women?"

"Oh, yes. Many, including fine, rich ladies. They bought medicine for female troubles."

The proprietor relaxed, glad to turn the conversation away from murder, but Hirata's heart sank. "Was one of the ladies tall, very beautiful and elegant, about twenty-nine, with a large bosom and lots of hair ornaments?"

"Could be, but not recently." Eager to dissociate himself from the crime, the proprietor added, "Come to think of it, there haven't been any messages or visitors for the old man in ages."

A young, pimple-faced waiter, passing by with a tray of food, interjected, "Except for that samurai who came here just after we finished serving the morning meal yesterday."

"What samurai?" Hirata and the proprietor said in unison.

The waiter distributed bowls of rice and eel. "The one I saw in the alley when I took out the garbage. He threatened to spear me if I didn't help him find the peddler. So I told him where the old man lived. He left in a hurry." The waiter looked stricken. "Was that who killed him? I guess I did the wrong thing."

"What did he look like?" Hirata asked.

"Older than you. An ugly fellow." The waiter thrust out his jaw, scowling in imitation. "He hadn't shaved, and even though his clothes were the kind gentlemen wear, they were dirty, like he'd been sleeping outside."

Elation buoyed Hirata. The description of the man and his weapon matched Lieutenant Kushida, placing him in the area at the time of Choyei's death; he could have donned the hood and cloak later, as a disguise. His potential as a suspect outweighed that of Lady Ichiteru. Hirata ate his food and thanked the proprietor and waiter with large tips. Leaving the restaurant, he sent a messenger to Edo Castle with orders to search for Kushida around Daikon Quay. Then he rode toward the marketplace where an assassin had almost felled Lady Harume with a dagger.

"I'll show you where it happened," said the priest in charge of security at Asakusa Kannon Temple. A former Edo Castle guard, he had the powerful features of an iron war mask and a vigor undiminished by the amputation of an injured left arm, which had ended his past career. Hirata had called on him to review the official account of the attack on Lady Harume. Now he and the priest left the temple and walked along Naka-mise-dori, the broad avenue that led from the main worship hall to the great vermilion Thunder Gate.

Asakusa, a suburb on the bank of the Sumida River, straddled the highway that led to all points north. Travelers often stopped to have refreshments and make offerings at the temple. This convenient location made Asakusa one of Edo's most popular entertainment districts. Noisy crowds thronged the precinct, gathering around stalls that sold plants, medicines, umbrellas, sweets, dolls, and ivory figurines. The scent of incense mingled with the toasty smell of Asakusa's famous "thunder crackers," made of millet, rice, and beans. Consulting a clothbound ledger, the priest halted outside a teahouse. Nearby, audiences cheered three acrobats who spun iron tops on the rims of their fans while balanced on a plank perched atop tall bamboo poles supported by a fourth man.

"According to Lady Harume's statement, she was standing here, like this." The priest positioned himself at the corner of the teahouse, just inside the adjacent alley and half-turned away from the street. "The dagger came from that direction"—he pointed diagonally across Naka-mise-dori—"and struck here." He touched a narrow slit in the plank wall of the teahouse. "The blade pierced Lady Harume's sleeve. Any closer, and she would have been seriously injured—or killed."

"What happened to the weapon?" Hirata asked.

"I have it here."

From the ledger, the priest took a paper-wrapped package. Hirata opened this and found a short dagger with a tapering, sharply pointed steel blade, the haft wrapped in black cotton cord. It was the sort of cheap weapon used by commoners, easily hidden beneath clothing or under the bed . . . and sold everywhere.

"I'll keep this," Hirata said, rewrapping the dagger and tucking it under his sash, though he had minimal hope of tracing the owner. "Were there any witnesses?"

"The people nearby were all looking in the other direction, at the acrobats. Lady Harume had become separated from her companions and was very upset. Either she saw nothing, or fright made her forget. Vendors down the street noticed a man in a dark cloak and hood running away."

Hirata's heart gave a thump of excitement. The attacker had worn the same disguise as Choyei's killer!

"Unfortunately, no one got a good look at the culprit, and he escaped," the priest said.

"How?" This surprised Hirata. The Asakusa security force usually maintained order and subdued troublemakers with admirable efficiency. "Didn't anyone chase after him?"

"Yes, but the incident occurred on Forty-six Thousand Day," the priest reminded Hirata.

Hirata nodded in glum comprehension. A visit to the temple on this summer holiday equalled forty-six thousand visits on ordinary days, incurring the equivalent in blessings. The precinct would have been jammed with pilgrims. Additional stalls selling Chinese lantern plants, whose fruit warded off the plague, would have hindered the pursuit, while the confusion allowed the would-be assassin to flee. Sighing, Hirata gazed up at the overshadowing bulk of the temple's main hall, the tiered roofs of the two pagodas. He envisioned the shrines, gardens, cemeteries, other temples, and secondary marketplace within Asakusa Kannon's precinct; the roads leading through the surrounding rice fields; the ferry landing and the river. There were countless places for a criminal to hide, and just as many avenues for escape. Lady Harume's attacker had chosen both time and place well.

"Do you have any other information?" Hirata asked without much hope.

"Just the names of everyone in the Edo Castle party. I gathered the women and their escorts at the temple and took statements from them, according to routine procedure."

He held out the ledger, and from the list of Harume's fifty-three companions, one entry leapt out at Hirata: Lady Ichiteru. A sick feeling engulfed his stomach. Pointing to his erstwhile lover's name, he said, "What did she tell you?"

The priest turned pages and found the statement. "Ichiteru said she was having tea alone down the street when she heard Lady Harume scream. She claimed not to know anything about the attack, or who might have been responsible."

But Ichiteru was a liar with no alibi. When Harume survived, had Ichiteru resorted to poison? However, Hirata didn't want to prove her guilt, not even for the sake of closing the case, or the satisfaction of seeing Ichiteru punished. The prospect of success and revenge lost appeal when he imagined living the rest of his life knowing he'd been tricked by a murderer.

"Let me see that list again." Finding Lieutenant Kushida noted there, Hirata experienced great relief. Kushida fit the assassin's general description. The dagger wasn't his preferred weapon, but he might have chosen it because it was more easily concealed than a spear. "What was Kushida's story?"

"He was so distraught over his failure to protect Lady Harume that I couldn't determine his whereabouts during the attack," said the priest.

"Had anyone else seen him?"

"No. They'd split up to escort various ladies around the precinct. Everyone assumed Kushida was with a different group." The priest frowned. "I know the lieutenant from my days at Edo Castle. I had no reason to believe he was a suspect in the attack, or that he would become a fugitive from the law. Otherwise I would have tried to trace his movements. I'm sorry to be of so little help."

"Not at all," Hirata said. "You've told me what I wanted to know."

He was convinced that the same man had flung the dagger at Lady Harume, poisoned her, and silenced Choyei. Lieutenant Kushida had had plenty of opportunity to commit the crimes, and no alibis. Hirata foresaw his triumphant return into Sano's good graces and his own self-respect.

All he had to do was find Lieutenant Kushida.

In the daimyo district, a party of soldiers escorting a lone palanquin halted outside the gate bearing a double-swan crest. The commander announced, "The wife of the shogun's *sōsakan-sama* wishes to call on Lord Miyagi."

One of the Miyagi guards said, "Please wait while I inform the daimyo that he has a visitor."

Inside the palanquin, Reiko trembled with happy excitement. Her detective career had truly begun. Earlier this morning, she'd talked to Eri, who had promised to arrange a meeting with Lady Ichiteru later. Now came her first chance to match wits with a murder suspect. How she hoped that Lord Miyagi was the killer, so she could have the triumph of proving it! As she waited, Reiko fidgeted with a box of sweets she'd brought as a courtesy gift to the Miyagi. Circumstance had provided her the perfect excuse to call on them. She could probe for dark secrets, and Lord Miyagi would never suspect her true purpose. Though Reiko tried to settle down and concentrate on the task ahead, a smile kept breaking out on her face, and not only because she'd achieved her dream.

Her first night with Sano had added new dimension to life. Despite the soreness between her legs, love had given her an exhilarating sense of physical and spiritual well-being. The world seemed full of tempting challenges, and Reiko felt ready to take on all of them. Impatiently she peered out of the palanquin at the Miyagi's gate.

Finally a manservant emerged. "Lord and Lady Miyagi will receive Lady Sano in the garden," he said.

Clutching her gift box, Reiko alit from the palanquin. She told her entourage to wait outside, then followed the servant into the daimyo's estate. In the enclosure formed by the retainers' barracks, only two samurai sat in the guardroom. An inner courtyard surrounded a mansion with half-timbered walls and tile roof. A lone guard stood by the entry porch. The place was eerily deserted. Sano had warned Reiko to expect this, and now her heart began to race with anticipation. Surely Lord Miyagi's abnormal manner of living indicated a shady character. Was she going to meet the murderer of Lady Harume?

Reiko followed her escort through another gate, into the private garden. Pines stood like grotesque monsters, their trunks and limbs artificially contorted, the foliage pruned to emphasize their twisted postures. The ornamental boulders were thick, phallic pillars with rounded heads. From a cluster of shrubs rose the black statue of a many-armed hermaphroditic deity whose hands touched its naked breasts and erection. This morning Sano had briefed Reiko on the Miyagi's strange household, but mere words hadn't prepared her for the reality. Sexual initiation had expanded her senses, making her keenly aware of her surroundings. The garden's atmosphere was curiously hushed. Sunlight, filtered through the deformed trees, cast deep shadows. Reiko's nostrils flared at the putrid taint of rot in the air.

A pretty young woman raked neat parallel lines into a bed of white sand. Another tossed crumbs to orange carp in the pond. In the pavilion, an older woman with a plain, severe face sat and sewed. A middle-aged man, dressed in a faded blue cotton coat, knelt by a flower bed, ladling something out of a wooden bucket.

Suddenly Reiko was afraid, even with her guards waiting outside. She'd never interviewed a murder suspect before. Her knowledge of criminals was confined to the ones she'd watched safely in the magistrate's court. Now the sinister ambience of the Miyagi estate alerted Reiko that she was out of her depth. Could she get the information she wanted, without exposing her role as Sano's partner? To keep his respect, to serve honor and love, she must succeed. Was Lord Miyagi really the killer, and what would he do if he discovered her subterfuge?

"The Honorable Lady Sano Reiko," announced the servant.

Everyone turned toward Reiko. The rake halted in its tracks; the girl feeding the fish paused, arm extended. Lord Miyagi held his ladle in midair, while his wife's hands stilled on her embroidery. As they all observed Reiko in expressionless silence, she could almost see the bonds that joined them, like the skeins of a web. The daimyo and the two young women moved to stand beside the pavilion where Lady Miyagi sat. Reiko had the sense of separate parts of the same alien creature uniting against a threat. Suppressing a shiver of distaste, she approached her hosts.

Lady Miyagi bowed. "Your presence does us honor." She smiled, showing her blackened teeth.

The familiar ritual of introductions that followed restored Reiko's composure somewhat. "I've come to thank you for the beautiful sewing chest you sent me as a wedding present," she said, giving the ostensible reason for her visit. "Please accept this token of my appreciation."

"Many thanks," Lady Miyagi said. One of the concubines took Reiko's package. To the other, Lady Miyagi said, "Wren, fetch some tea for our guest." Both girls hurried into the house. Lady Miyagi flexed her shoulders. "One grows stiff from sitting too long, and I am sure you must be restless after traveling by palanquin. Come, let us take a turn around the garden."

Rising, she descended from the pavilion. She moved with a jerky, unfeminine stride; her gray kimono hung on her angular body. Hovering close beside Reiko, she said, "We are delighted to make your acquaintance."

Earlier, Reiko had hoped that the Miyagi would welcome a chance to curry favor with Sano through her, and hence give her more than the usual few moments allotted for a courtesy call. Now, though the scheme was working, she longed to finish her business and leave as soon as possible. Lady Miyagi's flat black eyes glittered with predatory interest. Reiko edged away—and bumped into Lord Miyagi, who had come to stand at her left.

"As lovely as spring snow on cherry blossoms," he drawled, sighing through moist lips.

Pinned between her hosts, Reiko felt increasingly alarmed, and not at all flattered by the compliment, which suggested the spoilage of beauty. She found Lord Miyagi repulsive, with his loose skin, droopy-lidded eyes, and slouching stance. Was he the father of Lady Harume's child? How could she have tolerated his touch? The stench Reiko had noticed didn't mask the intimate, musky odor that wafted from husband and wife. Inwardly she recoiled from its aura of mysterious, unhealthy practices. After consummating her marriage, she'd fancied herself very adult and experienced. Now her happy delusion crumbled before the perverse sophistication of the Miyagi.

"A walk in the garden sounds wonderful," she blurted.

Eager to put some distance between herself and the couple, she started down the path. But Lord and Lady Miyagi stayed so close that their sleeves touched hers as they strolled. Reiko could feel the daimyo's hot breath on her temple. Lady Miyagi was a barrier that prevented her from breaking the formation. Had Lady Harume felt this fearful unease while ensnared in the couple's erotic web? Would they dare make designs upon the wife of a high Tokugawa official?

Reiko wished she'd brought her guards. Nervousness drove from her mind the plans she'd made for questioning Lord Miyagi. She fumbled to start a conversation that might produce the answers she wanted.

"I admire your garden," she said. "It's so—" Seeking an apt description, she noticed another statue: a two-headed winged demon with the corpse of a small animal in its claws. Reiko shuddered. "So elegant," she finished lamely.

Lady Miyagi said, "But I imagine that the *sōsakan-sama*'s garden is far better?"

Hearing genuine curiosity in the conventional reply, Reiko guessed that the daimyo's wife had mentioned Sano because she wanted to find out what Reiko knew about the murder case. Reiko seized on the opening. "Unfortunately, my husband hasn't much time to devote to nature. Distressing matters occupy his attention. You may have heard about the incident that interrupted our wedding festivities?"

"Indeed. Quite shocking," Lady Miyagi said.

"Oh, yes." The daimyo sighed. "Harume. All that loveliness destroyed. Her suffering must have been extreme."

Lasciviousness crept into Lord Miyagi's smile. "The knife cutting her soft skin; the blood welling; the poisoned ink seeping into her young body. The convulsions and madness." Lord Miyagi's hooded eyes sparkled. "Pain is the ultimate sensation; fear is the most intense of all emotions. And there's a unique beauty in death."

Reiko experienced a frisson of horror as she realized that Lord Miyagi's tastes ranged even farther beyond the boundaries of normality than she or Sano had thought. She remembered a trial her father hadn't let her watch, that of a merchant who'd strangled a prostitute while they coupled, achieving the ultimate carnal satisfaction in the death of his lover. Had Lord Miyagi sought the same with Lady Harume, reveling in her agonies from afar?

Pretending not to notice anything unusual about his response, Reiko said, "I was very much saddened by Lady Harume's death. Weren't you?"

"Some women are wayward creatures who tease, torment, and entice in a continual flirtation with danger." A dark, morbid excitement roughened the daimyo's affected drawl. "They invite killing."

Reiko's heart jumped. "Did Lady Harume do that?" she asked. *With you, Lord Miyagi?*

Perhaps aware that her husband spoke too freely, Lady Miyagi cut in, "What progress does the *sōsakan-sama* make on his investigation? Will he make an arrest soon?" Eagerness sharpened her voice: She, unlike the daimyo, seemed worried about the outcome of the murder case.

"Oh, I don't know anything about my husband's business affairs." Reiko spoke with blithe unconcern, not wanting the couple to guess that she knew Lord Miyagi was a suspect.

Neither Lady Miyagi's expression nor bearing changed, but Reiko felt her relax. They reached the flower bed where the daimyo had been working. He picked up the bucket, which contained a lumpy red and gray slop, the source of the unpleasant odor. Flies buzzed around it. "Ground fish," Lord Miyagi explained, "for enriching the soil and making plants grow."

Reiko's stomach turned. As the daimyo ladled the mixture onto the ground, his limpid gaze caressed her. "From death comes life. Some must die so others may survive. Do you understand, my dear?"

"Um, yes, I guess so." Reiko wondered whether he was referring to dead animals—or Lady Harume. Was he justifying her murder? "It's the way of nature," she improvised.

"You are as perceptive as you are beautiful." Lord Miyagi brought his face close to hers and smiled, his wet lips baring discolored teeth.

Rigid with distaste, Reiko tried not to cringe from the dawning infatuation in his bloodshot eyes. "A thousand thanks," she murmured.

At the sound of the door opening and footsteps on the veranda, Lady Miyagi said, "Tea is served."

"Tea! Oh, yes!" Reiko exclaimed, giddy with relief.

They sat in the pavilion. The concubines brought hot, damp cloths for washing their hands and laid before them an extravagant repast: tea, fresh figs, bean-jam cakes, pickled melon, boiled chestnuts in honey, sliced lobster arranged in the shape of a peony. As Reiko politely sampled the refreshments, she thought of the poisoned ink. Her throat closed; a surge of nausea roiled her stomach. She felt a growing conviction that Lord Miyagi was the killer. The crimes against Lady Harume, which had involved no physical contact, suited the daimyo's habits. He'd sent her the ink bottle. The tea tasted bitter in Reiko's mouth, and the sweets saturated with the taint of dead flesh.

Lounging beside her, Lord Miyagi chewed slowly, amid much lip-smacking. As he ate petals of the lobster peony, his gaze moved over Reiko as if peeling off her clothes with his eyes. She blushed under her makeup, forcing down a gulp of tea. Her stomach lurched, and for one awful moment she feared the liquid would come back up.

The daimyo intoned:

"High on the bough hangs the ripe fruit,
Safe beyond the reach of man; untouched
A wasp pierces her downy flesh
And drinks of the sweetness within—

From below, I celebrate the wedding
With my own ecstasy."

He bit into the rosy pulp of a fig, never taking his gaze from Reiko. With a sinuous movement, he lifted a hand to her head. Reiko gasped. The concubines tittered; Lord Miyagi chuckled. "Don't be afraid, my dear. A leaf has become tangled in your pretty hair—let me remove it."

His fingers trailed over Reiko's temple and down her cheek before falling away. There was no leaf in them. The daimyo's touch left a damp sensation, like a snail's track. Hot with angry embarrassment, Reiko looked away. As a sheltered upper-class girl, she'd had little contact with men outside her immediate household, and none had dared treat a magistrate's daughter with such disrespect. Thus, she had no idea how to handle Lord Miyagi's vulgar attentions. The only thing she could think to do was pretend she didn't know what he was doing.

"You have an admirable turn of phrase," she said weakly, then looked to Lady Miyagi for assistance. If the woman had any pride or sense, she would stop the daimyo's outrageous flirtation now! How could any wife bear seeing her husband make advances toward another woman? Reiko herself would kill Sano if he ever behaved this way.

Yet Lady Miyagi merely watched and nodded; her stiff smile never wavered. If she felt any jealousy, she kept it well hidden. "Do you enjoy poetry, Lady Sano?" Sunlight slanted through the pavilion's lattice walls, revealing the mustache hairs on her upper lip. At Reiko's helpless nod, she said, "So do I."

They discussed famous poets and quoted classic poems. Lady Miyagi recited some of her own verse and invited Reiko to do the same. Licking his fingers, Lord Miyagi watched. Reiko hardly knew what she was saying. As the food soured in her churning stomach, her mind whirled with questions. What had happened between the couple and Lady Harume? Was this how it had started? Had it led to the concubine's death?

However, Reiko had lost whatever control she'd had over the interview. None of Sano's explanations or advice had prepared her for the actuality of this situation. She couldn't figure out how to direct the conversation back to the murder case without arousing suspicion. Despair worsened the sickness that washed over her in hot and cold waves. The morning took on the dimensions of a nightmare. Lady Miyagi's eyes shone as she recited haiku. Reiko squirmed beneath Lord Miyagi's tactile gaze. At last she could bear her distress no longer.

"I've imposed upon your hospitality for too long," she choked out. "Now I must be going."

The daimyo sighed regretfully. "So soon, my dear? Ah, well . . . partings are inevitable, the joys of life ephemeral. The frost claims even the freshest, loveliest blooms."

Again the dark excitement swelled in his voice. Reiko felt the spirit of Lady Harume hovering over the garden. Her gorge rose.

Then Lord Miyagi's eyes brightened, like sunlight reflecting off polluted water. "Tonight we are making a trip to our villa in the hills, to view the autumn moon. Would you be so good as to accompany us?"

No! I never want to see you again! Let me out of here! The vehement refusal would have burst from Reiko's lips, had she not been pressing them together in an attempt to contain her sickness. She knew the danger she courted during every moment spent with a man who found pleasure in the death of a young woman.

"Please do come," Lady Miyagi urged. "Your poetic talent will find much inspiration in the beauty of nature."

Sano had told her to be careful, and the thought of going anywhere with the Miyagi terrified and repulsed Reiko.

"The occasion will provide us a chance to become better acquainted, my dear." The daimyo's lazy smile suggested a night of bizarre, forbidden thrills. "So far from the city, nothing shall disturb us."

Yet Reiko had no proof that Lord Miyagi had poisoned Harume. Her own certainty wouldn't convict him. She needed evidence, or a confession. To obtain either, she must take advantage of the chance to see Lord Miyagi again.

"Thank you for the kind invitation." Reiko forced the words past the sour bile in her throat. "I gladly accept."

Fighting nausea, her skin cold and clammy, she nodded as her hosts discussed and settled upon travel arrangements. "Now I must be on my way to finish my calls and prepare for the journey. Good-bye!"

The walk through the daimyo's estate to the street lasted an eternity. Dizzy and faint, Reiko jumped into her waiting palanquin, not at all sure she could control herself until she got home. As the vehicle bounced with the bearers' steps, her stomach heaved.

"Stop!" Reiko cried.

Leaping out, she ran into an alley, crouched, and vomited, raising her sleeve to shield herself from public view. Relief was instantaneous, but dread followed immediately. How could she bear to spend an entire night with the Miyagi? Stumbling back to the palanquin, Reiko consoled herself with the knowledge that she had the rest of the day to prepare for the ordeal. She couldn't let Sano down, when failure to solve the case would ruin them. Somehow she must deliver Lord Miyagi to justice.

If only her courage—and stomach—didn't fail her.

34

The Tsubame Inn, where Lady Harume and Lord Miyagi had trysted, was located in a quiet lane on the outskirts of Asakusa, away from the busy Kannon Temple precinct. Its low, thatch-roofed buildings clustered behind a high bamboo fence. Across the street, an earthen wall surrounded a minor temple. The blank façades of warehouses comprised the immediate neighborhood.

Dismounting outside the inn's gate, Sano surveyed the empty street. A short distance away, birds soared above rice fields. Harume and the daimyo could not have chosen a more private, out-of-the-way place for a rendezvous. However, Sano hadn't come here to investigate their affair. He was playing a hunch.

He stepped through the gate. Inside, an artfully landscaped garden of evergreens, cherry trees, and red-leafed maples signaled a high class of clientele, none of whom was visible. The buildings' doors were closed, their windows shuttered. But Sano heard the murmur of voices through thin walls; he could smell food cooking. Steam issued from the bathhouse. Sano suspected that a raid on the inn would expose the illicit liaisons of some of Edo's most prominent citizens. He hoped that the solution to the mystery of Lady Harume's murder also hid here.

The entranceway of the front building sheltered an alcove tastefully decorated with branches of red berries in a black ceramic vase instead of the usual list of prices for room and board. When Sano rang the bell, the proprietor emerged from his living quarters.

"Welcome to the Tsubame Inn, master," he said. "You wish lodgings?" His grave mien and somber black kimono conveyed the utmost discretion.

Sano introduced himself. "I need some information about one of your former guests."

The proprietor's haughty eyebrows lifted. "I'm afraid it's against our policy for me to supply any. Our clients pay for privacy, and we take pains to ensure it."

Sano understood this to mean that the man paid the authorities not to look too closely into the inn's operations. However, his own power superseded that of petty local officials. "Cooperate, or I'll arrest you," he said. "This is a murder investigation. And since the guest in question is dead, she can hardly mind if you talk about her."

"All right." The proprietor shrugged in annoyed resignation. "Who was she?"

"Lady Harume, the shogun's concubine. She came here to meet Lord Miyagi of Tosa Province."

The proprietor brought out the guest register and made a show of consulting it. "I'm afraid that those individuals have never patronized this inn."

"There's no use hiding behind a list of false names." Sano knew that the proprietors of such establishments took care to find out who their clients were. Guessing the reason for the man's evasion, he said, "Don't worry about Lord Miyagi punishing you for talking to me. I'm not interested in him right now. What I want to know is this: Did Lady Harume meet anyone else here?"

If she'd had a secret lover, the concubine would have had to see him outside Edo Castle. She'd had limited freedom, little money of her own, and probably nowhere to go for illicit meetings. How better to arrange liaisons than during the same outings when she'd escaped her guards to meet Lord Miyagi, at the inn where he'd paid for the room? Therefore Sano had come to the Tsubame Inn in search of an unidentified potential suspect. Now creative deduction reaped its reward.

"Yes," the proprietor admitted, "she did meet another man."

"Who was he?" Sano asked eagerly.

"I don't know. Lady Harume sneaked him in. I only found out about him by accident—the maids heard a man and woman coupling in the room, which was unusual, because Lord Miyagi always stayed outside. Later I had the man followed, but was unable to learn his name, occupation, or where he lived, because he always got away."

Was jealousy of Harume's lover the daimyo's motive for killing her? "What did the man look like?" Sano said.

"He was a plainly dressed samurai in his twenties. That's all I can tell you. He was careful to avoid observation—as are many of our guests." The proprietor gave a sardonic smile. "I'm sorry I can't be of more help."

So the lover wasn't Lieutenant Kushida, but definitely a man, not a woman. Sano said, "Can I see the room they used?"

"It's occupied now, and has been thoroughly cleaned since Lady Harume's last visit."

"Would you recognize the man if you saw him again?"

"Maybe." The proprietor looked doubtful.

He might be someone from Edo Castle. Sano considered taking the proprietor there to try and pick out Harume's lover. But he might also be someone she'd met outside, or known before she became the shogun's concubine. "I'll post a detective here in case the man comes again," Sano told the proprietor. "Don't worry; your guests won't be bothered."

As Sano left the inn, disappointment drained his initial elation. Confirming the existence of Harume's lover brought him little closer to solving the case. Other troubles weighed heavily on his mind. He wondered whether he'd done the right thing concerning Hirata. Should he have removed Hirata from the investigation, lest he cause more problems? Or assigned other detectives to check his results on the scene of Choyei's murder and the dagger attack on Harume? But that would betray their mutual trust, possibly driving Hirata to ritual suicide. And as for Reiko . . .

Sano's heart swelled with love for his wife. But love brought worry, like a net that arrested the joyful flight of his soul. He yearned to know how she was faring with Lord Miyagi. Though he couldn't think what else he could have done and still preserved the spirit of their marriage, he regretted sending Reiko on such a hazardous mission. If the daimyo was the killer, he'd already destroyed one young woman. Reiko, like Lady Harume, was beautiful and sexually appealing—tempting prey.

Then Sano's practical side countered his fears. Reiko had promised to be careful. The daimyo wouldn't dare attack the wife of the shogun's *sōsakan-sama*. In any event, the more likely suspect was Lieutenant Kushida. However, it was all Sano could do to keep from rushing off to defend his beloved. He fought the impulse, reminding himself of the promise he'd made Reiko and the cost of betrayal. Then he forced his attention back to the matter at hand.

He couldn't help believing that the key to the mystery lay in this place that had harbored Lady Harume's secrets. Instead of mounting his horse, he looked around. His gaze lit on the placard hanging from the gate across the street. It read, "Hakka Temple." Sano recalled the printed prayer he'd found in Harume's room. She must have bought it there before or after meeting Lord Miyagi at the inn. With a sense of impending discovery, Sano entered the temple precinct.

The humble worship hall stood in quiet isolation, with no entertainment district to attract crowds. All the priests must be out begging alms. Yet Sano felt Lady Harume's presence, like a ghost tugging at his sleeve. Heading toward the hall, he heard voices from the rear and followed them to a small cemetery. The leafless boughs of willow trees drooped over the grave markers; stone shafts nestled in dead grass. Four men stood by one large marker, conferring over something spread upon its flat top. Two wore dirty, ragged clothes. Their grimy faces bore the stamp of poverty. The other men looked clean and well fed, dressed in padded cloaks. As Sano approached, he heard one of these say, "Five *momme* for the whole lot."

"But these are fresh, master," said a ragged man. "We got them yesterday."

"And they came from a young woman," added the other. "Perfect for your business, masters."

The second customer said, "I'll give you six *momme*."

An argument ensued. Moving closer, Sano saw the objects of trade: ten human fingernails, arranged in a row beside a pile of black hair. Sano recalled the nails and hair he'd found in Lady Harume's room. He felt a glow of satisfaction as a piece of the puzzle dropped into place.

The dealers were *eta* corpse handlers who robbed body parts from the dead. The customers were brothel servants, buying the relics for the courtesans to give clients as love tokens, so they needn't mutilate their own hands or coiffures. Lady Harume must have wandered into the temple after leaving the inn. She'd found the *eta* and bought their wares to give men, as her mother the nighthawk prostitute must have done. Sano's initial guess was confirmed. But what, if anything, did this have to do with Harume's murder?

Silver coins changed hands; the customers departed. The *eta,* catching sight of Sano, prostrated themselves on the ground. "Please, master, we weren't doing anything wrong!"

Sano understood their terror: a samurai could kill outcasts on a whim, without fear of reprisal. "Don't be afraid. I just want to ask you some questions. Get up."

The *eta* obeyed, huddling together, eyes respectfully downcast. One was old, the other young, with similar bony features. "Yes, master," they chorused.

"Did a young, pretty lady dressed in fine clothes ever buy hair and fingernails from you?"

The younger blurted, "Yes, master."

"When was this?" asked Sano.

"It was in the spring," said the young man, despite his companion's frantic shushing gestures. Wide, dull eyes gave him a look of naïve stupidity.

"Was a man with her?"

The older *eta* hit the youth, who said, "Ouch, Father, why did you do that?" He withdrew into hurt silence.

"Tell me what you know about the lady," Sano said.

Something in his voice or manner must have emboldened the young man, because he cast a defiant glance at his father, then said, "Our chief happened to be with us that day, making his tour of inspection."

In Japan's rigidly controlled society, every class was organized. The samurai occupied ranks under their lords; merchants and craftsmen had their guilds; the clergy their temple communities. Peasants belonged to groups of households that governed one another. Every unit had a leader, and not even the *eta* escaped regimentation. Their chief held the hereditary name and position passed down from father to son. It was his privilege to wear two swords and don ceremonial dress when he appeared before Edo's magistrates on official business. With this honor came the responsibility of monitoring the activities of his people. Now Sano had a premonition of how the outcast chief fit into the mystery.

"While we were bargaining with the lady," continued the young *eta,* "she kept looking at our chief. He looked back at her. They didn't speak, but we could tell that something was happening between them, couldn't we, Father?" The older man cowered, hands over his face, obviously ruing his son's betrayal of their superior and wishing himself far away. "After the lady bought the hair and fingernails, our chief ordered us to go away. She stayed.

"But we were curious, so we stood outside the wall and listened. We couldn't hear what they said, but they talked for a long time. Then she went to the inn across the street. He waited at the back gate until she let him in."

Delight filled Sano. His hunch had paid off. Lady Harume's ghost had led him to the surprising identity of her secret lover: Not a high official with a good reputation to protect, but a man whose outcast status had appealed to the low taste Harume had learned from her mother.

Danzaemon, chief of the *eta*. His two swords had misled the innkeeper to believe he was a samurai.

"Honorable Master, I beg you not to punish our chief for violating a lady from the castle," the older *eta* pleaded. "He knows he did wrong. Everyone tried to warn him of the danger. If the shogun found out, soldiers would kill him! But he couldn't help himself."

"They went on meeting. And now she's dead." The youth sighed. "Such a beautiful story," he said wistfully. "Just like a Kabuki play I once heard while I was cleaning the street in the theater district."

The beautiful forbidden love that had endangered the outcast leader had threatened Lady Harume no less, Sano knew. Any infidelity would have incurred the shogun's wrath, and resulted in Harume's death. But an affair with the *eta* chief? Punishment would have also included brutal torture at Edo Jail; an angry mob hurling stones and insults at Harume and her lover along the way to the execution ground; their bodies displayed by the highway for passersby to revile and mutilate, as a warning to other criminals. Now Sano understood the true meaning of phrases from the hidden passage in Harume's diary:

"Lying together in the shadows between two existences"; "Your rank and fame endanger us"; "We can never walk together in daylight . . ."

To risk the terrible consequences of discovery, Lady Harume and Danzaemon must have been deeply in love. Had the affair turned sour? Was the chief of outcasts her killer? Sano wondered whether he was getting close to the truth about the murder at last.

"Where can I find Danzaemon?" he asked the *eta*.

A painted map of Japan covered an entire wall of Chamberlain Yanagisawa's office in the palace. In a rich blue ocean floated the large landmasses of Hokkaidō, Honshū, Shikoku, and Kyūshū, as well as minor islands. Black characters designated cities; gold lines defined the boundaries of provinces labeled in red; white lines traced highways; brown peaks represented mountains; blue patches and squiggles were lakes and rivers; green meant farmland. Yanagisawa stood before this masterpiece, holding a lacquer box of pins with round heads made of jade, ivory, coral, onyx, and gold. While he waited for the messenger to bring news that Sano had accused Lady Keisho-in of murder, he planned his glorious future.

He didn't really expect Keisho-in to be convicted or executed. The shogun would never kill his own mother, or precipitate such a scandal. But neither would their relationship ever be the same. The gentle Tokugawa Tsunayoshi would recoil from the taint of suspicion that would cling to Keisho-in. Knowing what she stood to lose if he begot an heir, he would always wonder whether she was capable of murdering his concubine and child. Yanagisawa could easily persuade him to exile Keisho-in to . . . The chamberlain smiled as he stuck a coral pin on the remote island of Hachijo. After the shogun's mother was out of the way, he could execute the next phase of his plan. He began sticking pins in the sites of major Buddhist temples.

During the ten years of Tokugawa Tsunayoshi's reign, a fortune had been squandered on the building and upkeep of these institutions; on food, clothing, and servants for the priests; on extravagant religious ceremonies and public charity. Priest Ryuko, acting through Lady Keisho-in, had convinced the shogun that the expenditure would bring good fortune. But Yanagisawa saw a better use for the money and property. He would expel the clergy and take over the temples, staffing them with men loyal to him. The sites would become his power bases in the provinces. He would establish himself as a shadow ruler—a second shogun, commanding a *bakufu* within the *bakufu*. For his headquarters he chose Kannei Temple, situated in the hilly Ueno district north of Edo. He'd always liked its halls and pavilions, its beautiful pond and spring cherry blossoms. Soon it would be his private palace.

Pushing in a gold pin to mark his territory, Yanagisawa chuckled. The first thing he'd do once he took possession of Kannei Temple would be to host a huge party to celebrate the execution of the traitor Sano Ichirō. Already he tasted the exhilaration of being free of his rival, secure in his unlimited power. He could almost feel grateful to Sano for unwittingly making everything possible!

Dreams of triumph restored the equilibrium that Shichisaburō's declaration of love had upset. Cradling the box of pins in his palm, Yanagisawa looked ahead to a future where the old hurts and needs of his past no longer mattered.

At the sound of a knock at the door, his heart leapt. A tingle of anticipation vibrated within him. "Come in," Yanagisawa called, unable to keep the excitement out of his voice. The news had come. The future was here.

Instead of a messenger, in walked Priest Ryuko, saffron robe flowing, brocade stole glittering, an insolent smile on his face. "Good day, Honorable Chamberlain," he said, bowing. "I hope I'm not disturbing you."

"What do you want?" Yanagisawa's disappointment turned to anger. He hated the upstart priest who had parlayed an affair with a foolish old woman into a position of influence. Ryuko was a leech, sucking up Tokugawa wealth and privilege while hiding his ambitions under a cloak of piety. As much a rival for power as Sano, he was a major part of the reason Yanagisawa wanted Lady Keisho-in gone.

Ignoring the question, Ryuko strolled around the room,

looking at everything with great interest. "You have a most attractive office." Inspecting the alcove, he said, "A four-hundred-year-old Chinese vase from the Sung dynasty, and a scroll by Enkai, one of Japan's master calligraphers." Ryuko examined the furniture. "Teak chests and lacquer cabinets from the days of the Fujiwara regime." He fingered the tea service on Yanagisawa's desk. "Koryu celadon. Very nice." Opening the blinds, he beheld the garden of moss-covered boulders and raked sand paths. "And a most beautiful view."

"What do you think you're doing?" Furious, Yanagisawa stalked over to the intruder. "Get out of here. Now!"

Priest Ryuko trailed his fingers over the silk embroidery of a folding screen. "I need an office in the palace. Lady Keisho-in has told me to choose whichever room I like. Yours shall do very well."

Such unbelievable audacity! "*You*, take *my* office?" Chamberlain Yanagisawa said with an incredulous laugh. "Never!" Someone was going to pay for this affront. Yanagisawa would punish his staff for letting Ryuko in, then begin a campaign to persuade the shogun to banish him. "And take your hands off that screen!" Seizing Ryuko's arm, he shouted, "Guards!"

Then he gasped as the priest's fingers locked his wrist in a bruising grip. Smiling straight into the chamberlain's eyes, Ryuko said, "It didn't work."

"What?" An unsettling sensation crept through Yanagisawa, as if his internal organs were shifting position.

"Your plot to frame my lady and destroy the *sōsakan-sama*." Gloating in triumph, Ryuko spoke with slow, exaggerated clarity, driving home his point while relishing Yanagisawa's dismay: "It—did—not—work."

He explained how a music teacher had seen Shichisaburō sneaking around the Large Interior; how the *sōsakan-sama*'s wife had deduced that the actor had planted false evidence; how the news had arrived just in time to prevent Sano from making an official murder charge against Lady Keisho-in. As Ryuko's spiteful voice went on and on, Yanagisawa's surroundings seemed to recede in a tide of shock and nausea. The lacquer box fell from his hand. Pins scattered across the floor.

In a desperate attempt to dissemble, Chamberlain Yanagisawa said haughtily, "Your story is absurd. I have no idea what you're talking about. How dare you accuse me, you avaricious parasite?"

Ryuko laughed. "It takes one to know one, Honorable Chamberlain. And the truth is written all over you." Looking at the map, he sneered. "You might as well forget about any schemes to take over the country." He began yanking out pins, tossing them on the floor with the others. "*Sōsakan* Sano and Lady Keisho-in have resolved the misunderstanding caused by your trick. Soon the shogun will hear of your heinous attack against his mother and favorite retainer." The priest's desire to gloat had apparently overcome any misgivings about serving advance notice on Yanagisawa. "His Excellency shall come to recognize your true character at last."

Removing the coral pin from Hachijo, Ryuko said, "I can guess whom you planned to send there." He took Yanagisawa's hand and placed the pin ceremoniously in his palm. "Here. You can trade this bauble for food and shelter when you arrive on the Island of Exile."

Horror rendered Yanagisawa Chamberlain speechless. How could his clever plot have backfired so horribly? Fear turned his bowels to rice gruel. Finding his voice, he shouted, "Guards!"

Footsteps pounded the corridor. Two soldiers entered. Yanagisawa pointed at Ryuko. "Get him out of here!"

The soldiers moved to seize the priest, but Ryuko sailed past them toward the door, saying over his shoulder, "I shan't outstay my welcome." Then he paused and turned. "I just wanted you to know what's going to happen to you," he said, puffed up with his own moral superiority. "This way you can suffer a little longer for trying to harm my lady."

With the guards following, Priest Ryuko strode out of the room. The door slammed. For a moment, Yanagisawa stared after the harbinger of evil. Then he crouched on the tatami, arms wrapped around his knees. He felt himself shrinking into the miserable little boy he'd once been. Again his back ached from the blows of his father's wooden pole. The sharp voice echoed down through the years: "You're stupid, weak, incompetent, pitiful . . . You bring nothing but disgrace to this family!"

Yanagisawa breathed the desolate atmosphere of his youth—that amalgam of rain, decaying wood, drafty rooms, and tears. Now the past had caught up with the present. Ghastly scenarios crowded Yanagisawa's mind.

He saw Tokugawa Tsunayoshi's face, pinched with hurt and anger; heard him say, "After all I've given you, how could you treat me this way? Exile is too good for you, and so is ritual suicide. For your treasonous act against my family, I sentence you to execution!"

He felt iron shackles lock around his wrists and ankles. Soldiers dragged him to the execution ground. A jeering horde threw rocks and garbage, while his enemies applauded. Gawkers surrounded him as the soldiers forced him to kneel beside the executioner. Nearby waited the wooden frame on which his corpse would be displayed at the Nihonbashi Bridge. Chamberlain Yanagisawa realized that his father's prediction had come true: his stupidity and incompetence had brought him to the ultimate disgrace, the punishment he deserved.

And the last thing he saw before the sword severed his head was Sano Ichirō, Japan's new chamberlain, standing in the place of honor at Tokugawa Tsunayoshi's right.

Hatred for Sano seared Yanagisawa like a red-hot skewer twisted through his innards, rousing him from his paralysis. Anger flooded him like a healing tonic. With great relief, he felt himself expand to fill his adult persona and the world that his intelligence and strength had created. He surged to his feet. He didn't have to yield to Sano, Lady Keisho-in, or Ryuko. He wouldn't give up life without a fight, as his brother Yoshihiro had. Chamberlain Yanagisawa paced the room. Action restored his sense of power. Now he focused all his energy on solving his problem.

Sabotaging the murder investigation was the least of Yanagisawa's concerns, although he still hoped Sano would fail and disgrace himself. Instead Yanagisawa devised a strategy for combating Sano and Lady Keisho-in's retaliation. Again the plan would accomplish a double purpose. Again it would involve Shichisaburō.

The actor had ruined Chamberlain Yanagisawa's first brilliant scheme. Yanagisawa regretted becoming so entangled with him. He should have discarded the boy long ago; he should never have let infatuation blind him to the danger of using an amateur instead of a professional agent. In a rare moment of honesty, he acknowledged his mistake. Pathetically hungry for love, smitten with the actor, he'd suffered a fatal lapse of judgment. The howling emptiness still yawned within him; he teetered on the brink. His own weakness and need were his greatest enemies.

Then Chamberlain Yanagisawa placed the blame where it truly belonged: on the inept, naïve Shichisaburō, whom he despised almost as much as he did Sano. Relief sealed the abyss. This time his plan would work. A perfect expression of his genius, it would save him, while ending his disastrous relationship with the actor. His dream of ruling Japan, though deferred, was still possible.

Yanagisawa's breath came in gasps, as if he'd just fought a battle; exhaustion weakened him. But his smile returned as he gathered up the scattered pins and replaced them on the map.

On his way to see Lady Harume's secret lover, Sano stopped at Edo Jail. The *eta* settlement was unfamiliar territory to him, and he needed a guide who could introduce him to Chief Danzaemon. Mura, assistant to Dr. Ito, was the only *eta* Sano knew. They traveled to Nihonbashi's northern outskirts, Sano on horseback and Mura walking behind him. Beyond the last scattered houses of Edo proper, they traversed an expanse of weed-infested wasteland where stray dogs foraged through piles of trash. On the opposite side was the *eta* settlement, a sprawling village of huts surrounded by a wooden fence.

Mura led the way through a gate that consisted of a gap in the rough plank fence, then down narrow, crooked lanes awash in mud. Beside these ran open gutters full of reeking sewage. The houses were tiny shacks assembled from scrap wood and paper. In the doorways, women cooked over open fires, scrubbed laundry, or nursed babies. Children ran barefoot. Everyone gaped, then dropped to their knees as Sano passed: Probably they'd never seen a *bakufu* official enter their community. Clouds of smoke and steam billowed over the settlement, creating a foul miasma that stank of decaying flesh. Sano tried not to breathe. He'd eaten a hasty meal before leaving Asakusa, but now, as nausea gripped his stomach, he wished he hadn't.

"It's the tanneries, master," Mura said apologetically.

Sano hoped he could hide his distaste for the settlement when he questioned its chief. Such different worlds Lady Harume and her lover had inhabited!

Following Mura down a dim passage, Sano looked into a courtyard. A lye pond full of carcasses bubbled. Men stirred it with sticks, while women sprinkled salt on freshly flayed hides. Cauldrons steamed on open hearths; a partially butchered horse oozed blood and viscera. When a gust of wind wafted rancid fumes toward Sano, he nearly vomited. Feeling immersed in spiritual pollution, he resisted the urge to flee. How could Lady Harume have ignored society's taboos to love a man contaminated by this place? What had brought her and Danzaemon together "in the shadow between two existences"?

Mura halted. "There he is, master."

Toward Sano came three adult male *eta,* walking with brisk, purposeful strides. The middle, youngest one immediately drew his attention.

Thin as a sapling, his body carried no excess flesh to soften the hardness of bone and muscle. Strong tendons stood out like cords in his neck. Sharp-edged planes carved his face into a pattern of angles. His thin mouth was compressed in a resolute line. Thick, cropped hair grew back from a deep peak above his brow like a hawk's crest. Head high and shoulders squared, he projected an aura of fierce nobility at odds with his patched, faded clothes and *eta* status. The two swords he wore proclaimed his identity.

Danzaemon, chief of the outcasts, knelt and bowed. His two companions did the same, but while the gesture humbled them, Danzaemon's dignity elevated it to a ritual that honored himself as well as Sano. Arms outstretched, forehead to the ground, he said, "I beg to be of service, master." His quiet tone, while respectful, bore no obsequiousness.

"Please rise." Impressed by the chief's poise, which would have done a samurai proud, Sano dismounted and addressed Danzaemon politely. "I need your help in an important matter."

With athletic grace, Danzaemon stood. At his command, his men also rose, keeping their heads inclined. The *eta* chief turned a measuring gaze on Sano, who saw with surprise that he wasn't more than twenty-five years old. But Danzaemon's eyes belonged to someone who'd seen a lifetime of toil, poverty, violence, and suffering. A long, puckered scar down his left cheek bespoke his fight for survival in the harsh world of the outcasts. He was handsome in a tough, savage way, and Sano could see the appeal he'd held for Lady Harume.

Mura performed the introductions. Sano said, "I'm investigating the murder of the shogun's concubine Lady Harume, and I—"

At the mention of her name, instant awareness flashed in the *eta* chief's eyes: He knew why Sano had come. His men sprang to attention, unhooking clubs from their sashes. They evidently thought Sano had come to kill Danzaemon for violating the shogun's lady. Although the penalty for attacking a samurai was death, they were prepared to defend their leader.

Raising his hands in a gesture of entreaty, Sano said, "I'm not here to hurt anyone. I just need to ask Chief Danzaemon some questions."

"Stand back," Danzaemon ordered with the authority of a commanding general.

The men retreated, though Sano could still feel their hostility toward him, a member of the dreaded samurai class. He faced Danzaemon. "Can we talk in private?"

"Yes, master. I'll do my best to assist you."

Danzaemon spoke in the same soft, respectful voice with which he'd greeted Sano. His speech was more cultured than Sano had expected, probably because of his contact with samurai officials. Now Sano found himself subjected to the *eta* chief's scrutiny. A kind of mutual scenting occurred, as if between two animals from different packs. A crowd of *eta* gathered to watch. Sano sensed in them a reverence for their leader that matched any his own people felt toward their lords. Looking at Danzaemon across the vast barrier created by class and experience, Sano knew in a flash of intuition that under different circumstances, the two of them could have been comrades. Danzaemon's slight nod acknowledged that he realized it, too.

"You're the friend of Dr. Ito," he said. The statement sealed their understanding. "We can go to my house. It's nicer there." His manner conveyed a stoic acceptance of his squalid domain and Sano's authority over him.

"Yes. Please." Sano gave his relieved assent.

The house to which Danzaemon led Sano and Mura was

larger and in better condition than the others. It had solid wooden walls, an intact roof, and untorn paper panes behind the window bars. Danzaemon's lieutenants stood sentry outside, while Mura tended Sano's horse. Inside the house, people of all ages, far too many for them all to be family members, filled the main room. A blind man and two cripples sat against the wall. Mothers cradled babies who looked too frail to live. Men awaited Danzaemon's counsel. A young pregnant woman passed out bowls of soup. Upon Sano's arrival, all activity and conversation ceased. The adults prostrated themselves, and the mothers pressed the infants' small heads to the floor.

Danzaemon ushered Sano into a smaller, vacant room. Cheaply furnished but spotlessly clean, it held a desk, a chest, and open cupboards. One cupboard held folded bedding and clothes; the two others, full of ledgers and papers, suggested that the only literate member of his caste devoted more time to work than rest. The window overlooked a yard where men were butchering an ox. Evidently Danzaemon's clan supported itself by practicing a trade; he didn't abuse his position by extorting money from his people. Sano felt awed by the young chief's responsibilities. Did many samurai lords have more, or attend to them with any greater apparent dedication?

Perhaps Lady Harume had admired this trait as well as Danzaemon's looks and manner. Never before had Sano seen such strong proof that character transcended class.

Danzaemon knelt on the mat. Sano took the spot opposite him. "You're here because you've found out about my relationship with Lady Harume," Danzaemon said without straining their relations by inviting a samurai to eat and drink with an *eta*. "Thank you for sparing my life. I've committed an inexcusable crime. I deserve to die, and it's your right to kill me." The *eta* chief's mouth thinned in a bitter smile. "But if you did, you wouldn't get the answers you want, would you?"

In spite of the young man's controlled tone and expression, Sano observed signs of grief: the bleakness in his eyes; lines of strain around his mouth. Danzaemon mourned Lady Harume as no one else did.

"Love may not be a good excuse for breaking the law," Sano said, "but it's a reason I can understand." He would do anything for Reiko, risk any danger, betray any other loyalty. "I won't punish you for loving unwisely. If you tell me about you and Lady Harume, I'll try to be fair."

The current of mutual empathy again flashed between them. Danzaemon inhaled a tremulous breath and released it in a shuddering sigh. Sano watched his need to speak of his lover warring with the reluctance to compromise himself and his people by saying something that might tax Sano's tolerance. Need triumphed over prudence.

"We met by chance. At a temple in Asakusa." Danzaemon spoke haltingly, looking down at his hands, clasped in his lap. "Even though a long time had passed, I recognized her at once. And she recognized me."

"You knew each other before?"

"Yes. When we were children. My uncle used to take me to Fukagawa to gather shellfish on the beach every month. He met Harume's mother and became her client. We would go to her houseboat. While I waited for them to finish, Harume and I played together."

So he'd been correct in guessing that part of the solution to the mystery of Lady Harume's life lay in her past, Sano thought. Blue Apple, the nighthawk prostitute desperate enough to accept *eta* clients, had unwittingly set the course of her daughter's future.

A slight, tender smile curved Danzaemon's lips. "Harume was so small and pretty, but tough, too. She was six years younger than I, but not afraid of anything. I taught her to throw stones, fight with sticks, and swim. It never mattered to her that I was *eta*. We were like sister and brother. While I was with her, I could forget . . . everything else."

His hands turned palms up, as if accepting a burden—an eloquent gesture that conveyed the young boy's unhappy knowledge of his destiny. "Then Harume's mother died. She went to live with her father. I thought I would never see her again."

This was because Danzaemon was one of the low-class companions from whom Jimba had separated Harume,

Sano realized. Yet the horse dealer had not reckoned with the power of fate.

"When we met in the cemetery, at first it seemed as if no time had passed at all," the *eta* chief continued. "We talked the way we did in Fukagawa. We were so glad to see each other." Then he uttered a humorless chuckle. "But of course everything was different. She was no longer a little girl, but a beautiful woman—and the shogun's concubine. I'm a grown man who should have known better than to go near her. But what we felt for each other was so sudden, and strong, and wonderful . . . When she said she had a room at an inn and asked me to go there with her, I couldn't refuse."

Sano marveled at the attraction so powerful that Harume and Danzaemon had courted death to consummate their desire. A centuries-old taboo, defeated by the even more ancient force of sex.

"It wasn't only lust," Danzaemon said, reading Sano's thoughts. He leaned forward, his sharp face alight with the wish to make Sano understand. "What I found with Harume was the same thing she gave me all those years ago: the chance to forget that I'm dirty and inferior, less than human; an object of disgust. When I held her, I felt like a different person. Clean. Whole." Looking away, he added sadly, "It was the only time I ever felt loved."

"Your people love you," Sano pointed out, wondering if Danzaemon's passion had led to Harume's death.

With a pained grimace, the *eta* chief said, "That's not the same. My people are all contaminated with the same stigma as I. Underneath, we all despise one another the same way everyone else despises us."

Raw pain hoarsened Danzaemon's voice, as if he were tearing all the unspoken thoughts of a lifetime from his soul. Probably he'd never met anyone else willing to hear, or capable of appreciating his insight. "Even my wife, whom I betrayed for Harume, can never give me what she did—the kind of love that eased my own self-hatred."

Sano hadn't known that the outcasts themselves embraced society's prejudice. This case had opened his eyes to the realities of worlds besides his own, and his own unwitting participation in human misery.

"What did Lady Harume get from the affair?" he asked.

Anger flared in the *eta* chief's eyes, quickly extinguished by his formidable self-control. "I know it's hard for you to imagine that I could give her anything besides trouble. But she was so alone. Her father sold her to the shogun and considered himself well rid of her. The women in the castle snubbed her because she was the daughter of a prostitute. She had no one to listen to her problems, to care how she felt, to love her. Except me. We were everything to each other."

Here Sano spied a possible motive for murder. "Did you know that Harume was meeting another man at the inn?"

"Lord Miyagi. Yes, I knew." Embarrassment painted red slashes across Danzaemon's cheekbones. "He wanted to watch Harume pleasuring herself. She let him, then threatened to tell the shogun he'd violated her unless he paid her to keep quiet. She did it for me—she gave me all the money. I didn't want her doing something so risky and demeaning. I didn't want blackmail money. But she was hurt when I tried to refuse. She wanted so much to give me something and couldn't believe that her love was enough."

The *eta* chief shot Sano a defensive look. "I won't deny that I took the money to buy food and medicine for the settlement. If accepting a woman's ill-gotten gold makes me a criminal, then so be it."

He laughed, a single sharp note that spoke worlds of the humiliation he must battle daily in trying to better the lot of his people. Then he bowed his head in obvious shame at betraying his emotions. Even as Sano's heart went out to the young *eta* chief, he saw that Lady Harume had given Lord Miyagi a strong reason for wanting her dead. Sano thought of Reiko with the daimyo, and a chill crept through him. Resisting the impulse to hurry to his wife, he weighed Danzaemon's statement. Everything the *eta* had said resonated with honesty. He had truly loved Harume, sincerely regretted her death. But was there a darker side to the story?

Sano said, "Lady Harume was pregnant."

Danzaemon's head snapped up. Shock paled the surface of his gaze like a sheet of ice over deep water.

"You didn't know, then," Sano said.

Closing his eyes briefly, the *eta* chief said, "No. She never told me. But I should have known it could happen. Merciful gods." Horror muted his voice to a whisper. "Our child died with her."

"You're sure it was yours?"

"She told me that the shogun couldn't . . . and Lord Miyagi never touched her. There was no one else but me." Danzaemon added, "I have two sons, and my wife . . ." Sano remembered the pregnant woman he'd seen in the outer room—proof of Danzaemon's potency. "I suppose it's just as well that the child didn't live to be born."

For the sake of the investigation, Sano couldn't accept at face value the apparently genuine sorrow of the *eta* chief, whose survival skills must surely include the ability to deceive. "If the child had been born, and been male, the shogun would have claimed it as his heir and made Lady Harume his consort. She would have been in a position to give you much more than just blackmail money from Lord Miyagi. And your son could have become the next ruler of Japan."

"You can't be serious." Scorn tinged Danzaemon's gaze. "That could never have happened. You found out about Harume and me; eventually someone else would have. There would have been a scandal. The shogun would never accept the child of an *eta* as his own. It would have been killed along with us."

"Is that why you poisoned Lady Harume? To end her pregnancy, avert the scandal, and save yourself?"

Danzaemon blinked, as if stunned by the conversation's unexpected turn. Then he leapt to his feet, protesting, "I didn't poison Harume! I told you how I felt about her. I didn't know about the child. And even if I had, I would sooner have killed myself than them!"

"Kneel!" Sano ordered.

The pupils of his eyes pinpointed with fury, the *eta* chief obeyed. Sano had no doubt about which man to whom Harume had pledged her love. That Danzaemon also knew this,

Sano could tell from the expression of defeat that came over his face. He had motive for Harume's murder, and she'd died tattooing herself for him.

"Think what you will," Danzaemon said. "Arrest me if you want. Torture a confession out of me. But I didn't kill Harume." Defiant conviction lifted his chin and burned in his eyes. "You'll never be able to prove I did."

And there lay the fatal weakness in Sano's case against Danzaemon. According to the results of his detectives' inquiries, the ink jar had not been tampered with along the way from the Miyagi estate to Edo Castle. Therefore, the ink had to have been poisoned at one end of the journey or the other, where no *eta* could ever go. Danzaemon had had no opportunity to commit the murder.

"I know you didn't poison Harume," Sano said. "Now I want your help." Danzaemon regarded him warily. "You said Harume talked to you. Can you remember anything she said that might tell us who killed her?"

"Since I heard the news of her death, I've gone over every conversation we had, looking for answers. There was another concubine who was cruel to Harume, and a palace guard who annoyed her."

"Lady Ichiteru and Lieutenant Kushida are already suspects," Sano said. "Was there anyone else?"

"The assassin who threw a dagger at Harume."

"She told you about that?"

Memory darkened Danzaemon's eyes. "I was there when it happened. We'd just left the inn. She always went first; I would follow at a distance to make sure she was safe. Usually I saw her as far as the Asakusa Kannon precinct, then went on my way. But that day I couldn't bear to let her go. I followed her into the marketplace. I stood outside a cracker stall across the street and watched her step into the alley next to a teahouse. She turned her back and raised her sleeve to her face." A barely audible tremor inflected Danzaemon's voice. "I knew she was crying because she missed me.

"Then Harume screamed and fell. I saw the dagger sticking out of the teahouse wall. People started yelling. I forgot about pretending I didn't know Harume and started toward her. Then someone ran straight into me. She was wearing a dark cloak with a hood. She was in such a hurry to get away, I knew she'd thrown the dagger."

After the thrill of learning that the assassin resembled the person who'd murdered the drug peddler, Sano belatedly registered Danzaemon's choice of pronoun. " 'She'? You mean it was a woman?" Choyei had described his attacker as a man . . . or had he? Now Sano recalled the peddler's agitation when asked what the man looked like. Sano had attributed it to Choyei's fear of death. Had he really been trying to say that a woman had stabbed him? "Are you sure?"

The *eta* chief nodded. "Her hair was covered, and the cloak hid her clothes. She had a scarf over her nose and mouth. But I saw the rest of her face. Her eyebrows were shaved."

In the fashionable style of noblewomen, Sano thought. His heart began to race with the excitement he always felt when nearing the end of a successful investigation. "You never told the police," he guessed.

The *eta* chief shrugged helplessly. "When Harume saw me coming, she called, 'No. No.' I knew what she meant. We couldn't let anyone see us together and suspect that we weren't just strangers who happened to be in the same place at the same time. We couldn't have the police asking me what I was doing there or why I wanted to get involved in something that was none of my business. So . . ."

His harsh sigh expressed the tragedy of a man prohibited from aiding his beloved. "I just turned and walked away. Now I live with the knowledge that if I'd come forward and reported what I'd seen, the police might have caught the assassin. Harume might still be alive." He added in his emotionless voice, "But that's just the way things are." Sano wondered how many times a day he fought for and achieved this impassive acceptance of fate. "I can't go back in time, or change the world."

"What you've told me will help deliver Lady Harume's killer to justice," Sano said. "You'll have the satisfaction of avenging her death that way."

From the hardening of the *eta* chief's mouth and the

despair in his eyes, Sano knew this was small consolation. He thanked Danzaemon for his trouble and rose to go.

"I'll see you to the gate," Danzaemon said.

They left the house, retrieved Sano's horse, and walked through the settlement in silence, with Danzaemon's lieutenants and Mura as an escort. At the gate, Danzaemon bowed in farewell. After a moment, Sano did, too. Thanks to the *eta* chief's clue, Sano now believed he knew who had killed Lady Harume. As he started across the field, he turned for a last look at Danzaemon.

Flanked by his lieutenants and Mura, the chief of the outcasts stood proudly before the fetid settlement that teemed with thousands of people, young and old, who honored and depended on him. But for the misfortune of his low birth, what a fine daimyo he might have made! It was a blasphemous thought, but Sano could more easily imagine Danzaemon commanding an army than Tokugawa Tsunayoshi.

37

"Lady Ichiteru is the logical culprit," Sano said. "A woman threw the dagger at Harume in the Asakusa Kannon Temple precinct. Ichiteru was there, with no alibi. She had access to Harume's room, and could have bought the arrow toxin from Choyei when she got the aphrodisiac she used on you, Hirata."

The young retainer's face was haggard with misery. "I can't believe Ichiteru is the killer," he repeated for the third time since he and Sano had met outside Edo Castle and compared the results of their inquiries. Now, as they rode into the Official Quarter, he stubbornly championed his seducer's innocence. "Maybe Danzaemon is wrong about what he thinks he saw."

Controlling his impatience, Sano cast his eyes up the hilltop. The late-afternoon sun bronzed the palace rooftops and enflamed the trees in the forest preserve. Blue shadows crept outward from the barracks that lined the street, immersing the district in premature dusk. Sano was tired and hungry; he wanted a hot bath to wash away the pollution of the *eta* settlement. He longed to see Reiko and share with her the successful conclusion to the case. The last thing he needed was more trouble from Hirata.

"Ichiteru isn't going to evade interrogation any longer," Sano said with an air of finality. "By now Lady Keisho-in will have explained to the shogun about our misunderstanding. He'll have reopened the Large Interior to us." He paused, then added, "There's too much evidence against Ichiteru. You'll have to give up your partiality toward her whether you like it or not."

"I know." Hirata's hands twisted the reins. "It's just—I can't accept that I could be so wrong about someone who

. . . I still have this feeling that she didn't do it. All day I kept hoping to find some evidence that would prove I wasn't a fool. I convinced myself that Lieutenant Kushida was the killer, and I've been looking all over town for him." They dismounted outside Sano's estate. In the courtyard, a groom took their horses. A pained sigh issued from Hirata. "But now . . ."

Outside the barracks, the detectives and their families often socialized before the evening meal. Today a group of boys fought a mock battle with wooden swords, while the men cheered them on and women chatted. A mother played ball with a toddler. Sano said, "Everyone makes mistakes, Hirata. Let it go."

But Hirata wasn't listening. He stood frozen in the courtyard, staring at the mother and child, a stunned look on his face. "Oh," he said, then repeated with strange emphasis, *"Oh."*

"What's wrong?" Sano asked.

"I just remembered something." Excitement animated Hirata's face. "Now I know Lady Ichiteru didn't kill Harume."

Sano regarded him with exasperation. "Hirata, don't. Enough is enough. I'm going to get cleaned up and have a word with Reiko. Then we'll go to the Large Interior."

Turning, he entered the house. Hirata ran after him. "Wait, *sōsakan-sama*! Let me explain." As they exchanged their shoes for cloth slippers in the entryway, he said, "I think I saw the killer the other day."

"What?" Sano paused with his hand on the door.

Words tumbled from Hirata in a rapid, incoherent flood: "When I went to see the Rat, I thought it was something different, but now I see what was going on, I should have guessed." Fairly bouncing with anxiety, he burst out, "She wasn't selling anything, *she* was paying *him*!"

"Slow down so I can understand you," Sano said. "Start at the beginning."

Hirata gulped a deep breath. He patted the air in an effort to subdue his agitation. "I paid the Rat to keep an eye out for Choyei. Later I went back to see whether he'd learned anything. There was a woman in the room with him. They were bargaining—making a deal. When the Rat came out, he said she'd just sold her deformed child to his freak show." Speaking with deliberate slowness, Hirata explained, "Seeing Detective Yamada's wife playing with their son reminded me.

"Then the Rat told me he couldn't find Choyei. He returned the money I'd paid him. I suspected that he'd actually found Choyei, who had bribed him to keep quiet. Now I'm positive it was the woman I saw—offering the Rat money, not the other way around. She disappeared while we were talking. It must have been the killer, not a mother selling a child. She must have seen the crests on my clothes and guessed who I was and what I wanted, when I asked the Rat about Choyei."

"But Ichiteru is the only female suspect." Even as Sano spoke, he recalled otherwise.

The light of vindication shone in Hirata's eyes. "I've never met Lady Miyagi. What does she look like?"

"She's around forty-five," Sano began.

"Not very pretty, with a long face and droopy eyes and a deep voice?"

"Yes, but . . ."

"And black teeth and shaved eyebrows." Hirata laughed exultantly. "Just think, I had the evidence all along!"

"That's an interesting theory," Sano admitted. "Choyei's landlord thought he heard a man in the room where the peddler died; he could have been fooled by Lady Miyagi's voice. But we haven't placed Lady Miyagi at the scene of the dagger attack. She could have poisoned the ink, but we've no proof that she did. And what's her motive?"

"Let's go and see if I can identify Lady Miyagi as the woman I saw," Hirata pleaded. "The Rat must have found out she was Choyei's customer and tried to blackmail her. She probably meant to kill the Rat the way she did Choyei. I probably saved his life by arriving just then."

Hirata bowed. "Please, *sōsakan-sama*, before you decide Ichiteru is guilty, give me a chance to prove I'm right. Let me question Lady Miyagi!"

Seeking to avert a chase in the wrong direction, Sano

said, "Reiko went to see the Miyagi today. Let's find out if she learned anything." He entered the corridor, where a manservant came to greet him. "Where's my wife?"

"She's not home, master. But she left this for you." The servant proffered a sealed letter.

Tearing it open, Sano read aloud:

"Honorable Husband,

I had a very interesting visit with Lord Miyagi, and I believe he killed Lady Harume. He and his wife have invited me to view the autumn moon with them at their summer villa tonight. I must use this opportunity to question the daimyo further and obtain proof of his guilt.

Don't worry—I've taken Detectives Ota and Fujisawa along, as well as my usual escorts. We'll be back tomorrow morning.

With love,
Reiko"

Suddenly the idea of investigating the daimyo's wife didn't seem so bad. If there was any chance that she was the killer, Sano didn't want Reiko traveling to a remote location with her, even under armed guard.

"I guess Ichiteru can wait a little longer," Sano said. "We'll try to catch up with Reiko and the Miyagi before they leave town."

In a thunder of hoofbeats, Sano and Hirata arrived at Lord Miyagi's gate. Sano cast an anxious glance up and down the street. "I don't see Reiko's palanquin," he said, "or her escorts." Against his will, he began to believe that Hirata was right—Lady Miyagi was the killer they sought. And Reiko, who didn't know about Danzaemon's evidence, thought it was Lord Miyagi. A band of worry closed around Sano's heart.

"Calm down," Hirata soothed. "We'll find her."

Leaping off his horse, Sano accosted one of the two gate

sentries. "Where's my wife?" he demanded, grabbing the man's armor tunic.

"What do you think you're doing? Let go!"

The guard shoved Sano; the other gripped him in an armlock. Hirata rushed to explain. "The *sōsakan-sama*'s wife was supposed to go to the villa with Lord and Lady Miyagi. We want to talk to them. Where are they?"

At the mention of Sano's title, both guards tensed and stepped away from him, but didn't answer.

"We're going inside," Sano told Hirata.

The guards blocked the gate, expressions fearful but obstinate. Their defiance triggered an alarm in Sano: Something was wrong here.

"There's no one home," said a guard. "Everyone's gone."

Seized with an overwhelming fear that something had happened to Reiko in the house, Sano drew his sword. "Move!" The guards leapt aside, and Sano threw open the gate. With Hirata following, he ran across the courtyard, through the inner gate, and into the mansion, calling, "Reiko?"

Silence veiled the long, dim tunnel of the corridor. The ancient smell of the house filled Sano's lungs like a noxious gas. He pounded along floors that groaned under his footsteps, calling his wife's name. He heard the guards shouting at him to stop, and Hirata holding them off. Forging ahead, he found himself alone in the family living quarters. This wing was as cold, dark, and damp as a cave. The mullioned paper walls were gray squares of waning afternoon light. The Miyagi's musky odor saturated the air. Pausing to catch his breath and get his bearings, Sano saw no one. At first he heard nothing except his own labored breathing. Then came a thin wail.

Sano's heart lurched. *Reiko!* Panic burgeoned in him as he followed the sound, hurrying past the closed doors of unoccupied rooms. His aversion toward the Miyagi couple turned to fear as he imagined Reiko their victim. The wailing grew louder. Then Sano rounded a corner. He halted abruptly.

Lamplight spilled from an open doorway. Outside knelt

the manservant Sano remembered from his first visit. Head bowed, the man wept. At Sano's approach, he looked up.

"The girls," he moaned. Tears glistened on his wrinkled face. Raising a shaky hand, he pointed into the room.

As Sano rushed through the door, a disturbing, familiar scent hit him: fetid, salty, metallic. At first he couldn't make sense of the scene that greeted his dazed eyes. Twisted white shapes contrasted violently with black swirls and gleaming red puddles on the slatted floor. Then Sano's vision focused. In a bathchamber furnished with a sunken wooden tub and bamboo screen lay the naked bodies of two women, curled side by side. Their wrists and ankles were bound with cords. Deep gashes across the throats had nearly severed their heads. Crimson blood drenched their long, tangled black hair and pale skin. It had splashed the walls, run over the floor, and dripped over the sides of the tub into the water.

Horror paralyzed Sano. He felt the turbulent thudding of his heart; a cold sickness gripped his stomach. As vertigo dizzied him, he clutched the door frame. He heard a rasping sound, like a saw against wood, and recognized it as his own breathing. With nightmarish clarity, the faces of the dead women stood out from the carnage. Both bore Reiko's delicate features.

"No!" Sano blinked hard, rubbing his eyes to rid himself of what seemed a case of shock-induced double vision. "Reiko!" Moaning, he fell to his knees beside the women and seized their hands.

As soon as he touched the cold flesh, awareness penetrated his agony. Sano realized that his inner sense of Reiko remained intact. He was still attuned to her; he could perceive her life force, like a distant bell that was still ringing. The illusion dissolved. These women's bodies were larger and fuller than Reiko's. He didn't recognize their faces. Sobs of relief wracked his body. Reiko wasn't dead! His stomach convulsed, and he retched, as if trying to vomit up the needless terror and grief.

Hirata rushed into the chamber. "Merciful gods!"

"It's not her. It's not her!" In a frenzy of joy, Sano

jumped up and threw his arms around Hirata, laughing and weeping. "Reiko's alive!"

"*Sōsakan-sama*! Are you all right?" Hirata's face was a picture of frightened bewilderment. He shook Sano hard. "Stop that and listen to me." When Sano only laughed harder, he smacked Sano's cheek.

The blow jolted Sano out of his hysteria. Quieting immediately, he stared at Hirata, surprised that his retainer would ever strike him.

"*Gomen nasai*—I'm sorry," Hirata said, "but you have to get hold of yourself. The guards told me that Lady Miyagi killed her husband's concubines. She tied them up. They thought it was a game. Then she cut their throats. When the guards and servants heard screaming and came to see what was wrong, she ordered them not to tell anyone. She and Lord Miyagi left to meet someone at the castle gate so they could travel to the villa together. That was two hours ago."

Fresh horror drowned Sano's relief. Though he couldn't begin to fathom Lady Miyagi's reasons for killing the daimyo's concubines, her brutal act surely confirmed her, not Ichiteru, as the murderer of Lady Harume and Choyei. Gazing at the bloody tableau, Sano fought the resurgence of panic.

"Reiko," he whispered.

Then he was running and stumbling out of the mansion, with Hirata supporting him.

Above the western hills outside Edo, a tapestry of golden clouds wove across a sky awash with fire, ensnaring the radiant crimson orb of the setting sun. The distant mountains were shadowy lavender peaks. On the plain below, the city lights flickered under a veil of smoke. The river's great curve gleamed like molten copper. Temple bells echoed across the landscape. In the east rose the full moon, immense and bright, a mirror with the image of the moon goddess etched in shadow upon its face.

The Miyagi summer estate occupied a steep hillside off the main road. A narrow dirt trail led through the forest to the villa, two stories of vine-covered wood and plaster. A dense thicket of trees nearly obscured the roof. Lanterns burned in the stables and servants' quarters, but the other windows turned blank, shuttered eyes to the twilight. Except for the evening songs of birds and the wind rustling dry leaves, quiet engulfed the property. Beyond the villa, the terrain climbed through more forest to a bare promontory. A small pavilion topped the rise. In this, Lord Miyagi, his wife, and Reiko sat facing a perfect view of the moon.

Lattice walls at the back and sides of the pavilion shielded them from the wind; charcoal braziers under the tatami floor warmed them. A lantern lit individual desks furnished with writing supplies. A table held refreshments. On a teak stand were the traditional offerings to the moon: rice dumplings, soybeans, persimmons, smoking incense burners, and a vase of autumn grasses.

With a provocative gesture, Lord Miyagi picked up a brush and offered it to Reiko. "Will you compose the first poem in honor of the moon, my dear?"

"Thank you, but I'm not ready to write yet." Smiling

nervously, Reiko wanted to move away from Lord Miyagi, but Lady Miyagi sat too close at her other side. "I need more time to think."

In truth, she was too frightened to apply her mind to poetry. During the journey from Edo, the presence of her palanquin bearers, guards, and the two detectives had eased her fear of Lord Miyagi. But she hadn't foreseen that the moon-viewing site would be so far from the villa, where her escorts now waited. She'd had to leave them behind because ordering them to stand guard over her would have aroused Lord Miyagi's suspicion. Trapped between the murderer and his wife, Reiko swallowed her rising panic. Only the thought of the dagger hidden beneath her sleeve reassured her.

Lady Miyagi laughed, a gruff caw tinged with excitement. "Don't rush our guest, Cousin. The moon has not even begun to approach its full beauty." She seemed strangely altered since morning. Her flat cheeks were flushed; the prim line of her mouth quivered. Her eyes reflected pinpoint images of the lantern, and her restless energy filled the pavilion. Fidgeting with a brush, she smiled at Reiko. "Take all the time you need."

What a pathetic fool, obtaining vicarious thrills by abetting her husband's interest in another woman! Hiding disgust, Reiko politely thanked her hostess.

"Perhaps you'd like some refreshment to fortify your creative talents?" Lady Miyagi said.

"Yes, please." Reiko swallowed hard.

The thought of eating in the Miyagi's presence again brought a wave of nausea. Reluctantly she accepted tea and a round, sweet cake with a whole egg yolk baked inside to symbolize the moon. A sense of imprisonment worsened her discomfort. She could feel night closing in, obliterating the trail leading down the wooded slope to her protectors. Outside the pavilion ran a narrow gravel path. Beyond this, the ground dropped off steeply to the boulder-strewn bank of a stream. Reiko could hear the water rushing far below. There seemed no escape except over the precipice.

Crumbling the moon cake on her plate, Reiko got a tenuous hold on her poise and addressed her host. "I beg you to write the first poem, my lord, so that I might follow your superior example."

Lord Miyagi preened under her flattery. He contemplated the view, then inked his brush and wrote. He read aloud:

> *"Once the moon rose above the rim of the mountain,*
> *Casting its brilliant light upon the landscape.*
> *I raised my eyes over the windowsill,*
> *And, with my gaze, caressed the loveliness within.*
>
> *But now the old moon has waned,*
> *Beauty has turned to ashes—*
> *I stand alone in the cold, cold night,*
> *Waiting for love to come again."*

He aimed a suggestive look at Reiko, who could barely conceal her revulsion. The daimyo was twisting the moon-viewing ritual to serve his own purpose, issuing a blatant invitation for her to replace the lover he'd killed.

"A brilliant poem," Lady Miyagi said, although her praise sounded forced. Her eyes burned feverishly bright.

Ignoring Lord Miyagi's innuendo, Reiko seized upon the tiny opening his verse offered. "Speaking of cold weather, yesterday I went to Zōjō Temple and almost froze. Did you go outside, too?"

"We both spent the entire day at home alone indoors together," Lady Miyagi answered.

That she should give her husband an alibi for the time of Choyei's murder didn't surprise Reiko. However, Lord Miyagi said, "I did go out for a while. When I came in, you weren't there." He added peevishly, "You'd gone and left me all alone. It was ages before you returned."

"Oh, but you're mistaken, Cousin." A warning note sharpened Lady Miyagi's voice. "I was attending to some business in the servants' quarters. If you'd looked harder, you would have found me. I never left the house."

Reiko concealed her delight. If the daimyo was stupid enough to break his own alibi, then coaxing a confession from him should be easy. From the food table, Reiko selected a radish pickle and took a bite. The acrid morsel filled her mouth with saliva; imagining poison, she almost retched as she swallowed. "This is delicious. And think of how far it must have traveled to reach this table! When I was young, my nurse took me to see the vegetable barges at Daikon Quay. It's a very interesting place. Have you ever been there?"

Lady Miyagi cut in brusquely. "I am sorry to say that neither of us has ever had that pleasure."

The daimyo had opened his mouth to speak, but she silenced him with a glance. He looked confused, then shrugged. It was obvious he'd been to Daikon Quay. Certain that he'd stabbed Choyei, Reiko hid a smile.

"Why don't you try a poem now?" Lady Miyagi said to her.

Such pitiful attempts to prevent her husband from making incriminating remarks that the shogun's *sōsakan-sama* might eventually hear! Reiko turned a classic theme to her advantage. She wrote a few characters and read:

> *"The moon that shines on this pavilion*
> *Also shines on Asakusa Kannon Temple."*

Before she could continue questioning Lord Miyagi, the daimyo, inspired by her verse, recited:

> *"In the night, a worm secretly bores an apple,*
> *A caged bird sings out in ecstasy,*
> *The moonlight's milky celestial fluid*
> *streams down through my hands.*
> *But in the graveyard, all is still and lifeless."*

His crude sexual symbolism and morbid obsession with death appalled Reiko. Inwardly recoiling from Lord Miyagi, she said, "Asakusa is one of my favorite places, especially on Forty-six Thousand Day. Did you go this year?"

"The crowds are too much for us," Lady Miyagi said. Though the constant interference annoyed Reiko, she was grateful for Lady Miyagi's company, because surely the daimyo wouldn't hurt her in the presence of his wife. "We never go to Asakusa on major holy days."

"But we made an exception this year—don't you remember?" Lord Miyagi said. "I was having pains in my bones, and you thought that the healing smoke from the incense vat in front of Kannon Temple would help." He chuckled. "Really, you're becoming very forgetful, Cousin."

Thrilled that he'd placed himself in Asakusa on the day of the dagger attack on Lady Harume, Reiko sought to establish his presence in Harume's vicinity. "The Chinese lantern plants in the marketplace were splendid. Did you see them?"

"Alas, my health did not allow me the pleasure," the daimyo said. "I rested in the temple garden, leaving my wife to enjoy the sights alone."

With obvious annoyance, Lady Miyagi said, "We are straying from the purpose of our trip." She turned her brush around and around in trembling fingers; her musky odor grew stronger, as if increased by the heat of her body. "Let's compose another poem. I'll begin this time.

> *"I shall let the brilliance of the full moon*
> *Cleanse my spirit of evil!"*

The sky had darkened, immersing the city in night; stars glittered like gems floating in the moon's diffuse radiance. Inspired by a myth about two constellations that cross once a year in autumn, Reiko dashed off a verse:

> *"Behind the veil of moonlight,*
> *On the River of Heaven,*
> *The Herd Boy and Weaver Girl meet."*

Lord Miyagi said:

> *"As the lovers embrace,*
> *I rave at the sight of their forbidden rapture,*
> *Then they part, and he continues on his journey—*
> *Leaving her alone to face my censure."*

The cold hand of fear closed over Reiko's heart as she considered the significance of his words. Surely she was sitting beside a murderer who acted out the evil fantasies implied. "Forbidden love is very romantic," she said. "Your poem reminds me of a rumor I heard about Lady Harume."

"Edo Castle is full of rumors," Lady Miyagi said acerbically, "and too few of them true."

Lord Miyagi ignored her. "What did you hear?"

"Harume was meeting a man at an Asakusa inn." Seeing a flash of concern in his moist eyes, Reiko kept her expression innocent. "How daring of her to do such a thing."

"Yes . . ." As if talking to himself, the daimyo murmured, "Lovers in such a situation risk dire consequences. How fortunate for him that the danger has passed."

Reiko could hardly contain her excitement. "Do you think Harume's lover killed her to keep the affair a secret? I also heard that Harume began a second romance," she improvised, wondering whether Sano had traced the mystery lover and wishing he could see how well her interrogation was going. "She was really pushing her luck, don't you think?" Did you watch them, Lord Miyagi? Reiko longed to ask outright. Were you jealous? Is that why you poisoned her?

Lady Miyagi burst out, "What difference does it make what Harume did, now that she's dead? Really, I find this subject very repugnant."

"It's only natural to take an interest in one's acquaintances," Lord Miyagi said mildly.

"I wasn't aware you knew Harume," lied Reiko. "Tell me, what did you think of her?"

The daimyo's eyes blurred with reminiscence. "She—"

"Cousin." Glaring, Lady Miyagi spoke through clenched teeth.

The daimyo seemed to realize the folly of speaking about his murdered paramour. "It's all in the past. Harume is dead." His oily gaze slid over Reiko. "While you and I are alive."

"This morning you said Harume flirted with danger and invited killing," Reiko persisted, intent on concluding her case against Lord Miyagi. She had his statement placing him at a crime scene; she needed his confession. "Were you the one who gave her what she deserved?"

Even as Reiko spoke, she knew she'd gone too far. Seeing Lord Miyagi's nonplussed expression, she hoped that he was too dense to realize she'd virtually accused him of murder. Then Lady Miyagi seized her wrist. Gasping in surprise, Reiko turned to her hostess.

"You didn't really come here to view the moon, did you?" Lady Miyagi said. "You befriended us so you could spy for the *sōsakan-sama*. You're trying to pin Harume's murder on my husband. You want to destroy us!"

Her face had undergone a startling transformation. Above blazing eyes, frown lines cut deep slants into her brow. Her nostrils flared; a snarl bared her black teeth. Reiko stared in astonishment. It was like the pivotal moment in a No drama when the actor playing a nice, ordinary woman reveals her true character by changing masks and becoming a ferocious demon.

"No, that's not true." Reiko tried to pull away, but Lady Miyagi's fingernails dug into her flesh. "Let me go!"

"Cousin, what are you talking about?" mewled Lord Miyagi. "Why are you treating our guest this way?"

"Don't you see she's trying to prove you poisoned Harume and stabbed the old drug peddler from Daikon Quay? And you won't let me protect us. You fell right into her trap!"

The daimyo shook his head in befuddlement. "What drug peddler? How can you attribute such vile intentions to this sweet young lady? Release her at once." Leaning over, he tried to pry his wife's fingers loose. "Why should we need protection? I didn't do those terrible things. I've never killed anyone in my life."

"No," Lady Miyagi said in a voice full of quiet menace, "you haven't."

Suddenly the truth hit Reiko like a blow to the stomach. The broken alibis didn't incriminate Lord Miyagi alone. His wife's lies had been intended to protect herself as well. "You're the murderer!" Reiko exclaimed.

Lady Miyagi chuckled, a low growl deep in her throat.

"If it took you this long to figure it out, then you're not as smart as you think."

"Cousin!" As realization dawned on Lord Miyagi, he fell back on his knees. His face seemed to cave in, the soft flesh sinking around the holes of his gaping mouth, his horror-stricken eyes. "*You* killed Harume? But why?"

"Never mind," rasped Lady Miyagi. "Harume isn't important anymore. This one is the problem now. She knows too much." Her lips curved in a malicious grin directed at Reiko. "Do you know, I'm actually quite glad you turned out to be a spy. Now I feel even more justified in doing what I've been planning all along."

"What—what's that?" Still stunned by her discovery, Reiko shrank from the hostility that dripped from Lady Miyagi's voice.

"I didn't let you come here so you could steal my husband's affection. No, I brought you because I saw the perfect chance to get you out of our life for good. Just the way I did with his two concubines."

Lord Miyagi gasped. "Snowflake? Wren? What have you done to them?"

"They're both dead." Lady Miyagi nodded in smug satisfaction. "I tied them up and cut their throats."

Horror flooded Reiko in a sickening gush. Seeing the maniacal fury in her hostess's eyes, she regretted wasting her fear on the wrong person. The daimyo was innocent and harmless. The real danger lay in this woman whom Reiko had dismissed as his insignificant shadow. Now she yearned for the knife strapped to her left upper arm, but Lady Miyagi kept her right hand immobilized. She couldn't reach the hidden weapon.

"But why, Cousin, why?" Lord Miyagi said. White with shock, he stared at his wife. "How could you kill my girls? They never did anything to hurt you. Surely . . . surely you're not jealous?" Amazement lifted his voice. "They were just harmless diversions, like all my other women."

"I know better," Lady Miyagi snapped. "They could have taken you away from me and ruined everything. But I got rid of them. And now I'm going to make sure this one never comes between us, either."

The urgency of demented purpose must have been building rapidly inside Lady Miyagi since Harume's death, driving her to murder again and again. Sudden panic infused Reiko's body with strength. Now the woman meant to kill her, too! Wrenching out of Lady Miyagi's grip, she sprang to her feet and lunged toward the open front of the pavilion. But Lady Miyagi caught the end of her sash and yanked, whipping her around. She grabbed Reiko's ankle. Losing her balance, Reiko fell backward across the table. Food and crockery went flying. As the crash shot pain through Reiko's spine, Lady Miyagi jumped on top of her.

"Snowflake, Wren," the daimyo moaned, huddling in the corner. "No, no . . . Cousin, you've lost your senses. Stop, please. Stop!"

Reiko tried to throw off the daimyo's wife, but her arms were ensnared by the voluminous folds of her kimono, her legs twisted between Lady Miyagi's. She couldn't reach the dagger. She thrashed helplessly as the older woman grappled for her throat. Butting her forehead hard against Lady Miyagi's face, she felt the painful crack of bone against bone. Her vision went black for an instant. Lady Miyagi cried out and reared back. Reiko heaved herself upright, but Lady Miyagi recovered before she could grab the knife. Blood streaming from her mouth, front teeth broken at the gums, she flew at Reiko, eyes crazed. Together they crashed against the lattice wall, splintering it. Cold air rushed into the pavilion.

"Cousin, stop," keened Lord Miyagi.

With great chagrin, Reiko realized that she, a believer in the power of women, had underestimated the daimyo's wife. Lady Miyagi's urge to protect her husband equalled Reiko's determination to share Sano's work. Sano had considered Lady Miyagi a mere slave of her husband and not a serious suspect; like a thoughtless fool, Reiko had followed his example. She'd dismissed Lady Miyagi as old and weak, hardly capable of violence or killing. Now Reiko deplored her own stupidity. She'd correctly placed the blame for the murders within the Miyagi household, but failed to identify the actual culprit. She'd mistaken Lady Miyagi's murderous mania for sexual arousal, overlooking every clue provided by her behavior. Even the poem, an oblique, chilling confession, had slipped past Reiko. Social mores had blinded her as much as Sano.

"Help!" Reiko shouted. At this moment, she would welcome the protection of a man. "Detective Fujisawa. Detective Ota. Help!"

Lady Miyagi laughed breathlessly as she clawed and kicked and pummeled. She tore at Reiko's hair, scattering pins and combs. "Scream all you want. They won't come."

She clamped a hand over Reiko's chin, forcing it back. Reiko fought to free herself, but Lady Miyagi possessed the unnatural strength of madness. Her knees pinned Reiko down. She whipped a dagger from beneath her robe and held the blade to Reiko's face, touching her lips.

At once Reiko ceased struggling and went rigid. Eyes riveted on the length of sharp steel, she couldn't breathe. She pictured the two concubines, slaughtered like animals, and felt her whole spirit recoil from the blade that could spill her own blood. The only other time she'd faced such danger was during that long-ago sword battle in Nihonbashi. She'd felt invincible then—she'd been so young, so foolish. Now the terrible fact of her own mortality struck Reiko. Yearning for Sano, she bitterly rued the error of confronting a murderer alone. But Sano was back in Edo; regrets wouldn't save her.

Reiko forced herself to look past the dagger at Lady Miyagi, who knelt atop her, face hovering so close that Reiko could see the jagged edges of her broken teeth, the red veins in the whites of her hate-filled eyes. "Please don't hurt me." Despite her effort to sound brave, Reiko's voice came out a tearful whisper. "I won't tell anyone what you did, I promise."

Lord Miyagi cried, "See, she wants to cooperate. Set her free. We can all go home and forget about this."

"You mustn't believe her lies, dearest Cousin." Tenderness momentarily softened Lady Miyagi's voice as she addressed her husband. "You must trust me to take care of everything, the way I always do." She angled the knife downward, until it lay across Reiko's throat.

"Please, let her go," the daimyo moaned. "I'm scared."

His fascination with death had either been just a pose, or hadn't withstood the spectacle of real violence. "I don't want any trouble."

"I told my husband where I was going," Reiko said, longing for her own, inaccessible weapon. "You may get away with killing Harume and Choyei, but not me."

Lady Miyagi laughed. "Oh, but I'm not going to kill you, Lady Sano." Keeping the knife positioned, she eased sideways off Reiko. "You're going to do it for me."

She wound a thick skein of Reiko's hair around her free hand, then stood. Yanked upright, Reiko cried out as pain shot through her scalp. She stumbled to her feet. Lady Miyagi held her tight; the knife grazed her neck.

"You were so enchanted by the moon," the daimyo's wife said, "that you decided to take a walk along the precipice." Breathing hard, she forced Reiko to walk over scattered food and poems, past the cowering Lord Miyagi. "You tripped and fell to your death."

"No!" Fresh horror weakened Reiko. "My husband will never believe it."

"Oh, yes, he will." Ruthless determination filled Lady Miyagi's voice. She propelled Reiko down the steps of the pavilion and into the vast, windswept night. "So tragic, but accidents do happen. Move!"

"I should never have let Reiko go anywhere near the Miyagi!" Sano shouted over the pounding of his horse's hooves.

"But there was no way you could have foreseen this happening," Hirata shouted back.

They were galloping up a winding road into the hills. Burning lanterns swayed on poles attached to their horses' saddles. Their shadows flew over the packed earth. Stone embankments and dark forest blurred past on their left; to the right, lower hills cascaded down to the city, now invisible except for specks of brightness at Edo Castle, neighborhood gates, and along the river. His voice jarred by the gait of his horse, Sano called to Hirata, "I should have gone home to see Reiko after leaving Asakusa, instead of heading straight for the *eta* settlement. Then I could have prevented her from going on the moon-viewing trip."

"But if you hadn't seen Danzaemon, you wouldn't have known that it was a woman who threw the dagger at Harume." Hirata's words echoed across the night. "And I wouldn't have made the connection between the Rat and Lady Miyagi. We wouldn't have found the dead concubines. We would have thought it was safe for Reiko to go to the villa."

Cold wind tore at Sano's cloak; oily smoke from the lanterns filled his lungs. The full moon followed them like a malevolent, gloating eye. "I wouldn't have let her go alone," said Sano, refusing comfort as if it would only make him feel better at Reiko's expense. "I'd be with her now."

"They don't know she's working for you," Hirata said. "She'll be all right."

"If we don't get there in time, I'll kill myself." Sano couldn't bear the thought of life without Reiko. How he wished he'd stuck to his original position, even if it meant imprisoning her at home and alienating her forever. At least she would have been safe. "I never should have agreed to let her help with the investigation!"

His rash decision, made at a moment when love had impaired his judgment, could destroy Reiko. She was brave and smart, but also inexperienced and impulsive; it was his responsibility to protect her, and he'd failed. Forging ahead, Sano steered his horse into a narrow cut that angled off the main road. Before leaving town, he'd forced the Miyagi guards to give him directions to the summer villa. Hirata had sent a message summoning detectives to help, but they couldn't afford to wait for reinforcements.

The trail grew steeper and narrower until they had to dismount, leading their horses between endless borders of tall trees. The scent of pine and dead leaves saturated the air. Traveling within the pool of light from the lanterns, Sano had a nightmarish sense of climbing and climbing just to remain in the same place. His muscles strained; his chest tightened with his labored breathing. Was Reiko all right? How much farther to the villa?

A crunching noise moved through the forest nearby. From behind Sano, Hirata called, "What was that?"

"We must have frightened some animal," Sano said, intent on reaching his destination. "Never mind. Hurry."

Finally they reached a level clearing, where the villa loomed dark and silent. In front of the stable stood two empty palanquins, one of which Sano identified as his own. "Hello!" he called. "Anyone here?"

Taking the lanterns and leaving their horses, Sano and Hirata entered the villa through the unlocked door. Weapons hung in racks on the wall of the entryway. Recognizing two sets of swords, Sano rushed into the drafty corridor, shouting, "Ota! Fujisawa! Where are you? Reiko!"

No answer came, though Sano felt her presence, not far away. On the right yawned a cavernous kitchen. "There's smoke coming from the stove," Hirata said. "They must be around somewhere."

Then Sano heard a low, raspy hum that rose in pitch and ended in a sigh. The sound repeated, emanating from a room beyond the kitchen. Sano burst through the door.

Twelve men lay sprawled on the floor amid trays of half-eaten food. Sano recognized Reiko's escorts, and his two detectives. Ota snored—the noise Sano had heard.

"They're asleep," Hirata said.

Sano shook Detective Ota. "Wake up! Where's Reiko?"

Ota groaned and slept on. "They're all drunk," Hirata said in disgust.

Then Sano caught a whiff of Detective Ota's breath. Instead of liquor he smelled a peculiar sweetness, like spoiled apricots. He grabbed Ota's cup and sniffed. A trace of the odor lingered there. "It must be sleeping potion." His fears for Reiko coalesced into the awful certainty that Lady Miyagi planned to kill her. Why else disable the men? "Come on, we'll search the house."

They did, and found no one.

"Lord and Lady Miyagi must have taken Reiko outside to view the moon," Sano said, running out the back door.

The garden was deserted, but on top of the forested slope, the moonlight silhouetted a small building against the night sky. A light glowed within this. "They're up there," Sano said.

Carrying the lanterns, he and Hirata plunged into the woods, toiling up an elusive, overgrown path. They thrashed through low boughs, slid on pine needles and fallen leaves, clambered over rocks and fallen branches.

"I think someone's following us," Hirata said.

Sano ignored the warning. Breathless, he emerged from the forest and saw, above him on the grassy hilltop, a pavilion with a thatched roof. A lantern glowed behind lattice walls. Voices came from beyond the pavilion, where land met a great expanse of star-studded sky.

"Please, Cousin. Killing her will only make things worse." It was Lord Miyagi, his voice ragged with despair.

"We have no choice," Lady Miyagi said.

As Sano and Hirata staggered the remaining short distance up the incline, Lord Miyagi began to sob. "You can't get away with this. And it won't do for you to be executed for murder. How would I get along without you?"

"You couldn't." Bitter triumph rang in Lady Miyagi's voice. "For thirty-three years I've served you, always fulfilling your wishes, protecting you from the consequences. I killed that girl from next door because she caught you spying on her in the privy when we invited her over. I was afraid she would make trouble, so I poisoned her tea. This is just one more thing I must do, so that no one ever separates us."

Then Lady Miyagi had committed the unsolved murder that Magistrate Ueda had mentioned. Even as fear licked at Sano's heart, wild hope surged within him. It sounded as if Reiko was still alive. Panting, he rounded the pavilion and skidded to a stop. His lantern shone upon three figures, defining them in flickering highlights and deep shadow. Lord Miyagi knelt on the path, which bordered a precipice and ended at a sheer drop into a dark abyss. From far below this came the rush of water. Some ten paces away, Lady Miyagi stood near the edge, holding Reiko by the hair. Wind swirled their brilliant robes.

"Reiko!" cried Sano.

The daimyo turned a tear-stained face to Sano. Lady Miyagi spun around. She held a dagger to Reiko's throat. Reiko's face was a mask of terror. When she saw Sano, gladness filled her eyes. She started to speak, but Lady Miyagi jabbed her with the tip of the blade, rasping, "Quiet!"

"Drop the dagger," Sano ordered Lady Miyagi, trying to keep the panic out of his voice. Dread assailed him. "You're under arrest for the murders of Lady Harume and Choyei." He guessed that Reiko must have somehow discovered the truth, provoking Lady Miyagi's attack. "Killing my wife won't help you." Setting down his lantern, Sano beckoned. "Let her come to me."

"Do as he says, Cousin," begged Lord Miyagi.

The weapon wavered in Lady Miyagi's unsteady hand, but she still gripped Reiko tightly. Desperation glazed her eyes. Her long hair whipped in the wind. Sano barely recognized the prim matron he'd met two days ago. Cheeks flushed, chin bloodstained, and teeth bared in a grotesque rictus, she looked like a madwoman. And Reiko's life depended on his ability to reason with her.

"*Sōsakan-sama,* my wife is not really a bad person," said Lord Miyagi. "It's Lady Harume who was evil. She was blackmailing me. My wife only wants to protect me."

Sano said to Lady Miyagi, "If you let Reiko go, I'll advise the shogun to take the special circumstances into account. I'll recommend a lighter sentence." His spirit recoiled from the thought of letting a murderer escape justice, but he would say anything, do anything, to save Reiko. "Just come away from the precipice, and let's talk."

Lady Miyagi didn't move. Sano saw Reiko's throat contract, heard her breathing accelerate, and saw the glassiness of her eyes. "Relax, Reiko," he called, fearing she would die of terror. "You're going to be fine."

"Listen to the *sōsakan-sama,*" Lord Miyagi beseeched his wife. "He can help us."

But Lady Miyagi's red-eyed gaze bypassed Sano as if he didn't exist, fixing on her husband. "Yes, Harume was evil." Replete with sincerity, the words issued from some dark, secret place inside her. "She had the audacity to conceive your child."

"My child?" Confusion lifted Lord Miyagi's voice. "Whatever are you talking about?"

"The child Harume was carrying when she died," Lady Miyagi said. "I saw her at the shrine of Awashima Myōjin." This Shinto goddess was the patron deity of women. "She hung a prayer tablet beside the altar, asking for a safe delivery of the child. I poisoned the ink—to kill them both."

"But I never even touched Harume!" The daimyo crawled past Sano to kneel near his wife. "Cousin, you know what I am. How can you think I fathered a child on her?"

"If it wasn't you, then who else?" Lady Miyagi demanded. "Not the shogun, that impotent weakling." Glaring down at her husband, she lowered the dagger. "All these years, I've tolerated your affairs with other women and never complained, because I didn't think you would touch them; didn't think you could. I believed that in your heart you were true to me."

Dividing his attention among Lady Miyagi, the dagger, and Reiko, Sano eased closer, sending his wife a silent message: *Just a moment more, and I'll save you!*

"I thought we were spiritual lovers. Mated forever, like the swans on our family crest. Sharing everything." Lady Miyagi's mouth turned down; tears spilled over her face. "But now I know better. You sneaked away and bedded Lady Harume without telling me. You betrayed me!"

"Cousin, I never—"

"I know how much you want a son. I couldn't let Harume's child be born. That would have encouraged you to beget another, from one of your ladies. She would become your new wife, and the child your heir. You would have cast me aside. How could I survive without your protection?"

At last Sano understood the true reason for Lady Harume's murder. A misunderstanding had fostered jealousy. The unborn child, not the mother, had been the intended victim of the poison. Quietly Sano crept up on Lady Miyagi and Reiko.

"You killed Wren and Snowflake so they couldn't have sons by me." Dumbfounded, Lord Miyagi shook his head. "But why kill a drug peddler?"

Conviction hardened Lady Miyagi's teary gaze. "I did it so he couldn't identify me as the person who bought the poison. I was going to kill that odious freak-show proprietor who found out and tried to blackmail me, but I lost the chance. Don't you understand that I did it all so everything would stay the same between us?"

"Cousin, I would never cast you off," Lord Miyagi wailed. "I need you. Maybe I've never said so before, but I love you." He extended his clasped hands. "Please, give the *sōsakan-sama* his wife, and come to me!"

"I can't." Lady Miyagi took a step closer to the edge of the precipice. Sano's heart banged against his rib cage; he halted in his tracks, throwing out an arm to keep Hirata back. Any movement might goad Lady Miyagi into hurting Reiko. "I've watched you look at her. I know you want her. The only way I can make sure she never bears you a son is by killing her."

She yanked the dagger up, poking the tip into the soft flesh under Reiko's jaw. Terror shot through Sano. "Listen. Your husband wasn't the father of Harume's child," he said, fighting to keep calm. "He didn't betray you. Harume had another lover. And Reiko is mine. She's not available for Lord Miyagi's use. So give her to me, now."

Lady Miyagi met his plea with a blank stare. Deep in her own world of skewed perception, she seemed impervious to logic. Slowly she turned away, dragging Reiko to the brink of the precipice.

"No!"

Sano rushed toward the women, but Hirata leapt in front of him. The young retainer grabbed Lord Miyagi in a double armlock. "Lady Miyagi, if you hurt the *sōsakan-sama*'s wife, I'll throw your husband over the edge," Hirata yelled.

It was a strategy that hadn't occurred to Sano; his mind had been focused on Reiko. Now he held his breath as he watched Lady Miyagi's head jerk around. When she saw the daimyo, she froze, drawing a sharp hiss of breath.

"Cousin, help, I don't want to die!" Sobbing, Lord Miyagi kicked and struggled in Hirata's grip.

"You can save him," Sano said. A pool of hope spread in his heart. "Just drop the dagger. Then walk this way." Moving down the hillside, he gestured for Lady Miyagi to follow. "Bring Reiko to me."

Lady Miyagi's gaze flashed from her husband to Sano, then Reiko. An anguished moan escaped her. Sano felt indecision weakening her resolve, like cold water cracking hot porcelain, yet she didn't move.

"Hirata?" Sano said.

The young retainer hauled Lord Miyagi to the edge. "Help, Cousin," the daimyo mewled.

No one else spoke. No one moved. Only the sounds of wind and rushing water broke the silence. The great wheel of the heavens seemed to stall, halting moon and stars on their celestial paths. Deranged by jealousy, Lady Miyagi apparently wanted to save her husband, but not without securing her position in his life. Perhaps she also needed to punish him for his imagined betrayal. Sano felt the night expand, vast and dark and terrible as the impasse that the negotiations had reached. Despair overwhelmed him.

Then a series of crashing noises came from the forest. Running footsteps pounded up the slope. Beyond Lady Miyagi and Reiko, a man burst into view. He wore a soiled kimono and carried a spear.

"Lieutenant Kushida." Wonder hushed Sano's exclamation. He saw Hirata stiffen with surprise, and heard the daimyo utter a startled grunt. Lady Miyagi turned slightly, eyes darting, trying to watch everyone at once.

"It must have been him following us in the woods," Hirata said. "What's he doing here?"

The lieutenant ignored Sano, Hirata, Reiko, and Lord Miyagi. Pointing his spear at Lady Miyagi, he shouted, "Murderer!" His monkey face was streaked with dirt; his matted hair hung loose around his shoulders. "Day and night I've hunted the killer of my beloved Harume. At last I've found you. Now I shall avenge her death, appease her spirit, and reclaim my honor!"

Now Sano understood why Kushida had gone to Daikon Quay. He'd tracked down Choyei and forced the dying peddler to reveal the identity of the customer who had bought the arrow toxin. He was the man whom the landlord had heard in Choyei's room. Then he'd stalked Lady Miyagi. Before Sano could react, the lieutenant lunged at Lady Miyagi. She shrieked and lurched sideways across the path toward the pavilion. The spear blade ripped through the sleeve of her robe. Cursing, Kushida attacked again. As Lady Miyagi lashed out with her dagger in an attempt to defend herself, Reiko broke free. She stumbled along the path, trying to avoid Kushida's vicious thrusts. When Sano rushed to help her, the shaft of the spear banged him on the shoulder.

Hirata flung Lord Miyagi aside. Drawing his sword, he charged at Lieutenant Kushida. "I'll take care of him, *sōsakan-sama*. You save Reiko."

Thrusting and dodging, he drove Kushida down the hill. Sano reached for Reiko, but Lady Miyagi slashed his arm with the dagger, shrieking, "Get away!"

Sano drew his sword and chopped at Lady Miyagi's blade. Reiko drew a dagger from her sleeve and joined the battle. Then Sano felt someone come up behind him. He whirled and saw Lord Miyagi waving a sword.

"I won't let you hurt my wife." His droopy features tightened by fear, the daimyo took an awkward swipe at Sano.

Sano dodged the strike. He battered at the daimyo's sword, intending to subdue rather than kill. "You can't win, Lord Miyagi. Surrender."

Reiko slashed at Lady Miyagi, who parried. Their slender blades clashed with a sweet, steely ring. Whirling and feinting at the edge of the drop, amid billowing robes and hair, they engaged in a dance of violent grace. Reiko fought with practiced skill, Lady Miyagi with reckless ferocity. From down the hill, Sano heard Lieutenant Kushida shouting at Hirata, "Leave me alone. I must avenge Lady Harume's death. It's the only way I'll ever know peace."

Lord Miyagi struggled against Sano's superior skill. Sweat glistened on his woeful face. A lifetime of self-indulgence had left him ill suited for combat. Quickly Sano knocked the sword out of his hand. Helpless, he cowered on the ground. He looked at his wife, whose robes hung in bloodstained tatters where Reiko had cut her. A groan of misery issued from him. Sano could see his vision of life without a devoted slave; jail, exile, or confiscation of the family estate as punishment for his wife's crimes. Then Lord Miyagi raised his hands in a gesture of surrender.

"I accept defeat," he said with quiet dignity. "Please allow me the privilege of committing *seppuku*."

The daimyo drew his short sword, gripping it in trembling hands, the blade pointed at his abdomen. Closing his eyes, he murmured a prayer. Either he was taking the coward's way out of a difficult situation, or some vestige of samurai honor lived within him. Then he gulped a deep breath. With a piercing scream, he drove the sword into himself.

"Cousin!" Lady Miyagi rushed over and knelt beside her husband, who writhed and moaned in the agonies of death. Dropping the dagger, she caressed the daimyo's face with her bloody hands.

A great convulsion spasmed his body. He looked up at

his wife, and his lips mouthed unintelligible words. Then he went limp in her arms.

"Oh, no. My darling. No!" Ugly, choking sobs wracked Lady Miyagi.

Panting from exertion, Reiko joined Sano. Gingerly he crouched, reaching for Lady Miyagi's dagger, though he didn't think she would resist arrest now. Then her hand shot out and grabbed the weapon, pointing it at him. Grief twisted her mouth; her face was livid with anger, smeared with blood and tears. "You destroyed my husband," she whispered. "You'll pay for this."

Sano raised his sword. But instead of attacking him, Lady Miyagi assaulted Reiko, crying, "You took away my beloved. Now I'm going to take yours!"

Caught off guard, Reiko dodged too late; the blade missed her heart, but cut her shoulder. Then they were fighting again, with Reiko's back to the precipice and Lady Miyagi between her and Sano. Sano sheathed his sword and seized Lady Miyagi from behind, locking his hands around hers on the hilt of the dagger. As they grappled for control of the weapon, she fell forward on top of Reiko. Sano fell with her. They landed at the very edge, heads extended into empty space.

Reiko screamed, slashing Lady Miyagi's face with her dagger. Lady Miyagi howled. Sano wrenched the weapon away from her. At the same moment, she bucked, throwing him free. Then Reiko gave an enormous heave. Like an acrobat in a street show, Lady Miyagi flipped heels over head. Hands clawing wildly at Reiko, she soared into the air over the precipice and seemed to hang there for an instant. Sano threw himself on top of Reiko, anchoring her. Then Lady Miyagi plummeted out of sight. A high, thin scream followed her. There was a series of diminishing thuds as her body struck the rocks. Then silence.

Sano helped Reiko to her feet. Arms tight around each other, they peered down into the darkness. The moonlight gleamed faintly on Lady Miyagi's robes. She didn't move.

Hirata ran up to them, carrying Lieutenant Kushida's spear and his own sword. He bled from cuts on his hands, arms, and face. "Kushida is wounded, but he'll live. What happened here? Are you all right?"

Sano explained. Then he, Reiko, and Hirata were suddenly locked in a fierce embrace, faces pressed together. A catharsis of weeping shook them. As their blood and tears mingled, Sano experienced a deeper satisfaction than ever before at the end of a case. His wife was safe, his dearest comrade restored to honor. Each of them had played a crucial role in the investigation. Their shared victory was infinitely sweeter than the lone heroics of Sano's past.

"Let's wake up our troops and go home," he said, wiping tears from his cheeks.

Still embracing, with Sano in the middle, they started down the hill.

40

Three days after the death of Lord and Lady Miyagi, a guard captain escorted Chamberlain Yanagisawa to the shogun's private audience chamber. A banner printed with the characters for secrecy decorated the entrance, indicating that a meeting of extremely confidential nature was in session. Sentries stood outside, ready to repel intruders.

"Please go right in, Honorable Chamberlain," said his escort. "His Excellency awaits you."

Somewhere in the city below Edo Castle, a funeral drum beat. As the guards opened the door, Yanagisawa swallowed the metallic taste of fear. His destiny would be determined here and now.

Inside the chamber, Tokugawa Tsunayoshi knelt upon the dais. On the floor to his left, Lady Keisho-in and Priest Ryuko sat side by side. The shogun's mother glared at Yanagisawa, then turned away in a huff. Ryuko flashed the chamberlain a glance of smug triumph before respectfully lowering his eyes. Opposite them, in the place of honor at the shogun's right, knelt *Sōsakan* Sano, his expression carefully neutral.

A volcano of jealous hatred erupted in Yanagisawa. The sight of his enemy occupying his own usual position seemed a realization of his worst nightmare—that Sano had replaced him as their lord's favorite. Yanagisawa wanted to rail against the outrage, but a crude display of temper would ill serve his interests. His whole future depended upon skillful handling of the situation. He needed to remain in absolute control. Kneeling before the dais, he bowed to the shogun.

"Good morning, Yanagisawa-*san*," said Tokugawa Tsunayoshi. His voice held none of its customary affection, and he didn't smile. "It is unfortunate that this session must interfere with your, ahh, administrative duties."

"On the contrary—I'm honored to be called to your presence at any time." Although the chilly reception filled him with dread, Yanagisawa spoke as if he had no idea that this secret meeting had been called because his plot against Sano had backfired and he was now facing treason charges. "My service is yours to command."

"I have summoned you here to resolve some, ahh, serious issues that have been raised by *Sōsakan* Sano and my honorable mother," said the shogun, nervously toying with his fan.

Chamberlain Yanagisawa's heart thumped like a wild creature trying to escape the cage of his body. Though he'd envisioned this scene countless times since Ryuko had come to his office, the reality was still terrible. He must conquer his fear and concentrate on repairing the damage he'd done himself.

"Certainly I shall cooperate in any way I can, Your Excellency." Yanagisawa made his expression reflect puzzlement and a somber eagerness to please, inserting just the right note of innocence into his voice. "What seems to be the problem?"

"It appears that you have, ahh, tried to frame my beloved mother for the murder of Lady Harume, and to ruin my dear, loyal *sōsakan* by forcing him to accuse her. This is not only treason of the, ahh, highest order, but also a personal betrayal." Tokugawa Tsunayoshi's voice was high and tight; tears glistened in his eyes. Lady Keisho-in muttered angrily as she patted her son's hand. Ryuko smiled ever so slightly at Yanagisawa, while Sano watched everyone with wary alertness. "For fifteen years I've given you everything you desire—land, money, power. And you repaid my, ahh, generosity by attacking my family and my friend. This is an outrage!"

"It would be if it were true," Chamberlain Yanagisawa said, "but I can assure you that it is absolutely not." Sweat drenched his armpits and his hands turned to ice, but he knew exactly what he must do. Letting shock and hurt register on his face, but careful not to overact, he said, "Your

Excellency, whatever led you to believe I committed such heinous acts?"

"Ahh—" The shogun gulped and blinked. Overcome by emotion, he gestured weakly toward Sano.

"You ordered Shichisaburō to plant a letter written by Lady Keisho-in among Harume's possessions for me to find," Sano said.

The *sōsakan-sama*'s cautious tone signaled his knowledge that the battle wasn't over, despite Keisho-in's smirk and Ryuko's veiled gloating. While Sano explained how the ruse had been discovered, Yanagisawa shook his head in dismay, then let feigned anger harden his features.

"Shichisaburō acted without my orders or my knowledge," he said.

Lady Keisho-in gasped. "Incredible!" Ryuko's eyes narrowed. Sano frowned.

"Is that so?" Hope lifted the shogun's voice. "Do you mean that it's all the boy's fault, and you had nothing to do with the, ahh, plot against my mother and the *sōsakan-sama*?"

Chamberlain Yanagisawa felt the weight of victory shift in his direction. Tokugawa Tsunayoshi still cared for him, desiring reconciliation as much as justice. "That's exactly what I mean."

The shogun smiled in relief. "It seems we've misjudged you, Yanagisawa-*san*. A thousand pardons."

Now the double purposes of Yanagisawa's plan came together. Shichisaburō would take the blame for the failed plot, and the natural course of events would end their affair. No longer would he awaken dangerous cravings in Yanagisawa, or undermine his judgment and strength. Yanagisawa bowed, humbly accepting the shogun's apology, preparing for the next round.

Just as he'd expected, Sano said, "I suggest that Shichisaburō be allowed to tell his version of the story."

"Oh, very well," the shogun said indulgently.

Soon Shichisaburō was kneeling before the dais at Yanagisawa's side. Worry pinched his small face. He looked to Yanagisawa for reassurance, but the chamberlain refused to meet his lover's gaze. He couldn't wait to be rid of the despicable creature.

"Shichisaburō, I want you to tell us the truth," Tokugawa Tsunayoshi said. "Did you, upon your own initiative, without, ahh, directions from anyone else, steal a letter written by my mother and hide it in Lady Harume's room?"

Of course the boy would spill the whole story, Chamberlain Yanagisawa knew. But it was a humble actor's word against his own, and he could easily make Shichisaburō look like a liar.

"Yes, Your Excellency, I did," said Shichisaburō.

Yanagisawa stared at him, astonished. Excited mutters arose from Lady Keisho-in and Priest Ryuko; the shogun nodded. Sano said, "Your Excellency, I think that the present company is intimidating Shichisaburō. We'll have a better chance of learning the truth if you and I speak to him privately."

"No!" Shichisaburō's cry rang out. Then his voice dropped. "I'm all right. And I—I am telling the truth."

Confusion rendered Chamberlain Yanagisawa speechless. Was the actor crazy, or just stupid?

"Do you realize that you are admitting that you, ahh, tried to frame my mother for murder?" the shogun asked Shichisaburō. "Do you understand that this is treason?"

Trembling visibly, the boy whispered, "Yes, Your Excellency. I am a traitor."

Tokugawa Tsunayoshi sighed. "Then I must condemn you to death."

While guards chained Shichisaburō's arms and legs for the trip to the execution ground, Tokugawa Tsunayoshi looked away from the distasteful sight. Lady Keisho-in burst into tears. Glaring at Yanagisawa, Priest Ryuko comforted her. Sano's face mirrored dismay and resignation. Chamberlain Yanagisawa waited for the actor to plead for his life, to incriminate his master in an effort to save himself, to protest the betrayal. Yet Shichisaburō passively accepted his fate. As the soldiers led him to the door, he turned to Yanagisawa.

"I'd do anything for you." Though his complexion had gone as white as ice, love blazed from his dark eyes; he spoke with reverence and joy. "Now it is my privilege to die for you."

Then he was gone. The door slammed behind him.

"Well," said Tokugawa Tsunayoshi, "I am glad that the, ahh, misunderstanding has been cleared up and this unpleasant business resolved. *Sōsakan* Sano, move over. Come and sit by me, Yanagisawa-*san*."

But Chamberlain Yanagisawa, stunned by what had just happened, sat staring after Shichisaburō. For his sake, the actor had willingly made the ultimate sacrifice. Instead of relief, Yanagisawa experienced an agonizing onslaught of grief, regret, and horror. He realized that he'd just destroyed the only person in the world who truly cared for him. Too late, he perceived the value of Shichisaburō's love, and the desolate void it left behind.

Come back! he wanted to shout.

Yet even as he considered admitting that he, not the actor, had instigated the plot, he knew he wouldn't. Selfishness outweighed his capacity for doing what was right—and for love. Now he saw the ugly flaw in his character. He was as worthless as his parents had claimed. Surely this was why they'd withheld their affection from him.

"Yanagisawa-*san*?" The shogun's peevish voice penetrated his misery. "I told you to come here."

Yanagisawa obeyed. The howling emptiness inside him eroded his soul, growing deeper and darker, never to be filled. Ahead of him stretched a life populated with slaves and sycophants, political allies and enemies, superiors and rivals. But there was no one to nurture his starved heart, or mend his damaged spirit. Unloving and unloved, he was doomed.

"You look ill," Tokugawa Tsunayoshi said. "Is something the matter?"

Seated opposite Yanagisawa in a hostile trio were *Sōsakan* Sano, Lady Keisho-in, and Priest Ryuko. He could tell that they knew the truth about Shichisaburō's confession and his own role in the plot. They didn't intend to let him get away with attacking them. This battle was over, but the war continued—with his rivals united against him.

"Everything's fine," Chamberlain Yanagisawa said.

* * *

Hirata walked through Edo Castle's herb garden, where he'd ordered Lady Ichiteru to meet him. A blanket of murky cloud covered the sky, with the sun a diffuse white glow above the palace rooftops. Soaring crows cawed. Frost had withered the beds of herbs, though their pungent scents lingered. Gardeners swept the paths; in a long shed, the castle pharmacist and his apprentices prepared remedies. Lady Ichiteru's attendants waited at the gate. This time Hirata had deliberately arranged circumstances to preclude seduction, while providing enough privacy for what he intended to be their last conversation.

He found Ichiteru alone beside a pond in which lotus bloomed in summer. Standing with her back to him, she contemplated the tangled mat of foliage. She wore a gray cloak; a black veil covered her hair. Hirata could tell by the way her spine stiffened that she was aware of his presence, but she didn't turn. So much the better: he could speak his mind without succumbing to her allure.

"It was you who gave Lady Harume the poison that made her sick last summer, wasn't it?" Hirata said. "It was you she feared, and begged her father to rescue her from."

"So what if it was me?" Indifference dulled Ichiteru's husky voice. "You have no proof."

She was right. Hirata had spent the past three days investigating the incident, and had eliminated the other palace residents as suspects. He knew Ichiteru was guilty, but he'd found no evidence against her, and since she was obviously not about to confess, there was nothing he could do. Ichiteru had gotten away with attempted murder, as well as making a fool of him. Angry humiliation stung Hirata.

"I know you did it," he said. "Since you didn't kill Harume, it's the only explanation for how you treated me. You were afraid the *sōsakan-sama* would discover that you were responsible for the earlier poisoning, and you wanted Lady Keisho-in convicted of Harume's murder. So you used me."

Seething inside, Hirata continued, "I bet you're pretty pleased with the way things turned out. But hear this: I know what you are—a murderess in spirit if not in fact. And I'm warning you: Cause trouble again, and I'll come after you. Then you'll get the punishment you deserve."

"Punishment?" Lady Ichiteru gave a disdainful laugh. "What can you do to me that's worse than the future that already lies ahead?"

She turned; her veil slipped. Hirata stared in shock. Ichiteru wore no makeup. Her eyes were red and puffy from weeping, her pale lips bloated. Her bare skin looked mottled and sallow, and she wore her hair in an untidy knot devoid of ornaments. Hirata barely recognized this plain figure as the woman who had captivated him.

"What happened to you?" he said.

"Tomorrow, fifteen new concubines arrive in the Large Interior. I was just informed that I am one of the women who will be dismissed to make room for them—three months short of my official retirement date!" Lady Ichiteru's voice shook with fury. "I've lost my chance to bear the shogun an heir and become his consort. I shall return to Kyōtō with nothing to show for thirteen years of degradation and pain. I'll spend the rest of my life as an impoverished spinster, a despised symbol of the imperial family's failed hopes for a restoration to glory."

Sneering at Hirata, Lady Ichiteru said, "I apologize for what I did to you, but you'll get over it. And whenever you think of me, you can laugh!"

Hirata's need for vengeance dissolved. His attraction to Ichiteru had vanished with the artificial trappings of fashion and manner; her bitterness repelled him. Finally he could forgive and even pity Ichiteru. Her fate was indeed her punishment. His own concerns seemed trivial in comparison.

"I'm sorry," he said.

He would have wished her luck, or offered polite words of comfort, but Lady Ichiteru turned away. "Leave me."

"Good-bye, then," Hirata said.

Walking back through the garden, he felt years older than when he'd begun the investigation. The experience had fostered wisdom. Never again would he allow a murder suspect to manipulate him. Yet the departure of the strong emotions he'd had toward Ichiteru left a vacancy in his spirit. He should attend to other cases before Sano's wedding banquet, scheduled for that evening, but Hirata was too restless for work. Filled with vague yearnings, he entered the forest preserve, hoping that a solitary stroll would clear his mind.

He'd no sooner started down a path when a hesitant voice spoke behind him. "Hello, Hirata-*san*."

Turning, he saw Midori approaching. "Hello," he said.

"I took the liberty of following you from the herb garden because I thought—I hoped—you might like company." Blushing, Midori fidgeted with a lock of her hair. "I'll go away if you don't want me."

"No, no. I'd be grateful for your company," Hirata said, meaning it.

They wandered between birches that dropped golden leaves upon them. For the first time since they'd met, Hirata really looked at her. He saw the beauty in her clear, direct gaze, her guileless behavior. He could understand his infatuation with Lady Ichiteru as a sickness that had blinded him to good things, including Midori. Thinking about the conversations he'd enjoyed with her, Hirata remembered something.

"You knew that Ichiteru tried to kill Harume last summer, didn't you?" he said. "And you tried to warn me that she planned to use me to make sure she would never be arrested for the murder."

Hiding her face behind the shiny curtain of her hair, Midori looked at the ground. "I wasn't sure, but I suspected . . . And I didn't want her to hurt you."

"Then why didn't you say so? I know I must not have seemed very eager to listen, but you could have spoken up, or written me a letter, or told the *sōsakan-sama*."

"I was too afraid," Midori said unhappily. "You admire her so. I thought that if I said anything bad about her, you'd think I was lying. You'd hate me."

That a highborn girl could not only care about him, but also want him to think well of her, amazed Hirata. Now he realized that she'd liked him all along. She didn't care about his humble origins. Midori's honest tribute lifted him free of the prison of insecurity. It no longer mattered that he lacked noble lineage or cultured elegance. His life's achievements—the true manifestations of honor—would suffice. Hirata suddenly wanted to laugh with exultation. How strange that his most humiliating experience should also bring the gift of revelation!

Touching Midori's shoulder, he turned her to face him. "I don't admire Lady Ichiteru anymore," he said. "And I could never hate you."

Midori regarded him with wide, solemn eyes full of dawning hope. A smile trembled on her lips; her dimples flashed shyly, like sunlight glinting on pearls under water. Hirata felt a spring of happiness as he saw a possible answer to his longing.

"What are you going to do now that Ichiteru is leaving?" he asked.

"Oh, I'll be lady-in-waiting to one of the other concubines," said Midori. She added, "I'm supposed to stay at Edo Castle until I marry."

Or perhaps even afterward, Hirata thought, if he remained stationed here and their fortunes coincided. But that was rushing things. For now, he was satisfied to know they would both be at the castle long enough for the future to unfold.

"Well," Hirata said, grinning. "I'm glad to hear that."

Midori gave him a radiant smile. Sleeves touching, they continued along the path together.

"It is my pleasure to open the celebration of the marriage of *Sōsakan* Sano Ichirō and Lady Ueda Reiko," announced Noguchi Motoori.

The go-between and his wife knelt upon the dais in the reception hall of Sano's mansion. Beside them, Sano and Reiko, dressed in formal silk kimonos, sat beneath a huge paper umbrella, symbol of lovers. Wall partitions had been removed, expanding the room to accommodate three hundred banquet guests—friends and relatives, Sano's colleagues, superiors, and subordinates, representatives of prominent daimyo clans. Glowing lanterns hung from the ceiling; the atmosphere shimmered with the scents of perfume, tobacco smoke, incense, and cooking.

"Like rain after a drought, these festivities are much delayed and therefore all the more welcome," Noguchi said. "Now I invite you to join me in congratulating the bridal couple, and wishing them a long, happy life together."

Musicians played a cheerful melody on samisen, flute, and drum. Servants passed out sake decanters and cups, proffered laden trays of delicacies. Cries of *"Kanpai!"* arose from the guests. His heart brimming with joy, Sano exchanged smiles with Reiko.

The murder investigation was over, albeit not as comfortably as he would have liked. The violent deaths of Lord and Lady Miyagi still disturbed him. Lieutenant Kushida had been transferred to a post in Kaga Province, where he might or might not recover from his obsession and build a new life. Also, Sano felt that he should have guessed that Chamberlain Yanagisawa would sacrifice Shichisaburō, and somehow saved the actor.

However, there would be plenty of time later to review the case, to apply the experience toward better results in future. Relative harmony had returned to Edo Castle. Tonight offered a happy respite from agonizing over the past. How much more significant this celebration was now than if it had taken place right after the wedding! To Sano it seemed a fitting tribute to the bond forged between him and his bride during the investigation. Under cover of their flowing sleeves, they clasped hands.

Magistrate Ueda stood and made the first speech. "Marriage resembles the joining of two streams—two families, two spirits coming together. Though turbulence often results when the waters mix, may they continue to flow forever in the same direction, two forces united for mutual benefit." Beaming proudly at Sano and Reiko, the magistrate raised his sake cup. "I toast the allegiance between our two clans."

The guests cheered and drank. Maids poured liquor for Sano and Reiko. Hirata spoke next: "During the eighteen months that I've served the *sōsakan-sama,* I have found him to be an exemplary samurai and master. Now I'm glad that he has a wife of similar honor, courage, and fine character. I pledge my service to them for as long as I live."

More cheers; another round of drinks. Then an official

entered the room and announced, "His Excellency the shogun, and his mother, the Honorable Lady Keisho-in."

In walked Tokugawa Tsunayoshi, regal in his brilliant robes and tall black cap. Keisho-in minced alongside him, smiling. Everyone bowed low, but the shogun gestured for them to rise. "Relax, we're all, ahh, comrades here tonight." Eschewing formality, he seated himself and Keisho-in before the dais. He said to Sano, "My mother wishes to present you with a special wedding gift."

Four priests wrestled a huge Buddhist altar through the door. As Priest Ryuko directed them to set it in the corner, the assembly stared in awe. Garish carved dragons, deities, and landscapes adorned the teak doors of the ceiling-high *butsudan*. There were columns inlaid with mother-of-pearl, and a gilt pagoda roof. It was a masterpiece of ugliness.

"Wherever shall we put it?" whispered Reiko.

"In a prominent place," Sano whispered back. The gift sealed the alliance between him and Lady Keisho-in. With her support he hoped to convince the shogun to enact reforms that would reduce government corruption and benefit the citizens' welfare. And they needed each other to counteract the influence of Chamberlain Yanagisawa, who was conspicuously absent from the banquet. After the failure of his plot, Yanagisawa would be more eager than ever to ruin them. "That's the most glorious *butsudan* I've ever seen," Sano declared. "Many thanks, Honorable Lady."

Keisho-in giggled. The audience murmured polite praises, and Priest Ryuko led his brethren in a chant of blessing. Sano studied the handsome priest with interest: Ryuko, too, was a valuable ally. In the space of a single investigation, he'd built a strong power base from which to further his search for truth and justice.

More speeches followed, with much eating, drinking, music, and merriment. Guests approached the dais to wish the bridal couple well. During a lull, Sano turned to Reiko.

"Happy?" he asked.

Reiko smiled. "Very."

"Me, too." This was truly the best day of Sano's life. Of course he knew that such perfect contentment couldn't last. There would be more dangerous investigations; the ongoing fight to maintain his position in the political battlefield of the Tokugawa regime; the serious and minor crises of life. But for now, Sano basked in serenity. With such good friends and allies, future success seemed assured. And right beside him was the source of his new optimism.

"Let's make a promise," he said. "Whatever happens, we'll always be lovers."

Reiko squeezed his hand; her eyes sparkled with mischief. "And partners," she added.

TURN THE PAGE FOR
AN EXCERPT FROM

THE SAMURAI'S WIFE

THE NEXT EXCITING NOVEL
FROM LAURA JOH ROWLAND,
NOW AVAILABLE IN HARDCOVER
FROM ST. MARTIN'S PRESS . . .

Prologue

Nine hundred years ago, the city was Heian-kyō. Capital of Peace and Tranquility, founded as seat of the emperors who ruled Japan. Now, long after the reigning power had passed to the Tokugawa shoguns and their stronghold in Edo far to the east, it is simply Miyako, or Kyōto—the capital. But the shadows of the past haunt the present. The Imperial Palace still dominates the city, as always, forever. There the current emperor and his court exist as though suspended in time, masters of no one, human relics of bygone splendor. After centuries of war and bloodshed, of fallen regimes and changing fortunes, the eternal antagonisms, forgotten secrets, and ancient dangers still survive. . . .

In the imperial enclosure, the palace's innermost private heart, a warm summer midnight enfolded the garden. Over flowerbeds and gravel paths, the foliage of maple, willow, cherry, and plum trees arched in dark, motionless canopies. The evening rain had ceased; a full moon glowed through vaporous cloud. The calm surface of the pond reflected the sky's luminosity. On an island in the pond's center, a rustic cottage stood amid twisted pines. Inside burned a lantern, its white globe crisscrossed by the window lattice.

West of the garden loomed the residences, ceremonial halls, offices, storehouses, and kitchens of the emperor's household. Their tile roofs gleamed in the moon's pallid radiance. From a passageway between two buildings, another lantern emerged. It swung from the hand of the left minister, chief official of the Imperial Court.

He strode along the pond toward a stone bridge leading to the island. Heat hazed the air like a moist veil. Fireflies twinkled feebly, as if the humidity quenched their light. A waterfall rippled; frogs croaked. The chirps of crickets and shrill of cicadas blended into a solid fabric of sound stretched across the night. The lantern cast the shadow of the left minister's tall figure dressed in archaic imperial style—wide trousers and a cropped jacket whose long train dragged on the ground. Beneath his broad-brimmed black hat shone the sallow face of a man in middle age, with the arched brows and haughty nose inherited from ancestors who had held his post before him. As he followed a path between the trees toward his secret rendezvous, anticipation increased his pace. A smile hovered upon his mouth; he drew deep breaths of night air.

The drowsy sweetness of lilies and clover drifted heavenward over the pond's marshy scent, masking the rich summer odors of damp earth, grass, night soil, and drains. A sense of well-being intoxicated the left minister, heady as the night's aromatic breath. He felt as vigorous as in his youth, and extraordinarily alive. Now he could look back through years of anguish with detachment.

Fifteen years ago, an unfortunate convergence of fate and deed had condemned him to serve two masters. Birthright had placed him in a station at the heart of palace affairs, in a position to know everything worth knowing. A crime committed in passion had rendered him vulnerable to persons outside the sequestered world of the court's five thousand residents. His two best qualities—intelligence and a gift for manipulating people—had doomed him to live in two worlds, an impotent slave in one, isolated from family, friends, and colleagues in the other. He'd been an actor playing two opposing roles. But now, having reclaimed the power to shape his own destiny, he stood ready to unite his two worlds, with himself at their summit.

Tonight would bring a taste of the rewards to come.

The light in the pavilion kindled the left minister's eagerness. He walked faster as a surge of sexual arousal fed his new sense of omnipotence. Although uncertainty and danger lay ahead, he was buoyed by confidence that soon he would realize his highest ambitions, his deepest desires. Tonight everything was already prepared, an advance celebration of his triumph.

Along the pond, a bamboo grove rustled in the breezeless air. The left minister paused, then dismissed it as the movement of some harmless feral creature and continued on his way. But the rustling followed him. Hearing footsteps, he frowned in puzzled annoyance.

The imperial family, their lives circumscribed by tradition, rarely ventured outside so late. Desiring privacy for his rendezvous, the left minister had ordered everyone else to stay out of the garden tonight. Who dared to disobey?

Reluctantly he stopped again. The bridge lay a hundred paces ahead; across the silvery pond, the cottage lantern beckoned. The left minister peered into the dense thicket of bamboo.

"Who's there?" he demanded. "Show yourself!"

No answer came. The moving bamboo leaves stilled. Angry now, the left minister stalked toward the intruder. "I order you to come out. Now!"

An abrupt change in atmosphere halted him ten paces short of the grove. Here the night seemed charged with energy. A soundless vibration pulsated through the left minister. The insect shrills receded to the edge of his hearing; the darkness paled within the space around him. His skin tightened, and his heart began to thud in deep, urgent beats. The will of the person in the bamboo grove seemed to close around the left minister's mind. Inexplicable fear seized him. Icy sweat broke out on his face; his muscles weakened.

He knew that the person must be a member of the emperor's family, a servant, courtier, or attendant—a mortal human. But the strange force magnified the left minister's image of the intruder to gigantic size. He could hear it breathing monstrous gulps of air.

"Who are you?" His query came out sounding weak and timorous. "What do you want?" Somehow he understood, without word or gesture from the anonymous presence, its evil intent toward him.

The ominous breathing came faster, louder. The left minister turned and fled. On north and south, fences sealed off the garden. To the east, a stone wall separated the imperial enclosure from the estates of the court nobles. Vacant audience chambers, locked at night, cut him off from the shelter of the palace. There was no refuge except the island cottage. The left minister ran toward the lighted window, which promised companionship and safety, but his legs felt clumsy, his body weighted with the heavy malaise of nightmare. He stumbled, dropping his lantern. His stiff, cumbersome garments further hampered movement. Close behind, he heard the breathing, a vicious, predatory rasp. The ghostly grip on his mind crushed his courage.

"Help!" called the left minister, but his pursuer's will strangled his voice. Now he was sorry he'd banned everyone from the garden. He knew he could expect no help from the cottage's lone occupant.

As he struggled on, the eerie force enclosed him like a bubble. Desperately he zigzagged, trying to escape, but the awful pulsating sensation followed him. The weakness in his muscles increased. Glancing over his shoulder, he saw, through the force's pale halo, the indistinct silhouette of a human figure advancing on him. His heart pounded; his lungs couldn't draw enough air. He reached the bridge without the strength to run any farther. Falling to his knees, he crawled. The rough stone surface abraded his hands. He heard the chilling tap-tap of the intruder's footfalls coming closer. Reaching the island, the left minister dragged himself across sandy grass. He clutched the railing of the cottage veranda and pulled himself to a standing position. The three steps to the door loomed like towering cliffs. In the window, the lantern glowed, a mocking symbol of hope denied. The left minister turned to face his pursuer.

"No," he gasped, raising his hands in a futile attempt to ward off the undefined threat. "Please, no."

The intruder halted a few steps away. The noisy breathing stopped. Waves of panic washed over the left minister as he cowered in the sudden awful silence. Then, in the blurred oval of its face, the intruder's mouth opened—a darker void in darkness. Air rushed inward.

The scream shattered the night: a deafening wail that encompassed the full range of sound, from deepest groan to shrillest whine. The ghastly, inhuman voice blasted the left minister. Its low notes thundered through him with rumbles a million times stronger than an earthquake. The left minister's limbs splayed as sharp cracks like gunfire shot along his bones. As he howled in pain, sinews snapped. Terror combined with wonder.

Merciful gods, what is this terrible magic?

The scream's middle notes churned his bowels into liquid fire. The wail resonated in his heart, which beat faster and faster, swelling inside his chest. As his lungs ballooned, he breathed with harsh gasps. He fell, writhing in agony. The scream's shrillness arced along his nerves; convulsions wracked him. In the final moment before pain devoured reason, he knew he would never make his rendezvous. Nor would his dreams ever come to pass.

Now the left minister's insides erupted. Hot blood surged into his throat, filled his ears, choked off his breath, and blinded him. The scream's vibrations escalated until his brain exploded in a cataclysm of white-hot light.

Then death extinguished terror, pain, and consciousness.

The scream echoed across the city, then faded. A lull in the normal night sounds followed in its wake. For an eternal moment, time hung suspended in dead quiet. Then the doors and gates of the palace slammed open; lamps lit windows. The compound came alive with the clamor of voices, of hurrying footsteps. Flaming torches borne by guards converged on the imperial enclosure.

A breath extinguished the flame of the lantern in the cottage. A shadowy figure crept through the garden, merging with other shadows, and disappeared.

From the attic of a shop in Edo's Nihonbashi merchant district, Sano Ichirō, the shogun's *sōsakan-sama*—Most Honorable Investigator of Events, Situations, and People—conducted a secret surveillance. He and his chief retainer, Hirata, peered through the window blinds. Below them lay Tobacco Lane, a street of tobacco shops and warehouses, restaurants and teahouses. As the summer twilight deepened, the peaked roofs turned to dark silhouettes against a rosy sky. Tobacco Lane, recently bustling with daytime commerce, was now a corridor of blank facades, its storefronts hidden behind sliding doors. Lanterns burned over gates at either end of the block. Across the city echoed the usual evening music of dogs barking, horses' neighs, the clatter of night-soil carts, and tolling temple bells. The only sign of activity came from the Good Fortune Noodle Restaurant, a tiny establishment wedged between two shops across the street. Lamplight striped its barred window. Smoke wafted from the kitchen.

"Dinner's long past," Sano said, "but I smell fish cooking over there."

Hirata nodded. "She's definitely expecting someone."

"Let's just hope it's our man," Sano said.

Nearby, Sano's wife, Reiko, stood amid bales of fragrant tobacco. Her pastel summer robes glowed in the faint light from the window and open skylight. Twenty-one years old, with eyes like bright black flower petals and long, lustrous hair worn in a knot, she was small and slender. Since their marriage last autumn, Sano had defied convention by permitting Reiko to help with his cases. Even though both of them knew that a proper wife should be waiting for him at home, he'd learned that Reiko could question witnesses and uncover evidence in places where a male detective couldn't go. Now here to witness the climax of this investigation, Reiko joined Sano and Hirata at the window. She tensed, listening, her lovely, delicate oval face alert.

"I hear someone coming," she said.

In the street below, an old man shuffled into view, leaning on a cane. The lantern at the gate illuminated his straggly white hair; a tattered kimono hung on his stooped body.

"That's the Lion of the Kanto?" Surprise lifted Reiko's voice. The notorious crime lord ruled a band of gangsters who ran gambling dens, robbed travelers, operated illegal brothels, and extorted money from merchants throughout the Kantō, the region surrounding Edo. "I expected someone more impressive."

"The Lion travels in disguise," Sano reminded her. "Few people know what he really looks like. That's one way he's managed to evade capture for so long."

His other methods included bribing police to ignore his activities, killing his enemies, and keeping on the move. Attempts by Sano's detective corps to infiltrate the gang had failed, and their informants had refused to talk. Hence, Reiko had used her special communication network, composed of wives, relatives, servants, and other women associated with powerful samurai clans. They collected gossip, spread news and rumors. From them Reiko learned that the Lion had a mistress—a widow who ran the Good Fortune Noodle Restaurant. During a month's surveillance, Sano's detectives had observed that men of different descriptions regularly visited after the restaurant closed. Guessing that these were all the Lion in various disguises, Sano had planned an ambush and taken over this shop as his headquarters.

Now he said to Reiko, "If that old man is the Lion and we catch him, we'll have you to thank."

Sano felt excitement and anxiety surging through him. While he yearned to end the Lion's reign of crime, he was worried about Reiko. He wished she were safe at home, though what possible harm could come to her from merely watching through the window?

* * *

Up a curve in the road, another watcher peered out a different window, this one in a half-timbered mansion with a tile roof and high earthen wall. From his position in the lamplit second-floor parlor, Chamberlain Yanagisawa had a perfect view of Tobacco Lane, the Good Fortune Noodle Restaurant, and the shop where Sano and his comrades hid. Over silk robes he wore an armor tunic; a golden-horned helmet framed his handsome face. Inhaling on a long silver pipe, he savored the rise of anticipation. He turned to his chief retainer, Aisu, who squatted on the tatami floor nearby.

"Are you sure they're in there?" Yanagisawa asked.

"Oh, yes, Honorable Chamberlain." A slender man several years older than Yanagisawa's own age of thirty-three, Aisu had tensely coiled grace and hooded eyes that gave him a deceptive look of perpetual drowsiness. His voice was a sibilant drawl. "I climbed on the roof and saw Sano, his wife, and Hirata through the skylight. Six detectives are in the shop below. The side window is open." Aisu grinned. "Oh, yes, it's the perfect setup. A brilliant plan, Honorable Chamberlain."

"Any sign of the Lion yet?"

Aisu shook his head.

"Is everything ready?" Yanagisawa asked.

"Oh, yes." Aisu patted the lumpy cloth sack that lay on a table beside him.

"Timing is critical," Yanagisawa reminded him. "Have you given the men their orders?"

"Oh, yes. Everyone's in place."

"How fortunate that I managed to learn about Sano's plans in time to prepare." A smug smile curved Yanagisawa's mouth.

Today he'd received a message from his spy in Sano's household, describing the ambush. Yanagisawa had quickly organized his own scheme, commandeering the mansion of a rich tobacco merchant for a lookout station. If he succeeded, he would soon see his rival destroyed. The misfortunes of the past would end.

Since his youth, Yanagisawa had been the shogun's lover, influencing the weak Tokugawa Tsunayoshi and winning his post as second-in-command. As the ruler of Japan in all but name, Yanagisawa had virtually absolute power. Then Sano, the upstart scholar, martial arts teacher, son of a *ronin*—masterless samurai—and former police commander, had been promoted to the position of *sōsakansama*. The shogun had developed a high regard for Sano, who now commanded a staff of one hundred detectives and had gained influence over the *bakufu*, Japan's military government. Yanagisawa faced opposition from Sano whenever he proposed policies to Tokugawa Tsunayoshi and the Council of Elders; they sometimes took Sano's advice instead of his own. Sano's daring exploits overshadowed Yanagisawa's own importance, making him crave the adventure of detective work. And those exploits often meant serious trouble for him.

A case of double murder had led to Sano's discovery of a plot against the Tokugawa regime; he'd saved the shogun's life and won a post at Edo Castle. During his investigation of the Bundori Murders, when a madman had terrorized Edo with a series of grisly killings, Yanagisawa had been taken hostage by the murderer and nearly killed. Last year he'd exiled Sano to Nagasaki, but Sano had returned a hero. The final outrage had come when Sano, while investigating the poisoning of the shogun's concubine, had caused the death of Yanagisawa's lover.

Now Yanagisawa couldn't stand the sight of Sano and Reiko's happiness together. Tonight he would be rid of them. There'd be no more competition for the shogun's favor; no more humiliation. And as a bonus, he would steal Sano's reputation as a great detective.

A movement in the street outside caught Yanagisawa's eye. The foreshortened figure of an old man with a cane passed beneath the window. Yanagisawa beckoned Aisu, who glided swiftly to his side. They watched as the old man approached the noodle restaurant.

"Go!" Yanagisawa ordered.

"Oh, yes, Honorable Chamberlain." Aisu snatched up the cloth bundle and vanished without a sound.

* * *

Reiko said, "Look! He's stopping."

The old man beat his cane on the restaurant's door. It opened, and he disappeared inside.

"Let's go," Sano said to Hirata, then told Reiko, "We'll be back soon."

Her face shone with excitement. "I'm going with you!" She pushed up her sleeve, revealing the dagger strapped to her arm.

Consternation halted Sano. The problem with their partnership was that Reiko always wanted to do more than he could allow; to go places where a respectable woman could not be seen, risking social censure and her own life for the sake of their work. Always, Sano's desire for her assistance vied with his need to protect her. Sympathizing with Reiko's desire for adventure didn't ease his fear that their unusual marriage would provoke scandal and disgrace.

"I can't let you," he said. "You promised you would just watch if I let you come."

Reiko began to protest, then subsided in unhappy resignation: Promises between them were sacred, and she wouldn't break her word.

Sano and Hirata bounded down the staircase. In the dim shop, six detectives, waiting by the tobacco bins, sprang to attention. "The Lion is inside," Sano said. "We'll surround the place, and—"

From above the ceiling came a clatter, as though something had hit the floor upstairs, then the *whump* of a muffled explosion, followed by a scream.

"What was that?" Hirata said.

"Reiko!" Sano's heart seized. He turned to run back upstairs.

A fist-sized object flew in through the window. It landed in front of Sano and erupted in a cloud of smoke. Sulfurous fumes engulfed the shop. Coughs spasmed Sano's chest; his eyes burned. Through the dense haze, he heard the men coughing and thrashing around. Someone yelled, "A bomb!"

"This way out," Hirata cried.

Sano heard Reiko calling from the attic, but he couldn't

even see the stairway. "Reiko!" he yelled. "Don't come down here. Go to the window!"

He rushed outside and saw Reiko climbing down a wooden pillar from the balcony. More smoke billowed out the window and skylight. Gasping and wheezing, Sano reached up and grabbed Reiko, who fell into his arms. Coughs wracked her body. From a nearby firewatch tower came the clang of a bell. Carrying his wife, Sano staggered down the street, where the air was fresh and a crowd had gathered. The fire brigade, dressed in leather tunics and helmets, arrived with buckets of water.

"Don't go in there!" Sano shouted. "Poison fumes!"

The crowd exclaimed. The fire brigade broke down the shop doors and hurled water inside. Sano and Reiko collapsed together on the ground. The detectives joined them, while Hirata stumbled over to the Good Fortune. He went inside, then returned. "There's no one in there. The Lion has escaped."

Sano cursed under his breath, then turned to Reiko. "Are you all right?"

Sudden shouts and pounding hoofbeats scattered the crowd.

"I'm fine." Coughing and retching, Reiko pointed. "Look!"

Up the street ran the man who'd entered the Good Fortune, no longer stooped and white-haired but upright and bald. The torn kimono flapped open, exposing muscular arms, chest, and legs blue with tattoos—the mark of a gangster. Mounted troops wearing the Tokugawa triple-hollyhock crest galloped after him. His face, with the broad nose and snarling mouth that had earned him his nickname, was wild with terror.

"It's the Lion!" Hirata exclaimed.

Sano stared as more soldiers charged from the opposite direction. "Where did they come from?"

The leader, clad in armor, slashed out with his lance. It knocked the Lion flat, just a short distance from Sano. Instantly soldiers surrounded the Lion. Leaping off their horses, they seized him and tied his wrists.

"You're under arrest," the leader shouted.

Sano recognized his voice at once. Shock jolted him. "Chamberlain Yanagisawa!"

The chamberlain dismounted. Removing his helmet, he triumphantly surveyed the scene. Then his gaze fell upon Sano and Reiko. Dismay erased his smile. He stalked away, calling to his troops: "Take my prisoner to Edo Jail!"